The Seduction of Sunni Sinclair

Glass House Books

Noel Mealey skilfully blends well researched true stories and compelling characters to create entertaining and captivating fiction. From dealing with mega-rich entrepreneurs to associating with wanted criminals, crooked police and corrupt politicians, Noel has lived a varied life that allows him to build characters such as bent clergy, wily journalists, gangsters and murderers.

An Engineering graduate, Noel was inspired to write by his father, who had a wonderful talent for storytelling. Those stories, told under the stars on humid summer nights, focused on the eccentric personalities he knew and encouraged Noel to create characters that share some traits with his real life associates.

Noel's first books *Murder and Redemption* and *The Icon Murders* were published by HarperCollins.

I0652349

GHB

Glass House Books
Brisbane

The Seduction of Sunni Sinclair

Noel Mealey

Glass House Books
an imprint of IP (Interactive Publications Pty Ltd)
Treetop Studio • 9 Kuhler Court
Carindale, Queensland, Australia 4152
sales@ipoz.biz
http://ipoz.biz/shop
First published by IP in 2024
© 2024, IP and Noel Mealey

Printed in 16 pt Avenir Book on Caslon Pro 12 pt.

ISBN: 9781922830555 (PB) 9781922830562 (eBook)

A catalogue record for this book is available from the National Library of Australia

To my wife, Thérèse, who allowed me to dream
and encouraged me to turn my dreams into reality.

Acknowledgements

Book design: David P Reiter
Cover art: Design by Committee

I have lived a lucky life and am grateful to have been surrounded by a great network of friends and family.

While I was writing, my wife Thérèse did not once complain about the time I spent sequestered in my office. She assisted me by offering suggestions and positive criticism. Without her, this book would never have been started.

I want to acknowledge, from the beginning, David, Tuddy, George, Shammie and Merv for my early education, Frank and Joe for their mentoring, Maurice for his enormous help in my life, Anna & Chris and Emma for their early input into my first writing experiences, Kevin & Margaret and Rossa for their friendship through thick and thin.

Thanks to my family, David, Sarah, Emma and Eliza, for their care, enthusiasm and good humour.

I am grateful for the support and encouragement of the extended families on my and Therese's side, my engineers, and Hilda and Rosie, all of whom continued their enthusiasm and interest through my arid years.

I have used excerpts from Henry Lawson's poem, "Taking His Chance", from *In the Days When the World Was Wide and Other Verses*, Sydney: Angus and Robertson, 1903 [first published 1896].

Kate Goldsworthy is an outstanding editor who put me on the right track. Anna Valdinger played a massive part in keeping up my morale.

Dr David Reiter from Interactive Publications has given the right advice through the publishing process. His forty-plus years of experience in the industry has been of enormous help in his fine editing of the text and his knowledge of all aspects of modern publishing.

Josh Durham made a lovely cover for the book.

Theatre, film and television actor Fiona Press, the rich and commanding voice behind Sunni in the audiobook, has been delightfully skillful in her interpretation of Sunni, and audio engineer Martin Gallagher has edited it to perfection.

Contents

1. Trouble Finds Her   1
2. A Hitman's Shock   4
3. Illegal Casino Time   10
4. Becker's Criminal Reflex   18
5. Justice, Vigilante-style   23
6. What Becker Does to Impress   31
7. Search Warrant Time   44
8. Who's Doing Who in the Sauna?   49
9. Clawing Back Consciousness   58
10. Vengeance is Mine   69
11. Becker Near the Edge   76
12. A Daring Rescue, A Romance   81
13. Hang the Getaway Driver   91
14. Pit Pony Underground   97
15. Challenging the Sydney Mob   108
16. Boss Gangster Inside Track   118
17. Who's a Feminist?   125
18. King of the Kids   130
19. Sinister Red Eyes   141
20. Making Like Solomon   146
21. Becker Gets Fit   151
22. Royal Chats at Randwick   154
23. The Best Laid Plans   157
24. Committed at Last?   166
25. Calm Before the Heist   170
26. Queen Elizabeth II & Lesser Distractions   179
27. Our Getaway   194

28. Après Heist   200
29. Living It Up with Suspicion   206
30. Treasure Trove Revealed   211
31. Payback Time   214
32. The Great Pretender   219
33. A Prayer, an Engagement and Jealousy   222
34. Why Did the Cock Crow Thrice?   227
35. Timebomb Walking   232
36. Take Only What You Can Carry   237
37. No Time for Love   242
38. Razor's Edge   246
39. Baser and Higher Desires   259
40. A Pitch for Love   268
41. Captured?   275
42. The Chase   280
43. Here's Missing You, Kid   287
44. Rush of Pale Men   291

1. Trouble Finds Her

Dudley, NSW. Monday, December 28, 1953.

The game kicked off in fading daylight three days after Christmas '53 when Becker fled, leaving the police sergeant bleeding out in a dark alley between towering silos at Newcastle's coal wharf. I'd never heard the name Franz Becker. But, within a week, he would burst into my life like a firecracker in the henhouse, and I would emerge from the explosion, battle-stained and hardened, a wanted outlaw with a target on my forehead.

If you believed the sensationalised stories spun by Sydney's newspapers, I was the notorious Sunni Sinclair, a glamorous escort catering to the wicked desires of the wealthy and powerful. While that may have held some truth four years ago, it was no longer the reality. I escaped Sydney and invented a new identity—the hard-working publican up to her glamorous elbows in soap suds or serving beer to sweaty coal miners and tradies in overalls or grimy singlets. They flocked in at first, moths to the limelight glow, but lingered on, contented puppies basking in the radiance of the empty stage.

Ten miles from where the sergeant lay dying in torrential rain, The Dudley was alive, with Happy Hour in full swing below the same thundercloud racing south. Behind the bar, I bustled about, lively, animated, cheeking my regulars, flirting with the unattached, flattering the timid, topping up empty schooners and offering impromptu marriage counselling to those in need. But, while my feet and fingers danced to the tune of taps and glasses, my mind sometimes took off on a different trail away from the routine daily grind.

The batwing doors squealed open and click-clacked shut, and a tall, lanky stranger stepped into the cigarette-smoke haze. Lightning behind glass window panels advertising Toohey's ale wreathed him in their multi-coloured glow and held his face in shadow. He wore a brown wool fedora with the brim snapped down, a pinch in front and a tiny blue feather nestled in its golden band. The gorgeous hat knocked me over, and he pushed through to the bar before I registered the polished tan shoes, the crisply starched blue and white check dress shirt and the sharply creased beige wool trousers.

A hush spread through the crowded bar as it does on those rare occasions when a furious wife bursts in to drag her husband home, and I swear the crush of coal-lined and grease-stained miners opened before him as if Moses himself had parted the Red Sea in little old Dudley.

Hesitantly, he fronted the bar and said quietly, 'Hello, Sunni. Remember me? Lou?'

He was late forties, tallish, with a good body, and, up close, I recognised him from Sydney, where sometimes I would see him in one dark hangout or another consorting with Kitty Balushi. Upright citizens knew nothing much about the goings-on of Kitty's razor gang, preferring to live like the three monkeys. But nasty stuff happened in the dark lanes of Sydney's Kings Cross, and Lou was often somewhere nearby. From time to time, the police would arrest someone close to me—a client or a gangster of repute, and the papers would paint a bleak picture, darker than the truth. We blamed the war and carried on.

Lou's face appeared pale, his high cheekbones casting him as the scary twin to Jack Palance. He put out a nervous, jittery energy and wanted to stay for a week or two, and I wondered about that. However, he sparked my curiosity, and I sensed his loneliness, so I slid him a Tooheys Old, ran a cloth over the bar, and acted out a show, bustling about nearby.

Evenings can be dreary in a country town, so I gave him the

key to a ground-floor room across the hall from my suite. After my customers packed and headed home to wife and family, I appreciated a man's company.

I closed and tidied up. The bar grew silent, but Lou lingered on a stool, staring at his beer, watching the head fade. I stayed on, hoping to get the latest scuttlebutt on Kitty. The war had changed everything for Lou. It worked him over well and truly. Like many returned soldiers, he relived the murders and mutilations of his war but couldn't handle the peace, and, with no one to love him, he turned to crime.

'Troubles?' I asked, sensing his mood.

'You'll read about it in the paper. Sergeant Moran is dead, and Albie Fowler killed him. Becker drove the car, and now they're after me because I witnessed the murder. Fowler and Becker. I need to lie up for a week or so. Until things quieten.'

And so it began.

I'm no stranger to trouble. It's like those old friends you invite home for dinner, and they stay on until their feet are permanently beneath your favourite chair, and your journey is their journey, and they think they own your future. I should have kicked Lou out that night and lost the key.

2. A Hitman's Shock

Monday, January 4, 1954.

I backed away, pressing an open palm to my mouth. 'Dead?' The word stuck in my throat, and, when I finally grasped its meaning, I flicked away a tear, pressed a finger to my eyelid, and poured a beer slowly and deliberately to get my head together. My regulars had gathered in untidy groups, their eyes snapping sideways across the rims of their schooners, to me, then to the police.

'It's okay,' I called, flapping a cloth at those nearest me and somehow relieving the tension with a laugh. 'Nothing to worry about,' and gradually, their conversations resumed while they listened in to mine and looked to me to refill their glasses.

'Dead?' I repeated quietly. 'You did say it's Lou who died?'

Detective Inspector "Tommo" Thompson nodded solemnly, wiping the beer foam moustache from his lip. 'Yes. The coroner's best guess is that he died between midnight and dawn. Pretty hard to be more accurate.'

A uniformed constable rested his notebook on the bar and scribbled with an indelible pencil while I served a round of three beers and kept my eye on a young fella in a striped T-shirt and jeans who got punchy after four schooners.

It was the Monday following the New Year long weekend, near six o'clock closing time, and, on the other side of the bar, they jostled for space and juggled schooners to avoid spilling beer on the floor. My profit came from happy hour. With my assistant away, Tommo had reluctantly agreed to talk to me in the corner, hoping for privacy.

The constable raised his eyes from the notebook to ask, 'For the record, Sunni, what's your full name?'

'Sunni Sinclair.'

'Not von Liebling, then?' he said, with a mischievous grin.

'Get away, Jack. You know that was my professional name.'

Jack pushed a fist against his lips to stifle a grin. Everyone old enough to read the *Herald* knew me—Kitty's highest-paid escort during the war and for five years after Japan surrendered. I made heaps, tax-free, and so did Kitty. She took fifty per cent plus first dibs on the jewellery for providing the contacts, tax accounting and protection.

I caught the constable's snicker. 'Pity,' he said, his ears blushing. 'Von had a certain ring to it in the war years. I'll write here that you're thirty-two, five-foot-nine, grey-green eyes, auburn hair, and,' averting his eyes, 'with a full figure.' He sighed. 'Sorry, I'll have to add that you're a card-carrying member of the Communist Party.'

'Rubbish. Where'd you get that from?'

'Read it in the paper.'

'Don't be silly, mate.' I said, pulling a face. 'It's the press. 'Those journos. It's not my fault the crowd jeered at me outside the Royal Commission or the press labelled me a bolshie bombshell for supporting the miners in the '94 strike. And, no, Jack, I don't carry a party ticket.'

Tommo waited until I caught my breath, then repeated his question, 'Now, Sunni, tell me about the deceased.'

'Lou booked in for one week and said he might stay two.' I didn't bother to tell Tommo that Lou was reluctant to go to the fete with me until I pressed him. Hell, it was New Year's Eve, and I wanted a fling with a good-looking man, so rather than sit at home thinking about Gabe, I dragged Lou out first to the casino then to the fete.

'We had such fun until this kid assaulted us—a young fella, cocky as a blue-ribbon rooster, and his overgrown mate with a face he shaved with a hammer and chisel. If Lou is truly dead, you should look at those two.'

'Drowned in the surf at Stockton Beach,' Tommo said.

Tommo shuffled about on a bar stool and grumbled. He was a good-looker, too. A smart dresser like Lou, usually in a fawn or brown suit, white shirt and tie, and, of course, a hat. A six-footer. When he was younger, he played second row for the rugby team, and there was no mistaking him for anything but a copper. He took a mouthful of beer and wiped his lips with his finger and thumb. 'The super is kicking arse to be ready for the Royal Tour,' he said. 'I need to write this accident report and get to the station.'

'Accident? Come off it, Tommo.' During my years with Kitty, violence was my constant companion, but I shivered at the dark aura I sensed around Lou's death. 'This is no accident. It's murder.'

Tommo put a hand to the side of his neck and contorted his face. 'Murder? No, Sunni. Not murder. No. That's not what the coroner said.'

'But Lou was not the sort to swim in the middle of the night. I saw that young thug assault him at the fete. And him with a weak heart.'

Tommo said, 'There, ya go. Accidental drowning brought on by a heart attack, like the coroner said. I wouldn't be talking to you in the bar if I thought it was murder. Can you describe your friend to me?'

'He arrived about closing time the Monday after Christmas—'

'Certain it was Monday?' the constable asked. 'The day Sergeant Moran died?'

'Of course I'm sure. Lou was preoccupied. Write that in your book if you can't think of anything better to ask. Depressed, too.'

Jack was a wiseacre and needed putting down from time to time.

6

I spread full glasses for a trio of plant operators, including the young bloke in the T-shirt who had shuffled closer to Tommo's corner and was unashamedly eavesdropping on our conversation. I rang up the sale and waved a hand in a circle over three piles of coins, asking who would pay. A death is a death, but life goes on, and I had a mortgage and creditors to pay.

Tommo said, 'Early surfers found the body at Stockton Beach this morning. The coroner says he went for a swim with a bellyful of whisky.' He smirked. 'Reckoned he could swim like Jon Henricks.'

'No. Not Lou.'

'Yes. Lou. He had heart disease, and the surf was too much for him. That's the end of it.'

Lou had tried to tell me he was in the racing game. He raised his glass to a framed poster on the bar wall—a bay gelding stretched out in a gallop the jockey's whip held high. 'Rising Fast,' he said, trying to prove something. 'Jack Purcell on him, winning the Melbourne Cup.'

Of course, I recognised Lou as one of Kitty's mob but brushed away doubts about having him in my bar. My life behind The Dudley's batwing doors was far from the wildness of Sydney and Kitty's savagery. Through good luck, I escaped with my life after I refused to go along with her cruelty, and yet, strangely, when I thought of Sydney, I laughed aloud with delight when a memory came to me of its lustiness and the lavish lifestyle the city had offered me.

I acquired The Dudley—bars, bottles, barrels and beds— three years ago, a deliberate move to distance me from Kitty Balushi. It was a miner's pub built on a honeycomb of mined tunnels on a corner in Ocean Street, the main road leading out from Dudley. The Burwood coal mine was two miles south. Half an hour north was the port of Newcastle, and a three-hour drive separated me from Sydney and the lingering spectre of Kitty Balushi.

Tommo slapped a hand sharply on the bar. 'Wake up, Sunni. You drifted off there. Anything you can add to your statement?'

If Tommo forgot to mention Sergeant Moran again, then so would I. There was no future in tangling with Kitty's mob. 'Yes. I have something to add,' I said. 'Lou was too fit to drown.' And, upset they thought so lowly of him, I gave them a touch of the spur. 'His tummy muscles were hard as tree stumps.'

'He was a swine,' the constable said. 'Tummy muscles and all.'

I had miffed Jack by speaking sharply to him, so I slid a schooner of Toohey's Ale in front of him and gave him my best smile calculated to pacify. Drinks for the police come free of charge at The Dudley.

'He deserved a hanging,' Tommo bristled, his eyes hard. 'He was an enforcer for Kitty's gang.'

The bar noise dropped while those nearest sucked in air, and Jack covered a gassy eruption in his free fist.

Some would argue that Lou was a violent crook, but I can tell you everyone is bent to some degree. Saint or sinner, you are entitled to justice and a fair hearing. His death looked to me more like a gang execution, and Ms Kitty will be in it up to those diamond earrings that should be mine.

'Gotta go.' Tommo slapped his empty glass on the bar and sighed, 'Does Billy have a tip for Saturday?'

Billy was our SP bookie. He came with The Dudley, welded to the bar.

'Hey, Billy.' I waved him over to join us.

Illegal SP bookies provided a better service to the customer than the on-course bookies or the Tote, and, besides, he attracted customers to my bar. Racing was about the press, the police and the tax man versus racecourse owners and Protestant churches. Everyone came out on top and made money.

He sauntered over and, lowering his voice, suggested Pride of Egypt was a champion in the making—a big chestnut by Nilo from Civic Pride. 'Get on him for The Westminster Juveniles at Randwick. February 6th. He's a cert. I'm not taking your bet, but you'll get fifteens if you're quick. The odds are falling.'

'Thanks,' Tommo said, preparing to leave, then hesitating. 'I'll return the favour, Sunni. There's to be a clean-up before the Royal Visit to rid the town of race-fixing, SP bookies, and the rest.' He jerked his head to the guest lounge as though I had a convention of enslaved coal miners lurking there. His eyes swept the bar, and he lowered his voice. 'We'll be here with search warrants. Billy, get lost for the next few weeks.'

'You're getting on my nerves, mate,' I said. 'There's no illegal betting in this bar.'

I had renovated my bar into a cozy, warm and inviting place. It's nothing flash. Timber-panelled walls, pressed-metal ceiling, green mosaic floor tiles and a fireplace tucked into the corner. 'I put my heart and soul into making this pub a success, not to mention my hands and fingernails. You can't stamp around in your big boots and your warrant—'

'Hold on, Sunni—'

I rushed to the other end of the bar to serve a young bloke whose wife had left him for an American soldier. And also to cool down. Tommo was a friend.

I returned and said more evenly, 'The miners come here because they love me, not Billy.'

Tommo waited until he had my full attention once more. 'You're gunna make a commotion about Lou, so you better front into the station tomorrow and make a statement.'

3. Illegal Casino Time

Newcastle, NSW. Tuesday, January 5.

An interior decorator on Death Row must have designed the interview room. Straight-backed kitchen chairs were hard and unyielding, the pine table a rough slab chipped and stained with spilt ink, and God knows what else, a tape recorder. The contrast was glaring—the colonial beauty of Newcastle Police Station from the outside and the prison-like bleakness inside.

Tommo handed over a microphone. 'Hit the button and talk, Sunni. I'll be out making tea.'

'Where should I begin?'

'You're the one wanting to make a statement.' He was impatient to get to his tea, I suppose, but I didn't much like the way he said that. 'Just say how you ended here and who tagged along. Give me all the details. I'll trim out the fat, hand you the script, and give it to you ready to sign.'

I gave him my full-frontal snake eyes. 'No need to be so sulky.'

The walls, a cold two-tone of government cream and deathly green, closed in on me. The air reeked of stale cigarettes and deep-fried chips, though a frosted glass window offered a crack of breeze, allowing enough oxygen to keep alive the blowfly buzzing madly against the glass and a sliver of light, barely enough for me to check my make-up in the tiny mirror in my compact.

I half-expected Tommo to whip out the thumbscrews. But he adjusted his tone to speak with his police voice into a microphone to record the introduction. 'Tuesday, January 5th, 1954. Statement by Miss Sunni Sinclair commences,' and he flicked a finger at me.

I glared at him, plumped my hair, leaned into the mic and spoke into it with my best voice.

It was New Year's Eve. I drove with Lou on streets sparkling with decorative lamp bulbs, banners and bunting in preparation for the Royal visit in six weeks. Shopkeepers had hung Australian, British, and American flags in their windows, and the footpaths were busy with families window shopping and taking the cool night air.

Excited children chewed on toffee apples; miners with coal-black in the lines of their faces held children on their shoulders; teenagers rocked and rolled in the street outside The Palais dance hall, and a queue jostled and shouted in front of The Royal while they waited at the box office to buy tickets for *The Desert Rats*, starring Richard Burton. The war was eight years behind us, but people had not tired of war movies.

I spoke into the mic. 'The nightclub on the seventh floor was legal, but the casino was not.'

'Hang on, Sunni.' Tommo smacked the stop button and rewound twenty seconds of tape. 'You can't talk about the casino. That will get me and everyone else into trouble.'

'What, then?' I asked abruptly. Men take a risk when they try to walk over me.

'Talk about the nightclub and not the casino.'

Why would I care that the casino was illegal or a front for prostitution and after-hours drinking? Am I expected to judge everyone's behaviour—their morals? The government designed gambling laws to keep profit and power among the wealthy capitalists.

I banged my finger on the button and gave him the look.

The nightclub entrance was busy and lit with coloured neon lights. A bellboy in striped cuffs and a matching inch-wide red stripe down the side of his trousers opened the car door, and a spiv in a leather vest and gold bangle leaned on a two-tone Chrysler New Yorker at the kerbside.

We entered through the flashy ground floor lobby of a seven-storey, cream brick hotel on Hunter Street, across from the Foreshore Park and the Stockton ferry terminal. A doorman in the same uniform opened the door onto a beige and chocolate striped carpet, tan high-backed leather chesterfields, and art deco lamps that added nothing to the dim lighting. A fountain splashed in the centre, a grand staircase and on the left, polished brass lift doors reflected the lights. It was so over the top, but Lou said wow, so I didn't share my opinion.

The 7th floor is by invitation only. Strangers wait for Rosco to decide if they're sober, properly dressed, and a free-spender-and-generous-tipper or a tight-arse, and, if they pass inspection, he lets them up the lift.

Rosco loomed before us, recognised me, and raised his chin to Lou. With attitude, I thought. He said 'Good Evening' and led us straight to the lift driver, a large man sporting a boxer's nose and cauliflower ears, wearing a white dinner jacket and black bow tie and showing a lot of teeth. Rosco pressed me firmly towards the lift. 'Friend of Gabe's,' he growled, and, after I tipped them each a florin, we rattled off to the seventh floor before I had time to ask if Gabe was there tonight.

Tommo slammed the recorder's stop button. 'I've never been in there,' he said, his envy on display. 'What's it like?'

Starched white tablecloths. Imported champagne in shiny ice buckets. More flowers than a florist shop, and beautiful women swanning around wearing handsome men on their arms, posing for a page in *The Queen*, drinking Cognac in brandy balloons or exotic cocktails with olives skewered on toothpicks.

'Nothing to write home about.' I said, still sulking with my friend Tommo.

There was live jazz, cigar smoke, happy noise, spotlights on green baize tables, and expensively dressed women, outnumbered by men willing and able to throw away their money. An Alpha woman gave Lou a come-on look—powerful, confident, the centre of other female attention, but I managed to stand in front. Blocked his view.

I leant across and pressed the button to stop the recorder and think about how to describe a casino without mentioning the word. Six o'clock closing triggered violence against women because the men came home drunk from sinking their beers too fast. I testified to the Royal Commission about that, while illicit drinking and gambling behind closed doors grew like mushrooms after a storm. The secrecy led directly to prostitution, bribery, corruption, alcoholism, and tax-free wealth for the nightclub owners.

Illegal fun. I had teetered barefoot in the centre of that world in Sydney with Kitty; she was in it up to her damned diamonds, too. Sly grog was the real deal. Legitimate hotels bought more beer and spirits than needed and slipped it to illegal nightclub owners at a healthy margin. And where else can you find a drink after six?

Nightclubs morphed into casinos. Nature at work. Blackjack, roulette and baccarat. Adrenaline pumping. Men in dark suits and grey moustaches. Women in the latest from Paris and diamonds. Oh, the jewellery! To make you swoon. Local and state politicians, big business, farming, mining, property, racing personalities, those with money and those in debt, men and women, some from as far away as Sydney. Everyone in on the secret. All liable for a prison term in the eye of the law.

I enjoyed my night out, mixing with the crooks. Circulating, hugging, pecking cheeks, patting shoulders, stretching a glass of champagne to last an hour. It was all easy-going and how's-your-Bentley.

I consulted my watch and searched the room for Gabe. I asked Lou if he was ready to leave and go to the fete. But, in Gabe's absence, he was enjoying himself, so we stayed on.

I tapped the Start button, ready to forgive Tommo. 'I noticed a young bloke, twenty, twenty-one, wearing a cheap navy suit that probably came from the Red Cross, and his friend might have run up her knee-length dress that afternoon. We had passed them in the car while they danced in the street outside the Palais, and they were as out of place here as a rooster in the barber's chair. He was handsome enough but too untidy. Maybe a journalist. Then I remembered her. She had worked in my kitchen at The Dudley over her school holidays and was no more than nineteen. Jessica. Her friend was full of confidence, wandering around with champagne, watching the blackjack dealers, laughing at the enthusiasm of a woman at the roulette wheel who I recognised as one of Kitty's escorts who had gone to seed, needed a drink, and should not have worn a short skirt.'

Gabe's voice called, saying 'Hello, Sunni. I've missed you. Did you leave a little profit for me tonight?'

'Gabe!' He was right beside me and hadn't changed. He stood out in a crowd, a good looker, borderline overweight, with thick black hair above a round, cheerful face. A millionaire. At least a millionaire. He'd shared my bed for six exciting months, and I'd fallen more than a little in love with the bastard.

That reminded me of Kitty. I stopped the recording and said, 'Tommo, did you know Kitty started her career as a streetwalker?'

She married into the Balushi criminal family and made a massive fortune from six o'clock closing. Her razor gang terrified Sydney. Who likes to have their face slashed or splashed with acid? But the Tax Department caught on, and she had to lay low or go to prison.

As her fortunes dipped, Gabriel Rosen's star rose like a full moon to fill the vacuum.

Gabe's arm was around a tall movie starlet, and I noticed a diamond ring on his pinkie finger that must be five carats and set with rubies. I wore my most chic calf-length Mainbocher, drop-earrings and the diamond rings I skimmed from Kitty's take and refused to be intimidated by the King of the Cross and his jumped-up supermodels, even if he did own the place.

I gave him an enormous smile, mostly because he noticed me. Was my voice too eager? His eyes flirted with me, but he offered his thin lips to Lou. His other arm circled my waist, and he bent for an air kiss.

'Evening, Mr Rosen.' The young man in the Red Cross suit stepped between Gabe and me. I stepped on his foot, but he said 'excuse me,' moved aside and tossed me a cheeky wink. It pays to be happy, and good manners don't cost anything.

Gabe flicked his eyes to someone behind me and inclined his head. 'And, Sunni,' smiling as though he had not been interrupted, 'you're looking a million dollars. Remember, you promised me a dinner date?'

'Not tonight, Gabe,' I said. There'd be no invitation coming my way while he had that skinny sexpot squeaking in his wake, so I gave her my eyebrow flash to dampen her enthusiasm. 'I'm taking Lou to the fete, but ask me again soon.' I wanted to scowl at his dieting fashionista but smiled as I would to an inconvenient child.

To my intense pleasure, Gabe took my elbow and steered me away while the lift driver landed a heavy hand on the young man's shoulder and growled in his raspy voice. 'Ya got ya ten-bobs worth,' he said. 'Quietly, now, or I'll whip ya arse on the way down.'

'I've missed you,' Gabe said, teasing my backside with the same subtle touch I remembered. 'Why don't you come to the track? Friday morning for the dawn gallops. I've got a winner for the Cup. We can catch up over breakfast.'

I left the nightclub, happy as a Labrador chasing a ball, and, already, my mind was at the track watching Gabe, not the horses.

Out in the street again, we saw the shop windows were alight and the footpaths busy, and at the fair, canvas-covered street stalls sold party foods and knickknacks. You could buy toffee apples and the new chocolate-coated Two-in-Ones from Peters Ice Cream, fairy-floss on a stick and doughnuts, second-hand books, and Welcome to Newcastle postcards with pictures of curvy women frolicking on the beach in revealing costumes. There was street art, poetry reading, homemade ginger beer, hot dogs, and novelty booths where a happy customer propelled a monkey up a pole on a water jet to win a doll or guessed which moving cup covered the pea.

We passed the Hall of Mirrors, and Jessica was there, giggling at the distorted reflections that made her short and obese. Her friend admired himself in a true mirror, beaming at his reflection and clapping his hands. Fit would describe him. Beautiful, too. A rugged angel with a bent nose. No hips, tall, oval-faced, soft jaw, black hair and hazel eyes that jumped out of his face with their enthusiasm. Not that I noticed.

He practised a smile in the mirror. Good teeth. A sparse three-day growth on his cheeks and upper lip made him look like a boy practising to be a man. I'd have given him a run for free when I was in play. He flicked back the thick hair he had brushed in a pompadour, high at the front with a subtle parting and inch-long sideburns that gave him the Montgomery Clift look. He brushed fingers across his hair, glared at himself and narrowed his eyes. If he was trying out the intimidating look, he failed.

Jessica ragged him for taking too much time in front of the mirror. Becker, she called him, and I recalled the name but didn't make the connection to Moran's killing. It had a ring and carried more weight than a first name.

'Becker, you look like Richard Burton in *The Robe*,' she said, clapping her hands in delight. 'Soooo handsome.'

'Don't be ridiculous. I'm not looking at me.'

16

'Hah.'

As I strolled away with Lou, Becker said to Jessica, 'I'll shove Gabe Rosen aside before he can say boo.'

4. Becker's Criminal Reflex

I heaved a sigh when Tommo suggested I take a break. We relaxed back in our chairs with the casual ease of old friends discussing the upcoming Royal Tour, the Randwick races, Pride of Egypt, and race-fixing, which inevitably brought the conversation to Gabe. I asked the question that had troubled me since I realised at the casino the extent of his wealth and influence. 'Give me the low-down on Gabe, Tommo. How come he calls the shots in Newcastle when he's been in town for only three years?'

He dunked his VoVo and blushed when I leant across and slapped his wrist. He told me Gabe had made his fortune in Sydney three years ago by befriending and corrupting everyone from the Police Commissioner to the doorman at Tattersalls Club and even Kitty Balushi, who had no friends at all.

As it happened, Kitty was the source of Gabe's success in Newcastle. She had been fighting off the Tax Department, terrified she'd finish like Al Capone in prison for eleven years over tax evasion, and, to add to her problems, her old adversary Kate Law was preparing for an all-out war with her. With so much to distract her, Kitty had lost control of her gang in Newcastle and had to send Lou to sort it out.

'They called him Shanks,' Tommo said, studying my face for a reaction, 'because he would knife you as soon as look at you. No one had told her he was too ill to do the job.'

So, Kitty made a deal with Gabe. He would take over her Newcastle clubs, massage parlours, and gambling and racing interests in exchange for one of his properties in Sydney, whip her razor boys into shape, manage their finances for seventy per cent of the take, and return them to Kitty, fully house trained and reliable, after two years.

'But,' Tommo said, 'after the heart attack, Shanks couldn't beat an egg, and Gabe fired him. Shanks had to find a new gang.'

We put the teacups aside and got on with my statement. 'Where was I?' I asked.

Tommo reminded me, 'At the fair with Lou.'

I pressed the button and spoke into the mic.

We came off the Ferris wheel, eating hot potato chips from paper cones. My Mainbocher was over the top for a fair. So what? I enjoy being the centre of attention. And there they were again, across from the Dodgem Cars, near the drinks booth, Jessica and Becker, shaking their hands high and laughing and pirouetting to a jazz band, her skirt flaring out to make all the men goggle-eyed. They were twenty yards away when a bruiser with a corrugated face joined them.

'That would be Albie Fowler,' Tommo said, startled. 'An informant told me Albie joined Becker's gang in November, but I thought it was unlikely, Becker being so green.'

I swung about to speak to Lou, but he was nowhere to be seen, and the bruiser, Fowler, threw up his arms and was about to rush after him when Becker exploded. His face blazed, he spun about searching the crowd, drew away and spat words at Fowler, smashing the side of one hand into the other, then raising his hands and shoulders to toss a question at him.

Fowler pointed at the street and shaded his eyes while he jumped and twisted as though searching a crowd.

Becker would have none of it. He planted his legs wide and cut Fowler off with a stiff hand chop.

'What was that about?' Tommo asked.

'It looked like Fowler came to the fete searching for Lou and, spotting him, wanted to run him down. Becker was furious with him.'

Jessica appeared to be mildly alarmed. She spoke a few words and held a finger to her chest, introducing herself to Fowler. She hadn't noticed me, and I hadn't heard from her in over a year. Lou was by my side again, tugging at my arm, so I allowed him to slip away with me in tow.

But Jessica followed us, hollering, 'Miss Sinclair. Miss Sinclair.' She waved and skipped towards me from the Dodgems, excited to recognise me.

Fowler was in a state, waving and pointing. He tore his arm away from Becker and almost knocked Jessica over. 'Shanks,' he shouted, rushing at Lou. 'Here you are. Dolled up like a peacock.' He swung a punch, but Becker grabbed his arm. 'Not here, Albie. Leave it to me.'

Jessica was closing in on me, hollering again, 'Miss Sinclair. Miss Sinclair.' Becker told her to shut up. And she was red-faced at that. Told him she wasn't a child and not to tell her to shut up.

But Lou was off at a gallop, glancing behind to check who might be following, skulking in the shadows and searching faces mixing in with the mob, hunching his shoulders and keeping his head down until, after a while, I lost him. I said hello to Jessica, and nice to see you again. To distract attention away from Lou, I suggested we all join the queue to buy an ice cream.

'Oh, Miss Sinclair, you haven't forgotten me?'

I remembered her well. She helped me out in my kitchen over her school holidays.

Jessica told me she was a third-year trainee nurse at the Redhead coal mine. Rescue and First Aid. She commenced there after leaving school at sixteen, and her training would count when she was old enough to apply for nursing at the hospital.

Lou had lost himself in the herd for a few minutes, but Becker hadn't bothered with ice cream. He chased after Lou and finally caught up with him. From fifteen yards away, I saw Becker poking Lou in the chest and shouting at him.

'What's going on?' I yelled and started towards them, with Jessica following. 'Who are you?'

'Oh, this is Franz Becker,' Jessica said and faltered when Becker took a grip on Lou's jacket, pulling him off-balance, his finger pounding hard into Lou's chest.

'Who does Franz Becker think he is?' I said, dodging a group of elderly couples.

'He works part-time at the mine. I haven't spoken to him since he walked away from school, and....' Her words tapered off.

I shoved through, closing the gap fast, a four-master heading into battle with the pirates. 'What's going on, Lou?' My cannons were primed and ready for action.

'Lou?' Becker's thug bellowed, his lips pulled back, teeth clenched. 'It's Shanks, not Lou.' And he shook Lou like a terrier with a rat until Becker hauled him off.

'Come on, Lou,' I said, glaring at the thug. But he frightened me, and I gripped Lou's elbow to tug him away. 'We're outta here.'

'Shanks,' Becker steered away from Fowler and closer to me. His voice was light to avoid Fowler hearing, 'Albie will be waiting. He has plans for you.'

'I'll pay,' Lou muttered, 'and we'll be quits.'

'I'll take your money,' Becker said, lowering his head close to Lou's ear. 'But Fowler wants your head. Get outta town while you can, and don't come back.'

I stepped in, trying to separate them. 'Get away, boy, or I'll call the police.'

'Come away, Sunni,' Lou said while Jessica stood, feet apart, chin up, fists clenched, surrounded by screeching people and tinny music from a loudspeaker.

Teenagers milled about near us, taking notice, open-mouthed, long legs exposed in knee-length shorts. Another bruiser in a blue singlet and sandals, hopping from foot to foot, was on the verge of joining in, but his wife grabbed his elbow while he decided which side to take. 'Come on, Kev. They've had too much to drink. Let's mind our own business for once.'

Becker had cooled off. He released Lou's shirt and smoothed his tie. 'Stay outta sight, Shanks. Fowler's on the warpath. If he finds you, you are a dead soldier.' He made a gun with two fingers, pointed at Lou, and, cool as a lime drink, puffed his cheeks and 'Pashouu,' like a gunshot.

He gave Lou a scornful haw-haw and raised his fingers to me, 'You'll not call me a boy again, missus. Pashouu.'

I swear my eyes widened, and my nostrils distended. I put all my weight into my open hand and slammed him on the side of the head. 'Don't talk to me like that, you twerp.' And when he raised a hand to his ear, I thought he intended to hit me, so I swung at him again. 'Police! Police!'

The heavyweight in the blue singlet skittered about to join the melee, but his wife took over, and they disappeared into the throng, and two police officers came pushing through. Lou told the police not to worry. 'Thanks,' he shouted. 'A bag-snatcher,' acting out a drama of searching, and the police made a few polite noises and pushed away through the crowd to look for the thief.

Lou, defiant now, jutted his chin and pushed back his shoulders. 'Let's go to The Dudley,' he said, brushing away invisible dandruff.

And, as easily as that, Fowler discovered where Lou had been hiding.

Lou hurried ahead of me to the street and the bright lights and, panting, flagged a passing taxi. I held his hand, searched his eyes, bent my face to him, and brushed my lips on his. In sympathy for the poor man, you know. 'Poor Lou,' I said, wondering whether I kissed Shanks or Lou, and who was this Becker to be consorting with crooks like Lou and Gabe Rosen?

'And that ends my statement, Tommo. With that evidence, you can nail Becker and his thug. Get cracking, then.'

5. Justice, Vigilante-style

Wednesday, January 6.

I came out of the surf at Dudley Beach under a brilliant blue sky and bent to draw air deep into my lungs. A ten-foot wave had dumped me, rolled me over, beat my face into the sand, and held me down until my lungs were ready to burst. But the earth was beneath my feet where it belonged. I danced on one foot, hitting my head with the heel of my hand to shake the water from my ear, and a magpie sang in the fir trees behind the beach. I had fought once more and won against the crashing breakers and their power over life and death and lived to feel the sparkle flood into my life and enjoy another day. But a near-death experience with the dumper had scattered the tedium and aimed me directly at Becker and Fowler. I decided on the spot that, from that day, since no one else was interested, I would go to war for Lou.

At breakfast, Billy attempted to hold me in check. He lived on the ground floor and occasionally would share my bed. Not exclusively, thank God. In any case, he had never shown a desire for marriage. 'Leave it to the police,' he said. 'Why do you need to prove Lou was murdered? You were not a close friend.'

I hesitated while I mulled that over. 'I can do right by Lou and maybe get back at Kitty, that's why.'

The truth is, my daily routine was stifling me. The nine years of knocking around with Kitty's gang had been full of excitement and turmoil, and I itched for something more exciting than the smell of spent gas in the kitchen and stale beer in the bar.

I topped up the teapot, refilled my cup, and stood at the window, remembering Kitty, but not with kindness. After a while, I sat opposite Billy at the table. 'Four years ago,' I said, brooding, 'Kitty introduced me to a businessman of considerable importance and a pillar of the church. Content in his marriage, he was, but looking for a temporary seachange. Something different.

'I met him in April, 1950. He was Managing Director of one of Melbourne's big department stores with branches in Sydney and Brisbane, and he would fly from Melbourne for a weekly conference with his State Manager. He always stayed at The Australia. I met him in the bar, and it grew from there into regular weekly meetings. But never again at The Australia. He chose to meet at The Rex in Cammeray, which was discreet but inconvenient for him.

'So, he would vanish on Tuesday afternoons and stay with me. Sometimes, he invented a reason to be in Sydney, and we would spend all day together, wandering about, shopping at Mosman, or wrapped up in our winter woollies walking by the harbour at Manly, but he always caught the afternoon flight to Melbourne and home.

'From the start, he took pains to ensure I understood he loved his wife, didn't want to hurt or humiliate her, and would never leave her. Men confided that to me so often. They loved their wives. It was about sex, not love.

'But he set it out like a contract: clause one, no emotional fuss. Clause two, he would open a bank account in my name and deposit the money monthly. He would set the time and place for our assignations, and, once a month, we would have a blood test and show each other the results.

'I admired his loyalty to his wife and family. He had his needs, which his wife couldn't or wouldn't satisfy, but I did. So, it was ethical sex with high principles. He treated me like royalty, unlike others you probably know. We discussed business, politics, the stock market, sport, and even fashion. His passion was cricket, and my game was football. If more wives listened to the cricket on the wireless and read the *Financial Review* or *The Bulletin*, my kind would be out of business.

'I know a lot of intelligent men. Academics, surgeons, clerics, millionaires, but this man was in a class of his own.

'It was late July and cold. After romping with me at The Rex, he took a shower, and while tucking in his shirt, ready to go home to Melbourne, he said, "I would like to buy a flat and have you exclusively for me. Would you do that?"

'"Your fancy woman?"

'"My lover," he said. "I want you permanently in my life."

'How much I loved him for that. Damn. If it would be with any man, it would be with this one. My thirtieth birthday was around the corner; young, long-legged beauties were on the way up. Temptation called.

'I told him he had taken me by surprise, and I would like to think about it. But Kitty had discovered how wealthy he was and urged me to take it further.'

I glanced at Billy, finding it difficult to meet his eyes. 'It's no secret that the right woman can mould a man like a handful of a child's plasticine. You can make them laugh, cry, fall in love with you or stop them from falling.' Billy covered a grin with his hand, but I persisted. 'It's true. Keep a man talking about himself long enough, shower him with flattery, make him feel young again, solve his petty marital problems, and take him to bed. He's yours until you don't want him anymore.'

My eyes bounced around the room. 'I didn't set out to do that with this lovely man. I hadn't wanted him to fall in love.' I rubbed the back of my neck and shook my head, but Billy insisted I continue my story, and I wanted to end it.

'But this upright and decent man—'

Billy almost fell off his chair in his haste to interrupt. 'He's not that decent, is he? Playing up with you while his wife stayed home cooking for him?'

'We are all sinners, Billy, and he was no different. Who are we to pass judgment on others? Judges, government ministers, bankers, lawyers, professors, philosophers, bishops,' I waved my hand to encompass the world, 'all came to me with different excuses, but all wanting the same little fleeting thing.'

Billy said nothing, but that was of no concern to me. He was my true friend and would be until the world blew apart.

'Kitty threatened me.' My voice quivered, and I paused to get it under control. 'She swore she would remake my face with acid if I refused to advance the affair. So, while she plotted and conspired, he fell for me, and I fell more than a little in love with him. As I did with some clients.'

'Wait.' Billy flushed, and his tongue stumbled. 'Are ... Are you t-telling me you fell in love with your clients?'

'Men feel that under the circumstances, they can have their way with another human without love, though it may be only for a moment. Where there's no love, there's no life, so find something else to occupy your time.'

Perhaps Billy thought about it, but he didn't join that discussion. Instead, he said, 'Kitty, no doubt, employed a photographer to follow you and snap his camera at your secret romantic dinners or the shops and through the window. Did you know about that?'

'No. Well, not about the photographs. I suspected Kitty had a plan up her bloomers, but she hadn't shared it with me.'

'So, then she blackmailed him.'

Silent for ages, I waited for Billy to drop the question. Finally, he said, 'And—?'

'He refused to pay, confessed to his wife and shot himself dead.' I jumped up and stared through the window, facing away from Billy, not ready to meet his eyes. 'You can imagine how ashamed and dirty I felt. I had nightmares for weeks. So, I ran. Lucky for me, Hector Larcombe diverted her fury. He was my lawyer and client, and he made an enemy of Kitty over this affair. Without Hector's help, I would have lost my face to a cup of acid.'

I slumped in my chair. 'Now, in Dudley, people respect me for what I am. But I sometimes wake at night thinking of that poor man who shot himself and the part I played in it. I could make up for it if I trace Lou's killer to Kitty and make certain she gets her comeuppance.'

'That's foolish,' Billy said. 'Kitty has a heart as hard as agate and as black. She's lethal. You can only lose if you fight her.'

'It's a chance for me to forget what I did. I have friends in high places and know my way around the dark world. I can stay clear of her. Lou's murderer should face justice, and Kitty should be exposed. The police are not interested. I'll make them take notice.'

'Who will run the hotel while you gallop about playing the detective? There will be expenses.'

Back to my usual self, I laughed. 'Pride of Egypt will take care of the finances as you assured me she would.'

'It's a big gamble. You can never rely on tips, no matter the source. Anything can go astray.'

I jumped up from the kitchen table and put the dirty dishes in the sink. 'Come on, mate. Let Bad Billy out.' My arms were open to give Billy an unexpected hug. 'I'll go now and lay the bet with Tom Halley.'

In the car, I sucked the sea air into my lungs, fidgeted in the seat with my mind on the dangers of dealing with Kitty, and the gulls swooped and soared,

I squeezed into the corner to study Billy's face. 'You pay for protection,' I said. 'I've seen Bart Evans come on Tuesdays, and the look in your eye when you hand over your cash to him… Now that I'll be taking on Kitty in a fight to the death, she'll be on my case in a flash. Do I need protection? Who will protect me? How much do you pay? Can I afford it?'

The car slowed at an intersection. Shoppers sauntered on the pavement, school kids licked ice creams from dripping cones, and off-shift miners carried string bags filled with produce for their wives. I felt a sense of dislocation, yet Billy was unusually talkative since our chat about sin and the intimacies of life. I always knew he had a conscience; he sometimes polished it on me.

He said, 'Personal protection is one of those things you reckon you can do without until the day comes when you need it. Gabe has goons with him day and night. You can't afford that.'

'What's with Bart Evans? What does he do for you?'

'It's like this. On a good Saturday, I take twelve hundred pounds. On Melbourne Cup Day, maybe twice that. Suppose a journalist decides to write about the evils of gambling and how it takes money from poor coal miners' families. Politicians would have to react. Tell everyone how they'll come down hard on the gambling industry. Then, the Racing and Gaming Department would have to audit the books of registered bookies like Tom Halley, and the Tax Department would ask why he's not paying enough tax, and the police would raid the illegal SP bookies. Tom would have to pay tax penalties, and the Opposition would berate the Government to no one's benefit. I'd be out of business for months, losing thousands before life returned to normal. The poor miners would drink more, and their families would be no better off.'

'So,' I said, 'you pay Kitty to keep the journalist quiet.'

'And all the others in the chain. That journalist needs only to come up with a good headline, and Tom Halley is wondering how to pay for his new Jaguar. Tom takes thirty, forty thousand in bets every Saturday.'

We passed through a five-way intersection where a police constable stood in the centre waving his arms and moving about in a lively dance, occasionally shouting impatiently at a driver whose inattention held up his precious traffic.

'But,' Billy continued, 'many people can't make it to the track. They prefer to talk to an SP bookie, ask for a tip, and discuss form. Hundreds of small people bet with me. Market farmers love to gamble. Graziers, mine managers, doctors, dentists. I have an ice cream vendor who'll drop two hundred to win four. Melbourne Cup week, I've had a thousand to win five from a butcher. A bookie expects to make three quid profit for every five he takes. All things going well.'

Instantly, I respected Billy more. I peered sideways at him, his hands on the Ford's big steering wheel and his eyes on the road ahead. 'So you take twelve hundred hundred a week? And tax-free? A decent house near the beach at Merewether goes for three and a half thousand pounds. That's what... not five week's profit for you?'

We drove in silence for a long time at a leisurely pace, stopping at traffic lights, the Ford swaying on soft springs. Billy accelerated to pass a double-decker bus before the traffic light changed. 'There's a new bloke, a kid, muscled in on the action. Now, there'll be hell to pay.' A boy on the corner selling newspapers out of a hessian sack hanging on his shoulder held up a *Newcastle Sun* headline and shouted it: 'WEST INDIES BY A HUNDRED AND FORTY RUNS. Read all about it.'

Billy curled his lip. 'Gabe has a monopoly on casino gambling and sly grog, but I hear the new kid is a dangerous little bugger. He wants to take over all that and the protection racket, too.' Suddenly, he got excited and shouted, 'There he is.'

I twisted about in my seat.

'There.'

'Gabe?'

'No, the new kid.'

I searched the crowd, looking for a thug. 'The kid in jeans?' I asked. 'The boy licking chocolate ice cream in a cone? A good kick up the backside would straighten him out.' That's when I remembered him. 'That's the brat who terrorised Lou at the fete. His name is Franz Becker, and he has a friend, Jessica.'

I felt a buzz. Shanks had brought excitement into my life, successful standover merchant or not.

A half-hour later, that same young brat would cut Tom Halley in his sitting room and frighten the life out of me.

6. What Becker Does to Impress

Tom opened his door to me in sharply-creased fine wool trousers and a grey, summer-weight, houndstooth jacket. 'Sunni,' he hooted and, hands thrown out in welcome, opened the door and drew me inside. 'You have finally recognised the inevitable and come to live in sin with me until my divorce comes through.'

Tom Halley, registered bookmaker, happily married with no thoughts of divorce, lived near the top of the hill in a heritage-listed colonial mansion with a much-envied view of the rolling Pacific and the white surf breaking on creamy sand. Billy had dropped me at the kerb, and, after I stood for a while open-mouthed peering up at the seven separate gable roofs and four chimneys, I trod the long, curved sandstone path past the fish pond and up the steps to the stained-glass front door in deep shadow from the afternoon sun. I rang the bell and waited under the portico. I'm not a gambler, but I thought there were enough favourable omens to begin my gambling career on February 6th, the same day the Queen and Prince Philip would attend the races at Randwick.

I simpered a little. I loved Tom. 'Oh, you wish,' I said. 'Go on, Thomas. You'll have to drag yourself out of penury first. I'm here only to lay a bet with you. Pride of Egypt in the Westminster Juveniles.'

He gave me that cheeky grin that I loved so much. 'But you came in person when you might have phoned.' He scratched his nose and winked. 'Like old times, Sunni.' He lifted his shoulders and raised his eyes to the ceiling and the bedroom.

'You'll kink your neck, you duffer. Old times have long gone for you. I'll take twenty to one and give away twenty-five quid to help you out of your financial problems.'

'That's a lot of hoot, mate. I've had a run on Pride of Egypt over the last week, but I'll give ten to one to a special friend.'

'Sixteen, then,' I said, with a mental thank you to Billy.

'Give it here.' He held out his hand and counted the notes.

I stepped to the window and listened to the gulls and the surf breaking on rocks far below, then took in the room with its cream, embossed wallpaper, silk tasselled window coverings, deep carpet, elegant antique furniture, bookcases overflowing with old books, comfortable cracked-leather chair, a walnut sideboard, diamond-leaded bay window overlooking a view of the ocean and a dozen red roses in a cut-crystal vase.

Not that I noticed.

I felt the quality of the drapes. Silk. Pressed my toe into the carpet—pure wool. I checked for dust on the beautifully inlaid walnut sideboard and was tempted to say it was a lovely house, but I restrained my tongue because my mum told me only common people said that.

So, I said, 'Sixteens, Thomas. Gabe would have taken the bet at twenty. If I had gone to him.' Tom gaped, his face turning red. 'Steady on, mate,' I said. 'You look like you saw a fly in your whisky.'

Tom said, 'Count your jewellery after you shake hands with Gabe.'

'I can count my jewellery on one finger.'

'Don't joke about him. He's dangerous. Doesn't play by the rules. He hasn't shown his true colours in this town, but there are stories out of Sydney would turn your hair grey. Murder, arson, top people helping him. What would you expect of Kitty's friend?' He opened his mouth to add something, paused to reconsider, and moved on. 'A new kid in town reckons he can take Gabe on and beat him. Unfortunately, he's too young to offer a match.'

'Would that be a Franz Becker?'

'Yes. How did you come by that name?'

Like Tom, I held off while I thought of Becker. The word wary comes to mind. 'Unhappily, I met him at the fete. He's a strange one. Looks like a teenager but swaggers like a street brawler. I saw him for only a few minutes before I gave him a whack across the ear. He's overflowing with aggression. Good looking, though.'

Tom cleared his throat. 'Cheeky young bastard he is. I'll tell you a story and let you judge for yourself. You know Joe Parker, the car man?'

'Yes, I know Joe.'

'He has a heritage house at Meriwether. Not far down the road. Nice place, two-storey weatherboard and sandstone, set thirty yards from the beach behind high hedges. Friday night, no moon, Becker and friend went in through the gate, along the path and up the steps. Joe's wife is ill, and, sometimes in summer, he sleeps on the verandah in a squatter's chair overlooking the ocean where he can get the breeze and smoke his bloody cigars.'

Tom crinkled his nose and waved a hand in front of his face. 'Anyway,' he said, 'Becker waltzes up to the front door. As he raises a hand to knock on the glass panels, a gust rattles the door, and he has to speak loudly above the noise of the wind. Joe wakes when Becker tells his friend that Parker must have a half-acre here and can afford more than two quid a month, so what's he complaining about?

'Joe got a bit excited about this. He bellowed, like, what in hell's name are you boys doing here, waking me at this hour? But Becker banged on the door anyway. Loudly, Joe told me, to show he meant business. Dogs in the street woke and barked, but Becker didn't care. Joe hadn't locked the door. It swung open.'

Tom made a sound that might have been a laugh if it had lasted longer. 'Joe is not a threatening figure at the best of times. His pencil moustache and salesman's smile. To make it worse, he was barefoot, wearing cotton pyjama shorts and a silk dressing gown.

I snorted. 'Joe in shorties. That's a sight.' Joe was tall, skinny as a pick handle, and had trained an Errol Flynn-style moustache to sit on his upper lip. He waved a big fat Cuban cigar wherever he went and trailed the stink of used cigar smoke.

Tom took up his story. 'Becker told Joe they were there about their money and barged into the house. Joe squealed. It was midnight, and his wife was in a bad way, but Becker carried a baseball bat. He rapped it on a glass panel in the door and told Joe to come inside, or he'd have to break something. I expect Joe would have lost his smile by then. He told them to be quiet and to wait there while he checked on his wife upstairs. They were too smart to fall for that, and, according to Joe, Becker's mate demanded to come too and make sure Joe didn't chat to his friends on the telephone. Then he shoved Joe and demanded the two quid he owed, or he'd pay the hard way.'

I missed part of Tom's story while my mind was stuck on Joe Parker. I disliked that man. He sold second-hand cars and was cruel to his wife, putting her down in public as though she were simple-minded. Should I have any sympathy for him? No. It was high time someone took him to task.

Tom was saying, 'Joe tried to talk his way out of it. Told them he didn't have two quid. Business wasn't good, and the war was barely over. The recession and all that. Blah, blah, blah. Said they hadn't done anything to earn two pounds and kept calling them kids.

'Joe says he was distracted by Becker swinging his baseball bat—practice hits, his back foot pivoting, leading his hips through. Joe smirked his contempt for their threats, and he thought that calling them kids got at Becker.'

On the edge of the chair, enjoying Tom's tale, I clutched the empty brown envelope. 'Joe Parker is an arrogant bugger,' I said, trying to keep the smirk off my face. 'He gets under my skin with that pompous sneer. It's no wonder the kids took offence.'

'Teenage wannabes, Joe called them and told them to run

along as you would a naughty child. He said he was paying the syndicate for protection, and there was no room for Becker. That did it. Becker swung the bat and cleared a hall table of silver-framed photographs and porcelain figurines. They were Joe's pride and joy. Lladro. He said he had paid big and told Becker he'd have to reinburse the cost.'

Tom was enjoying the story. 'Talk about insult to injury. Becker stepped into the living room and swung the bat at a crystal flower vase on the coffee table, then spun on his heel and stepped towards Joe with the bat raised, ready to slam him one. Joe is his own worst enemy. He called Becker 'Kiddo' and told him to get out, and that's when Becker tossed the bat, whipped out a knife, and Joe was clapping a hand to his face, reeling. Blood leaking between his fingers, he told me, splashing on the carpet and his silk dressing gown. Becker demanded two quid for last month and four from then on for welshing. "Run and get it," he told Joe. "Now. And no phone calls, or you'll be bleeding from your throat."'

I concentrated on Tom's story and didn't register the doorbell ringing the first time.

Tom laughed, 'I wish I'd been there to hear Joe scream.'

The bell rang a second time, and he went off to open the door.

I heard a commotion in the hallway. Tom shouted something and tried to close the door, grunting with the effort. He shouted again. 'Get your fucking foot outta my door.'

'There was a scuffle and more grunting, and I rushed to the rescue. Tom shouted, 'You're the kid who slashed Joe Parker. Get outta here.' But Becker was inside the house, and the door slammed behind him.

'I've come to do you a favour, Mr Halley,' he said, moving forward, and I yelled something at him as I ran to get to them. Tom took two quick steps backwards to a silky-oak hall table, tore open the drawer and swung around with a revolver in his hand. 'Get out. Out!' all the time putting space between himself and Becker. 'Take one step, and I'll shoot you dead.'

But Becker sauntered forward, mocking Tom. 'You won't shoot, Mr Halley. The revolver doesn't look right in your hand, and you don't want blood on your clothes.' He half turned to me and spoke easily, cool as a sailboat on a wintry day. 'Stay there, Miss Sinclair. You will make things the worse.' He had a deep, vibrant voice. To avoid provoking him, I waited.

'Good people,' Becker said, as though speaking to a priest or lecturing a class of school children, 'will not shoot until they are frantic. It is not easy to pull the trigger, especially if the gun's on a young, good-looking bloke like me.'

Becker's attempt at humour fell flat. Tom stepped away.

'Be sensible, Mr Halley. No, mate, you'll not shoot me.' He followed Tom, forcing him against the wall with the revolver pointing directly at Becker's heart a yard away.

Tom's voice was shaky. 'You're threatening me. I have every right to shoot. One more step, and I'll fire.'

'No, you can't shoot me, Mr Halley. Have you ever killed a man? It takes more than anger to kill a man. Give me the gun.'

'I'll shoot you in the leg,' Tom said, lowering the barrel. 'Cripple you.'

'Nah. Don't be silly. Here.' Becker held out his hand and moved forward to an easy arm's length. 'Give it to me,' he said. He held the barrel with two tender fingers, gentled Tom's passive arm until the gun pointed away, then took it from unresisting fingers.

But Becker's Adam's apple wobbled as he swallowed his spit, and outside sounds came to me as though through earmuffs.

'Sit down, please, Miss Sinclair, Mr Halley,' Becker said, walking uninvited into the lounge room and guiding Halley to a comfortable chair. 'There now.' He dropped the gun on the coffee table. 'You are pale. I'll bet you'd like a drink.' He turned to a trolley against the wall. 'Scotch?'

But he had underestimated Tom, and, while Becker fussed with the bottles and poured, Tom recovered, spun off the chair, grabbed the revolver and backed away, shouting, 'Stop. This time I *will* shoot.'

Becker ran at him, knocked the gun from his hand and flashed a blade. Tom cried out and slapped a hand to his face, blood trickling between his fingers.

'That was stupid,' Becker said, breathing fast. 'Now, look what you've done.' He ripped a cotton runner from the coffee table and handed it to Halley. 'Hold that on your face.'

It happened in a flash and with such force, I stopped open-mouthed and speechless. When the blood flow slowed, I managed to say, 'Let me look at that. Keep the pressure on it, Tom. It's not a deep cut.'

'A nick. A pinprick,' Becker said, an adult speaking to a child as though he had often experienced knife wounds.

Tom sat, holding the cloth against his face. Becker had poured him a single malt Scotch. Tom's hand was steady, and his lips didn't tremble. I admired him for that.

Becker said, 'I should have known an old bookie would not give in easily.'

Tom examined the cloth for blood and held it back on his face. 'I should have shot you when I had the chance.'

We waited while Becker inspected a collection of framed photographs and paintings hanging above the trolley, with his back to us but the gun in his pocket. I thought of lion tamers turning away from the animals to prove they were in control.

Becker ran his fingers on the glass of a framed photograph. 'You were in the Air Force?'

'The Great War, 1917,' Tom said.

'I would not have taken your gun if I'd known. You've broken a few heads in your life. I'm lucky. You might have shot me. Is this you?' He touched the black and white photograph of an Air Force sergeant holding a cigarette, standing casually with a hand on the wing of a twin-engine biplane. The flyer wore khaki shorts, a cotton bush jacket with two breast pockets, and a buttoned, baggy pocket on each hip. He had a leather flying helmet on his head with bulbous earmuffs and goggles, the chinstrap dangling open. His boots were heavy with mud, and the laces open below puggarees to his knees. He was a handsome young bloke in those days.

'What's the plane?'

'It's a Handley Page 0/100.'

'You were the pilot?'

'Navigator and gunner. You can see a Lewis gun in the open cockpit.'

'Shoot anyone?' Becker asked.

'We bombed rail yards and telephone exchanges, German ships. Strafed ground troops.'

'Belgium?'

'No. Middle-East. Beersheba and Megiddo. Nineteen-sixteen to eighteen.'

'Is that the pilot with you?'

'Yes.' In Halley's voice, the long-remembered anguish. But he shrugged. 'We were too young.'

'Killed in action?' Becker ventured.

'Pilots died every day. I'm ashamed when I forget their names.'

'Doesn't matter. You escaped.'

'It matters.' Halley patted his face with a handkerchief and inspected it. 'Where did you learn to face a gun like that?'

'Korea. It's funny, but I'm not scared of guns after being wounded. Do you think killing counts when you're in the army or air force?'

'The Air Force was not personal. Not up close like infantry. They returned fire, so it wasn't like murder. Were you infantry?'

'Special Forces,' Becker said. 'Does it worry you?'

'Yes,' Tom said, following Becker's eyes, interested. 'You?'

'Some of it, yeah. When I least expect it, my captain's corpse floats by like he was lazing on Bondi Beach, and I hear the screaming inside my head after Maryang. Does it ever go away?'

'Not after thirty-five years. I read about Maryang. Heroes, according to the papers.'

'Don't know about heroes,' Becker said, as returned soldiers do when put on the spot. 'Life is a poker game. You pick up the cards, then bluff and gamble your way through.'

Silence descended on the room. I thought, who the hell does this kid think he is, offering his opinion on life to a successful man like Tom?

Becker said, 'I thought you were an old bloke and knew nothing.'

'That's not a bad description of me.'

We laughed at that, the tension easing.

'Sorry.' Becker gestured at the handkerchief Tom held to his face. 'It's a nick. I'm Franz Becker, by the way. I prefer Becker because it makes me appear more serious.' He inspected a glass-fronted bookcase. 'I left school at sixteen and went straight to war. Always carried a book to read when we sat about with nothing to do. Mind if I look?' his finger tracking a line along the cabinet door.

Tom said, 'You're the one with the gun. Do what you like.'

But Becker turned away.

'Go ahead,' Tom said, the essence of a cultured man embarrassed. 'That was a bit surly of me.'

Becker opened the glass door of the case. He fluttered a finger along the books' spines and took out a handsome, slim, leather-covered, gold-tooled volume. 'Collected Poems of Henry Lawson.'

'Look,' Tom said, reaching for reasonableness. 'I can't pay you for protection. I pay the syndicate, and they'll be after you for Joe—and now for me.'

'I walk in here, cut you, and where's the protection? What do they protect you against?'

'From the police,' Tom said. 'From judges, newspapers, churches, taxation. Are you able to do that?' He waited for an answer, but Becker remained silent. 'No, you can't. On the other hand, you seem smart enough. How old are you?'

'Twenty.'

'So, what's it about?'

Becker shrugged, indifferent.

Tom said, 'You were too young to join the army. War has twisted your mind like it did with many soldiers. We get scared out there, and that little mad bastard kicks off in our heads. Plenty of twenty-year-old soldiers came apart in the war and never got it together again. You were how old?'

'Sixteen, when I joined up to go to Korea.'

'Is it any wonder you're disturbed? But that's curable if you would give yourself a second chance.'

Becker said, 'I want my slice of the world, is all—and I don't mind taking a risk. Who wants to die a boring old man?'

Or a boring old woman.

Becker rifled through the Lawson book. 'Hey, listen to this.'

I stared at him. Was he interested or playing a game? But, too absorbed to take his eyes off the page, he read to us:

> They stood by the door of the Inn on the Rise;
> May Carney looked up in the bushranger's eyes:
> 'Oh! Why did you come? —it was mad of you, Jack;
> You know that the troopers are out on your track.'
> A laugh and a shake of his obstinate head —
> 'I wanted a dance, and I'll chance it,' he said.

I laughed. But Becker said quietly, 'I want to dance, too, and I'll chance it.' His unguarded face revealed the inexperienced youth who fought a war too early in his short life.

Tom shuffled unsteadily on his chair. 'You had better read

the rest of the poem. The troopers always win.' He smiled grimly then and asked, 'See yourself as a bushranger, do you?'

'Nah. I've never ridden a horse, and stagecoaches are out of fashion.' Becker chuckled at his joke.

But Tom turned away, biting his lip. 'You're young. Looking to find yourself. At some time, everyone asks, who am I?'

Becker busied himself reading another poem.

Tom raised his hands to hold up the sky. 'You're looking only in the shadows, son. But there's as much interest on the lighter side of life.'

'How's your face?' Becker asked.

'A bit of pain, but I'll survive. No thanks to you.'

'Get a tetanus shot. It will not leave a scar. Sorry about that.'

'Korea, eh?' Tom said. 'Listen, Franz. You're off on the wrong path. Bushrangers finish dead at the side of the road, and nobody cares. I will find you a job with a future. Do something with your life.'

Becker glanced around the room. 'I need a house like this, on a hill like this, with a car like yours and money to spare to pay for skiing trips to Switzerland and to run with the wealthy ones. That's what I want to do with my life.'

Tom raised his face and thrust out his jaw. 'I had nothing when I left the army thirty-six years ago.'

Becker said, 'That was too long ago. Gabe took only six years. Life is short.' He waved the book, once more the arrogant youth. 'I will do the dance and chance it.'

Tom told him to stay clear of Gabe and people like him. 'That's not for you,' he said. 'Come and talk to me at the races. I'll start you off.'

Becker placed the book on the coffee table.

'You can borrow it if you like,' Tom said, standing closer and making a friendly opening. 'Read it and return it when you finish.'

'Thanks, Mr Halley.' With the book in his hand, Becker made for the door, 'but I'll buy one to keep. Goodbye, Miss Sinclair, Mr Halley. I'll leave the gun and the book on the hall table. I'll not bother you again. There are plenty other stagecoaches to rob.'

When he left, he took all the air out of the room. I looked at Tom, and he raised a corner of his mouth. 'Impressive,' I said, smiling, nodding acceptance of my assessment. 'This kid could teach me a lesson or two.'

'He may be twelve years younger than you, but he's not a kid.'

'But what an adventurous spirit. He'll get there.'

'Except,' Tom said, 'he's on the wrong track, and it leads only to a sticky end. The world is changing and needs kids with his vitality, but not with his scrambled brain. Steady will get him there if he would just understand that.'

'Time to get on the right track when you're forty,' I said. 'The right or wrong track is a matter of your perspective.'

'Sunni. Ugh. You, of all people, must know how hard and dirty life can be. Stick to your hotel. Ten years from now, you will have all the money and fame you can handle.'

'It doesn't work as easily as that.'

'Danger's like a red rag to you. I know you too well. It's there in your eyes. Please don't allow yourself to be seduced by the excitement and adventure of Gabe's world or Becker's dreams.'

I had never thought of seduction in that context.

The sun was low in the west and happy hour was busy when I arrived back at The Dudley. The television was blaring a re-run of the third race at Canterbury—a mid-week meeting.

Moving swiftly, I filled glasses and checked my watch, too busy to talk or listen, and after a flurry of refills, taking coins and pound notes and counting out change, I slipped out from behind the bar to have a few minutes to think about Becker away from the noise.

I stepped out through the batwing doors onto the footpath to take in the evening breeze. Why should I care if Lou was murdered or died in an accident? He was a bit of fun in a string of one-night stands. Something caught my eye, and I peered across the street at a movement in the shadows. Nothing. I'll see his murderer punished, then move on from Kitty.

And, across the road, a brute I recognised emerged from shadow into the light. Albie Fowler glared at me while I stood transfixed for a full minute. My mouth went dry, and my leg muscles were weak. 'Get out of here. I'm calling the police.'

I grabbed a half-brick and threw it with all my strength, and it clanged on his motorbike's tank. I shouted, and three customers piled through the door, attracted by the alarm in my voice.

The motorbike burst into life, U-turned and sped past and away.

'What's wrong?' Billy charged around the corner.

'Nothing.' I shooed my customers inside with a laugh to finish their drinks. 'False alarm.' And, quietly to Billy, 'Looks like I'm about to get that excitement in my life.'

Until that moment, I believed in my courage and independence. Fowler's appearance changed that. He threatened me. He intended to hurt me. Why?

7. Search Warrant Time

Thursday, January 7.

Billy was not in his usual corner answering the telephone. He was at the bar with his mates when Tommo came through the door with his search warrant.

'Sorry, Sunni,' Tommo said, 'but we've gotta tear your place apart looking for books or betting slips. For some reason, the Queen and SP bookies can't live in the same town.'

To make the most of the Royals, the City of Newcastle had scheduled a week-long Race Festival at the Newcastle racecourse. The Hunter Valley Trophy Festival was to be three race meetings over two weeks, kicking off with the Newcastle Stakes on the 23rd of January, followed by the Golden Guineas meet on the last Saturday of the month. The big day in the racing calendar would be the Royal Hunter Valley Gold Trophy on February sixth, the same Saturday the Royal visitors would grace Randwick Racecourse in Sydney for the Queen Elizabeth Stakes.

One constable probed behind the bar; one went off to the guest lounge and another to the kitchen. 'Sunni, you're not busy. Can Billy take over from you? We need to talk.'

I called Billy to the bar, and Tommo asked, 'Who won the third, Billy? It was too noisy outside. I had two quid each way on Blue Ocean.'

'Came in second to Lancaster. You'll be up by five bob.'

We sat at the kitchen table— cheese and crackers, a beer for Tommo, and tea for me. 'Well, what have you got to tell me?' I asked while I reached for a cracker.

Tommo swallowed half a glass of cold beer before he said,

'We have spent a lot of time on your case, Sunni. We checked with every taxi driver in the area, and no one drove Lou to Stockton Beach or the ferry. Are you certain he arrived without a car or motorbike?'

'Not certain, but, if he did, it was well hidden out of sight.'

'Did you notice any strange cars early on the Sunday morning, before dawn?'

'No.' I said. 'I've asked Billy and all the house guests the same question, and no one noticed anything.'

Tommo tapped his fingers on the table, shuffled in his chair, and searched the ceiling. 'We went door to door in Dudley and Redhead. Nothing. The coroner has reviewed his findings at our request and was not too happy to oblige us. The bruises are consistent with a pounding in the surf and being washed onto rocks, though he says he cannot rule out foul play. We interviewed Becker and threatened him. He laughed at us, and we got nowhere. We have spoken to our criminal contacts. Nothing. How he got there is a mystery, but what do you expect us to do? And don't say investigate because we've searched under every stone.'

I jumped to my feet, paced to the window, and brandished a cracker at Tommo. 'What about that thug, Fowler? He came here to intimidate me.'

Tommo cut into a Gorgonzola and smacked his lips. 'Albie Fowler is a suspect in the murder of Sergeant Moran, and we know how to take care of cop killers. If there was foul play with Lou, it will come to light, and we will act. The night Shanks died at Redhead Beach, Fowler was with friends, including your Becker. An early morning swimmer spotted them Monday morning. They'd spent the night fishing and slept on the beach, miles away from Stockton, and had a bag of fish. One of the group is a respected licensed surveyor, who has never come to police attention and swears they were together all night.'

I drummed my fingers on the table and let my eyes wander about the room. 'Becker paid for Lou's funeral. Why would he do that?'

'Loyalty to a friend?'

'Loyalty? I wonder.'

With a trace of a smile, Tommo said, 'That's it for now. Life goes on.' He waited for a decent interval, then, 'Is Pride of Egypt on for the Juveniles.'

'Yeah. Billy says she'll be running.'

'I put ten quid on her at sixteen to one.'

'She's now down to tens.'

Tommo's voice was filled with envy. 'It will be a big day for you when she wins.'

'Tom Halley says it will be a record settlement day.'

While my hands and feet were on the move to keep the glasses filled, take cash, give change and swap cheek with the wags at the bar, my subconscious must have been working because I had a sudden vision of the Eiffel Tower and me. Together. And, somewhere in the mist, shadows sat with Billy at the centre, counting a mountain of pound notes. I worked my mind on it, but it kept slipping away.

Lou was Lou until he died; then he became Shanks, the riddle. I would swear he wasn't the sort to swim in the dark. He was like two people—an identical twin hiding inside him—a doppelganger. Don't we all have one?

'Am I wrong? I asked Billy later after I closed the doors, and we sat together in harmony, with brandy nightcaps in hand. 'About the boy murdering Lou?'

'Did you find out anything from the girl?' he asked.

I sighed and checked the clock. It had been a long day. 'I visited Jessica at the mine. It's not exactly Disneyland.'

Twin winding wheels were constantly in motion, five feet in diameter, sixty feet above the ground on a steel truss pithead. A steel cable unwound to launch men and materials to the coal face nine hundred feet below and reeled in the skips filled with coal. Seventy feet high, a chimneystack poured out dirty-coloured smoke to drift over the Pacific Ocean, and a steam train hissed and panted and puffed out steam and dense, black, sulphurous smoke waiting for a rotary dumper to fill its wagons. The entire yard and the surrounding field were covered in fine coal dust.

'You know,' I said to Billy, 'Jessica was a bit put out by my visit. I suppose after working all day in the first aid room. She spun about to run off when she saw me waiting at the reception counter. I called her name, and she had to come to me. But she was impatient, shifting from one foot to the other. I suggested we go outside where it would be quieter, and we sat on a seat under the Norfolk pines overlooking the ocean.'

'Was she nervy? Suspicious? Spiteful? Angry?'

'I put her at ease by talking about nursing and made a joke of telling her she might meet a nice young doctor. When I dropped in a sneaky question, she tossed an eye in my direction, which I took to mean that Becker has hang-ups about sex.'

'Gay?' Billy asked.

'Perhaps. Jessica told me Becker knocks around with a young bloke she called Skeet, who dotes on him. He has a mind, young Franz has, though it's in a mess after his war in Korea.'

I told her Lou had died and that he had been one of Franz's gang, but she denied knowing anyone named Lou, then jumped up, cupped her forehead, to look for the bus. I grabbed her elbow and spoke sharply. Had Becker frightened her, threatened her? She denied that but offered that he was awfully young to have fought in a war.

Billy grimaced and heaved himself up on the pillow. 'The way they take in underage kids. It's criminal.'

'She wrenched herself away from me and rushed to the bus without looking back.'

Billy said, 'She's a witness who can place Becker and Fowler with Shanks at the fete.'

I turned my head to look at him. 'So?'

He reached to the bedside table and poured another brandy. 'You should be frightened after Fowler came to the hotel.' He raised the bottle and his eyebrows to me. 'You're not just any bystander. You're a witness, too. If someone did kill Lou, you're putting yourself in danger, running about, recklessly asking questions. Stirring the pot like that, you might as well paint a target on your forehead. You are likely endangering the girl, too. You're too conspicuous. Drop it, Sunni. Shanks doesn't mean anything to you.'

I gaped at the ceiling, an intricate pattern in pressed metal, sheaves of wheat reflecting the dull glow from a dim security lamp above the external door. 'Would you please go to the hardware in the morning? We need a brighter bulb above the door and a stronger lock.'

8. Who's Doing Who in the Sauna?

Friday, January 8.

The sun hadn't yet raised its head. I stood outside the training track, my fingers in the chain wire gate, dragging in the cool air and the smells of manure and chaff. Harnesses creaked and jingled, men and women spoke gently as they led horses out in the pre-dawn gloom, and the soft glow of daylight spread behind the stable roof.

I had been to the dawn gallops a few times and knew to wear trousers and rubber boots and to leave my jewellery at home. Naturally, I had gone to my hairdresser yesterday and climbed out of bed this morning in plenty of time to do my face for Gabe.

As a member of the Newcastle Jockey Club, I rubbed shoulders with Gabe and other crooks and came to the races often, but not to throw my money away on the horses. People talked. I didn't try to quash the rumour that we were partners. It surfaced whenever we appeared together in public. It wasn't entirely true, but it offered me some protection against the men who wanted a one-nighter. A picture blew into my mind. Me at next year's Academy Awards in a long evening dress—bright, sparkling green—and Gabe in a dinner suit with those slick sharkskin lapels.

The rising sun was warming the air, and Gabe stood nonchalantly in a thin ground mist, his foot on a rail, watching horses cantering, warming up. Others snorted and danced under their strappers' control, impatient to be out on the course. Over average height, he wore rough clothes—jeans, T-shirt, muddy rubber boots, leather jacket—and managed to look like a millionaire. His smile acknowledged me, but he ambled over to a trainer standing with a grey mare, clapped the strapper on the shoulder, the horse on its neck, and shook hands with the trainer.

I stood watching, within earshot, but the conversation was no more than good mornings and what the weather would be like for the rest of the day.

Gabe patted the trainer on the shoulder and came over to me. He looked like he had won the Gold Cup and owned the horse, the racetrack, command of the morning gallops and the rising sun. His hand came out from three yards away, drew me to him and threw an arm around my waist like a long-lost lover or an eccentric millionaire.

I heard this cheerful voice calling, 'Morning, Mr Rosen.' It busted straight into the space between Gabe's arm and my waist.

I found Becker standing behind me, as he had at the casino. 'Are you following me around?' I asked him, not in a pleasant tone, after he interrupted my smooching with Gabe.

He smiled, 'Morning, Miss Sinclair,' and stood back so I couldn't stand on his toe again.

'Franz Becker,' Gabe said, pulling him into a hug despite kicking him out of the casino. 'I know about you, Franz.'

Becker recoiled from the embrace, wrenched himself free and croaked a good morning again. Gabe lifted his hands loosely to ask who cared.

When Becker found his breath, he said, 'They call me Becker.'

'Then, Becker it shall be.'

A gaggle of young women stood around—Grace Kelly look-alikes in rollnecks and beige or camel breeches and knee-high boots—preening, heads together whispering, their eyes following Gabe, sniggering about me until they grasped who was who in the steam room, then patching on their snottiest smiles.

50

One day, I'll make them pay for that. Moving constantly, two men in cheap, wrinkled suits checked Becker over and scorned him with unseeing eyes.

'Sit here with me,' Gabe said, drawing us into a circle of broken cable spools near a pile of pungent straw and fresh manure raked from the stables. Producing a flask, he rinsed enamel mugs and poured hot tea smelling of horse sweat and whisky. 'Make yourself comfortable. Drinks are on me.'

'You own these stables, Mr Rosen?' Becker said, waving a hand that cut across my sightline to Gabe.

He moved his foot to stop me from standing on it and demanded Gabe's attention. After all, Gabe had invited me, and Becker acted as though he was unexpected, his eyes searching the shadowy stables, a long passage with stalls on each side where horses stuck their heads out to be part of the action and stable hands were busy mucking out, saddling and grooming. A lively young woman in a white shirt and jeans held a conversation with a grey horse, its head stretching out over the stable door, its lips moving, nose snuffling.

Gabe chuckled. 'They're my horses. I'm negotiating to buy the property. All this will be mine by next week.'

'Twenty stalls.'

'Twenty-four. You're younger than I thought.'

'Old enough,' Becker said, 'to be wounded in Korea and to know how to handle life outside the army.' He laid his head on the side and smiled bleakly. 'Some think my age makes me a pushover, but they shouldn't forget I've been killing people since I turned sixteen.'

'Korea, eh? You joined up young to the army, same as me.'

According to the press, Gabe was a sexual athlete—the impresario who was always accompanied by ravishing strippers and dancers and had enticed Frank Sinatra, Elizabeth Taylor and Mario Lanza to tour Australia and perform in his nightclubs. 'I left school at fifteen,' he told Becker, 'and got into a bit of mischief. My mother wanted me to be a surgeon. What about you?'

Becker said, 'The headmaster in Newcastle told me I had no future to speak of, so I left and bummed about for two years. My parents were dirt-poor.'

I sipped my tea and raised my eyebrows to Gabe over the rim of the cup.

At least he had parents. I didn't know my mother or father enough to make any judgements. A deep black hole dwells in my brain where others keep their parents. I didn't understand them, and my ways were a complete mystery to them. They were too busy fighting each other and making out to care about their one child. Dad told me once he thought he let me down, what with the drinking and the sex. Nothing he said could have impressed me. They were undoubtedly poor.

Gabe said to me, 'I invited Becker—'

'Not invited,' Becker interrupted, arrogant as always. 'Demanded with threats.'

'He got cheeky. Took a swipe at Joe Palmer, knowing I'm Joe's friend.'

Becker said, 'You sent your heavyweights around to beat up Albie Fowler and left a message for me to come here today.'

Gabe's voice was full of impatience for this kid. 'What did you expect? You took me on and thought I would let a child like you get away with it?'

'You'll find I'm no child.'

Gabe leaned forward to punch him casually on the shoulder. 'You surprised me when you visited Joe Parker and then had the cheek to come to my casino. Now you have Fowler and think you can muscle in on my business?'

Becker said, 'You told me to come here today. I came. What's up?'

I tried for a relaxed posture on the broken spool, but it wouldn't stay still, rocking every time I moved, keeping me off balance. Under that thick black hair, Becker had an open face with smiling, generous lips. Though his eyes were flinty, he was cool, calm and holding together, and his style impressed me more than a little, as it had at Tom Halley's.

'Shanks finally had his heart attack,' Gabe said, as though that was reasonable and logical, 'and Fowler should be in an institution. You're too young to know what's what and who's who. You don't know enough to understand your strengths, limits or capability. One minute, you're dancing to Rock 'n Roll or licking an ice cream, and the next, you're cutting Joe Parker. You're too young. A kid.'

Gabe came to his feet as a horse galloped past. He waved a semaphored message to a trainer and relaxed on his spool as though he'd never interrupted the conversation. 'Kids can be ruthless. Kill without thought or remorse like you did in Korea. When you mature a bit, well, you'll find there's a value on human life and a cost for the suffering. You're hardly out of your teens and don't seem the type to head up a gang. The only people you can lead are the weak, the desperate, the no-hopers. Who's the real boss?'

Becker took a swig of his whisky tea, pulled a face, spat on the ground splashing Gabe's boot, and said. 'If he hadn't tried to put one over us, Shanks would be boss. I'm running my own gang now.'

I sat open-mouthed at the disrespect he showed, and Gabe was silent for a long time. It may have dawned on him that there was more to Becker than he first realised.

A stable hand wheeled a barrow of soiled straw and dumped it in the reeking pile at our feet. Twenty yards away, a woman in a body-hugging beige jumpsuit leant on the timber fence, binoculars to her eyes, following the horses now cantering and galloping on the track. I rocked to and fro on my spool.

Gabe spat a crumb of tobacco into the air. 'Why did you go after Parker? You must have known I wouldn't let you get away with it. Or were you too callow to stop and think about it?' He blew smoke in Becker's face.

Becker waved a hand in front of his face. 'You'll die if you keep smoking like that,' he said, feet planted apart, eyes threatening.

Was I lining up on Becker's side? But which Becker? Becker, the gentleman gangster, quiet, polite, calling me Miss Sinclair? Becker the Lionheart, who faces up to Gabe while knowing he's out of his league? Or Becker the Hothead, who knifes you in an instant then offers first-aid and an apology? I tossed my cold tea into the filthy straw to join his, but Gabe shifted his foot in time.

Becker said, 'Parker's my client now. He knows you'll lean on him and threaten him, but he knows I'll hurt him.'

'You'll need a big gun.'

Becker laughed. 'I don't need a gun.'

'No gun. You reckon big talk will carry you through?'

Becker laughed again. 'Big talk got you here.'

I thought there was a lot of truth in what Gabe said. Big talk gets you nowhere unless you know where you're going and have a plan to get there.

'You have a death wish?' Gabe asked.

'Life is temporary. I learned that in Korea. It's a competition. You live with the permission of the bloke at the top. So I'll get to be the toughest, wealthiest bastard at the top of the coop and live the life any way I want to.'

'You wouldn't know where to start.' Gabe beckoned to the trainer as though he had no interest in Becker's ambitions.

Becker said, 'At the top. I'll start at the top. Everyone else will fall into place.'

Gabe laughed as though it was the funniest joke he'd ever heard.

The trainer came to where we sat, nodded toward me and jerked his head to question Gabe.

'You can speak freely,' Gabe said. 'We're all friends here.'

'Reckon we let Gold Label out a bit Saturday? She needs a win.'

Gabe shook his head. 'Gold Label looks good, but she's too young. Let her grab the running too early, and she'll blow out. She has a future but needs a year to show it.' To Becker, he added, 'Why don't you put two-bob on her for a place?'

'Yeah, thanks a lot,' said Becker, acting offended at Gabe suggesting he bet two-bob like a wimp.

'I gave the trainer good advice. It's good for you, too. You have a future, but you're not ready by a long shot.'

The trainer strode to the horses, where he hugged the two-ton horse and kissed it on the nose.

'I'm not into violence,' Gabe said at last. 'I'm not a standover merchant like you. I find it easier to persuade my clients I can protect them from people who would do them harm— journalists, politicians, police. Then, I concentrate on doing my business. You don't need to be unfriendly, kid.'

'Don't call me kid,' Becker smirked. 'You left Sydney and came to Newcastle because your business was down the drain.'

'I haven't left Sydney. I come and go. I'm a Sydney boy, see. Born in Leichardt. I own hotels in Sydney. Nightclubs. I came here to expand my business, and I need a goer like you.'

'How come you're a bookie, and everyone says you're not making money?'

'Well,' Gabe said, 'that's nasty talk to take me down. My parents came here from Poland to avoid the pogroms. Dad was Italian, and Mum was a Polish Jew, so I'm a ring-in to some, and they hold it against me. People want to stop me from succeeding. Ruin me, hurt me. But I know why my clients need protection. It's the personal experience, see?'

'Makes no difference to me if you are a refugee or the Duke of York. You asked me here to talk business, not family history. So?'

Gabe drew a deep antsy breath. 'The world is a violent place, and I need people who can handle themselves. I'm busy with this and that, and I don't have time to look after the business and protect my clients from people like you. Why don't you come and work for me? I'll teach you.'

Becker jumped aside as a half-ton grey mare on ballerina's legs, eager to be on the track, skittered about giving her strapper a hard time and trod on his foot. He said with a grin, 'You know what is funny, Mr Rosen? You offering me a job. It's my second offer in as many days.'

'I'm not joking. I pay well—tax-free cash. You'd stay in the hotel with the others, and they can teach you the ropes. You'll have all the women you can handle. It's the life for a young bloke, and you'll learn how we do it in the grown-up world.'

I recoiled and glared at Gabe. He hadn't listened to a word Becker said. Grown-up world? Who does he think he's talking to?

'I don't need a job,' Becker said, picking a clean straw from a bale of grass and brandishing it cheekily like a conductor's baton. 'I'm setting up in Newcastle. There's room enough for two.'

A chestnut gelding behind me sneezed and blew its spit over me. The smiles were in place, the manure pile growing as stable hands wheeled it out by the barrowloads. Gabe offered a cigarette, and when we passed, he lit a cigar and blew the smoke away from Becker's face. 'You are a cheeky young bugger.' Gabe held his hands open at shoulder height, the cigar smoke rising in the cool air. 'I'm hearing Fowler did Moran first, then Shanks. Your man is out of control. Boss.'

Becker was unfazed. 'Moran was bent as a buckled wheel,' he said. 'If you didn't knock him off, then who did?'

Gabe watched a horse gallop past, clicked a stopwatch and said without anger, 'Look, kiddo. You're wasting my time and heading for a messy end. You come here to meet me, but

56

you won't listen to sense, and you have nothing to offer but childish threats.' He consulted the stopwatch and smiled. 'You're punching above your class, boy. Take my offer or wear the consequences.' He shut his eyes, smiling, smug, King of the Cross. 'You're out of place and outgunned. Do not rely on Fowler to look after you. He's lost the plot.'

'I'll look for you at the track,' said Becker, making a move away.

But Gabe placed a restraining hand on his shoulder. 'Halley and Parker and the others are mine. Get it? I don't need to see you in trouble.'

'I hear what you said, but they're not yours, Mr Rosen. You'll have to fight me for them if you want them.'

Becker swaggered past the trainers and jockeys, past Gabe's bodyguards who shot him their dirtiest looks, nodding gravely to say you have it coming to you, mate, past the Grace Kellys and out to the gate where a hard man in a ball cap leaned against Gabe's black Packard and sneered.

For the first time, I thought of Gabe as a real-life gangster, not the pleasant companion I fell in love with. I had mixed feelings also about Becker. He made sense in many ways. A swellhead? A braggart? Absolutely. Even so, I understood what Jessica saw in him.

9. Clawing Back Consciousness

Sunday, January 24 to Tuesday, January 26.

Becker came out of a coma slowly, unsteadily, groaning. It was Sunday evening around seven, two weeks since he challenged Gabe at the dawn training gallops. His eyes shifted, rotated, searched, blinked. They were blank. There was nothing—empty space.

At dawn, Jessica had hammered on the side door at The Dudley to tell me that Becker was in dead trouble. She couldn't handle it alone and needed me, that minute, to help stitch him up. She raised a Red Cross bag and said Becker was hurt and please hurry because she had only me to help her. Fowler had saved his life and was looking after him at Stockton Beach. Weak in the head from partying late into the night with Gabe until I lost out to the skinny starlet and intent on pushing Jessica away, I closed the door. But she got under my skin, shouting that Kitty Balushi's razor boys had cut Becker up. I smelled opportunity, excitement, vengeance, and, like a half-witted hero in a racy Barbara Cartland novel, I followed Jessica for thirty minutes—she rode Fowler's motorbike—to halfway along Stockton Beach.

We slid off the gravel road into a sand trail leading to the ocean through a stand of red cedars at the base of a forty-foot-high dune. At the top, panting heavily from the climb, I saw through the salt mist a handful of rusting tin shacks half buried in the sand.

It was Monday morning and Becker had survived the night. I helped Jessica clean away most of the blood and sew up the deepest wounds and, after all that heavy nursing, I needed to swim, but hadn't brought my bathers. The locals called this part of Stockton Beach Tin City. I was cold and uncomfortable, squashed into a tiny space on the floor and drowsing against the tin wall of a dilapidated shack.

'Cold.' Becker's pathetic whisper raised no sympathy from me. And Jessica's voice was getting on my nerves, too. 'Franzi. Do you hear me? Franzi drink this water. Franzi this Franzi that.'

'Biscuit,' Franzi said. 'Chocolate cream.'

She held two fingers in front of his face. 'What do you see?'

'Smoke … Artillery.'

'Do you know who I am?'

'Mum. Dark.'

'He's out again,' Jessica said, and I stood from my uncomfortable position beside his stretcher and stomped through the door to the sun and the beach.

Surf booming like constant explosions broke on the beach, thundered, surged, and the vast ocean sucked it back across the sand. Everything smelled of seaweed and salt and as I paddled in the shallows the water was cool on my ankles, and the sun glared hot on my bare shoulders. The cream, sandy beach was endless. The Pacific Ocean stretched blue and deep thousands of miles from the Americas, washing my feet in white foamy surf. I paddled on.

In the early 1900s, shipwrecked survivors landed here without knowing where they were. There was no sign of civilisation, so they built shelters using material washed ashore from the wreck and lived off fish. Then, during the Great Depression in the 30s, out-of-work miners came here and built more shacks and fed their families off the fishing. They say twenty families lived here before the war. Only three huts remained constructed from scraps of corrugated iron nailed to tea tree branches taken from the bush behind the dunes. Sand and wind buried the rest. One half-buried already. A windy, eerie place.

I kicked at the sand for a while. There was something mystical about the place in the early light. As a girl, I used to slide down the steep dunes, and, lately, it had become my secret place to be alone when the hotel set me on edge. During the depression in the 30s, my father had often been out of work and would ride his pushbike towing a two-wheel trailer and come home with fifty fish—bream, tailor, whiting, and sometimes a swordfish. He sold most of what he caught because we didn't have an ice chest, but we ate so much seafood that I thought I must smell like a fish.

Three tar-paper and tin fishing shacks slumped rusting on the grassed sandhill, jerry-built and now abandoned or neglected. Empty window frames that once held Perspex panes from crashed World War Two bombers ventilated the huts. One hut had a door hanging crookedly in its frame. In '39, Aussie men and women went off to war in Europe. When they returned, sand had buried the huts, and fishermen later dug up these three for shelter. One builder had dressed up his place with metal advertising signs now corroded away but still advertising Wrigley's Juicy Fruit and Aeroplane Jelly, and a rusting enamelled picture of a blonde woman in a strapless one-piece bathing suit and helmet sold the delights of the Jantzen swimsuit.

I wrenched the door open, and Becker was lying on the cot, awake and wounded. His nose was broken and swollen. I asked him, 'What can you smell?'

'Seaweed … The sea. Cigarette smoke… Eucalyptus.'

His eyes opened to the soft light inside the shack. On the floor, empty bottles with weathered labels for brands no longer in production, old food cans, and crumpled cigarette packets. Fowler said, 'It's okay, Franz. Yah're alive.'

As long as Becker struggled for life, I had no need to fear Fowler. He was a mighty force within the shed, dedicated more even than Jessica, to Becker's survival.

'Alive.' Becker repeated the word like a parrot and tried to say more. He groaned. Jessica trickled water into his mouth. 'Where? ... Who—?'

'Tin City. Abandoned shed. There's no one about. You're safe.'

'How—?'

'Yah're a stubborn bastard,' Fowler said, rocking from one foot to another like a prize fighter. 'Somewhere to hide, ya said. Ya wouldn't let me call the ambulance. You was crazy and kept on about how you was skeered. Aye, and kept repeating that word and laughing crazy. Skeered?'

'Old movie... John Wayne.'

'And ya told me to take the steers to the girl's ranch, and she'd stitch you up. Ya said Stockton Beach, Stockton Beach, and passed out. Ya should be in the hospital.'

Becker raised a hand wrapped in a crepe bandage. 'What's the time—?'

'It's Monday. Yah'll survive. Jessica gave ya first aid, but ya need proper treatment, or yah'll have terrible scars. Hell, people die from losing so much blood. Who knows what internal damage? I'm taking ya to the hospital.'

'No.' Becker said. 'Jess will fix me.'

I bent to look at him. He lay on a folding army stretcher, on a floor made from offcuts of a conveyor belt thrown on the sand, and I smelt spent kerosene from the lamp hanging on a hook from the ceiling. He tried to scratch an itch. 'I'm naked. A baby.'

'Help me move him, Mr Fowler,' Jessica said, and rough hands rolled his body until he lay on his side. 'I'm giving you a tetanus shot,' she said, the needle jabbing deep into his backside.

'Pain,' Becker said. 'Getting worse.'

I unwrapped a paper envelope holding a coarse powder. 'Take this Bex and be brave.' I spooned it into his mouth with a trickle of water from a bottle. I helped with the bandaging, and we took turns wiping his forehead with damp cloths and checking his breathing, but he would have to handle the pain on his own. He probably deserved it.

'What happened to him?' I asked Fowler.

'A gang brawl after Saturday's races. A reg'lar riot. Police and ambulances settled the argument. Becker escaped.'

Jessica held the needle and thread out of sight. 'Your face needs stitching, or you'll never look in a mirror again. It's now or never. I don't have an anaesthetic.'

Becker closed his eyes, and I squirmed when the needle pricked his face. It would not compare to the pain in the rest of his body, but he faded away and I remained standing. Monday afternoon Fowler's drowsy voice, brought me out of a daze. 'He's awake.'

Becker struggled to come awake, to sit and open his eyes to Jessica's face.

'At least you're covered now,' I said and replaced the blanket.

He tried to smile but failed, so he raised a newly bandaged hand an inch to show appreciation. 'It's embarrassing.'

'I'm a nurse, remember?' Jessica said, surprising me with her worldliness. 'Or at least a trainee. It doesn't count.'

Jessica told him she'd cut off his clothes, and there was no way to get him dressed until he was much better; he'd have to run around naked until then. Bruises and cuts covered his body. There was a tremor in her voice when she said, 'I've never been in such a panic. I thought I can't do this. I'd kill you. I wanted to take you to the hospital, but you wouldn't have a bar of it.'

'Do they teach you that at the mine?' he asked. 'To sew faces?'

'No. I would never have done that except you flat refused to go to a doctor. You'll have a scar. I'm good at embroidery, so cross your fingers, and it may come out right.'

Jessica had borrowed proper suture needles and thread from the first-aid room and bandages and antiseptic. Lucky for Becker, she was on shift when Fowler called on her, but she'd need to replace them soon or risk a charge of theft. Plenty of tetanus shots were in stock; a couple missing would be overlooked.

She bustled around him for another minute. 'As soon as you are out of danger, you had better tell me what's happening here. Make it good if you expect me to stick around. Promise me.'

'Promise.'

Becker might have easily conned Jessica with his promise, but it would need to be some story to satisfy me.

'Fowler?' Becker asked.

'He fainted while I stitched you,' Jessica said. 'He's outside. He carried you up the sandhill, and he's been driving me to and from the mine. I'd better go now, or Security will catch me.'

Becker choked up. 'Thanks.'

The will to live is strong, and feeling the pain was a sign of his recovery. I had to hand it to him. He suffered without complaining, blustering or whining.

I got to The Dudley around one o'clock Tuesday morning, and, after a sleep and a late breakfast, I asked Billy to open the bar and drove directly to Stockton Beach.

Jessica and Fowler were there before me. Skeet introduced himself. Twenty-two, pale amber eyes, polished olive skin, black hair slicked and glossy as midnight silk. He was slim but well-built with muscles sculpted from weight-lifting and walked with the grace of a dancer. He had spent Saturday night and most of Sunday in the hospital but was at the tin hut when I arrived. He had come with the newspaper and a milkshake for Becker.

Skeet looked away, saying, 'Becker copped it worse than me. I only picked up some bruises. They beat us up,' he said. 'I copped some heavy punches, but the bastards attacked Becker with knives and razors. They meant to kill him. Only Kitty Balushi could be that vindictive.'

I said, 'I was at the races. I didn't see a brawl or a riot.'

I had arrived at the track before the first race to lunch with Tom Halley, check out the horses and chat with Gabe before he got too busy. We were in the Members' dining marquee, adjacent to the bookies' stands, entertained by colourful racing identities and the dips, damsels, and desperados puffed up and eager to risk their money.

'I searched for Becker but didn't see him,' I added.

Jessica and I hunkered on the floor in the hut and waited while Becker got himself together. Skeet crouched beside the stretcher looking concerned, and Fowler leant against the open door.

Becker lay on the stretcher, obviously in pain but seemingly determined to rejoin the world. 'Are you up to telling us what happened?' I asked him.

He was awake and surprised me. He had improved enough to string sentences together, but his voice was faint. 'I'll tell you,' he said. 'Skeet can correct me if I go wrong.'

He began slowly and surprised me how quickly he improved. The telling resuscitated him. He told us he went to the racecourse that Saturday to watch Gabe in action at the Newcastle Stakes, the first day of the Hunter Valley Trophy Festival, three race meetings building over seventeen days to the Royal Tour.

Movie actor Peter Finch was there to stir the undecided to attend with open purses. He played a Polish officer in the 1952 version of *The Miniver Story*. Chips Rafferty—he starred in *The Desert Rats*, currently in cinemas—would present the trophy and a thousand-pound prize. From mid-morning, buses and trams stacked to the gunwales poured crowds from the suburbs and nearby towns into the racetrack.

'The Stakes was Race Four on the programme,' he said. 'A 1200 yards gallop that would test every horse.'

Becker was on a roll, and his voice was stronger. 'When I arrived,' he told us, 'the public car park was jam-packed, and uniformed police kept the riff-raff away from the Members' enclosure and the VIP car park. Skeet was impatient—the horses were at the barrier for Race Two. I rummaged in the rear seat for my tie. Dress in the public area was optional, except that male guests were expected to wear a jacket and tie on a big day like this. Regulars came in loose shirts and crumpled trousers. I never wear a tie, except to the races, and I needed Skeet's help to tie it. I would have taken all day if I had known what was in store for me.'

Becker sighed. 'Skeet,' he said, 'was more interested in the movie stars than the races. I gave the security guard a two-finger salute as we jogged through the VIP car park. The latest model Oldsmobile two-door convertible got my heart pumping, and there was a Bentley among a handful of Jaguars, Hudsons, and Packards. The bookies would have a bonanza. I pushed Skeet on his shoulder. I told him I'd be parking my Olds here one day and sauntered to the bookies' stands past the band playing "Pop Goes the Weasel" as though the Olds was already mine.'

Becker lay on the stretcher and closed his eyes. It was stifling inside the tin shed. He took a sip of water and got on with his story. 'The crowd,' he said, 'was packed deep in front of us. Hooting and laughing, shouting tips as they surged towards the grandstand. I skipped past children playing hopscotch on the gravel path leading to the general public enclosure and past a disabled World War Two veteran displaying a peg leg and fumbling about on the strings of a mandolin. Smug and full of confidence, I dropped a half-crown among the pennies and threepenny bits in his hat.

'Skeet knew his horses. He rattled the *Herald* at me and told me Sydney papers were full of the Trophy Festival, and Pride of Egypt was a cert to run second in the Stakes and tipped to win the Juveniles at Randwick on the sixth. He was sure because

Egypt's jockey, his cousin, gave him the wink over a beer last Thursday.

'A terrier with a fresh rat could not have been more excited than I was. Looking about for Gabe, I spotted you, Miss Sinclair, in the Members' enclosure. You were in the white marquee. The stewards were all dolled up and serving champagne and wine. I suppose champagne cracks open the chancers' wallets to allow the bookies to get at their cash.

'Skeet went off to get a beer. The sun was out. It was too hot for a jacket and tie. Before each race, the band belted out the "Can-Can", "The Saints", and "Rule Britannia". It gets the punters' blood up to place last-minute bets. I hummed in tune with the band playing "Waltzing Matilda" on my way to buy a pie at the kiosk under the grandstand when a gent in a navy-blue striped suit shouldered me and swaggered on. It took me a second to recognise him in his flash suit, then I kept my eyes under control and touched the knife in my pocket. Bart Evans was Kitty Balushi's new enforcer and was not to be disturbed, troubled or discomfited in any way.

'I don't mind admitting that if anyone scared the shitters out of me, it was Bart Evans. He peeped over his shoulder with his dead-fish eyes, gave me a toothy smile, and then winked at me. I forgot about the pie and headed toward the brass band and safety, no longer humming. I came to the racecourse to watch Gabe and the bookies and certainly not to tangle with Bart. His appearance meant the game was on. I gave him the Italian salute. Behind his back.'

Becker bent his arm at the elbow but couldn't raise it. He grinned as he went on. 'Fifteen bookmakers shouted their odds, gestured to their runners, and got semaphored replies to tell them the best place to lay off their bets. Their assistants chalked the blackboard as the odds changed. Under umbrellas, the bagmen held their floppy leather cash bags and the bookies scribbled the odds on betting slips for the local races and meetings at Randwick, Flemington, and across Australia. The Stakes favourite, Deep Water, ranged from evens to twos.'

After a five-minute rest, the blood returned to Becker's face, and he continued his story from a prone position. 'The main event was twenty minutes away when Skeet asked if I had bet on the fourth race. I told him racing's a mug's game. If the owners and trainers don't nobble a horse, the jockeys will likely pull it. I'm not a gambler and had to speak loudly above the background noise. It's true. I came for the education and excitement, not for the gambling.

'Skeet said he'd drop into the TAB and lay a half-crown on Pride of Egypt for a place at five to one, so I took out my wallet and slipped him a ten bob note to shout him a beer and bring me a Coke.'

Becker grunted and shifted about on the stretcher. 'I don't gamble,' he said, 'but I like to watch the horses parading around the ring, and the punters making last-minute decisions before rushing off to lay their bets. Gabe joked with them, taunted them, and took their cash while the horses cantered to the line. Skeet bounced back, hooting, waving a betting ticket, telling me he was on at five to one and had run into Bart Evans. I told him not to worry. Bart didn't scare me. Skeet told me a woman was skiting about putting three quid on Pride of Egypt for a place and crowing how she'd put twenty-five on it to win the Juveniles at Randwick at sixteen to one. He said he should have put a quid on and then yelped and pointed out the woman who'd bet on Pride of Egypt.

Becker's voice rose an octave in his excitement. 'Skeet was shouting for me that the race was about to start. The band abruptly ended its piece, and the musicians jumped up to watch the horses line up at the stall gates. A pair of fractious horses refused the barrier gate, and a third fretted in the stall. "They're off," the commentator shouted. Thousands of voices roared, and a heavy hand landed on my shoulder. I spun on my heel, my hands coming up to defend my stomach and heart against a knife attack. Powerful hands tore my arms away and held them behind me. Then, a boot in front kicked my feet away, and strong hands bent me forward from the waist and suspended me on dislocated shoulders in terrible pain—I cried out and immediately thought Bart Evans had me. They toppled me forward. My wrists were cuffed behind and numb. A voice told me to be quiet, "Mr Becker, sir," and to stop struggling. He dragged my cuffed hands painfully high, forcing my head to my knees. I had no struggle left in me. I surrendered.

'Two uniformed officers from Track Security relaxed their hold until I stood upright to relieve the pain in my shoulders. They had Skeet also and frog-marched us quickly through the curious to a timber hut signed SECURITY, and, with an upward jerk on the handcuffs, forced me to enter and told us to make ourselves comfortable there until the race meeting was over.

'I demanded a lawyer, but they weren't interested. They offered to take the cuffs off if I promised to behave. My lungs heaved. I accepted the inevitable, and Skeet seemed relieved I had given up. I spotted Bart Evans, six-foot-two and fifteen stone, through the open door, laughing with a well-dressed man. Then the door slammed shut, and a key turned in the lock.'

Becker was pale as a hospital sheet. He lay back on the stretcher. 'Give me half an hour and a Sarsparilla,' he said, 'and I'll be good to go on.' His eyes closed.

But no one was going home until Becker finished his story. He had to explain how he came to have such terrible injuries and who was to blame.

'Was it Kitty Balushi?' I asked Skeet.

'No,' Skeet replied. 'But Gabe paid Kitty's razor boys to attack us.'

10. Vengeance is Mine

Wednesday, January 27.

I tracked the silver highway across the water to the waning moon, ploughed my bare feet into silky white sand, and squadrons of rain clouds formed on the eastern horizon. It was after midnight, and Becker was sleeping. Fowler had taken Jessica to her nurses' station at the mine, and I made out Skeet's silhouette a hundred yards away, paddling in the shallows.

Where was I, besides being sprawled out on Stockton Beach? I was lost in a wildly exciting escapade with no compass bearings to rely on and no wish to find my way home. Gabe, my once-upon-a-time pin-up boy, was exposed as a vicious barbarian, safe in the knowledge he was all-powerful—a Joseph Stalin, an Adolph Hitler, able to torture and kill at will, and he had opened my life to the light like an oyster shell and shown me to be grey, shallow, unremarkable, and tasteless.

I drifted off into a doze and dreamt of Billy sitting in an armchair made of banknotes, of Becker shooting Korean soldiers with an automatic rifle, and of old miners with coal ingrained in their wrinkled faces while they downed a beer in the coal tunnels beneath The Dudley.

I woke when Skeet squeaked through the sand and slumped beside me. 'I have never been to Tin City,' he said, waving a hand over his shoulder at the shed behind us where Becker rested. 'What is this place, a mirage?'

'I like it here,' I said, sucking in the cool sea air. 'Especially at night when the moon rises over the water, it's like you are the one person on earth.'

We sat alone on the twenty-mile beach, kicking at the wet sand in the shallows, and when I reached out to take his hand, he vibrated with happiness, and we lay in the darkness, exhausted. It's a different tiredness here to working at the Dudley. I am doing something useful, even if it is helping to stitch up a small-time gangster.

Though I had been here with the gang for only two days and nights, I found something special—comradeship, companionship, a certain intimacy I don't get from Billy or the regulars. Gabe and the others used me only when they wanted something.

Skeet broke the silence. 'I wish....'

'What? Spit it out.'

'I wish you had been there when I went to court. I had no one to stand up for me.'

'I don't know about that,' I said. 'Whatever it was, were you convicted?'

His voice cracked. I suppose he was relieved to unburden himself. Women are listeners.

'The coppers set a trap in the dark at Nobby's Beach. I had turned seventeen, over the age of consent. They knocked me about and demanded the names of the men who had been with me. They were looking for paedophiles, and, when I told them I knew no names, they dragged me to the police station and browbeat me. They called in my father. They charged me with indecent exposure in a public place. Dad was furious. He dragged me home and never spoke to me after that.'

'Did they put you away?'

'Nah.'

I peeped at Skeet, and he peered sideways at me. We lay quietly in the night until he said. 'I slept with the magistrate for six months. He found a technicality to let me off with a warning.'

I chuckled to show I appreciated the happy ending. 'How

did you get to sleep with a magistrate?' It was his business and his life to lead as he wanted. I waited, knowing he wanted to tell me.

'I worked as a steward at Tattersalls Cub,' he said. 'One Friday afternoon, the magistrate asked me—he left the Club after a boozy lunch—if I would like to earn some cash by helping him on his yacht. It needed work inside, painting this, changing that, blah, blah, blah. He was young to be a magistrate, and I caught his signals. The next day, I met him, and surprise, surprise, the boat needed no work, and it went on from there.'

I waited in the night to the sound of the surf and the smell of the sea. After a while, Skeet snorted. 'When my case came up, he talked about police entrapment and let me off with a lecture.'

He tried to throw an arm across my shoulder, but I ducked out of the way.

'Sorry, Sunni. I didn't mean anything. Are you sensitive about people touching you?'

'No,' I said. I thought Kitty's work had done something to me. Unexpected intimacy forced me back into that world with Kitty where I had no desire to be.

We walked a long way and paddled in the shallows, laughing as we skipped through the efflorescence. I waited, sensing that Skeet had more to say.

'It's getting too violent for me,' he said, fretting. 'I don't mind scratching a few cars or breaking windscreens, but Becker scared me when he cut Joe Parker like that. I thought he had killed Joe. There was so much blood.'

I thought about Becker cutting Tom Halley.

Skeet was fussing about Becker's attack on Parker. 'Would he have killed Joe? Like they say Fowler and Shanks did with others? Nah. Maybe. I don't know. A little cut, a little blood, that's all he needs to scare them. I don't know if Becker would kill someone. No.'

'No, you don't know?'

'Maybe if he snaps or goes overboard. He says he did in the war, but this is different. Is it? Different?'

We came to a light shining through cracks in the tin shed where Becker was sleeping. 'Fowler's different,' I said. 'For sure, he's different. He will carry on like this, doing what he does, forever. But if you're not like him, well it's not for you. There are other ways to live in grand style on the hill. You could too, if you stick with Becker.'

'Yeah? You think so? But I'm out if it comes to killing. I don't want Becker to hurt Albie. He's been my friend for as long as I can remember. They say Kitty's killed two men.'

He kicked at the sand, his back to Becker and the shed.

I took a little time to sort Skeet's rambling list of concerns. 'Fowler doesn't have what it takes to rise above petty stuff,' I said, 'and that's all crap about being Kitty's friend. Don't worry about her. Gabe Rosen is Becker's only competition.' The clouds were dispersing, and I wondered when I had become so offhanded about murder. Like a gangster, I thought. I spoke about killers and killing as though I were Fowler.

I stood at the door to Becker's hut, and the first glow on the horizon struck me as a good omen for the future. 'Have the police spoken to you about Saturday after the races? The newspapers are describing it as a riot.'

'Nothing connects it to Becker and me,' Skeet said, pushing past me and blocking the door. 'We're in the clear. Gabe's boys are not talking. The coppers know the real story, but with the races and the Royal Visit, they don't have time to scratch and don't want the press to know. They're saying it was kids, drunk after a family party, and they have it under control.'

Fowler was there when we stepped into the hut, and he introduced me to Rudy, the last of Becker's gang.

I unpacked the picnic hamper, handed out cold bacon and egg rolls, poured strong tea from a flask and asked Becker how he was feeling.

'He won't be up to robbing a bank for a few days,' Rudy said, chomping into his sandwich. 'Thanks. I didn't have breakfast.'

He interested me. Tall, lean, and twenty-six, he spoke with an educated accent and wore a brown leather riding jacket and a tie in the summer heat.

'What's your story, Rudy?' I asked.

'You're not supposed to ask,' he said, his smile removing any sting in the words.

'Rudy is brains plus, plus,' Skeet said in his naïve way. 'He was all screwed up when I first met him. You're still a bit that way, aren't you, Rudy? He was in Korea, like Becker, and he talks about getting even with the world for what the war did to him. He's more calculating and wanting revenge than crazy.'

'Another Aussie from the Korean War?' I said. 'How did that come about?'

'I came out from Ireland with my parents in thirty-six,' Rudy said. 'I won an Army scholarship to do a surveying degree at Sydney Uni, and they sent me to Korea when I graduated.'

Becker stirred. I checked his temperature with a hand on his forehead.

'Rudy works underground at Redhead,' Becker croaked.

'There's four of us,' Rudy said, mocking his gang. 'Not enough bodies to do anything worthwhile.'

I felt I'd become one of the gang, but he would have counted five if that were so.

'Rudy, you're smart,' Skeet said. 'You'll come up with something.'

No. He'll not come up with anything. None will come up with a plan. Not Becker, with all his swaggering and bravado. They'll go on talking about it until they're old men.

'What are the coppers doing?' Becker asked.

Fowler said, 'They're furious that Gabe pissed in their garden in the middle of the Festival, and they're privately blaming Kitty. I don't hear nothing about you.'

Rudy finally removed his leather jacket and loosened his tie. 'Anyway, Jessica made a job of stitching your face and arm. Lots of doctors couldn't do as well. You'll have a scar or two.'

'I'll be surfing tomorrow and ready to rob a bank,' Becker said, his voice firming.

'It's a bit early for that,' I said, laughing. 'And are you a little ambitious to be thinking of robbing banks? Looking like you do?'

He groaned. We sat quietly, chewing our breakfast and drinking our tea, and the long walk on the beach talking with Skeet had fired my brain cells. While the sound of surf carried away the rest of the world, I remembered my dream of Billy's riches and Becker's automatic gun and my mind regurgitated conversations I'd had the past few weeks.

'What day is it?' I asked.

'It's Thursday,' Skeet said. 'Becker woke yesterday. Today is January 28th. What's on your mind, Sunni?'

'Something as delicate as a duckling, and talking may kill it off. Skeet, I want you to come with me tomorrow.'

'What's on?'

'On the sixth, there's the Hunter Valley Gold trophy here in Newcastle and the Queen Elizabeth Stakes at Randwick. On the ninth, the Queen comes to visit us here. Right?'

Becker struggled to rise from the stretcher, his left arm strapped to broken ribs, his face looking like hell from the stitches, and his body yellow and purple bruised.

Fowler gently pushed him back, and Becker tried to rise again. In the dim light, the scene was like a staged melodrama. 'Tomorrow,' I gave Skeet a grin. 'We're getting up early to rob a bank the minute it opens.'

Rudy chuckled, Fowler and Skeet chuckled, and we howled

with laughter until I thought Becker would split his stitches and break apart at the seams.

My belly pained, my face hurt from laughing, and I would stop for a second and start over again, carefree but serious, confident but a little edgy like a woman wondering if she was pregnant, until I could laugh no more.

11. Becker Near the Edge

Thursday, January 28.

While Becker slept on the camp stretcher in the tin shed at Stockton Beach, I made my way to The Dudley, hoping to find some rest, but I had a sleepless night wrestling with my thoughts and emotions, excited by the ideas flashing in my head like unfocused moving pictures on a screen. One minute, flying as a detail fell into place, and the next, crashing with fear, sure it was insanity to tackle this escapade that had captured my imagination. I was too old, too over it, too slow, too weak, and my gang was too small or my spine too weak.

At dawn, alone on the beach, I waited for Becker to wake and get on with his story of the race day. 'You and Skeet were locked in the security room at the racetrack,' I reminded him.

Becker told us the door was solid, so they sat quietly on old kitchen chairs, listening to the races over loudspeakers. Eventually, the last race was over, the band had played their final number, and the punters had all departed, singing and hollering. Engines rumbled, owners loaded their animals into horse transports, and the clang of iron gates closing brought them to their feet. Finally, a glimmer under the door lit the room. A key scraped, and the door opened to the last of the sunset. The same security guard barrelled in and made it clear he was not happy to take the abuse Becker hurled at him. He said he did them a favour and that, after receiving a credible report of a plan to attack Becker during the race meeting, he took them out of circulation for their safety. He denied knowing Bart Evans and was clear that, if Becker made a commotion, he'd call the police, and they would charge Becker with carrying an offensive weapon, namely a knife, on the racecourse.

The guard refused Becker's plea to have his knife back and became hostile, so, as Becker told it, Becker tucked his shirt into his trousers, ran a comb through his hair, shot his cuffs and led Skeet out of the lock-up. They followed the guards to the side gates as the last horse float left.

Becker said, 'Everything stank of horse shit and humiliation. My stomach came up until I spat to get rid of the taste of surrender. Skeet reached out, but I shrank away, wanting to escape the guard's contempt. What was I to do? Threaten Gabe that he messed with me at his own risk? Come on, Skeet, I said, I feel like a hamburger, and a voice from the darkness asked if I was hungry. In the blink of an eye, I knew what was about to happen and prayed for rescue from a God I didn't believe in. Skeet made a strange gurgling noise. He bent forward, hands holding his belly, fighting for air.

'They came at me whooping—a bunched-up gang with razors. They slashed at my arms, my face. They hammered me to my knees—terrible pain. Boots thumped my balls and shoulders. Fists and knuckle-dusters broke my ribs, my nose. I came up swinging, but a fist crunched into my forehead, and I fell again. I screamed out. My body was paralysed, my brain frozen. I threw out a hand to protect my face, and the blade slashed across my knuckles.

'I tried to shout. I wanted to run, but there was no escape from the boots and the razors.

'Their leader kicked me in the belly and stomped on my face. I tasted blood in my mouth. He swung his boot to finish me, missed my head and smashed into my shoulder. Half a second was all I needed. Hand-to-hand fighting in the trenches taught me that. I swung a steel-toed boot hard into his knee and rolled away. His blade flashed. Slashed my cheek. I grabbed a wrist, twisted, caught the knife, and aimed for a killing stroke to the groin. Blood drenched my face. He pivoted away, but I had buried the blade deep into his thigh. The mob came at me again, but I won that half-second respite and brought another thug down on top of me.

'A crawl space opened. A razor aimed at my throat slashed a gash across my shoulder. Another caught me below the eye. I slid away from the kicking feet and faded into the dark, pressed a hand hard to my bleeding cheek, and a woman in a nearby house screamed.

'Sirens howled. The thugs split. Police rushed in. The bastards were on the spot, ready and waiting and standing aside until instructed to move in, knowing all the time what was happening. An ambulance siren moaned. I scrambled away from the bloody footpath, ducked into a bed of shrubs and left Skeet for the ambulance to look after him.

'I had no balance, with one hand holding my face together. But I ran. Fell over my feet. I cried out with the pain and stumbled straight into the arms of one of Kitty's cutthroats, waiting to block my escape. We backed off for a second, and then I dropped a shoulder, barged straight at him and stuck the knife in him.

'I needed both arms to run fast—no time to hold my face. Blood streamed across my cheek, blinding me. Saturated my shirt and jacket. I ran as I'd never run. Twisted into lanes. Through backyards. Three of Kitty's gang hollering, "Tally Ho," and "Holloo," and baying like hounds, having great fun. Concrete wheel tracks led into a car shed, and Kitty's men raced past. I bent over, hands on my knees, sucking air, and watched through a crack in the door as the third man halted. My mind came up with a blank. Winded and done. I wanted a place to hide away.

'I saw splashes of blood on the concrete tracks under the streetlamp. My blood pointing to me. I grabbed a shovel, held a dry rag to my face and returned to the door. All three stood on the footpath, panting and blowing and waving their arms.

78

I eased my shoulders and crept to a bunch of rags lying on the bench. At the door, I heard words without grasping their meaning. I wiped blood from my palms and from the slippery blade I held, fixed my eye on the door, and kicked the shovel. The clink of metal got me peering into the shadows of the shed. No windows. Was my face bleeding? My ankles throbbed, ribs were busted, a brutal pain in the hip. I vomited, grabbed a shelf for support, and dropped the shovel.

'My white shirt. I'd stand out like a target at the rifle range. I rolled, forced my knees to take my weight, and braced myself against the wall. Louder shouts now. They circled closer. I kept telling myself, 'Don't let go. Don't let go.' Through a crack, my eye searched the yard. Bushes. A bed of vegetables. A fence, too high.

'The shed was a trap. They'd zero in on the bloody path. Attack and I'd die fighting, I thought. Let them kill me. They'd get me as I cross the lawn. They didn't have guns. I would have to outrun them.

'There was no way I could get over that fence. It was six feet high. A wheelbarrow. In the corner. A step up.

'Car lights. They'd called in reinforcements. They were coming for me.

'I picked up a spanner, made a break while they went into a huddle facing away from me, tossed the spanner high and far towards the racetrack and ran for the rear yard. The fence loomed, the wheelbarrow—a high step. Thump, and over I flew and fell on my face.

'I heard, "Tally Ho." More baying. Car lights lit the shed. People ran, shouting. I fell over the next fence, plunged, rolled on my shoulder. It was torture, but I laughed at my escape. A booming shot, pellets flying high over my head. A dog barking. I kept off the footpath. Skipped through the next yard.

'The voices receded. I dived into a rose bush. Thorns. I yelped. Police sirens. Whistles. Shouting, "Police! Police!"'

'I felt my way through the dark yard, heading towards my car. I was a guerrilla again, in the darkness, waiting, moving into the dark forest, snaking through a mound of bricks and heaps of soil prepared for foundations.

'The car was where I left it.

'I came out of cover. A match flared; a cigarette glowed. I choked on the sour-smelling smoke. A shadow crouched ten yards away. 'My blood was up. I crept close with a brick in hand, needing to kill someone. Anyone. I whacked at a head, but my wounds weakened me, and I missed. Struck a shoulder. The man grunted and spun to face me.

'Fowler.'

'Get rid of that knife,' he said. 'There'll be fingerprints.'

12. A Daring Rescue, A Romance

Friday, January 29.

I leaned close to Becker, one hand guiding the bandage I wound around his chest and the other smoothing it into place, his breath wavering on my neck and face. Inside the tin shed at Stockton Beach, the air was thick with the scents of salty ocean and antiseptic from a plastic basin filled with water and Dettol, pink from Becker's blood.

He sat on a rickety kitchen chair, my fingers softly scratching his chest and belly muscles, as I applied the adhesive dressing to a shallow gash above his navel. He drew a sharp breath. The old shack trembled under the force of the wind, and I understood the tension in his body and slapped him lightly on the shoulder.

'Enough of that,' I said, suppressing a grin that might have challenged his manhood. Men!

Self-conscious, he held a torn tea towel on his lap, a feeble attempt at modesty. 'I'm sorry for causing you all this trouble,' he whispered.

I put a little distance between us, though I felt the pressure also. Jessica had left for the mine and asked me to wash and bandage him despite my protests that never in my life had I trained to be a nurse.

I dabbed at a cut on his shoulder, and he recoiled at the antiseptic sting. 'You're lucky,' I said, applying a fresh plaster to his shoulder. 'So far, none of your wounds are infected.' I tossed a bloodied rag into the basin. 'Who did this to you? Gabe or Kitty?'

Fowler, pushing through the door, heard the question. 'Kitty's razor boys beat him up. She took back her gang from

Gabe at the end of the two years. But it was Gabe who paid Kitty to do him.'

'Tried to kill me,' Becker said, shifting position on the chair as he checked a groan.

'No. Their orders were to beat ya real bad. Teach you a lesson, but not kill ya.'

'Huh?'

'Bart Evans and me,' Fowler said, 'we've been friends for years. Bart took the job as enforcer after Shanks was fired and went swimming. He's not happy working with Kitty. Says he can't trust her. He's making noises about joining us.'

'No way.' Becker pointed at the water bottle. Sipped and choked. Sipped and choked again.

Fowler went on, 'Bart told me Gabe has plans for you. He said he's furious they came close to killing ya. He ordered a bit of a belting, and that's all.' He placed a hand on the door. 'I have to go collect Jessica.'

The sea breeze raised dry sand in the shack, and the door slammed behind him.

'Gabe can shove his plans,' Becker said with less than his usual bravado. 'I'll stay out of his way. There's other money lying around for the taking. Gabe is past it. I'll do over a bank or an armoured car. Take my time to make enough and chase him out of Newcastle to Sydney, where he belongs.'

Becker didn't care that he shared his planned life of crime with innocent me. I said, 'You'll need a month to get well before you think of robbing banks.'

'I have a good nurse.' He put his hand behind my head and tried to draw me closer.

'None of that,' I said, moving my head. 'I'm not your nurse, certainly not your girlfriend, and not likely to be.' I tied off the bandage and slowly removed the covering from the cut below his eye. He paused my hand. 'Hold,' I said sharply, 'or you'll bust the stitching,' and he released my hand and remained quiet until

I raised his head to examine the wound. I looked to the side and shifted uneasily.

'Not pretty, eh?' His voice vibrated, and he closed his eyes tight. 'Did it cut me deep?'

I bent again to examine the wound, holding my fingers to measure off the length of the cut. 'Jessica said it's deepish. It's an inch long. She read the manual, put two rows of stitches inside your cheek and one outside, and used tiny stitches and tiny needles. Luckily, the razor missed your eye and facial muscles. The stitches are holding. There's no infection. There'll be a scar, but you can count your blessings this time.'

'Blessings,' the word evaporated as he spoke it. He was quiet, flirting. Arrogance forgotten, he sparked up. 'A swim and a walk on the beach are what I need.'

I remembered how we'd laughed before and grinned at him. 'No banks to be robbed today?' He must have had the same thought and lowered his eyes. I went on, 'It's not yet seven days. Don't risk an infection. There's lots of bad stuff in the sea. Dead fish and crabs and lice.'

'Lotsa bad stuff on land, too.'

'You should be in the hospital,' I said. 'Or in prison. But if you stay nice and quiet and behave, I'll think about what to do with you. Jessica is passing keen on you, so you can't be all bad.'

I'm not one for sentiment, that watery-eyed carry-on the way they do at football reunions and christenings, but he was all sliced, broken and chewed as though a tiger had mauled him, and something moved inside me. I paced around the shed, poked with my foot at an empty can and opened the door to look at the sea.

The hours passed while Becker rested, and I read the paper. A voice sounded outside. Bottles rattled. A foot stamped on the rotting stair, and the door shook and scraped on the floor as it cracked open on its broken hinge. I ran to the door and put my weight against it. 'Who is it?'

Sunset and the smell of salt and sea rushed in through the gap, and Fowler and Jessica filled the opening, her skirt blowing out in the breeze, her hair trapped in a floral scarf.

Though Fowler appeared to be tamed, I hadn't forgotten how he glared at me the night he came to The Dudley, a living witness to his threatening Lou at the fete. He said to Becker, 'The news on the wireless is making a big deal of the racecourse riot, and Sergeant Thompson is asking around after you.'

Jessica rushed to Becker and kissed his forehead. The look on his face told me she tasted like life and the sun. He grinned and reached for a bunch of grapes, but I gazed through the open door and watched the clouds forming on the horizon. He was a gangster, though a minor one, and she was only nineteen.

I leaned against the door, watching them for a while until my conscience, or was it jealousy, pushed me a step towards the bed. 'Jessica, you haven't fallen for this boy? He's not for you. You don't want to ruin your life by getting mixed up with gangsters.'

'Please don't say things like that, Miss Sinclair. I don't need you to upset my patient. Why do you care about me, anyway?'

'Face it, Jessica. He should have known that Gabe has muscles and sharp claws. This bloke isn't smart enough to stay away from the big bears. He's not for you.'

'Stop,' Jess cried, swinging about, her tousled hair flying, and pointing an accusing finger. 'Don't say that. If I want him to be my gangster, as you call him, he will be *my* gangster.'

She wriggled past me and pushed impatiently at the door until it came unstuck. She stood, arms straight, hands locked into fists, looking out into the glare of the falling sun. 'People can change,' she said sullenly. 'Leave us alone.'

Naked and too embarrassed to leave the chair, Becker said quietly, 'Gabe will find who has the sharpest claws.'

84

'I'll not leave you alone until you understand how dangerous this boy is,' I said. 'He knows more than he's saying about Lou's death and Sergeant Moran's. They were my friends.'

'Don't call Franz a boy. He doesn't like it. He's not a murderer. Look at him, and you'll see that.'

'No one murdered Shanks,' Becker said, his voice more robust than I thought he could muster. 'It was an accident. I told them to knock him about a bit, screw him for double-crossing us, but nothing too serious. Like the coroner said, he died of a heart attack.'

'And I suppose Sergeant Moran died of appendicitis?'

'He was on the take, and the syndicate paid off on him— nothing to do with me. But I happened to be there and recognise who did it.'

I looked at Fowler and then to Becker, but they kept their heads down and eyes on the ground.

'That's all,' Becker said, 'and it's the truth.'

Lying brat.

Perhaps understanding that she was not about to rid herself of me quickly, Jessica closed the door and stepped in to stand beside me. 'Franz is innocent. You must see that, Miss Sinclair. You've got him wrong. He's kind and thoughtful. He's badly hurt, and I will nurse him until he's better, and if he wants me, he'll learn to change his ways. Please give him a chance. He won't make any more mischief.'

I sighed. 'Mischief. Love has a weird sense of humour. Men play their games with us, push our buttons and spray their testosterone around until no one can see straight. I'll take some convincing Lou's death was entirely an accident, though I'm not one to judge others.'

I folded my arms and leaned against the door again. 'Let me tell you this. If love comes as a package with trouble, toss it. Walk away. A thousand good and honest men will do better for you than this crook.'

'I don't care what you say,' Jess replied. 'If I decide to love him, I'll love him, and it's not for you to say against it.'

The hut was suffocating. I opened the door for a breeze. Becker was too insignificant to fight over. 'Franz, no matter what you or Jessica say, you are only a boy. I'll take your word for her sake that Lou's death was an accident. I'll stop badgering the police about him and not tell anyone where you are. But, if you mistreat her—'

Fowler was at the door. 'We need to leave, or you'll be late for your shift.'

Jess bent to kiss Becker goodbye, and I smirked when he turned his face so she would buss him on the cheek.

'Jess,' Becker said, 'don't talk to anyone about meeting Shanks and Fowler at the fair.' His voice was maybe rougher than he intended because he added, 'Please.'

''Course, I won't talk.' She stood at the opened door; the sun glared, her face in deep shadow, and she crossed her heart with two fingers. 'What do you take me for? Your secret is safe with me.'

Then Jess was gone, the door slamming after her.

Becker struggled off the chair and held the door for support, dizzy, his face pale. Abruptly, his mood changed. He took a step, tripped, stretched a hand as though pleading his case to a jury and groaned. He dropped his head and sagged like a burst balloon. I felt nothing but disgust for Gabe Rosen, and his torture of Becker had crushed any love I may once have thought I had for him. Gabe was a monster.

Exhausted, embracing his broken ribs, Becker took one shuffling step after another, down the sandhill and across the sand until he stood in ankle-deep water, pointing and shouting unintelligibly. I let him go, knowing he would do whatever he wanted after I left. Sitting in water to his neck, crying, he allowed the waves to push him down, break over him, knock him off balance, and before I had time to react, the surf swept him into deeper water, and he was struggling.

Stripping to my underwear on the run, I hurdled waves and dived into the surf. The breakers were higher and held more force than I expected. A wave dumped me, plunged me to the bottom, flipped me, rolled past, sucking me towards the beach, and I exploded to the surface, kicking, searching. Becker had been swept farther out and held a hand high, struggling. I took a deep breath and swam to him in the fast rip. I grabbed him and held his head above water, his arms thrashing, legs kicking me, resisting with all his panicking strength, his floundering forcing me into the sweep, taking us out to sea. My heart raced with the effort. He strained to climb onto my back, pushing my head under, drowning me. He dragged me down. I kicked upwards, but he clung to me, and we sank into deep water. My chest tightened. Squeezed the air out of me. My lungs were on fire. I tore loose, let him go, kicked to the surface, twisted in mad circles until I spotted him, and thought let the bastard drown before he kills me too.

But I swam to him again, rolled, and held him away with my arm crooked around his neck to allow me to backstroke free of his flailing arms. My chest threatened to explode, and then we were in quiet water two hundred yards from the beach, rising and falling easily in the swell. I rested floating, bellowing at Becker not to struggle; we would let the rip take us where it wanted and bring us to the beach. I willed my legs to kick and keep us afloat, but they were heavy and wanted to surrender. My arms grew heavy. My body screamed out for rest. I ached and swallowed water.

I wanted to punch Becker's head for getting me into this mess and pleaded with the ocean gods to allow the rip to take us in to the beach. I wished I'd never met Becker and had not run into Jessica at the fair. We drifted for twenty minutes. It felt like hours.

My face would be salt-burned and ugly.

A wave broke onto my head, dragging me down, but my feet touched bottom. One last burst of adrenaline, and I forced my arms and legs to move. My muscles ripped, letting me know it was their last effort. I half swam, half waded to the beach, and, with his weight sapping my strength, I dragged him to the shallows and collapsed.

The slap of a wave brought us to our senses. 'I'll need new bandages,' he said, coughing up water. 'Jess will be mad at me.' He laughed then, and I laughed with him.

'Thanks,' I said.

'Why are you thanking me? I should be thanking you.'

'That's what I meant.' I fell back exhausted.

We lay on the wet beach, sand and the sea burying our legs. The sun sank below the horizon, the sky changed from deep orange to purple, and stars appeared shyly in their full brilliance. 'Why did you do such a stupid thing?' I asked him.

'What?' he said, a word to fill the space while he tried to come up with a lie.

'You went into the water because you wanted to drown. Why would you want that? Tell me the truth, or I'll drag you out to sea and leave you there.'

'A vision. It caught me off guard. I was attacking, facing the Chinese mortar bombs, knowing I was one of the walking dead. Then, my father sat above the waves coaxing a tune from a ukulele and flicking his head to invite me in. I thought I would let the tide float me out to sea. I would have died happy.'

'Is that what you were shouting about?'

He shrugged.

'You were too young. Too brave.'

'It was not like living,' he said. 'Every time I came out alive, I isolated the memory to somewhere it would not poison my life. Everything I experienced before Korea and after was no more than an outrageous dream.'

'Hallucinations. Concussion. I'm taking you to the hospital.'

'I've been whacked on the head many times. It always works out.'

My eyes opened to a million stars, my ears to the sound of surf and gulls. The city was far away; my mind drifted, my arms outstretched, my body caressed intimately by the rippling water. I thought that for his entire life, Becker had not experienced intimacy. He had stumbled from childhood to criminal with nothing between. Did he know right from wrong? Why did he choose to go wrong? That got me thinking about Gabe and Tom and Hector and all the Toms, Dicks and Harrys I allowed into my body. Society had bound me to a microscopic splinter of the world inhabited by politicians, magistrates, and wealthy crooks who believed in the mutual forgiveness of other criminals but punishment for those outside their globe.

It came to me in my exalted state that Becker and his gang had shown me a path to break free from my way of life. If I fought free of Society's constraints and went to war against the establishment, win or lose, maybe there would be the same nobility in my fight as in Lenin's defence of the powerless. Then I thought, well, that's a bit far-fetched.

Conversations arose from deep in my memory. A falling star flashed across the horizon. Another piece of the jigsaw came to me, and I must have nibbled around the edges of trouble for a while, or how would I have recognised, spreadeagled on the beach half-drowned, the opportunity to beat the shit out of Gabe Rosen and defeat all the men who ever messed with me. Or did a falling star tell me I was an insignificant mortal, and I should return to the world I left behind in Sydney and defeat it?

In the sky, I saw the glitter, the champagne, the politicians and judges, the grand piano and the Hollywood star caressing its keys while I stood by—the goddess in my Jean Pateau figure-hugging silver sheath with the glittering sequin leaves.

Sprawled on the sand, drained yet exhilarated, I turned my head to Becker. His eyes were closed, his chest rising and falling, the outgoing tide drawing water past his naked body: the dark hair, the rich, creamy skin, the beauty of his youth. I sat up, gazed out to sea and contemplated the grand design that had come to me in my dream. I would need Becker and his gang of amateurs because they were the only honest gangsters available, and I'd have to make the most of them.

Not to forget Kitty Balushi. There would always be Kitty Balushi.

13. Hang the Getaway Driver

Saturday, January 30.

A week had passed since the brutal attack on Becker, and he would have to recuperate quickly because an idea was forming in my head.

I sat with him, overlooking white horses on a choppy ocean and the ships lined up waiting to enter the port, a heady aroma of salt and seaweed from the sea. I found a seashell shaped like a cow's horn and washed it in the sea. I rubbed it with my thumb while I hesitated to find words that would not appear foolish.

'I have an idea,' I said, unsure if I had one or not. I have entertained some crazy thoughts in my life, but the recklessness of this one took my breath away and left elation in its place. 'Just the beginnings of one. A thought, a wispy notion. There is a king's ransom in it if I can work it.'

'How much?' Becker asked.

'One hundred and fifty thousand, maybe two hundred. Pounds.'

He tried to sit but fell back. 'Tell me.'

So, I told him. It took me a minute because I had no details. A concept. 'No one has attempted it before,' I said after that brief outline, 'and it would be the biggest haul in Australia since Ben Hall robbed the gold coach at Eugowra in 1862.'

'I'm in,' Becker said after a while, his voice more potent. He even laughed. 'It's a ripper of an idea. We'll split the proceeds. I'll run the job and take three-quarters.'

I'm not so good at mental arithmetic, but I laughed and went for it. 'I'll run it, and I'll take sixty per cent of the cash plus a hundred per cent of everything else of value. You split your share with your gang any way you like.'

He was so quiet I thought he may have lost interest. Was there any place for him in his present state? But I needed his gang, and I had twelve days to get him fit. 'Are you alive in there?' I asked him.

'Thinking,' he said, tapping his head. 'Okay. I'll go with that. Do you think you can be boss to six men?'

'I'll need you and Skeet and Rudy, but not Fowler.'

'Fowler is the muscle,' he said. 'Doesn't matter what the job is. You can't get by without muscle.'

'I don't like how he looks at me. Sergeant Moran's murder will explode in our faces.'

Becker, overconfident in his youthfulness, said, 'That's all blown over.'

But he hadn't convinced me. I said, 'You had better tell me what happened.'

Becker hesitated, frowning, screwing up his eyes long enough that I thought I'd walk away from him and my scheme. He stared into space and, stuttering at first, started to speak. 'I had just turned twenty and was full of myself, home from Korea and out to grab enough dough to make it all worthwhile. I knew I would have to take on the mob to get anywhere. The older types treated me like a snotty-nosed brat and dished out a few beatings to prove their point. But Australia was full of opportunities for young people like me. I thought about a heist. A bank, an armoured car, a gold shipment, diamonds, a caper big enough to retire and get out. The tricky part would be surviving to enjoy life before someone takes it off my dead body.'

'You got that right,' I said, but he rushed ahead excited at the action.

'At first,' Becker continued, 'I needed a gang, then, after a while, as I grew into it, I had to have muscle. With Fowler and Lou, we were five with the potential to reach beyond the petty stuff. We'd been robbing soft targets, putting the frighteners on Greek and Chinese cafe owners, and sometimes raising hell and maybe hurting someone a bit, but it wasn't enough.'

'Forget about your gang,' I said, digging into the sand with my toe. 'I need to know what happened with Sergeant Moran.'

He chewed the inside of his cheek for a while. 'Okay, but you won't like what you hear.'

I nodded. I had been with enough men to know that truth was a flexible concept to them, so Becker may have been lying his head off, but this is the way he told it.

'I drove my Plymouth,' Becker said. 'Fowler was in the passenger seat. We were twenty minutes early to meet Moran at the coal wharf and deliver his payoff, rolling slowly past unlit sheds and silos holding cement and fertiliser—nothing to worry about, the usual routine. The setting sun reflected off cranes and coal ships moored in the South Channel. A storm was brewing, and the lights were coming on in houses on Tighes Hill.

'Moran had arranged the meeting where no one was likely to see us pass the cash. But he had not bargained on us being early. As we rounded the bend into the wharves, the headlights lit a shadowy lane between two silos, and Fowler shouted, "Stop the car, Becker. Back up!"'

'I slammed on the brakes and reversed. Unable to understand what was exciting Fowler, I spun the wheel and brought the front around, and Moran and Shanks were there, shading their eyes from the headlights.

'Shanks was another lost soul. I thought he would be helpful, so I brought him into the gang in August. Fowler was screaming that Shanks was a bastard—a dirty bastard and two-timing us. Moran is mine, he bellowed, shaking his head, and the madness was in his eyes. I should have noticed it before.

'Fowler was out of the car in a flash, dancing about in his excitement speaking so fast I could barely understand. But I could see that Shanks was in trouble. He took off like a racehorse from the gates. Fowler slammed the car door and bolted after him, but Shanks had a fifteen-yard advantage. Moran was old and out of condition, lining his pocket for retirement, and no competition to Fowler in a footrace, so he stayed and waited. He was unarmed, and Fowler knew it. Police carry weapons only when authorised, and it's automatic prison time for anyone caught with an unlicensed firearm. They stepped around each other on stiff legs, Fowler talking and cracking his knuckles, Moran, shoulders back, sticking his chest out, moving in circles like a top-notch pigeon in a mating dance, and stepping closer into Fowler's face. I shouted something but nobody heard. I wasn't about to join the brawl, so I watched.

'I was in the car,' Becker continued, 'and saw the whole thing. Fowler's eyes were white in the headlight beam, his spit spraying, tossing a hand, rejecting whatever Moran said. Fowler planted his feet, cranked his neck from side to side, and limbered up, readying for a punch-up. But Moran was retreating, harking and spitting, tugging at his cuffs, ready to leave, and there wasn't anything to be concerned about. Then Fowler shouted again, threw out a hand, gripped Moran's shoulder, and let loose a king hit to Moran's head—one punch. Moran fell and belted his head on the concrete kerb. Blood spouted from a head wound, and, before Moran hit the ground, I was out of the car and sprinting towards them.

'I knew I was in big trouble. I took three paces, spun away, and leapt to the car. I kicked the engine to life, slid the gearshift into reverse by mistake and planted my foot on the accelerator. The car shot backwards. I hit the brakes. My lungs choked, I opened the door, put my head out, and sucked air while the car rolled forward on the incline. Fowler tried to jump into the moving car, his pupils were dilated, and the smell of blood was on him.

'Get out,' I screamed. 'Out! You'll get blood on the upholstery.' I slammed on the brakes. The open door knocked Fowler over.

I shouted at him not to touch the car and grabbed a handful of cotton waste and a bottle of kerosene from the boot and swiped an arm across my face to get rid of the sweat running into my eyes. 'Get that shirt off,' I yelled. 'Wipe the blood with kero. On your face, in your hair.' I pelted a beach towel at Fowler. 'Is he—'

'Don't know,' Fowler said, wiping his face and hands. 'He don't look good.'

'Put that stuff in the boot. I'll clean the rubber floor.'

'I just punched him once,' Fowler said. 'Hit his head on the concrete. I held his head. So much blood.'

'Get in,' I screamed. 'Keep your bloody fingers away from the seat.' We would make a run for it. 'Sheeeeet! What else was there to do? I jumped out again, wiped blood from the passenger side door and glass where Fowler had grabbed it, slammed the door, and Fowler crumpled into the corner, head hanging, hands over his ears, his sighs changing to mumbled complaints. My Plymouth was screaming in second gear. I took the corner too fast. We slid sideways, spraying gravel, spinning, tipping, and crashing onto four wheels. Raging at Fowler for putting me in danger of prison or worse, I held the steering wheel tight, my fingers hurting. I poked my head out the window and spat a wad of spew.

'I asked the crazy bastard what the hell happened, and he told me Moran called him a dumb Yorkshire yokel and to piss off and never come back, or Moran would make sure his mates would find him in the river with his throat cut.

'There was something wrong with Fowler. He was not upset or sorry. He just told me I was slowing down and to get moving. I was sweating. This was not the war. This was whacking a copper, and maybe he'd die. Fowler was eyeing me. He was not the German Shepherd I thought I'd bought. One who would growl and snarl then heel on my command. No. I had an uncontrollable pit bull terrier.

'Fowler said Shanks was a witness and had to be put down. It was as though Fowler had been at nothing more than a scrum at the footy.

'I yelped "What?" The car strayed. A horn blasted. I drove in silence until we came into the city steering one-handed, squeezed into the corner against the door, wanting to sink my teeth into Fowler's fat neck, rip and shred, and bang his thick head on the dashboard until there was nothing but a spongy mess of brain and blood. Fowler sat in his corner, his head against the window, his eyes shut. He giggled and said he'd find Shanks and chuck him down a mine shaft.

'I bellowed at him, "You'll be facing the hangman if Moran dies."'

But Fowler was awake, after all. He said, 'They always hang the getaway driver, too.'

14. Pit Pony Underground

Sunday, January 31.

After another agonising night sleepless in bed at The Dudley, I returned to Tin City at dawn the day after Becker almost drowned me. I bent forward, grabbed a clump of chalky grass, hauled my body to the top of the sandhill, and, dizzy for a moment, sat, hands crossed behind my head, with my back to a paperbark. I stared at the ocean and gathered my breath. Becker was a tiger's cub. Would he grow into a wildcat, untameable and unpredictable? Could I control him, or would he scratch me to death? Did he have claws?

The salt was heavy in the air, the beach already warming in the mid-summer heat, a coal ship riding high closed on the mouth of the Hunter River and entered through the breakwall to the port. I had found a few minutes to relax before a busy day, driving to Sydney and returning after dark.

A pair of midnight-black crows sliced across the early sun to take refuge in the next tree and kraal their anger. An omen? But Becker had the loyalty of the gang, and it was the only gang I had outside of Gabe's and Kitty's. An image popped up of Becker riding Gabe, taking the whip to him, but the innocence in his handsome face betrayed the picture. He was, after all, a kid licking an ice cream cone in the street.

My gang of four lived in separate rooms at Annie's boarding house at Cooks Hill, in the centre of Newcastle, and drove or rode to their day jobs at the Burwood mine, thirty minutes away. I lived in a similar room in the early days of the war before the Americans arrived and spread their money generously among the women of Newcastle. The only telephone was in the ground floor entrance lobby, where rickety timber stairs led to the second floor. The building was ramshackle then, and the war had left little spare cash for renovations. A thin fibro partition offered what little privacy there was. A French door led to a balcony shared by two rooms where, on summer nights, we would sit on the floor with our backs against the rusting cast-iron balustrade, the balcony floor bouncing like a boat in rough water.

I needed five, maybe six, to do the job. Becker was in because I took a shine to him and because he was their leader and my captain's choice. That made no sense, but, while von Liebling, the glamorous escort, was not allowed to fall properly in love, I, Sunni Sinclair publican and aspiring gang boss, could take into my heart anyone I wanted if that's the way things worked out. And besides, Franz was brave and chivalrous and switched me on.

Fowler was there for the threat of his violence and because I had no one else remotely menacing to add to my team.

Rudy and Skeet were the keys to a successful heist. Rudy held the critical knowledge stored in his head, and Skeet had the details of access and timing I needed if my primitive idea was to become a workable caper.

Skeet was intense, dicey, and risky, but I could count on his decency and honesty. But what sort of a man was Rudy? Did I trust him? He came away from the Korean War, so he must have teamwork skills and the instinct for spontaneous action when the plan goes belly-up, or he would not have survived. You have to look at the people around you and ask what they have done to stay alive and judge them on that. Time was short, and I needed to sleep, but what was my adrenaline for, if not to keep me awake?

I joined Rudy where he lay under the sparse shade of a redgum, hands clasped behind his head, watching the same coal ship. There was a breeze from the sea; cooler now but not by much.

We sat for a long time, Rudy in his shirt and tie combing

his hair, and spoke about the weather and Inigo Jones's latest forecast, the discovery of oil in Exmouth Gulf and Robert Menzies latest witticism.

When there was a lull in the conversation, Rudy asked, 'What are you doing here, Sunni? Why are you hanging about with a gang of junior wannabes like us?'

'Good question.'

'Soldiers don't have good questions,' Rudy said. 'They only have nasty ones they wish had ended differently.'

Becker's gang made barely enough from crime to keep food on their rented table, so they worked in the mine and wherever they found part-time jobs. But when I shared my life with Kitty and Gabe, we lived on the edge, glamorous and dashing, and that was the only way for me. After Gabe's savage attack on Becker, I recognised Lou for what he had been—Shanks, the killer—and he died because he chose to be a part of Kitty's world. My life in the good old days was often plain ugly, but as I sat on the beach with Rudy, I yearned for the good old parts.

Do I want to get at Kitty? Yes. Do I miss the excitement? Yes. Oh, yes. From their perch high above, the crows glared at me through black eyes and cackled.

I told Rudy I wanted to live the celebrity life again. Drink the champagne and wear the jewellery. But that wasn't the real reason for my discontent. I thought Kitty had cured me of that life, but the spirit of it must have lived on inside me. I have always hankered to steal from the rich, put them in their place and teach them a lesson. I suppose that's why I sympathise with the communists.

Rudy said, brushing aside my needs, 'For whatever reason, I'm making a grab for riches, and I'll take the risk that I get away unscathed. My choice.' He sank into silence again, but, after a while, 'You don't seem the type to join with Fowler and Skeet.'

'You don't include Becker?' I said. 'You think he's my type?'

Rudy said, 'Maybe he and I are the same—tired of being powerless. Tired of being kicked about like a football. In Korea, I thought we fought for a worthy cause.' He gave me a half-hearted laugh, and the crows joined in. 'The war released me from the restrictions of civilian life, the worry, the wondering if I had the intelligence to lead a revolution or influence my world as my parents and teachers expected of me. But when I came home from the war, the world treated me like another returned soldier. I could find no path through the maze. Stealing other people's money was the quickest way to become the kicker, not the ball.'

'Do you think you joined the right gang?'

'Becker's a go-getter,' Rudy said. 'He's got guts and brains. If I stick with him, opportunities will come my way.' He had been staring at the clouds while we spoke but then his eyes sought mine. 'Did you say you have an idea?'

'A heist,' I said, with all the confidence of a barefoot pirate dodging the black spot.

'Will I be expected to kill someone?'

'No.'

Rudy thought about that before he said, 'The possibility is there, though?'

'We can avoid it.'

Rudy didn't hesitate. 'Then you need Fowler, though you would be safer without him. Skeet and I would go to water if we had to kill. I don't know how Becker would react. He threatened to kill his best friend Benny in Korea, but there were circumstances. A threat is not murder.'

He steepled his fingers; the light behind him diffused through the trees, and he would not look me in the eye.

'It's Becker, isn't it?' I said. 'You are not confident of him.'

After a while, he nodded. 'Sometimes—it began in Korea after the bayonet fighting at the battle of Maryang—a black mood settles on Becker, and he loses it without any warning

100

or reason. Hits out. But Fowler's a cold-blooded killer. He has that way of controlling a situation simply by looking fierce and terrifying. If, say, a security guard wanted to make a show of earning his pay, maybe pull his gun, Fowler would enjoy shooting him and, as quickly, turn his gun on anyone who might get in the way.'

Rudy's cold portrait of Fowler disturbed me. 'His job,' I said, 'would be to rush the guard, shock him, drop him to the floor and convince him to stay there.'

'Fowler enjoys killing. Not me. Not anymore. Not after Korea. Without Fowler, everything would be safer. How much cash are we talking?'

'Two hundred thousand pounds.'

'Who carries that much cash?'

'People,' I said, 'who don't like keeping the sorts of records the Tax Department uses to get its jollies. That would be my low expectation. Maybe two hundred and fifty thousand.'

'What's my share?'

'I take sixty per cent. Becker said he'd split the forty per cent equally among the gang. There will be six or seven players, so conservatively eleven thousand pounds to you.'

'That would buy me fifteen acres of waterfront land at Southport. Subdivide that into sixty lots, sell them for two thousand each, and I'm wealthy. What's the job?'

I drew in a breath. The plan was taking on a shape. 'For security, each gang member will know only what they need to know. You will not take part in the heist. Your job is to take delivery of the cash and hide it for six months.'

'That means no one can splash the cash and draw attention to the gang for at least six months. Right?'

'Yeah.'

'That's clever,' Rudy said, and immediately boosted my confidence.

'Skeet says you know the old mine shafts better than anyone. Your first job would be to find a way to open a disused adit I have in mind.'

'Not a vertical shaft,' he said, 'but one exposed at ground level and sealed off? Is that what you mean? Some are secure against entry, and others are easier to access. When will I know?'

'When three more join the gang,' I said. 'That will happen tomorrow.'

A beach angler lofted a baitfish far into the surf, and a flock of gulls descended from nowhere to dive and screech until it sank out of sight. I liked Rudy—I trusted his judgement.

'Are you in?' I asked.

'Yeah.' Rudy didn't blink. Just Yeah.

'Can I trust Skeet?' I asked.

'Not to hurt someone.'

'Getaway driver?'

Rudy said, 'Skeet's moody since Shanks died and Fowler attacked Sergeant Moran. He thinks he would be on the scaffold, being one of the gang. Yesterday, we went down to the coal face—'

I interrupted him for a piece of vital information. 'How do you get there?'

Rudy laughed gently, 'You hurtle down nine hundred feet on a dolly carriage at the end of a one-inch steel cable—twenty others with you on cramped timber seats at forty degrees to the horizontal. In pitch dark, the wheels roar on steel rails, the wind whistles through the cage inches from the sides of the rock tunnel, dim lights at twenty-yard intervals streak past in a continuous line, your stomach loses touch with your body, and your ears block with the speed of the descent. That's how.'

According to Rudy, Skeet was claustrophobic and easily unnerved. The ride to pit bottom on the end of a rope always snatched the blood from his face and brought acid to his throat. Skeet hid it well because he needed to keep his job, but each trip was a nightmare for him. Skeet and Fowler usually worked the mine together as an electrical repair team, but yesterday was a minor job, and Skeet was on his own.

'Can you get me down to look at the mineshafts?'

He needed less than a second to say, 'No way. Security is too tight.'

'Describe it to me, then.'

'Really?' Rudy said, scoffing. 'Why would you want to know that?'

'I need to know what a mineshaft looks like if I decide to plant bags full of cash there.'

'Okay, then, I'll tell you. Yesterday, I needed to go to the level three office to update the mine plans. I joined Skeet and Becker while we collected our battery belts. Before starting down, Skeet whispered to me that Jessica had phoned Becker at the boarding house. Annie's.'

'Where's this story going?' I asked.

'Wait. At first, Skeet let the phone ring, but the jangling kept on until he finally ran downstairs to answer it. Jessica insisted on speaking to Becker, but he wasn't there, and when Skeet asked what it was about, she told him someone was asking questions about Becker and wanted to know if he had threatened her. Jessica said the caller told her someone had murdered Shanks.'

I held up a hand to pause Rudy's hurried words. 'I don't believe I said that. I might have said that his death was suspicious, but I wouldn't frighten her by using the word murder.'

'I guessed it was you,' Rudy replied, making it clear with a grunt that he had no interest in what I said to Jessica. 'Anyway, the trolley eased to a stop at pit bottom and bounced on the rope. We grabbed our tool kits, switched on our helmet lamps, tightened the battery belts, and stepped out into a space as big as a cathedral. The walls and ceiling are white, with banks of fluorescent tubes lighting the place like a power station. Skeet was trembling from the dizzying descent in darkness. That's when he told me he was scared they would hang him.'

I leaned back into heavier shade under the tree. 'Get off,' I said. 'They don't hang the driver. Don't you think Skeet's a bit of a tragic?'

Rudy shrugged. 'The overman told Skeet to sign the book and warned us to watch out for the blind pit ponies. He told Skeet there would be blasting at exactly fourteen-twenty and again at sixteen-thirty and to return to pit bottom before fourteen-ten whether he fixed it or not and sent him off.

'These were routine warnings, but Skeet grabbed my elbow and told me you were spreading the rumour Shanks was murdered. He said that Albie Fowler insisted you must be disappeared, but Skeet said he would have no part of that.'

'Good for Skeet,' I said, moving my leg out of the sun and wriggling my bottom to get comfortable on the sand.

Rudy gave me a grunt and took up his story as though I hadn't interrupted. He told me that Skeet had to go to Section Six, where the lights had failed, find the switchboard and repair the fault. At the entrance to an adit, Skeet rechecked his lamp and swore. His battery showed twenty-five per cent capacity, enough for only two hours. The system was supposed to be foolproof, with used batteries stored on separate hangers until fully charged, and only then returned to the battery room. But a used, uncharged battery had found its way to the hangers with fully charged batteries. Skeet was liable to cop a bluey for violating regulations and faced the sack. He hesitated, before shying away from the overman's office. He swore again, then hurried off to the coal face.

Rudy said, 'I told Becker about Skeet's battery and that he'd gone to Section Six. Becker said one of us should go after him, stay with him. So I went, and Becker told the overman I had gone to check a benchmark. So, Skeet hustled off along the well-lit main roadway—'

'Wait. A roadway?'

'A path for trucks and machinery. Busy with miners in blue overalls and reflective patches and muddy boots. Their eyes and teeth are white in faces black from coal dust. But I knew a shorter route, without roof lights, to Section Six.'

The way Rudy described the underground, I felt claustrophobic out in the blazing sun. Black coal walls, the floor and the ceiling, absorbing the light from helmet lamps, and even after a hundred descents, the most experienced miners sometimes found the darkness confusing, and section six was a recent opening.

Rudy said he trudged on to find the work face and, in the dark, thought about the phone call and Shanks and about Skeet worrying he would hang for murder. His throat was dry, the cross-through was closing in on him, the ceiling was lowering, and he came to a work face and a Y-junction with cuttings heading inbye. Pillars of coal three yards by three yards remained to hold up the roof over cuttings where miners had taken the coal, and ventilation passages formed by heavy, wet hessian curtains added to the confusion.

'I should have found the switch box by then,' Rudy said. 'I had allowed my mind to wander. I was lost. Which passage? Neither was signed. The air was filthy hot. I panted for lack of oxygen. Rats squeaked and scratched, and I lost my way for a moment.'

'Hold on,' I said. Rudy lost? I grabbed a fistful of my hair and pulled it until it hurt. My plan drained away like stormwater down the spout, and I crumbled. I thought if he could be lost so easily, then my plan was shattered. 'Wait!' I went on. 'I thought you knew your way around the mine.'

Rudy shrugged, groaned, spat. 'I know my way around, but this was a new section. I lost it for a second and shouted. "Hello." And again, "Helloooo," drawn out and louder, but the wet hessian absorbed my shouts. "You the electric?" a voice asked, while I struggled to escape from behind the heavy curtain. "Over here. Here's your switchboard."

'And through a joint in the curtains, a beam from my helmet lamp showed a team of miners stripped to helmets, boots, battery belts and loincloths, sitting in the dark to conserve their batteries and sharing their crib boxes with two pit ponies, and there was Skeet, arriving behind me. "Took ya time," one miner said to Skeet, his voice coming from the darkness. "Can't earn a crust when we can't see nothink." I stepped into the circle of Skeet's helmet light and said g'day, cool as a waterbag in winter. Miners are unforgiving of anyone scared of the dark.'

Rudy's description of getting lost in the darkness of tunnels and roads shook me, and I only half-listened as he lied about being cool and told me the rest of the story. Working with the glow from his helmet lamp, Skeet isolated the failed circuit and searched for the fault while Rudy sat on the floor in the dark with the miners.

When Skeet was done, and the lights were on, they trudged along the head passage, Skeet muttering into the darkness about how he didn't know, he didn't know. He freaked out, so Rudy went to the surface with him. He'd come back with a spare dumpy or something for an excuse to go to the surface and return.

Skeet was first off the trolley, sucking in the cool air, swallowing the whole sky, the freedom, the relief. He wanted to go straight to Stockton Beach to make sure he hadn't left anything behind. That's how murderers get caught, he said—a boot, a handbag, a sock even. Then he remembered fingerprints and wanted to go immediately to the hotel to wipe the window. Wipe the car. He was suffocating, tears clogging his eyes, and though his mouth was open, no words came out.

The crows kraaled, the seagulls cried, and the coal ship had travelled through the break wall to the coal port. Rudy wound to a halt and said, 'So you can make up your mind whether

Skeet can be trusted. Getaway driver maybe, but nothing more elaborate.'

I thought about Skeet. 'How can you hide the stuff with so much activity in the mine shafts?'

'There are hundreds of miles of unlit worked-out adits. They crisscross where no one would dare go. Except for the surveyor with a plan in his hand.'

15. Challenging the Sydney Mob

Monday, February 1.

At eight a.m., I paced anxiously around the property. The clock was running, and my plan was up the creek if this place was a no-go. I took in the timber cottage, the fenced acreage where the horses had roamed and the splintered ironbark-plank barn where they had sheltered from the weather. I slid down the slope to reach what remained of the old banana plantation and a ploughed paddock where rockmelons, cabbages and carrots grew wild. Never comfortable in the country, I stamped my boots to scare away snakes and spiders and pushed through the trees. A rusting ploughshare concealed in the overgrown bushes grazed on weeds and nettles like the ghostly skeleton of a primitive animal. I shuddered and returned to the barn where a two-wheeler, horse-drawn cart with solid rubber tyres on cast-iron wheels leant tiredly against the wall. Dusty cobwebs strangled busted shafts and wire chicken baskets, and pumpkin vines covered the cracked leather seat. I wore slacks for the occasion, and, at the top of the slope, I rested one R.M. Williams riding boot on the post and rail fence and surveyed the vista across hills and valleys to the sea.

'This will do,' I said to Skeet. He had come on his motorbike. 'You sure nobody followed you?'

'Yeah, right. I've watched the mirror since I left Redhead. Too early for the coppers to be up and about.'

I met Skeet last evening after his shift at the mine and explained the general concept. I set him off to search the south side of Newcastle from the railway station through Merewether and Charlestown to Kahibah, looking for a suitable out-of-the-way shed or old warehouse. The shed I described to him would be away from the main north to south highway, in an industrial area where unusual activity would not concern curious eyes. But, as Skeet discovered, the industrial zones with their sheds were north, where traffic and roadblocks would not favour a getaway car, and so he thought outside the box and came up with a farmer's shed.

'The barn is big enough to hold two vehicles,' I said, and Skeet savoured my approval. The bitumen road was too narrow for two cars to pass without getting off the sealed road onto the gravel, and its broken edges and spring-breaking potholes kept the volume of traffic low. A stand of trees gave privacy from passing cars. 'How'd you find it?' I asked.

'Last night,' Skeet said, 'I was half-asleep and remembered this place. My friend, the magistrate, thought he would buy it and build a big house for his wife and kids.'

'But you told me he was homosexual.'

'He's bi. During the war, the landowner leased part of the banana plantation to a market gardener to grow vegetables. Cauliflower, melons, pumpkins and stuff. It was a small allotment with good soil, enough to keep a family going and plenty left to sell. The farmer, Philip Lee Chin, delivered directly to his customers from this horse-drawn cart. My mother bought all our fruit and veg from him. One day, I came out with the magistrate to inspect the property, but he eventually lost interest. The barn was the packing shed. Now the property is in limbo, while National Parks fights about who owns it.'

'Will the magistrate recognise you? Is he likely to be a problem?'

'He'll be out of the way at Randwick chatting to the racing aristocracy.'

'Buy a padlock for this door,' I said, 'and drive out here over the weekend. Make sure nothing changes.'

'Should I lock the door?' Skeet asked.

'Not until we're ready. In case someone comes around. Wear gloves, and don't leave fingerprints on the padlock or door. Wipe everything you touched today. I need to get away.'

Skeet glanced at Becker lying in the Plymouth. 'Where are you going with Becker?'

I needed to get Becker to Sydney by noon, but there was no need for Skeet to know, so I fobbed him off. Told him Becker was coming with me for a drive in the country. That's what he needed to know and nothing more.

Becker was stretched out in the rear seat, occasionally groaning when we hit a bump or took a sharp bend. The wounds on his body were healing, but his silences and frequent hesitations told me something deep inside him was out of order. The Plymouth's suspension was not designed for transporting casualties, but there was no time to be gentle with him. I needed him in Sydney to talk to the two he had assured me could handle the job.

We drove for three hours towards Sydney, on the ocean road to Gosford, across the Hawkesbury, slowing on a narrow winding route through the Ku-ring-gai hills, heading for the Harbour Bridge, then Matraville—plenty of time for me to think about Fowler and Jessica.

I shouted over my shoulder to Becker. 'Jessica is at risk as a witness to Fowler's meeting with Lou shortly before he drowned. Are you worried about her?'

'Fowler swears he will not hurt her.'

'Can you trust her? You haven't mentioned our high jinx? I suppose, in any case, she'll have her suspicions.'

Becker raised his voice above the car noise. 'We can't let her become suspicious. I don't want her involved if it goes wrong.'

We drove on in silence until I twisted the mirror to check if he was awake.

'I'm here,' he said, trying to grin. Then, 'I don't recall Jess at school. Maybe a pair of pigtails and the teacher praising her for her homework. I think she may have topped the class. The only thing that interested me was getting out of school at the end of the day. I would roam the city, cheeking the coppers in the street and beating all comers at the billiard hall. I played for a shilling a game. My shoplifting expanded to joining a gang, stealing a car and driving it into a ditch when I was sixteen. I had no time for girls or for Jess.'

We twisted up the side of the range, and as we dived down off the mountain and through the forest to Hornsby, sunlight streaked through the grey sky, and I asked about Fowler.

'He was not the sharpest razor in Kitty's gang,' Becker said. But he's obsessive in his loyalty to me. He was so grateful when I picked him up after Gabe fired him. He's built like a milk-fed bullock. Must be over six feet. Handy to have around. We never get into a brawl because his broken nose and bushy eyebrows frighten the shit out of everyone, including me.'

'I noticed. What's with his accent?'

Becker said, 'Before the Great War, his family came to Australia from Yorkshire. He worked his way up the line in Kitty's gang until he was her chief in Newcastle.'

There was no point in getting Fowler off-side. We needed him unless I found someone to do his job, and I had a tight schedule. I had eight days to get everything ready. A gang needs a heavyweight who knows how to get things done and is prepared to go to the wire. So, I sucked it up, put on my best voice and asked, 'Do you carry a gun?' The question made me wonder, not for the first time, if in rushing to prove myself, my adventure had somehow leapt a barrier to become a reckless folly.

Becker deliberated before answering a different question, 'I always felt naked around Shanks and Fowler without a weapon. If I show a knife, most loudmouths will drop away. You don't have to kill anyone. Flash the blade, and they back off. But not those two.'

'Rudy seems a good bloke.'

'He's the peacemaker. All the time, combing his hair as though he'd like to tear it out by the roots. He fought like a fury in Korea, so I take notice when he speaks.'

'He says you threatened your best friend Benny in Korea.'

'Ah, shit,' Becker said. 'Did he tell you that? There was a lot of stress. Benny *was* my friend. We often talked about getting justice for what the war did to us and doing whatever was necessary to avoid boredom and get the dream life. When your friends are mutilated or killed, mutiny and violence come naturally.'

'Rudy is a good friend?'

'He's twenty-six, a qualified surveyor, always dresses in a business shirt and tie. He has this thing about plastering his hair with oil and tearing it out with a comb. The army psych said it was the war, and he'd get over it. He's one hundred per cent reliable and usually takes my side in an argument. Rudy saved me from a court marshall and arranged my job here when we returned. Set me up as his chainman. Soldiers stick together. He knows every twist and bend of the mineshafts. Like Swiss cheese, it would be without surveyors. No one knows the mine like Rudy and me.'

'What about Benny?' I asked. 'I need to know how he feels about you before we meet him today.'

'Never a hard feeling there.'

'And Skeet?'

'Skeet is Skeet. As loyal as they come. He was fourteen when he arrived from Italy and has never had a fair go.'

We arrived at Matraville, an up-and-coming Eastern suburb of Sydney with low unemployment among its mainly white-collar workers. Marty Ferguson lived in a rented timber cottage that needed a paint job ten years ago. The roof leaked, the yard was knee-deep in thistles and burrs, and the twenty-yard path leading to the outside lav turned to mud at the suggestion of a humid day.

Becker's health was improving. That's the best way to describe it. He limped in and introduced me. Marty was fifty-something, had a face like a weathered hardwood log, ears that stuck out from his short back-and-sides haircut. He wore a ragged lumberjack shirt and had the look of a man who enjoyed a good brawl.

Becker said, 'Marty saved my bacon more than once.'

'And you,' Marty said, 'returned the favour.' He brandished a bottle of Tooheys. 'Gotta be dangerous, mate, when you've driven three hours to talk to us looking like death warmed up. Whose throat do I have to cut?'

I stepped to the sink, picked up two glasses the worse for want of a clean, rinsed them under the tap, and held them out in the spirit of the occasion. Marty poured and talked at the same time.

'You gotta know this Becker bloke.' He flicked an eye at me, then to the glass. 'He's not everything he appears to be, mate.'

'How did you two meet up?' I asked.

'This little bastard was sixteen and hanging on to a rifle taller than him. After Tojo surrendered, I came home, and the writing was on the wall. Jobs were non-existent, and we lived on the dole. Me mates were gone hell west and crooked, and life at home was a bit hectic after a month. We all needed a holiday in the Blue Mountains. So, I volunteered to rejoin the army—three meals a day but boring. I knew if I stayed in the peacetime army, I'd have to cop those never-fired-in-anger officers. So, I put my hand up for Korea with the Third Battalion. Tough work, but I got paid. That's where I met me little mate Becker and his big rifle.'

I peeked at Benny Dean, a long-faced tram driver and a softer version of Marty. He had a prominent Roman nose bending to the left, wrinkles on his forehead and cheeks, thick black hair parted in the middle, and the eyes of a Basset Hound. His white shirt was starched, and he wore a plain blue tie.

'There was no future in the British army,' Benny said, wearing a doleful face, 'for a poor ignorant Brit based in Burma. But this hulking great Aussie sergeant took a liking to me and looked after me. So, I followed him to Australia. The government was bringing in boatloads of refugees and letting em take the jobs we should have had, so when he suggested Korea, naturally enough, I pulls out me clogs and mooches off with him. At Pusan, some foreign prick handed me a rifle. He had no English, so Marty snarled at me to come on, Benny, smarten up unless you want to get home with a bullet up yer arse. Now that I'm back on civvy street, the commies are busy again, and the government has betrayed me and shattered me fucking illusions.'

'Yeah, mate,' Marty said impatiently. 'I know all that. You've told me often enough about your delusions.'

Benny said, 'I christened Becker "The Kid" at Maryang-san, and we sort of adopted him. Look what's happened to the poor bastard now that I'm not around to care for him no more.'

Marty cracked another bottle. 'We were drinking mates and not exactly model soldiers. The army transferred us to Special Forces to get rid of us. After we got busted by a bunch of Chinese, the brass bundled us off to hospital in Australia.'

Benny nodded his agreement and downed his beer.

'Anyway,' Marty said, pouring for Benny, 'they called us heroes, demobbed us, and let us loose on the Aussie pubs. Here, Sunni, I'll fill your glass again.' He waved a hand around the kitchen, where they sat at a pine table. 'Look where I finished up. No job, no wife, no kids, no dough.'

A gas stove occupied a corrugated iron recess, and a fridge dripped water into a tray on the floral-patterned linoleum. From there, the water drained through a hole in the floor. A separate bedroom was barely big enough for the double bed, and a pink basin was falling off the wall in the bathroom.

'What you gunna do about this, Becker?' Marty asked. 'You always said we wouldn't put up with a lousy wage, and we'd live like kings or not live at all.'

'Yeah, Becker,' Benny had a sly expression. 'What sorta crooked deal did youse bring for us?'

'How does two hundred thousand sound?'

'Quid?' Benny asked.

'Yeah, maybe two hundred and fifty in cash, and maybe some jewellery and other shit.'

'Yeah? Have ya got any more detail to go with that lengthy presentation? Rob a bank, is it?'

'Yeah, a bank,' Becker said.

'Who's running the show?' Benny flicked his eyes sideways at me.

'Sunni's the boss.'

'A female? Well, things are certainly changing. Are you one of them—you know?'

'No, I *don't* know. I was a call girl and one of Kitty Balushi's gang. Now I own a pub in Newcastle.'

'Well,' Marty said. 'I suppose that qualifies ya. Ya can't do no university course in heists. Where's the job?'

'Newcastle,' I said. 'Next week.'

'All planned and everything?' Benny asked.

I leaned forward in my chair. 'Sorry, fellas. No more information until the day before the job. Then, if you don't like it, we walk away.'

'Ah, mate,' Benny, the sceptic, said. 'Nothing's that straightforward. Plans fall apart, and people get hurt. Give us a hint.'

'Two hundred thousand?' Marty said. He was pacing, excited. 'What's the split?'

'I take sixty per cent of the cash plus any stray jewellery and documents,' I said, expecting, for no good reason, gold rings and betting slips. 'You guys split the rest of the cash seven ways.

Three of Becker's mob are in Newcastle, plus I need you to find one other.'

'Seven blokes can do a job,' Marty said. 'That's for sure. But why do you get to keep the jewellery?'

'I will toss it in the deepest hole in the harbour. Jewellery is dynamite. We go to sell it, the police have a list of stolen goods, and boom, we're all locked up.'

'Yeah,' Marty was scribbling with an indelible pencil on his wrist. 'Good thinking. You sound as though you know what you're doing. That's what? Ten, eleven thousand each. Gets me a decent house at Maroubra or Brighton-le-Sands, a car and plenty left for drinking.'

Benny chimed in. 'You're joking, mate. Or you've been on the turps. Robbing a bank—that's stupid. I've never robbed a Salvo's collection box.'

'That's my lowest estimate,' I said.

'What's the catch?' Benny said.

'Catch is, I hold the dough for six months. Police capture too many robbers when they splash the cash. If they find one, they'll have all of us. I'll give you each twenty quid a month for six months, then, all being well, I give you the rest.'

Marty looked at Benny. 'Twenty a month is good pocket money on top of what you're getting for driving a tram.'

Benny shrugged, waving his hand around the kitchen. 'My place is no better than this. I've always wanted a farm where I grow grapes and make wine. I learned to like a glass or two in France but can't afford the good stuff. What do you want from us?'

'Automatic machine guns, handguns—'

'What's with the machine guns?' Benny's voice rose and vibrated. 'They gunna let us take the cash away because they're all dead. Is that it? I've had my fill of shooting people.'

'It won't come to that,' I said, crossing my fingers under the table. 'This is not a violent situation unless we make it one.'

116

They nodded at each other, scratched their armpits, and stretched. 'Next?'

I roamed the room for a minute wondering who I could trust, who would stick with me when things went wrong. They sat like soldiers waiting for the officer to tell them. So, I told them. 'We'll need a closed getaway van to carry six people and bags to hold the cash, a second truck—like a Landrover—with a cover over the rear. You have to swipe the vehicles from different cities, and I need you to find me one more soldier, ex-Commando, preferably, but any war will do. No previous convictions, and he needs to ride a motorbike and accept that he won't get his share for six months. After that, wire cutters, hammers and a few bits and pieces. A grenade. I'll give you a list.'

'Grenade? What grenade? Are you crackers?'

'Get it all together, bring it to Newcastle next Monday. Marty, you and the new bloke ride to Newcastle, but make sure they don't see your proper rego where I tell you to park. Benny and Skeet will drive the vehicles. We'll do a full-dress rehearsal, and, if you don't like it, we don't go ahead. Are you in?'

Benny gave a short, sharp laugh. 'I'll come to a dress rehearsal to find out what it's all about. But I won't be going any further than that. You're having me on, right?'

'Not joking. I'll do it with or without you, and it will work.'

Marty wanted to know the specifications for the truck.

'Here's a sketch of what I need. Do you have a pencil and paper? It's Monday already. Let's get to the details. The sooner we sort it out, the sooner we roll in the cash.'

16. Boss Gangster Inside Track

I rushed Billy up the stairs after he reluctantly agreed to swap his ground-floor room across the hall from my suite with Becker's, then drove the Plymouth to Tin City to reclaim my white Austin A70 sedan. Driving that zippy little car after manhandling the massive Plymouth through city traffic was a relief. Becker loved his Plymouth. He told me that, when he got home from Korea, he boosted the khaki-coloured staff car from a disposal yard where the U.S. Army had left stuff to rust and had a friend spray it a shiny black.

Distracted by thoughts of the heist and guns, grenades, and casualties, I slid to a stop outside the pharmacy, parked carelessly at the kerb and went in to buy the APC powders, bandages, and antiseptic washes Jessica needed. The sun had dipped below the horizon and cast an eerie pink shadow as I hustled through the streets and parked my A70 at the side of The Dudley, right on seven. Preoccupied with my meeting in Sydney, I reached for the door handle, but before I flipped it open, a sudden, sharp knock shattered the silence and my calm. And Tommo was glaring at me, tapping on the glass with a lemonade bottle in one hand and circling a finger, urging me to wind down the window. I panicked, suffocating, unable to speak. Had he somehow discovered my plan? Had Skeet opened his chatty mouth? Don't be stupid. You haven't done anything yet.

'Jeez, Tommo,' I managed to stammer. 'You frightened the bejesus out of me, sneaking up like that.'

Tommo scoffed at my accusation. 'I pulled in behind you and knocked. Do you want me to sound the siren whenever I visit The Dudley? Where have you been?'

His question hung in the air like black smoke from a bush fire until I rediscovered my wits. 'You can't ask me that, mate. I'm an upright citizen going about my business, which is confidential. Anyway, g'day.' My mouth running away without me. 'You're looking a bit over it today, and the night shift is hardly underway.'

I think my little joke raised his spirits. At least I got a short laugh. 'Bloody cheek. I will admit to a little exhaustion after being harassed all day by self-important bureaucrats organising the Royal Tour and other petty criminals.' I saw in my rear mirror that he had come in a marked patrol car with a uniformed constable. 'I've had a report,' he said, 'that you were driving a Plymouth, the same as Becker's. Same rego.'

Who reported that? It's no coincidence that Tommo pulled in behind me. He's been following me. He may have followed behind me all day. Not to Sydney. What has he found out? Nothing. Don't panic.

But Tommo pressed on. 'And I have a report on my desk that a witness observed you with Gabe Rosen during that Saturday night's riot. What can you tell me about the riot?'

Fatigue overcame me. Tired of the whole frolic and sick of being a criminal and playing hide-and-seek, I spoke more forcefully than I needed to. 'I wasn't at any riot, and you should be interrogating your precious Mr Rosen, not me. If you must know, we danced at the Festival Ball until some cute little, mousey adolescent tapped in. Then I came home in a sulk.'

'And Becker's car?' Tommo cried. 'What are you doing? You're old enough to be his aunty.'

'Old enough?' I shouted back at him. 'Old enough? Is that how you would describe me? Old enough to be his grandmother is what you want to say.'

'If I find Becker, I'll lock him away until after the Royals have come and gone, and longer if I am allowed.'

'Well, do it.' My blood was up. I'd give him old. 'I'm not interested in the Royal Windsors. Bloody aristocrats. For centuries, sending working-class men and women to war and taking a million lives to protect their wealth.' He wouldn't be talking Royal Tours if he was about to arrest me for conspiring to commit a crime. 'Becker got beaten up. Isn't that enough to satisfy Gabe?'

Tommo said, 'There's to be a procession along Hunter Street with speeches and partying from one-fifteen in the afternoon, eight days from now. We expect a hundred thousand loyal fans to line the street to watch their Royals streak past in the flesh. That's three hours of pandemonium.'

He offered a cigarette pack, which I rejected with a shake of my head. 'There'll be enough opportunities,' he said, 'for any mad Red to try an assassination. I need your help to find Becker.'

'Don't be silly, mate. Becker is not a mad Red. He fought the Communists in Korea, for God's sake.'

Tommo did a little angry dance shaking his head. 'But,' he said, 'he's not right in the head. Don't you see that? The way he speaks. His violence. I can't have anyone upsetting the applecart this side of the Tour.'

I invited him in for a beer. That resolves most problems.

'No, thanks. I'm on duty.'

Not a good sign, that. For the three years I've known him, Tommo has never been so much on duty as to pass up a beer.

'So?' I asked, sulking.

'It's come to the superintendent's attention,' Tommo said, 'that you are consorting with Franz Becker, an alleged gangster, whom you previously complained attacked your friend Lou, AKA Shanks, the alleged enforcer for Kitty Balushi's gang.'

'That's a lot of alleging and consorting for one little old aunty. And, anyway, that's all done with. Don't lose any sleep over it. As far as I'm concerned, it was an accident. You were right, and Lou died in his sleep.'

I may have pissed Tommo off a little.

'Cut the crap, Sunni,' he said. 'Have you got something going with Becker?'

'Are you asking if I am sleeping with him? You should know better than to ask about personal matters. But no. I'm not.' Not yet.

'But you are close to him and the alleged hit man, Albie Fowler.'

'Not close even. No. Not last time I allegedly checked.'

'I want no trouble leading to the procession,' Tommo snarled. 'No more brawling. No rigged races. No doped horses. Most of all, no disturbances between your friends and Mr Rosen. You should know better.'

I sighed theatrically.

'Give over Sunni. No need for attitude.'

Tommo waited, expecting some response from me other than a stare that went right through him and came out the other side. He was disappointed.

'The Federal Police will be all over the place,' he said. 'The international press will search through every horse's droppings. They'll look into every race winner, and they'll have spies at the track. You won't be able to walk without tripping over spies, coppers, reporters, and everyone looking for a scandal because they know the Queen is interested in racing and will have a quid on her selection. And that selection better win fair and square, or there'll be hell to pay. Right?'

'As if I'd do anything. I don't fiddle the nags or the bets. What are you on about? Did Rosen put you up to this?'

'Shit, mate. Give it away, will you? You're deliberately provoking me while I'm doing you a favour by warning you that you are running with a bad lot. Becker, Fowler. I know what's going on. They are toeing up for a barney with Mr Rosen. You're a businesswoman. It would help if you behaved accordingly. You're not a rebellious kid like Becker. He's a young reptile with ideas above his station, and you're patting the wrong end of the taipan. Well, I'm here with a message I want you to pass on to Becker. No more brawling. Not now and not in my bailiwick. Got it? No gang wars anywhere, especially not until the Queen leaves Australia. Right?'

'If you like.'

'Ten thousand miles away from here, the press is carrying on about the risk to their precious Royals, so stay away from the track until they're safely home.'

I stood. 'Have you finished mocking me, Tommo, mate? Don't tell me not to go to the track. I'll be there whenever I need a dose of fresh air. Tell Mr Rosen it is up to him to keep the peace.'

'Becker is up to his subversive little head in shit, and, if he goes against Rosen, I'll have another kid's body to investigate.'

'And he'd be going against your superintendent, too, if I read the rumours right. And don't call him a kid.'

'For God's sake, this is a friendly warning,' Tommo swung away on his heel, readying to leave in a fury. 'Do you imagine I care if Rosen feeds Becker to the fishes like you insisted someone did to Shanks? You are consorting with known criminals, and that—'

'I have to go.' I took a tentative step towards the door. No arrest. 'Shanks died from natural causes. A heart attack, and he drowned.'

'Yeah? Well, you've changed your tune. We're taking another look at it, too. I know Gabe can keep the town peaceful, and Becker cannot. That's why we give Gabe some rope.'

I fumbled with the door handle, my face burning from the humiliation he had handed me. 'I'll be off. One day, you'll find out,' I said over my shoulder. 'Becker may be only twenty, but he can handle Gabe Rosen with his eyes closed. Let the bodies pile up. It won't be his doing.'

'Why are you defending him?'

'He's a young bloke who deserves a fair go while you are acting like you're part of the ruling class.'

'I'll tell you what a fair go means. Sergeant Moran is dead, and we know Becker's mate, Albie Fowler, did it. There's not a copper in New South Wales who will let it alone until the murdering bastard is dead and buried. That would be what I call a fair go.'

'You wouldn't hurt a member of the public, now would you, Sarge?'

'Stay away from Becker. He's a bomb waiting to explode.'

Tommo marched to the patrol car and made a point of waiting while I did my best to appear innocent as Saint Thérèse and passed through the door.

Rudy delivered Jessica to The Dudley on the pillion of his bike and left. The less Rudy and I were seen in public together, the better. She checked the packet I brought from the pharmacy and told Becker to remove his shirt. 'I'll check you over. Your jeans, too. Sunni, you'd better stay. I don't want him to get any ideas.' And when he had stripped to his underwear, 'Hold still while I jab you. I told you to rest.'

He took the needle without complaint. 'With luck, it will help me get to sleep.'

'You are pale. Exhausted. Where have you been, Franz? You can't come and go like this. Bed rest is what I told you. It's what you need. If you don't, I'll not be coming again. I'm not doing this because I have nothing better to do.'

'Rest. I promise. Please go home now. You need to get some sleep.'

He'd learned to say please when Jessica was around. That was quick.

When she had gone, I told Becker that Tommo had followed me there. 'We need to keep our eyes open.'

I sighed. I might have wept, but big bosses don't cry. I'm ducking from the police after breaking any number of laws in the past week. I'm hiding a fugitive. I've put together a gang and a half-arsed plan to make a grab for someone else's cash. Does that make me a gangster? I think so. That was quick, too.

17. Who's a Feminist?

Tuesday, February 2.

The lounge bar at the Great Northern was busy with the after-work office crowd, sleek men in dark suits and a sprinkling of whispery women, circulating in a random dance, flirting with sultry eyes, taking care to line up their drinks before the end of Happy Hour. Pre-dinner couples chatted at marble-top coffee tables under the lights of four chandeliers and silver-grey lampshades on side tables.

'You're not accustomed to this intoxicating life, Billy,' I said with throaty undertones. 'Champers and cakes at The Great Northern.'

'It's my pleasure,' Billy said. 'You've been working far too hard, and you deserve to revel in a few luxuries.'

I leaned closer, purring, my thigh pressing his. 'Oh, my darling, what a lover you are. One day, I'll have enough to buy you the best decadent champers in the world.'

Billy's eyes, ignited with the promise of passion, locked onto mine. It worried me that I would be stealing from him, but warning him would put the entire project at risk, and, besides, he makes twelve hundred a week clear of tax. He could afford to lose a little.

I settled into the comfort of the blissful, Indian-red fabric cushion, wriggled my bare toes in the luxury of the deep red and gold carpet and regretted not wearing my cocktail dress and high heels. I raised a glass to an older man standing at the bar, who lifted his discreetly in return and slipped his head to indicate his wife standing beside him.

'Who's that?' Billy asked.

'Wine export agent. I met him occasionally in Sydney before I left Kitty.'

'And met Lou and Becker.'

'Becker is innocent of killing Lou,' I said. 'I believe that now, and I promised him I wouldn't tell the police he's hiding at The Dudley. I'm afraid Tommo is off on the wrong track. He thinks Becker wants to assassinate the Queen.'

'But the police are looking for him about the riot, and you promised Becker—'

'Only that I wouldn't reveal his hiding place.'

Billy said, 'I've never known you in three years to stay away from The Dudley so often. You need to mind your own business and not Becker's.' He bit into a chocolate éclair, poured champagne, and relaxed in his chair. 'What a splendid room, this is.'

'I've missed this life,' I said, twirling a finger around the room. 'Crystal and fine china and gracious people. Yes, ma'am, no, ma'am, have another chocolate, ma'am. I don't want to run into anyone I want to impress dressed like this. Buy me another champagne, Billy.'

'You'll break me.'

'Champagne is exhilarating. A little bit of mischief. You had such a great day at Saturday's races that you offered to shout Dom Perignon. So, order another bottle of that seductive French and pretend I'm on the game, and when you take me upstairs, I'll set fire to your soul.'

'Don't say that. Not here. You're speaking too loudly.' But the tension in his voice told me he got my message loud and clear.

'Oh, dear. We are inhibited today.' My well-practised smile took the sting out of the words. 'So strait-laced. Buy me another French. Don't be such a tight-arse.'

'Are you talking about me again?' Gabe looked me up and down while the Minister continued on until he reached the door and waited.

'Well, look who's here. It's my Gabe. And me in my overalls and old sandals.'

'Powder blue, silk overalls. Dior? And sandals from Milan or Florence, if I'm not mistaken? The hotel business must be looking up.' His eyes travelled the length of my body, then its width.

'An old thing I bought years ago.' I purred like one of his sex-starved pussy cats. And it *was* an old thing anyway. When I lived in Sydney, I had plenty tax-free cash to buy high-fashion clothes. They were an essential business expense. I hadn't bought any decent clothes since I came to Dudley. 'Come and sit here,' I said, patting the sofa beside me and batting lively eyes at him. 'You can buy champagne for me and make beautiful love to me in your beautiful polished shoes.'

Like hell, he can. Not after what he did to Becker. My chest tightened. I hid my contempt for him. I could play intrigue and seduction better than Marilyn Monroe.

'Hello, Billy.' Gabe stood beside me, his hand gently caressing mine. 'You are dangerously tempting today, Sunni. But I can't stay. The Minister is waiting for me, and you're embarrassing me.' He moved out of hand's reach. 'I have my entire harem to consider.'

'Blush away, darling.' Soon, I would emasculate him, and his skinny Minnie would not want to know him. 'It's fun to be alive today in this wonderfully materialistic world. Are you still mooning over that juvenile you were with at the Casino? You forgot to introduce me. Is she a—'

'Sunni, O Sunni, my witch of the wood, would I not die for you, dear, if I could.'

What a dick, what an arrogant prick. I would be coming for him sooner than he knew. Oh, Yes. His life was about to change. 'Oh, Gabe,' I said, 'you are such a romancer. Before you take me away to ravish me, I want to know if you will be in

Sydney next week. I'm taking a holiday there, and it would be fun to meet up.'

'Sorry, darling, I intend to stay here all week for the Golden Guineas, the Trophy, and the Queen. Now I have to go. You've had too many champers, and I have to run. Go home with Billy and sleep it off.'

Gabe swaggered to the door like an Olympic athlete and silenced the chatter in the Great Northern while breaths were held and eyes followed his departure. Good. He'll be here for the Queen.

I gasped a theatrical sigh. 'The light dimmed with his leaving. Did you notice that, too?'

Gabe glanced at me and waved. The world will live on after I break his heart and his wallet.

'This is far superior to The Dudley,' I slurred, stepping out of my sheer black-lace underwear. Gabe will not be running off next time I catch him. The carpets are easy on my toes, my beautiful, sensual toes. 'Look, Billy. Oh, Billy. You've gone to sleep.' Men! Bald and beaten, broken and brainless. I might as well have gone to the movies. Men don't deserve us. Not that I care, but Gabe doesn't deserve his starlet, and Jessica doesn't deserve Becker. Oops. I meant Becker doesn't deserve Jessica.

I lay on the bed beside Billy, my eyes closed, listening to faint music from the lounge, a piano playing a Vera Lynne medley. The tunes had a sadness about them, a walk through memory lane, and drowsy, my mind drifted.

I stirred at dawn when a seagull landed noisily on the windowsill. 'Morning, Gull, what's happening in the big world?' The ebbing tide troubled the seashells; the sun glinted on the foaming surf, and my gull soared and, with a flick of its wings, nosedived into the water to grab a fish. I cheered as it fought off the other squawking birds and cackling, perched on the windowsill to take its leisurely breakfast.

Much as I love him, there's something not right about that Becker kid. Something is playing with his head. I defied Kitty and found a new life. I did it, so *he* can do it. Right?

I knocked on the window glass, the gull fluttered, and I fell onto the bed, watching a movie play on my eyelids. Pride of Egypt winning the Juveniles at Randwick. 'Hey, Gull. Tell me Becker will not snap before my big event.'

18. King of the Kids

Wednesday, February 3.

The Queen and Prince were still on the high seas, approaching the coast, and the urgency of their arrival electrified the journalists to fill their newspapers with details of the highly anticipated Royal Tour set to arrive in Australia that very day. Aware of their mounting tension, I gathered the gang to exercise their minds, get them working on the heist, and give them the broad picture while withholding any details they might accidentally leak, then be on my way. Once again, I told them, as I had with Marty and Benny, that our target was a bank, that it had to happen next week, and when I saw hesitation and nervousness, I dangled the massive reward. Over eleven thousand pounds each after we brought in three of Becker's mates for the job. Enough to invest and live on for the rest of their lives.

We met around a picnic table at a popular waterside park on the shore of Myuna Bay, not far from the coal mine where a dolly carriage was launching materials on a steel cable to the coal face three hundred feet below the ground. I allocated tasks, described the artillery but not the grenade, and provided a rough picture of our escape without mentioning the geography, the route or the tricks I planned to use to camouflage our getaway.

There was silence when I finished my scanty briefing until Skeet, leaning his backside on the seat of an old BSA 500 that blew smoke and leaked oil, said, 'Fowler's right. We shouldn't have met this close to the mine.'

Rudy had carried Fowler on the pillion of his Honda Shadow, which was polished as bright as a cloudless sky, and its colour, he told me, was Ardent Red. Skeet bounced off his bike and landed a hand on my shoulder. I brushed him off and stepped away.

'Sorry.' His face fell as though I'd struck him. 'But many miners live in Wangi Wangi and work at Redhead, and if someone recognises us, the coppers will connect us with Albie Fowler and from him to Moran and Shanks.'

I hadn't thought of that. My car crackled and popped in the heat of the sun while I allowed time to pass. No more mistakes. Not even a small one like that.

Fowler raised his voice, 'We was nowhere near Shanks. We was drinkin' rum and talkin' bullshit on the beach until dawn, and we woke late. That's it. That's our alibi. We saw nothin', know nothin' about him.'

Alibi? So, they constructed an alibi. I believed Becker that it was an accident. Now that I'm a gang leader, they tell the real story.

Becker confused me. I hadn't found the words to put him together in my head, let alone describe my feelings to someone else. He was a wild child and children know how to be mean. But that wildness also made him kind, and I love him for that. Should I add liar to his catalogue of sins? Or was he the naked saint lying beside me on the sand after nearly drowning me? My partner in crime. Would he break? And how easily?

Rudy kicked viciously at a rock the size of a tennis ball. 'We shouldn't need an alibi,' he said. 'You were supposed to frighten him off, and that's all. You insisted Shanks had double-crossed you with Sergeant Moran and had to pay for it.'

Skeet shook his head vigorously. 'No. That's right. We agreed to put a scare in him, is all. Now, I risk being thrown into a cell for the rest of me life. No way.'

But Fowler jabbed a finger at Skeet. 'A scare. Shanks was tough as they come. Scared my arse. And don't anyone go soft on me.' Fowler hawked and spat. 'I had nothing to do with him, anyway.' Mocking me with a derisive grin that failed to meet his eyes. 'It was an accident. Reet?'

Fowler. My partner in sudden death and daylight robbery. How easily did I fall from grace? 'Tommo told me they are re-opening the case,' I said to put him in his place.

He removed his grey cap, ran a hand across a bony skull, scratching at the sides where the barber had given him a short cut and turned his attack on me. 'Tommo can go to hell. I never step away from a fight.' He was building himself into a rage. 'I'm like Kitty. I get the big deals done.'

'You wouldn't know a big deal from a dark-eyed dingo,' I said. 'So, belt up about Kitty.'

'You don't have no right to talk to me like that.'

'I'm boss until this heist is over. Suck it up or get out.'

Fowler recoiled, mumbling into his collar and slipped his thumbs beneath red braces, stretching the elastic with hooked thumbs. I should not have organised a meeting. They weren't listening to me—too busy squabbling. Though, I felt a particular pride that Fowler had backed off.

'Then tell us, where's this big deal you're planning?'

I wanted to squash Fowler but tempered my voice. 'After it goes down next week, you'll have eleven thousand quid to spend. That's all I'll tell you for today.'

'Come on, Albie,' Skeet said, sensing, I suppose, my need to keep Fowler on board. 'You'll be rolling in money, not shark food for the big operators like Gabe Rosen.'

'Rosen!' Fowler said. 'He treated me like scum.'

He was a brute and a thug, but he was my brute, the only one I had, and I thought then that I needed him. 'Albie, Albie,' I said. 'After we've done this one big deal, you'll never worry about people treating you right.'

Fowler stomped around with a hand behind his neck. 'I can spit from here ta The Dudley. That's where Shanks was last seen alive, and ya say the coppers have reopened the case. Investigating Lou will lead them to Moran, and I don't need some copper asking why we're hanging around here in the heat and writing my name in his book.'

I had to call his bluff and shut him down. 'Make up your mind, Albie. In or out?'

'Get moving on this so-called heist, or I'm out. I'm famished, I am. There's a café at Redhead Beach. Best fish and chips in the Hunter.'

Rudy said, 'Fish and chips.' He seemed keen to finish the conversation and get to work. 'Sounds like a good idea. I trust Sunni. Skeet and I have to get to our shift. You two sort it out. You dine on your fish and chips while we eat coal dust.' Rudy smacked his knees and laughed to relieve the tension hovering over Fowler like his personal black cloud.

But Fowler had a hook in and wasn't about to let go. 'Becker shouldn't a made a scene at the fete. The coppers witnessed him assault Shanks. Aye, they'll remember that. Shanks hid and watched me take out Moran, and later, two witnesses saw me with Shanks at the fete.'

Glaring at me. This scary thug meant to deliver that direct threat, and I reined in my temper. I would have to get Fowler on side or let him go. I looked out at the inky sea, clouds skating on the horizon, white horses in the gathering wind, a tic pulsing at the corner of my eye, everything inside me fragile. Al Capone or Gabe Rosen would have ordered their heavies to remove Albie for that remark.

Rudy had lost patience. 'Has anyone threatened to rat you out, Albie?'

'No, but—'

'Is someone harassing you?'

'No, but—'

'In that case, belt up. You have nothing to worry about.'

133

'I went to The Dudley,' Fowler said, 'to warn her off. All girlie and la-de-dah, she was, and I scared the shit outta her.' He glanced at me with a pleased grin.

He doesn't like me. If I keep him in the gang, I'll need to find a way to straighten that out.

A hand gripped my arm. 'Come on,' Skeet said. 'Don't take any notice of Albie. He's always furious.'

A shadow raced towards me across the sea, and I sucked in the salty air gusting from the beach, cool and damp with aromas of ocean and bush. I pressed my fingers to my lips, squinted against the glare and willed my rigid muscles to relax. Fowler was right—I couldn't afford to be weak. Unless I toughened up, we would all share a cell with him. If I were Kitty Balushi, I would not hesitate to drop Fowler in a mine shaft to avoid the risk that he would act on his threat. But I wasn't Kitty Balushi. Was I?

Rudy and Skeet had gone off to the mine. Their motorbikes disappeared towards the colliery, rear wheels raising dust, taillights flaring as they braked at the corner, and I strolled to my car and sat on my hands, rocking on the seat, and waited, hoping Fowler would walk home rather than come with me. No chance.

I parked, and we settled uneasily at the kiosk on the edge of Redhead Beach, unwrapped separate white-paper packages of fish and chips and chugged beers I had carried there in ice wrapped in towels in the boot. The relentless pounding of the surf made conversation difficult as if it wasn't already. The waves beating away at the face of the cliff, eroded caves and overhangs and brought down landslides as the soapy rock surrendered to a mightier force. We made no progress towards becoming more tolerant of each other. At least I had no thought of becoming his friend, and Fowler had not sent a peace pipe, or put up smoke signals offering his eternal loyalty.

'How high do you think?' I asked, gazing at the top of the cliff with a hand shielding my eyes.

'A hundred and fifty feet. Two hundred? Let's go and check it out. Come on.'

Like hell, I will. 'Look there. Those rocks have fallen recently.'

'Come on, don't be a chicken shit.'

But I had to prove something to Albie Fowler and, I suppose, to me. 'Okay, you're on.'

We drove the car to the top of the hill, and he was yards ahead on the narrow, muddy track through low scrub when we came to a grassy clearing and a safety fence with a sign: STOP. THE CLIFF FACE IS DANGEROUS. DO NOT ENTER.

'Come on,' he said, straddling the fence. 'Come on,' lifting his other leg over the wire, 'Come over this side.'

And because he challenged me and my tongue tied itself in a knot, I climbed the rickety wire fence and stood holding on to the fence post at the front of a shallow, red pea-gravel slope leading to the edge of a vertical drop forty yards away. It appeared innocuous enough.

Ten yards down the slope, he waved impatiently for me to join him. 'Come on. 'It's a thrill, or are you too chicken?'

'Wait,' I said.

'Ya reckon you can do a heist, but ya haven't got the guts. Come on.'

I smoothed my jeans with one hand, scraped a hand through my hair, pasted on a smile to camouflage my fear, released my death grip on the fence post and stepped off gingerly towards him.

Fowler said, 'Better stay there where it's safe, Pussy. I'm going to hang my legs over the cliff.'

'Too dangerous,' I said. And while I added 'It's also stupid,' he danced backwards, taunting me.

'Come away!' he said, but he had increased his lead, and, if I wanted to be the gang boss, I had to pass him. I raced to overtake him.

The slope was suddenly steeper than it looked. Fine stones rolled under my feet. Albie's legs came out from under him, and he was flailing his arms, falling, sliding. I caught up. Grabbed his arm. We fell and rolled, the slope getting steeper, and I lost my grip on his arm. He threw out a hand. I grabbed his wrist. Held on. We slid, accelerating on loose pea-shaped gravel toward the edge. Our spread weight acted as a brake and sent us into a slow spin, and we dropped two feet onto a level shelf. I grabbed an embedded rock with my free hand, and he jammed his foot against a cleft in the surface. We lurched to a stop at the edge.

My knee bounced out of control, my head shook to deny what my senses told me had happened, and I rolled weakly into a foetal position facing him, trembling, speechless.

A hundred feet below us, the surf crashed on grey rocks and black petrified coal, and the water swirled, hissed, foamed, and retreated to come barging in again and break once more to send spume fifteen feet into the air. Fowler sat at the edge, hiding the emotions he must have felt—fear, relief, acceptance—as macho people like Fowler do, and searched the horizon and then the rocks below, but he took his time to look at me.

When the gates had closed on my adrenaline and my shakes had stopped, I stared at Fowler until I wept. After the tears stopped, I gathered oxygen into my exhausted lungs, 'You tried to kill me.'

'No. I wanted to outdo ya. Show ya can't run a gang. Can't handle a heist.' He reached into his pocket and came up with a packet of cigarettes and a lighter.

A pulse opened in my eye; my blood was burning. I needed to move, run and jump. I grabbed his cigarettes and pitched them far out over the cliff. The packet plummeted and crashed into the rocks. The water captured it, swept it out to sea, carried it back, and smashed it on the rocks.

'Why did ya have to go and do that?' he said 'They cost me.'

My mouth was working, but it took a while for the words to come. 'Thanks, you saved me.'

'We saved each other,' he said. 'Yah've got guts, ya have.'

We brooded for a time, looking out to sea at white clouds chasing across the sky and seagulls diving for fish, screeching and quarrelling over scraps. The wind gusted hard. I slipped and screamed, and he grabbed me, digging in his heels and throwing his weight back to hold me. I screamed again. 'Get out of here.'

We bum-walked to the fence and sat in the car for a long time. He patted his pockets and grumbled that he had no cigarettes while I berated him for my stupidity.

Eventually, I said, 'I want the truth about Shanks and no lies, or you're out of the heist for good.'

'It's not fair,' Fowler, like me, was in shock and spoke like a schoolboy in front of the principal. 'I had no reason to kill Shanks. Why would I do that? No killing, I told them. We can get life or hang for that. Becker will remember. Skeet stayed in Becker's car while Becker and me waited for Shanks in his room at The Dudley. The wait was longer than I expected, and when Shanks finally arrived, he said he'd come quietly if we would give him a double slug of whisky. He didn't complain much. Allowed me to drag him through his bedroom window and toss him into the car.'

Fowler giggled. 'It was like carrying a bag of spuds. I whispered to Skeet to get moving, and he rolled down the hill before starting the engine, then drove to Stockton Beach with me and Shanks in the rear seat. The funny part is that people liked Shanks. Ya know? He can charm the white socks off a black cat. During that two-hour drive, he told jokes and stories and had us laughing fit to burst. Shanks and me go way back. We had worked for Kitty and swapped stories about the tricks she got up to. I had two bottles of Scotch whisky. We shared a bottle and had to hold each other up until we arrived at where Becker wanted to go. We staggered up the sandhill, laughing.'

'What time was this?' I asked.

'Maybe midnight,' Fowler said. 'We was too plastered to tell the time, but the beach was dark and deserted. The moon had set, only the stars for light, and the night air sobered me a bit. It was high tide, and while I pissed into the grass at the top of the hill, I barely made out the white surf and those broke-down fishing shacks. Skeet and Becker were stone-cold sober, but us two needed a rest to sober up, so we sat on the grass, drunk as shearers, while Shanks told more jokes.

'After a while, he said he knew we gotta give him a bit of a hiding—he was slurring from the whisky—but no need to go too hard on him. He admitted he deserved it but let us know he had a dicky heart. Swore he'd pack and leave town, and we'd never hear from him again. Becker had told me not to do Shanks any harm other than a smack on the knuckles, and I think he came to make sure I behaved. Shanks was pleading all right but half-laughing, too, and it crossed my mind he was putting on an act. I took a swig from the second whisky bottle, threw the empty away, sucked in the fresh air and flexed my fingers. Then Shanksy stripped off his singlet, cheeky bugger that he was, and said let's go for a swim before you knock me about. He called me mate. The whisky made me clumsy, and I moved in on him unsteady like. He told me I didn't need my blade, the sharks were in the Union and house-trained, so I could leave the knife behind.

Fowler interrupted his story to pat his pockets, searching for a cigarette, and when he didn't find one, he said, 'Come on, we'll get a smoke, then I'll tell you the rest.'

'No way, Albie. Finish the story. Then you can smoke all you want.'

He grumbled and hissed, then reluctantly got on with it.

'Becker was sober as always, and I think he twigged Shanks was making a break for it and, in his heart, wished him luck. I reckon Shanks planned to separate me from my knife, then into the surf, swim out to sea in darkness, and he was a strong enough swimmer to come in anywhere and hoof it to Sydney in his own good time. Yeah, I reckon that was his plan. Shanks was helping me get my shirt off in the dark, all the time cracking jokes to distract me. I was pissed enough to go along with him until the shirt covered me head, then Shanks ripped down me trousers around me ankles and took off down the sandhill laughing his head off that he wasn't a surfie. I pulled up me duds and raced after him. We went swimming, but Shanks didn't come back.'

That was the end of the story, so far as Albie was concerned. 'Well, how did he die?' I asked impatiently, remembering my near death in the same place.

'Shanks was cunning as a city rat. He dived in and swam straight out to sea. Well, I'm not a swimmer, am I? No way I would ride them surfboards. I went in, up to my knees, but it was too dark. Becker and Skeet had raced down to the water, and we spread out, searching the water's edge, hoping to find him splashing about. After half an hour, Skeet came running to say Shanks's body had washed up on the beach. He thought Shanks must have caught a rip that took him out to sea and brought him in again. End of story.'

It was a good story with no victims, only heroes—everyone exonerated, everyone clean as a lawyer's bible. I even took a liking to Fowler. I suppose you get used to the smell if you live near a sewage farm.

Back home at The Dudley, I stood under the hot shower for fifteen minutes, my mind filled with the horror of that slide down to the cliff face. Somewhere, I whispered, there has to be an answer to why I'm doing this. I wanted to be boss of the bedlam for a change, I whispered back, and now that I'm boss, I've come too far to retreat.

I had won my place as boss. Skeet was having a breakdown; Rudy was teetering on the edge of his conscience; Becker felt sorry for himself and was not much use to anyone. I had bested Fowler, and he would follow me wherever I led him. My Sydney team, Marty and Benny, were solid as rocks.

Gabe might be King of the Cross, but I wore a crown, also— King of the Kids, and I was on my way.

19. Sinister Red Eyes

Thursday, February 4.

Shaken and exhausted after my near-death encounter with Fowler and the cliff, I slept on and off, uneasy under the blanket like a hibernating bear. I needed a hug, and, specifically, I needed a hug from Becker. That would be nice. But, hugless, I stumbled through the day at home, distracted by a sense of impending disaster, to allocate tasks and rehearse the moves in my mind.

To uphold the illusion of life as usual and dampen any suspicion that might arise after the heist, I attended later that evening a committee meeting at St John's in Redhead, and we spent three hours discussing the annual school fete, which boiled down to whether I would make my usual donation.

I left the closing to Billy, and when I returned to The Dudley, everything was in darkness except for a dull glow from the lamp above the side door. As I steered into the carpark, my headlights washed over Skeet. His arm stretched to brace his body on the step, and a smashed glass lay on the path, an opened bottle of Bundy rum in a brown paper bag held upright in his hand. I sat beside him, my feet on the step below.

'Where have you been?' Skeet was weeping like a mother of the bride. 'I had the idea you had skipped town, or the coppers had arrested you.'

I took the paper bag, removed the bottle and held it to the light. 'Half-empty. Nice going.' I tipped the bottle, and the dark liquid drained away, my senses assaulted by the sweet smell of oxidated rum and Skeet's moaning. I crumpled the paper bag and tossed it and the empty bottle into the bin, and we listened to the glass smash against empty bottles. Hungry for the fresh ocean air, I sidestepped a few paces away from the smell of evaporating alcohol, then returned to squeeze a hand on his shoulder. 'What are you doing here, Skeet? Besides drinking.'

'You're here, at last,' slurring his words a little. 'Steve Crabbe said you talked to Tommo. Steve's my friend.' Skeet ran a hand through his hair, 'I've been worried. I don't feel good.'

'I've no time for nerves,' I said, making sure by the tone in my voice that he understood I held no sympathy for him.

'I want out,' Skeet pleaded.

'I chat with Tommo all the time. He was probably talking to me about the Golden Guineas.'

'Not about Shanks, then?'

'No. Not about Shanks,' I said. 'Let's walk for a bit. It's uncomfortable sitting here. A walk will do you good.' And when I had him on his feet, I held his elbow. 'Watch out for the pavement. There's a broken slab. Who is Steve Crabbe?'

'D'you remember I work at Tattersalls—when they're short-staffed? Like I told you, they need extra staff to handle the lunches on settling day. Steve works there, too, and sometimes we wait on tables at the Greek place across from the police station. They pay four bob an hour for the afternoon. Sometimes, I get another half-quid in tips. Gabe is the best tipper.'

'Gabe Rosen tips big?' I asked. I didn't care about tips, but Gabe's name focused my mind.

'Yeah. Some days, if he's done well, he'll sling me a pound note. He's there every week when he's not in Sydney, and his manager comes in his place when he's away.'

I held eye contact with him for a while. 'Jessica gave you a message on the phone. You might have told me. Quietly without involving the others.'

'Fowler was shouting at me.'

Skeet was irritating the hell out of me, but if I left him to wander off alone until he was sober, he'd finish under a tram.

'You need to be more careful, Sunni,' he said. 'Don't go near Stockton Beach. Fowler's not right in the head. He will draw attention from the coppers. I want out.' A tic opened in the corner of his eye. 'I'm too nervy for this, Sunni. I never intended to tangle with killing. I didn't do it, didn't know Fowler was gunna do it. I'll get life for driving the car.'

'It was an accident,' I said. 'Leave it.' Annoyed by then, I wanted to shut him down.

'Do you believe that? You said about Tommo—'

'That was for Fowler's benefit. The police believe—'

'I should disappear,' Skeet said, tears running down his cheeks. 'That's what I want to do,' fumbling to shake a cigarette from the Craven A packet.

'Disappear?' I said. 'What's that supposed to mean?'

'For a while. Go to Lismore. Stay with my mum. Have a holiday. Straighten my nerves. You can trust me, Sunni. I'm safe. I've always been loyal.'

'Nobody's safe.'

Skeet said, 'I'll come when it's all blown over about Shanks and Moran. I know the racetrack.' Hurrying the words, he added, 'I get good tips, and I know the horses. You can trust me.'

'Yes, but you have a loose tongue. That's a problem. Who will you speak to next?'

Skeet said, 'It's best for you if I'm gone. I'll go quietly, where nobody knows me. No need for Fowler to do a Shanks on me. Say the word, and I'm outta here.'

Did he just compare me with that savage, Kitty? 'No! Stay here.'

I needed him and would keep him on a rope like a loose cannon.

'Later,' I said. 'You can take a holiday. A bus to Coolangatta or somewhere. Visit your mother in Lismore. I'll sling you an extra two pounds a week if you stay. I can do with a friend who knows the track.'

Any friend would be good; he didn't have to know the track.

'So, stay on, but get yourself under control. Nerves mean trouble. And no more booze.'

'Yeah, Sunni. Yeah, if that's what you want.'

We arrived at The Dudley and stood outside. I'd heard enough, so I clapped him on the shoulder. 'If you can't handle the stress,' I said, 'your best out of the game. Later, though. After we do the job. Go to bed now. I need to sleep. I'll call a taxi to take you home.'

After Skeet had said goodnight, I switched out the light, peered at my face reflecting dimly from the mirror, and listened to his footsteps retreating gingerly to the unlit car park outside my window. I dozed, uneasy—Gabe on my mind in his tailored suit, drinking champagne with that slinky starlet in her skin-tight ankle-length dress.

After thirty minutes tossing about in bed, I switched on the lamp and opened Henry Lawson to a poem I hadn't read—I'd bought the book after meeting Tom Halley at his home.

A bushranger, yes. I enjoyed the idea I might be a bushranger. I came to the poem "Dan Wasn't Thrown From His Horse."

> The horse that Dan rode was a devil,
> The kind of a brute I despise,
> With nasty big eyelashes fringing
> A pair of sinister red eyes.

I had never ridden a horse and would need someone to manage my racehorses. I pictured the brute that nearly trod on my foot at Gabe's stables. Its eyes? Were they red? Sinister? Eyelashes?

I climbed out of bed and stood before the mirror to check my eyes. Blue. Dark eyelashes. I slit my eyes. Sinister.

I had been a bit rough on Skeet. His knowledge of horses

came only from the Form Book, but he was good to have around. Loyal. A friend. I would have to trust him. Only he has the information I need. It's time to reveal his part in my plan.

Skeet and Rudy were my family. The one family I have had since I left school. Maybe Billy, too. I smiled into the mirror, trying to look friendly. Friends? Becker? He made friends in the army and stayed in contact with Benny and Marty in Sydney. The kids I went to school with wouldn't give me the time of day or spare a wave if I passed them in the street. I'll stick it to them when I've made my pile.

I put my hands in my pockets, looking suave.

Sergeant Moran paid dearly, and Shanks may have died alone, unloved, and unwanted. Their bushranging days were over, but we are all entitled to a friend to help us on our way. Shanks had been my friend briefly, but I thought it best to disengage from him after I attended his funeral.

Nor did I know where I stood with Jess, and, as for Becker, well, I dearly wanted to be his friend, but he didn't give me any indication that appeared in my stars.

My last thought before sleep claimed my addled mind was about Hector.

20. Making Like Solomon

Friday, February 5.

I sashayed across the zebra crossing and slung a provocative glance at the driver of a red tram hissing and swaying along Hunter Street, a people-swallowing behemoth, one unbalanced wheel keeping time like a drummer's foot and its bell clanging angrily at the leisurely pace of a pedestrian on a zebra crossing.

To meet my friend, Judge Hector Larcombe, I had my hair trimmed to an edgier look and wore high heels and a below-the-knee, pleated skirt in shimmering gold and olive-brown, with a cinched waist and a lightweight knit jumper in a soft straw colour to flatter my silhouette and get this caper sorted.

A breeze carried the smells of fresh bread and doughnuts, and, next door, in the airline's window, a TAA poster invited the wealthy to follow the Royal procession around Australia on a special Electra flight. On the footpath, a returned soldier played the mandolin and sang "de Camptown Racetrack five miles long. Oh, doo-dah-day." Crutches leaning against his wheelchair told his story, and a handwritten sign dangled on a string—LOST MY LEG IN THE DESERT IN EGYPT.

I stood transfixed. Lady Luck had sent me an omen. I would win on Pride of Egypt. I left a ten-bob note in his hat.

I checked the address in my diary, twirled across the busy pavement to show off my long legs to anyone watching, and climbed the narrow stairs to the first floor above a milliner's shop.

Hector's office was small and unfurnished except for a water-stained timber filing cabinet, a desk that had seen better days, and a decomposing chair that once had a good pedigree. The young receptionist filed her nails long enough to inspect her visitor. 'Yeah?'

'I'm here for Judge Larcombe, and don't file your nails when you're speaking to a customer.'

The young eyes burned briefly and switched to the other door, standing half-open to her left. She screwed her face into a sulky moue. 'Sorry, he's not in.'

'Tell him Sunni's here.'

A voice erupted from the office. 'Tell her I'm not in.'

'I told you so. He's not in.'

'Tell him if he doesn't come out here lickety-split, Billy will send his goons around to collect on his bets.'

From the other room: 'Better tell her to come in.'

'You may go in, madam,' she added, with a wicked grin this time.

Shoulder bag swinging, hips swaying, eyes alight, I swished into his office, and, before he rose from his battered chair, leant across the desk, cupped his face in my hands and planted a kiss on each of his cheeks. He smelled of whisky. 'Now, be a good boy, and I'll tell you a story.'

Hector said, 'I'd prefer not to hear your story. It will bring me trouble from Kitty again. You're the reason I'm here in this lonely old room when I could be sitting high on a bench making like Solomon.'

I filled the room with laughter while casting a critical eye over the judge, dusty as his desk, a grey-haired, sixty, pasty-faced caricature of Humphrey Bogart wearing a blue shirt and a bow tie with yellow spots. 'How you wish you were young and silly and visiting me at Palmer Street.'

'Ah,' he said. 'The Tradesman's Arms. You were twenty-six, Kitty's most beautiful escort, and I, a bachelor, forty-six and infatuated.'

'You were married, fifty-six and in debt to Kitty.'

We were quiet for a time, sharing the same memories. I dipped into my bag and came out with the tattered front page of the *Newcastle Times*. 'They call it a riot,' I said, 'but it was a gang of a dozen thugs belting the hell out of my friend, Franz Becker.' And I launched into the story of a lovely man who was threatened at the fete and came up dead on Stockton Beach and the line that tied Lou to Becker, Kitty and Gabe.

The judge rubbed a finger across his teeth and harrumphed. 'What's this kid like—the one with whom you are playing Florence Nightingale?'

'It's complicated. He told me he plans to be the toughest, wealthiest bastard in the pigeon coop, then took me by surprise by paying for Lou's funeral.'

'That was an act of unusual generosity for a gangster.'

'It was a pine coffin,' I said, 'and no tea afterwards. Strangely, as the priest drew his homily to a close, I felt Lou's presence. I think Lou has a doppelganger.'

'Yes,' Hector said, 'you're crazy enough to believe that.'

'Maybe I have one, too. Two people in the same body, and I'm beginning to like the other me.'

I twirled across the room and straightened a dog-eared *Women's Weekly* with a dark-haired, forty-year-old hero on the cover. Nancy Wake.

Hector stood, straightened his tie and, coming around his desk, offered his hand. 'Will you allow me to take you to lunch at Tattersalls?' he said.

As though I hadn't planned it.

Tattersalls Club was the playground of the elite—owners, bookies, tipsters, touts and self-proclaimed patron saints of racing. Women were prohibited in the bar but reluctantly accepted into the dining room in the evenings or on special occasions when the Committee deemed it beneficial, and they declared a special occasion for the entire two weeks of the Newcastle Festival and

Royal Visit. The Club Secretary, a bookie, pushed it through in the vote when he declared it would encourage wives to excuse their husbands' inevitable losses at the racecourse.

In the rarefied air of the Club, my focus changed from Hector to Gabe, that arrogant, complacent, egotist, then to Becker.

Hector broke into my reverie. 'My days of reckless devilry are long gone.'

'Will there be anything more, Your Honour?' Our waiter, Skeet, in white shirt and chequered vest, black trousers and cummerbund, stood away after refilling Hector's cognac balloon.

'No, Skeet. Thanks for your assistance.'

I gave Skeet the sort of smile you give to a waiter, and, after he had taken himself off, Hector said, 'The waiter is Giambattista Fulvio La Rocca,' the name rolling off his tongue as though he sang the Canticles at St Peter's in Rome, 'also known as Skeet.'

'He has appeared before you in court?' I asked.

'Not that I remember.' He swirled the cognac, sniffed it and sighed. 'Now, business. Why did you phone, other than to wheedle an invitation to lunch?'

'Idle curiosity,' I said. 'Every woman in Newcastle is curious to get inside the Club. Is this where Billy comes to settle his accounts?'

'To the Club, yes. The settling room is upstairs.'

'Billy is always on about settling,' I said. Sneaky. All innocence, as though it was something to fill the conversation. 'How does that work?'

Hector gave me a smile, the tiniest uptick on one side of his mouth. 'When your Billy gets a big bet, he'll ring Tom and say he's holding three thousand on So-and-So, and does Tom want part of it? And Tom will take twenty per cent, or thirty. Then he goes to the Watts brothers, and they'll take fifteen, and so on, until he's covered his risk. The registered bookies come together here to settle their bets every Tuesday, and some of the bigger punters drop in to pay or collect.' But Hector didn't get to be a judge by being stupid. 'Why are you interested?'

Taken by surprise, I spluttered and stammered. 'I'm thinking of registering as a bookie.'

He barked a short laugh. 'The new kid on the block, Becker. Has he got you all hot and bothered?'

Blood rushed to my head. What made me think I could outwit Hector? Another mistake. 'Hector, I want you to be my lawyer for all my private and business dealings.'

'So, everything you say,' Hector said, 'or have said to me is privileged and cannot be used against you?'

Oh, God. Am I so transparent? How many mistakes can I make and still survive this heist?

'Consider me your lawyer, Sunni, and here is my lawyerly advice. You are like the biblical lamb to slaughter. Don't let Becker lead you astray. He will seduce you into his way of life and leave you to face the music.'

That word again. 'Please, Your Honour, I'd like to look around the rest of this place.'

Hector clasped his hands over his belly and sighed. 'I have no desire to have the Secretary kick me out of the Club, and I shall not show you around the premises. I told you: my foolhardy days are over.'

I replied, 'Over for you, perhaps. For too long, mine have needed a recharge.'

And Mr. Franz Becker is the boy who sparks my plugs.

21. Becker Gets Fit

Steering the Plymouth with one hand, I glowered at the pedestrian and relished the look on his face when I shattered the silence with a blast of the horn. It was late in the afternoon, and I'd had a glass or two of Champagne for lunch with Hector.

Becker said, 'A petty crim, Gabe called me. Ideas above my station. A viper. A kid. The contempt in his voice got my guts in a twist. The way he waltzed around those horses. I know, I'm kidding myself. I'm a loser, is what I am. Not in Gabe Rosen's class.'

I let that pass and eased the big, powerful V8 engine up to the speed limit while the air cooled my face and drained his frustration and passion. We drove on in mutually sulky silence.

'You are in a mood.' he said finally, 'I don't know where you're taking me.'

'I thought we'd drive to the beach.'

We had words at The Dudley when I insisted he come out with me and get some exercise. He was growing lazy lying in bed, feeling sorry for himself, and was not helping or even thinking. I threatened to kick him out and let him take his chances with the police until, groaning and complaining, he agreed to come with me. I needed his hands and feet to get the job done, and I needed him fit and eager. I intended to walk him and swim him until it was easier for him to enjoy it than to hide from me.

We drove on a sand track through Worimi National Park, where stringy scrub and palm trees sweltered in the February heat on our left, while, on our right, high dunes and the wide trackless Stockton Beach bordered the endless breakers and bottomless ocean. My fingers beat a rhythm on the steering wheel to music I didn't hear until gradually, mile following mile, I relaxed.

'I'm tired,' he said. 'This is far enough. I want to go home.'

I shielded my eyes against the afternoon sun and turned down the sun visor. 'Your home is a police cell. I should leave you to walk.'

'Stuff walking.'

'Walk on the beach, and I'll take you to The Dudley later.'

'Please. I don't like it here. I have a headache, and I want to go.'

I glanced at him. 'Do you get a headache often?'

'It comes and goes since Gabe's boys bashed me.'

I sauntered, and Becker limped along the beach, paddling barefoot in the shallows, and soon enough, the fresh air and exercise invigorated him. After walking for an hour, gradually increasing the pace, I allowed him to rest while we stood in knee-deep water.

'Time for a swim,' I said. 'You need to get your arms and shoulders moving.'

'I'd love to, but I left my togs in my room,' he said.

'It's walk or swim. You can go in the nude.'

'No way,' he said.

So, I pushed him hard, and he toppled into the water. He didn't know whether to laugh or complain until the surf knocked him over, and he came up spluttering and laughing.

I told him to swim to the hut, and he took off slowly, struggling against the shore dump.

Walking to the car, he was back to his old self. 'You remind me of my mother,' he said.

'Thanks. I've never been so flattered.'

'I remember her kissing me goodnight. "Sleep well, Franzi," she would say and kiss me on the forehead. My father would come home drunk at midnight, rush Mum to bed, then tear into her, slapping and punching. She would moan as he beat her but would not stop him for fear of worse while I pretended to sleep.'

Head down, he kicked at the sand, sometimes burying his heel or stooping to collect a shell. 'I hardly knew my mother, only the face she put out to the world. I loved her and wanted to protect her, but a child can't protect his mother against his father's aggression. Instead, I attacked my friends and teachers at school until no one wanted to be near me.'

Darkness swallowed the dunes. Surf crashed on the beach, and Becker laughed. 'That was good medicine,' he said. 'I'm ready to make money and take Gabe to the cleaners. Get even with him for messing with me.'

I drove Becker home and then checked if Skeet had his nerves under control. Rudy was steady. Fowler was Fowler. Skeet seemed okay.

22. Royal Chats at Randwick

Saturday, February 6.

Too pumped up with anticipation to attend to the bar, I brought in two assistants. My customers packed the place, and I cranked the wireless to maximum volume for those spilling out onto the footpath.

The race commentator at Randwick was dishing out the gossip on the Royal presence and the state of the horses in the first race, the Westminster Juvenile Handicap, scheduled for 12:53. 'Thousands are packed into the grandstand and on the lawn. Even-money favourite is Pride of Egypt, a three-year-old looking like a winner. After wild odds, dropping from fifty to one in October, today she's at evens after coming in second in her last race to Indian Empire in the Kirkham Handicap.'

I had intended to finance my investigation of Lou's death by winning on Pride of Egypt, but now there was no longer an investigation and no point asking Tom to return my money. Caught in the excitement of the race, I wanted a return on the twenty-five pounds I wagered. 'Billy,' I said. 'She has to win, Billy. Who's riding her?'

'Arthur Ward's on her today. Wardy knows how to ride a horse.'

'Who's she up against? Tell me, Billy. Don't just stand there with that silly grin on your face. Will she win, or will she not?'

Billy said, 'Pipes of Pan is a good runner on a dry track like today. He's on at seven to two and will give your nag a run for its money.'

'Blow me down, Billy. That's not what I need to hear. Tell me she'll win, or you'll need an ambulance.'

'She's a winner,' he said. 'Your money's as safe as it will ever be on a race.'

'I'm going outside for a walk. I can't stand this.'

On the footpath, I chatted to my customers, offering tips Billy had given me and opinions on the Royal visitors, asking after a new baby girl, and dipping into my pocket when the Salvos came by with their collection box.

Most drinkers had walked to the pub or ridden a bike or occasionally a motorbike, and it was rare for a black Plymouth to idle past and stop fifty yards down the road outside the fenced-off, vacant allotment adjacent to the hotel and owned by The Burwood Mining Company. When Becker opened the car door, I withdrew into the crowd and watched him limp across the footpath to lean against the fence. What was he up to, his hat pulled down, dark glasses, shirt collar high? I confined him to the shack at Stockton Beach for the day because he was too eager to leave his room at The Dudley, and I thought someone might recognise him.

Billy was shouting and waving from the door. 'Sunni. Come on. The race is about to start. Come on. Hurry.'

I ran to the door and pushed through the crowd as I heard, 'They're off,' and the commentator ran through the horses too quickly for me to keep up. Before I had my senses about me, he was shouting the name of the winner by two lengths.

'Who won? Billy, who won?'

I didn't hear the commentator or Billy for the noisy crowd. People cheered, shouted at each other, but I understood the triumphant smile on Billy's face, and I screamed.

'Who won the Juveniles?' I shouted, needing to be sure.

'Pride of Egypt first,' he said. 'Farquhar came in second, and Pipes of Pan third.'

I rushed out to check on Becker, but his Plymouth had gone. Why was he here? What does he know? Can I trust him?

The race commentator's voice was lost to everyone except those nearest the wireless. 'On the lawn at Randwick, the Band is playing their energetic rendition of *The Thunder and Lightning Polka*, the Queen and Prince Philip are entertaining a flock of monarchists and republicans alike, and now, they are walking across to shake hands with trainer Ted Hush and jockey Arthur Ward. The bookies will bag a record day today—more cash than any day in Randwick's history. More than at the Melbourne Cup.

23. The Best Laid Plans

Sunday, February 7.

Two weeks after Kitty's gang attacked him, Becker's body was healing. Cuts and bruises from boots, razors, and metal knuckles stood out less starkly, now purple and yellow, against his creamy skin in the bright reflection off the beach, and Jess had removed the stitches earlier in the week. But, after a closer inspection, I was more convinced than ever that something inside had broken. Time was short, and our deadline approaching like a speeding steam engine. It was two days before the Royal Tour arrived in Newcastle, and it appeared to me he was a frightened boy.

He eyed his reflection in the hand mirror I bought for him at the pharmacy. 'What a nightmare.' His face was contorted and twisted from the stitches. 'God, what a mess you made of me, Jess. You might be good at embroidery, but I will be Scarface to everyone.' He grimaced. 'But, then, Scarface might not be such a bad idea. Scarface: I think I like it.'

I waited until he was off guard, admiring his new image in the mirror, then asked what he was doing at The Dudley yesterday.

He gave me a crooked smile. 'You sprung me, then? Nothing to do at the beach except walk. I thought that, in disguise, I'd get away with a car trip. Then, you came out and spotted me. I wanted to be there with you, but when there was such a crowd between us, I thought better of it.'

I stared at him long and hard. It sounded off to me, and his eyes lied. I always watch the man's eyes. I've avoided trouble on many occasions by watching the eyes. 'You shouldn't have done that. You'll end up in a cell. I've told you often enough.'

'Fidgeting about in the shack, I have nothing to do but worry. Let's take a drive now. Get away for a while. I have a headache again.'

Rudy was avoiding attention but otherwise living normally. I hadn't heard from Marty and Benny and presumed they were doing their thing in Sydney. Skeet was having a nervous breakdown while doing the leg work around Newcastle, Fowler was waiting to unleash his anger on someone, and Becker was partially crippled and recuperating. My gang.

'Where to?' I asked.

'Too risky.' Fowler said. He was critical that I shared the general plan with him but not the details. As far as he knew, we and three mates from Sydney would soon be going after an unnamed bank. I explained the details of the split, and that was it. 'Stay inside until we're ready, is what ya told me. The coppers are everywhere, and they'd love to lock us in a room until the Royals have come and gone.'

'Why would they do that?' Jess asked. 'What's going on?'

Fowler tossed his head and drew air through his teeth.

'Come on, Jess.' I scowled. 'Fowler has a big mouth and doesn't know what he's talking about. I'll drive. We'll go north to Anna Bay.'

Fowler said, 'A hundred coppers are patrolling the roads around the airport for the Royal visit.'

'Then we'll stay clear of the airport,' Becker said. 'Skirt the town to Glendale. Come on, Jess.'

'What's going on?' Jess asked again. 'What has the Royal visit to do with anything? I don't intend to wait around when the police arrest you. Why would they be arresting you anyway?'

'It's Fowler. He's scared of the dark. Coppers are here to keep the city quiet. That's all. Come on.'

Jess grabbed Fowler's shoulder. 'No. This place is spooking me. Come on, Albie. Take me to work.' She stormed out, armed to the teeth with moral indignation.

I relented. Jess's abrupt departure, the argument and the holes in my plan plagued me and gave me an unusual headache that refused to retreat. Becker was up and down from cabin fever, and I did not want a depressed Becker on my payroll. To say nothing of his physical disabilities. Despite the intermittent reception and crackling static, we drove with blaring Rock to soothe him. Jess was a worrier, Fowler an ever-present danger, and Becker a high-maintenance prima donna. If I intended to do something about Fowler, it must be soon.

'Let's take a drive through the city,' Becker said. 'I can do that much. I need to get rid of this headache.'

And my headache, if anyone was interested enough to ask.

The city was razzle-dazzle—a fairyland of fancy lighting and decorations.

Yesterday at Randwick, bookies had doubled their usual Saturday profit, and, at Newcastle, the bookies had a bonanza at the Hunter Valley Gold Trophy. Tom Halley said it was the highest take on record, and the excitement of the race added to the public's thrill of celebrities on their doorstep.

Newcastle was a city of enormous enthusiasm for the Queen's visit on Tuesday. Families walking the streets held small children high to admire the window decorations, kids roamed licking ice creams, and teens danced on the footpath because it was too crowded and hot inside the Palais.

Finally, with a packet of fish and chips rolled in newspaper, I found a parking spot near the foreshore where the air smelled of family picnics, and hundreds played cricket and net games. I looked around, nervous that Becker might be recognised, but the crowd was so thick it was unlikely.

Later, we strolled beneath the leafy canopy, our steps heavy with unspoken tension, as Becker nursed the throbbing headache hanging like a storm cloud between us. On instinct,

I reached out my arm to circle his waist. He stiffened, startled, his surprise matching my own.

'That's nice,' he said. 'I like that. We can walk out together… I suppose.' He was probably picturing us at the Casino, surrounded by admirers.

'No,' I said firmly. 'You are going out with Jessica.'

His brow furrowed, 'Don't worry, I'm not coming on to you.' He lay on the lawn and closed his eyes on his world. On me and Jess.

Then, as though we had been discussing the subject, he blurted out, 'I was locked away in that tin shed. I don't like having Fowler involved. I don't trust him. The way he looks at Jess. He hasn't forgotten she's a witness to his meeting with Shanks. He will wait for the right opportunity and attack her. What can I do?'

'How's the headache,' I asked, without attempting to conceal my scepticism.

'Sorry. I'll handle it.'

Silence settled over us like a prickly blanket. I sat beside him, looking over the river, his headache taking over my heist. Despair overwhelmed me and drowned me as effectively as the ocean had. What to do?

'Forget the heist,' Becker said, his voice thick, as though he had a bone caught in his throat. 'We're not ready.'

I tried to placate him. 'You're suffering from last-minute nerves. There's no reason to cancel.' I sent him a quick, false smile, knowing he was right. There was no plan, only optimism and ambition, and to proceed was the definition of foolhardy.

Becker said, 'It's not a properly organised heist. I knew this would happen. The boys are all over the place, like a donkey's dinner. Skeet's nerves, Fowler's ready to explode, and I'm all banged up. No. I'll make a run for it. I'll take Jess and go. Perth. Singapore. China. Gabe will never find us in China.' He stood. 'C'mon. Let's go.'

'What's the hurry?' I thought if I remained calm, then he would also. 'It's nice here in the park, and she's safe until after the heist. Then, if you have to kill Fowler to stop him from hurting Jessica, you'll do it.'

'Come on! My head is hurting like a monster. Let's go. It's raining.'

The sky was clear. He stumbled.

'Franz. What's wrong?'

'No time to argue.' He hammered his fist into his hand. 'Get up! We're going.'

'What—?'

'My head! I can't think. Paralysed. Can't move my feet.' He pressed his fists against his temples. 'The sky's on fire. Air raid!' he screamed and fell to the ground, moaning. 'Artillery. It's a raid. No time! They'll hit us within minutes.'

He lurched off, swinging backhand at the cloud of birds following and bellowed, 'Run! Run!' Then the words stopped coming. He vomited in the gutter, fell heavily onto a bench and held tight.

Delayed shock and concussion, a doctor had called it when a client mugged me. Sitting still and riding it out in the hospital was his medicine.

Becker was on the run again. In case I had to call an ambulance, I followed him in darkness, through the narrow lanes from one pool of light under a streetlamp to the next. Past an infant wailing, a drunken man hurling abuse at his wife and children, a child practising the violin. And sweating in the sultry night, I remembered my ugly life with Kitty and asked why I was doing this.

Close behind, I followed Becker's meandering path to no known destination until we turned the corner, and I froze. Police cars shone spotlights on Annie's boarding house. An ambulance parked beside a collection of garbage bins, and I feared the flashing red lights would reawaken Becker's vertigo.

From outside the circle of light, I screwed my eyes to watch Sergeant Sharpe pacing and Tommo, his back to me, shaking a fist at Skeet and shouting words lost to the wind.

The crowd was eerily quiet, staring at the balcony, pointing, the front wall dingy in the harsh spotlights, its plaster spalling, a window cracked, and a six-foot space where the balcony railing had broken away. My eye followed gravity to the body covered by a canvas sheet and blood glistening on the footpath. Rudy. I elbowed Becker farther into the shadows and tried to grasp the impact of Rudy's death.

Without Rudy, my entire plan was on the garbage heap.

A mongrel dog lying in a doorway crept closer and wagged its tail. I kicked at an empty can, and it rattled and clanked down the hill until I thought the noise would never stop. Skeet's head swung sharply at the sound. He stared into my eyes, then looked back at the body. Tommo peered towards where I stood, but I moved into shadow.

Flashing lights sped past the lane where I hid, the ambulance taking the body to wherever they took the dead.

Becker said, his voice normal, 'I'm okay now. It has happened before. The psychiatrists have a name for it. They say it has to do with childhood trauma and the killings in Korea. I'll take my car to Stockton. Would you mind getting a taxi home?'

I held his hand, but he limped away, and I screamed inside for my opportunity lost.

Footsteps approached. I huddled behind a pile of rubble, the muddy ground carpeted with old newspaper and smelling like a public lavatory. Slow footsteps entered my lane, and a voice hissed, 'Sunni. It's me. Skeet.'

'What's up? What happened?'

'It was after midnight,' Skeet was whispering, 'So stinking hot and humid inside, I thought I'd walk in the fresh air. Rudy and Fowler had a few drinks and sat on the balcony discussing the job. I hung around nearby.'

I bristled. My chest tightened, I couldn't breathe and for a moment couldn't speak. 'You talked about the job.' I said, accusing him. 'Are you dim-witted? I told you not to tell anyone about our plan.' Not that it mattered. I had no gang left to carry it out. Becker was lost and Rudy dead.

Skeet's face collapsed. 'For Christ's sake,' he spluttered. 'I don't *know* your plan. You refused to tell me. I had to guess from the information you sent me to collect. I told them shit. But Fowler was drinking rum and getting snakier by the minute. You had treated him badly, he said. You wouldn't tell him your plan, only that there'd be a dress rehearsal on Monday, and you didn't trust him. Becker was supposed to take care of the witnesses, but they're still alive. Blah, blah, blah. Rudy said no one should know the whole plan in case the coppers picked them up, and that way, each of us knew nothing more than the part we needed to play.'

'That's right. That's how I played it. Now it's all over.'

'Here, take a swig of this.'

'What is it?'

'Whisky.'

'I don't drink whisky.'

'Yeah, but it's a good time to start.'

I grabbed the bottle, upended it and swallowed a mouthful. 'Ah, Jeez,' coughing, spitting, and dragging air into my lungs. 'Go on. What happened?'

Skeet said, 'Fowler hit the bottle hard and became more and more hostile about not knowing the plan. "What's your part," he asked Rudy, real belligerent, but Rudy disappeared inside. That's when I left. I ran a hundred yards but swung around when a car skidded to a stop at Annie's. Tommo jumped out and raced upstairs. Then he was on the balcony, and all hell erupted. Tommo was shouting about Moran, until Fowler swung a punch. Tommo backed him against the balcony rail, and I thought he would push him over. Then, there was a loud cracking noise, and the balcony rail crashed. Over he went. That's when Sergeant Sharpe flew out of Tommo's car, and a squad car arrived. Sergeant Sharpe rushed inside.'

'There's no one who can do Rudy's job. It's the end.'

'Rudy? You weren't listening. It wasn't Rudy fell. He had left Fowler on the balcony. It was Fowler.'

'Fowler's dead? Not Rudy?'

'Yeah. He went headfirst straight over the edge.'

'Fowler? Albie? Thank God for that.'

'What?' Skeet took a step away.

'I mean poor Albie, but we can keep going. Without Rudy, the plan was dead.'

Skeet was quiet for a long while. Then he added, 'Sergeant Sharpe called the ambulance, and more coppers came too.'

'What was Tommo saying to you? He shook a fist at you.'

'He said it was right that Fowler was dead because he had stabbed Sergeant Moran, and it saved the coppers from doing him. He wanted me to say Becker was on the balcony and had pushed Fowler. I reckon Tommo pushed him. I kept telling him I hadn't been anywhere near Becker since they hurt him at the racecourse. Then Sergeant Sharpe says he saw the whole thing from the car, and Rudy wasn't there when the brawl commenced. He passed no one on the stairs, so Becker was not there. He told me to go home, but I'm to report to the police station first thing tomorrow and make a statement about the accident. He said accident twice. It was an accident, a tragic accident, he said. But if you ask me, Tommo deliberately pushed Fowler over the rail. Sergeant Sharpe is from out of town, and he'll not understand that.'

'Where's Rudy?' I asked.

'Tommo's talking to him upstairs.'

'Rudy's safe,' I said. 'He won't talk. Thank God it was Fowler killed and not Rudy.'

'Ah, mate. That's a bit cold-blooded.'

'Yeah. Sorry. I didn't mean—Albie was loyal and waited for Becker after Bart Evans beat him up.'

Fowler was always going to be trouble. A temper tantrum and he might have shot Jess, me, or anyone else. I reckoned Tommo killed him as payback for Sergeant Moran, and I had to work out if we should go ahead with one man short—maybe two if Becker didn't straighten himself out.

If I walked away, no one would accuse me of surrender. But would there be another chance like this? I would live knowing I did not rise to the challenge when the opportunity came. Whenever I visited the racecourse or talked to Billy or Tom, I'd feel inadequate. How could I let the chance slip through my fingers without a fight?

24. Committed at Last?

Monday, February 8.

Albie Fowler was dead. At the tumble-down shack perched above the high-water mark, they waited uneasily for me to decide whether to go ahead or cancel. Jess had heard the news of Fowler's death and called Rudy to bring her urgently to Stockton Beach.

She had wavered between aggression and submission until Becker snarled, then she came out of the shed shouting at him, ten yards away at the top of the sandhill, hanging his head and aimlessly kicking his toe into the sand.

'Don't tell me I'm a panic merchant,' she said. 'You need proper medical treatment. If you don't go to the hospital, I'll go and not be back. I should have known better than to come in the first place. Mr Fowler was my friend.'

Becker settled for reconciliation. 'I'm pleased you came,' he said. 'I shouldn't have spoken so harshly. Not like that.'

He knew how to be polite when needs demanded it. The crows flapping overhead, landing on the shack and complaining did nothing to relieve the tension.

'You acted suspicious,' Jess said. 'I wanted to do a runner. Why am I still here?'

I admired her determination and courage in the face of her vulnerability. Her words hung in the air, uncertainty and doubt weighing on me. Becker raised the corner of his mouth, making him look more suspicious, and mumbled something I didn't hear above the sound of breaking surf.

'What?' Jessica shouted.

Becker raised his voice, but only a little. 'I expected never to hear from you again after I ran off last night. I'm sorry. You deserve better than that. I had a sort of a fit.'

'A fit?' A fit? What sort of a fit?'

'Delayed concussion,' he said. 'I spewed in the gutter.'

'Jessica is right,' I said. 'You should go to a doctor. Come with me to the hospital.'

Becker looked at me, and the way he held his belly and bent forward, he seemed concerned despite his words. 'Don't fuss. I'll be all right. I'll be okay,' he said again, but with a subdued tone.

Jess raised her voice, 'Mr Fowler's death was on the news— the accident. I only came to make sure you are okay.'

'I'm fine.'

'What happened?'

'He leaned on the rail,' Becker said. 'It was loose. The balcony needed mending. The timber was rotten.'

The crows flapped and complained. Jessica stared at her feet and said, 'If you are well enough tomorrow, why not come with me to watch the Royal procession?'

'What?' Becker said. 'Why would I want to go to a procession? I'm going away. Skeet is coming in a few minutes, and I'll be off.'

'Go where? Where are you going? You didn't tell me.'

'Sydney. For a few days. A holiday will help me. I booked a hotel in Woolloomooloo.'

It was a part of my plan to tell her where he was staying so the police would know where to look and he would have an alibi. But after his convulsion last night, I had backpedalled and challenged him. 'If you are not up to it, I'll find someone to take your place.'

Jess glared at Becker, staring him down. 'You might have let me know.'

'I'm sorry for not telling you,' Becker said. 'There I go again, apologising. After all the care you gave me. I decided to go last night after you left with Albie.'

'It's up to you,' I said, hoping he would be well enough to hold the plan together.

'You'll miss the Queen.' Jess crossed her arms on her chest, then threw them off and crossed them again. 'You get the chance every blue moon. What's going on?'

'There you go, being suspicious again.'

'You two are up to something,' Jessica said, thrusting a finger at me so hard she lost her footing in the sand.

Becker took off through the dunes. He ran for twenty yards and had to stop. Hands on knees, he gasped for air. The Plymouth's engine revved, and the horn tooted. Becker came upright and called to us as he limped off. 'I'm up for it. Here's Skeet. I'll be at the hotel in Wooloomooloo.' He waved, and they drove away.

It was not too late to cancel. But the gang was hyped and ready to run. If I stopped, I'd never get it up again. But the heist would be a disaster if Becker were to lose it on the day. The next day. Or Skeet. Too many buts and ifs.

Jess had gone; the sun was warm. I sat under the shade of a tree, shaded my eyes to watch a white-headed osprey circling on predatory wings a hundred feet above the water and plummet feet first until it submerged and seconds later rose with a silver fish wriggling in its claws and its hooked yellow beak feasting.

When the osprey disappeared into the trees, I returned my attention to the white clouds forming into familiar shapes, and I drowsed. Becker needed to get married. The crowd cheered and whistled and catcalled. I stood with gloved hands above my head, my foot on Gabe Rosen's throat. Who was boss now? I pointed to Gabe and then at a Cobb & Co coach. 'You. Get the hell outta my town.'

'Sunni. Sunni, wake up.'

Rudy stood over me and waited for me to stretch and groan. 'Will you be up for it tomorrow?' he said.

"Course, I will. Late night. What's wrong with you?'

'It would be better for us to postpone for a week. Becker was like this in Korea before threatening to shoot Benny, his friend. Another friend, Marty, stepped in and almost got himself killed.'

Rudy was not aware that Benny and Marty would be his partners in the heist. More and more, my gang feels like a mistake. As Becker said, bluff your way through.

I laughed to make light of it. 'The worst is over. He'll be right for tomorrow.'

Rudy joined in with a lopsided grin. 'I'd hate to cancel when we are this close to winning the lottery.' He lost the grin. 'If he goes off, we will all end in prison for life.'

This caper could not end well. It was written in the air-- how wrong it was to press on with a bunch of amateurs and a childlike plan. Yet the smell of success was around me, and like the osprey sighting a shoal of mullet in the water, I looked down from the heights at Gabe and Tilly, and there was no contest.

'We go,' I shouted.

25. Calm Before the Heist

The horse saw me approaching, galloped across, tossed its head, and whinnied cheerfully. I fed it with a handful of grass across a wire fence in a paddock across the bitumen road from the ominously named Murdering Gully, the site of a massacre of an Aboriginal clan in 1839, and some claim there are a dozen more recent murders and disappearances in the gully. The view from there to Glenrock Beach and Dudley across the top of the rainforest took my breath away.

Not that I knew anything about horses, but this one had come kicking its heels and prancing over, genuinely excited to welcome me. The sweet, creamy dun pony appreciated my offering. It snorted and tossed its head playfully until I raised the muster to reach across and warily pat the white blaze on its forehead. I handed over more grass and closed my mind to the fear of its teeth; thick lips softly nudged my hand, and the horse raised its face to snicker at my nervousness.

Behind me, a throaty engine revved. A flock of yellow-crested cockatoos rose, squawking their complaint, and a khaki-painted truck blasting black smoke from its exhaust clattered up the ramp, roared into the barn, and bounced to a halt with less than a foot separating it from the Volkswagen delivery van Skeet had delivered ten minutes earlier.

I ran to the door and slid it closed. The engine died, and the garden returned to its everyday quiet under the watchful eyes of the horse and two cows in the paddock across the road. It was four on Monday afternoon. There would be no lights in the barn tonight. The rehearsal had to begin soon. I peeped through the cracks in a weather-rotted timber plank wall to check if a neighbour or a passing car had taken any interest in our trespass and, satisfied, inspected the vehicles.

I said g'day to Becker and Benny, and Marty introduced a new face. I had ordered them not to use surnames when strangers were within earshot, so Marty said, 'This is Horlicks. He was with Second Battalion 3 RAR in Korea.'

Horlicks might have had his twenty-first birthday last week. He wore shoulder-length golden-brown hair crimped like a fox terrier's amputated tail. He had the long face of a terrier, too. His sharp eyes went with the snout, eyes too close together and would not settle on mine. But then, the whole scheme was a little crazy, and I accepted him without question.

'Second Battalion had the easy part of the job,' Marty added.

'Up yours, mate,' Horlicks said.

'You blokes waltzed in and sat on yer arses for three days until we came to ya rescue.'

Horlicks held out a hand to Becker. 'No one introduced you, mate,' he chuckled. 'Anyway, good to meet ya. What do I call you?'

'Call me Franz.'

'Woo, hoo,' Skeet called from across the shed. 'How ya doing, Franzi?'

Marty said, 'Horlicks is Polish with a name that would choke you, but he comes highly recommended for his special abilities. Horlicks is the closest we got to his family name.'

'The special abilities,' I said to Horlicks. 'Did they bring you to the attention of the police?'

'No, mate. Coppers don't know I exist.'

Marty said, 'Horlicks has made it his hobby to hot-wire cars—Jags and Chevys, that sorta high-end stuff. He takes them to a mate with a chop shop in Melbourne to be repainted and have their numbers fixed. Another mate finds a buyer, and they share the profit.'

'Good,' I said. 'No fuss, driving from Sydney?' Cool, calm and confident. That was the way to play it. I would not lose control today.

'Nah,' Skeet said. 'All good. I drove the VW with Franz. Marty came with the truck. Benny and Horlicks rode their bikes.'

'Did you leave your motorbikes where I told you, Benny?'

'Yeah. We booked into the pub at Charlestown for two nights. Left the bikes in their garage. Doctored the plates, like you said.'

'No fuss?'

'All good—'

'But what, mate?'

'I'm not in yet,' Benny said. 'It sounds too risky, and I don't have an urge to self-destruct.'

'You always thought hard before taking silly risks,' Marty said. 'That's true, Franz?'

"Course he did. But afterwards, they didn't seem all that bad. Let's see what the boss has for us this time.'

The old barn leaned away from the wind, and in the dim light, within its rusting corrugated iron roof, weathered timber walls, frames, and exposed roof beams, I would not have been surprised if an apparition of the ancient banana farmer had wished me a good afternoon. The two vehicles occupied one side, and Skeet had chalked on the floor the outline of a space fifteen yards by nine with a double-leaf entry door in the centre on one side, two windows on the side marked STREET, and a partition in one corner marked PANTRY. A bench made from iron sheets on timber trestles was the BAR. Pine fruit crates lay in neat lines at the room's perimeter, and Skeet had chalked a hallway and STAIRS with an arrow pointing DOWN outside the room leading to EXIT.

Chalk lines on the floor. It was such an amateurish undertaking. What childish folly had I led these poor, hesitant young men into? What suffering would there be when this misguided adventure comes to a sticky end? My high spirits collapsed like a child's balloon; one minute, a taut, bright, tethered cigar-shaped toy, hopping about with anticipation of its release to the wind; the next, shrunken, miserable, unrecognisable as the same plaything that had given me such joy and pleasure.

I raised my voice to quieten the banter and enthusiastic loud talk. 'Can the police trace the truck and van to us?' I asked. Was I hoping for a last-minute excuse for a reprieve?

Horlicks said, 'Acres of ex-army trucks are lying around in Sydney and Victoria, waiting for us to lift them.'

'Dodge WC-41,' Benny said, patting the truck's roof. 'They did most of the heavy work in Korea, and thousands came to Australia. They made good ambulances.'

'It's blowing a lot of smoke. Will it get us there?'

'Six years old,' Horlicks said. 'In good nick, has never been off the bitumen. Top speed of fifty, but will run all day carrying a ton. I put some juice in it and a new battery, dollied up a pair of military rego plates, and away we went. The army will not know it's gone for months. I'll return it after the job if that's what ya want.'

It was open-backed and painted khaki. 'Where's the rest? I can't go ahead without the modifications I specified.'

'Hey, Horlicks,' Marty said. 'Get it dressed up, will ya? Show the boss we're not idiots.'

Benny took two strides and opened the sliding door of the panel van. 'While he's on that, look at the van. This one was a bit harder. You wanted a van to travel from here to Sydney without attracting attention. What's better than a cream VW van, eh? Horlicks picked it up at the Dandenong station yesterday afternoon, changed the plates, drove through last night, swapped to his bike, and Skeet drove it from Sydney.'

Horlicks and Skeet had been busy with the Dodge.

Horlicks said, 'There ya go, mate. You can go anywhere, park anywhere in that, and we have four uniforms to go with it if that's what you decide.'

'But it stands out. I told you, reversible camo! This doesn't work.'

'Watch this.' Horlicks clambered into the truck, and we watched as the Dodge became a different vehicle within three minutes. 'Shazam!' he said.

'Do you have the guns?'

'Yep. Wasn't hard,' Marty said. 'Sydney is flooded with handguns from the war and Korea. You have to be careful, though. If the coppers catch you with one, you're gone for ten years. There are no Thomsons in Australia. They have to come from America. I managed two Stens and an Owen. Howzat?'

'Can't be traced to us?'

'Right. You're getting the picture, mate. Three steps from the supplier to us.'

'The grenade?'

'They're like snake wings,' Marty said. 'But we managed. You'll be happy with it.'

Skeet had primed a kerosene stove and was ready with mugs of tea. 'Sorry about no alcohol,' he said, 'but the boss said work first, then we can have a beer.'

'Where do we sleep?' Horlicks asked.

'In the truck and the VW. It's just for one night, so no complaints.'

They drank the tea and ate the sandwiches Skeet made by hacking thick planks from fresh loaves, spreading butter and mustard, and corned beef. 'I've made a beef stew for tonight, and there'll be ham and eggs for breakfast.'

Horlicks flapped a sandwich in the direction of the truck. 'How do we find our way to the bank? By the way, Marty said there'd be seven. I'm counting five.'

I said, 'One will not be at the bank. His job is to clear the place where I'll hide the cash. The less he knows about the plan, the better. The other died yesterday in an accidental fall.'

'So, after you take yours, we share among six, not seven, right?'

'That's up to Franz.'

'Yeah,' Becker said. 'You're on it.'

'Where's the bank?'

'You don't need to know that. We'll run through the details now, and I'll tell you before we go in.'

'Ah,' Horlicks said. 'Not sure I like that.'

'Stop with the griping, Horlicks,' Marty said. 'I told you. The boss will tell us when she's good and ready. Trust her. It's best we have tight security in case one of you blokes slips out tonight, gets a belly full of booze, and tells the first female he dances with. Right?'

'OK, but…'

Horlicks was getting on my nerves. 'Are you in or out? It's everyone in, or we don't go ahead.' Would he be another dud like Fowler and Shanks?

Horlicks said, 'Does that mean you intend to lock us in tonight like monks in a monastery?'

'Get with it, Horlicks.' The irritation in Marty's voice got through, and Horlicks looked downcast. 'Joking.'

'Let's get to work,' I said. The boss again. 'Skeet stays here while we do the business. He'll drive us to Sydney in the VW. I have rooms at a hotel in Woolloomooloo for Skeet and Franz. Their clothes are there and unpacked, the beds tossed. That's Marty's work. He checked them in yesterday under their real names.'

Horlicks had to be the one to say it. 'Marty doesn't look a lot like Franz.'

'My nephew made the booking,' Marty said. 'Same height, same build, hairdo. Put them in a white tee shirt, sunglasses, a red leather jacket, and short shorts with a sailor's cap, and they look alike. Receptionists and waiters don't take that much notice, but when the coppers come looking, they'll describe James Dean on a Saturday night splurge and his pal who kept in the background.'

My confidence leaped for no good reason except the job was unstoppable. 'Tomorrow, we leave here in the Dodge early, ten hundred hours, because we're heading into traffic.'

'It's a long wait,' Benny said. 'Two-forty, you said we go into action.'

'Yes,' I said. 'A long time to be exposed.'

Benny was coming around, like Marty said he would. And I had no way of knowing if Gabe would be there. If he didn't show, then half my fun would be gone. 'If the coppers spring us while we're waiting, it's over, and we go home. Don't worry. Everything will go to plan, and we will walk away with the cash and drop Benny and Horlicks at their motorbikes. Marty will ride pillion to Sydney. Okay?'

'So far, so good,' Marty said.

Horlicks said, 'You'll have the cash. When do we get to run it through our fingers?'

'You'll take twenty quid each before we reach Charlestown and the same each month for six months, and the balance as I told you.'

Horlicks tried to catch someone's eye, but none cooperated.

I pointed to the chalk marks. 'Here's the room. The important items are the door,' I mimed opening a door and walking inside, 'and the cashier tables,' banging a hand on one of the fruit boxes. Then I stepped to the space marked Pantry and said, 'The central cage here will hold the cash not in immediate use. I call it the pantry. There'll be cash on the tables, and lots of it. The lone security guard stands at the pantry door. It's Horlick's job to take him out within the first few seconds. And the service stairs from the floor below lead to this door.'

'Where will you be?' Horlicks asked. 'I suppose, a mile behind the action like all good generals.'

'Fowler's death meant I had to change the workload. Marty is taking his place, and I'll be making up the numbers in the room.'

'Ahh,' Horlicks said, 'give it up, mate. How you gunna disguise a body like yours—how you walk and talk?' He cupped his hands to his chest. 'Eh?'

'Padding, oversize overalls, floppy cap, and I'll not speak,' I snorted. Amateur Hour. 'I'll make it work. Now, to details.'

I woke, stiff and tired, on a thin cardboard mattress on the floor of the VW panel van. Watching the first streaks of daylight through holes and rusted gaps in the walls, I smiled at the thought of a chancer wanting to dance while troopers waited outside. Last night, I dreamt of every single thing in my life that had gone wrong and every friend who had died. Mine wasn't much of a gang. Without me, they were yobbos looking for trouble, not one with the imagination to steal a dollar from the poor box. I bet my life on making it work.

Marty and Benny were awake and moving about in the barn. Skeet had pumped a kerosene burner and boiled a can of water to make tea. Last night, Benny pointed out that success or failure depended on grabbing control within the first seconds. 'And,' he said, 'if anything goes wrong in the room, there's one way out. Down the stairs, and, if that's blocked, we go to prison for life.'

'That will not happen,' I told him. 'Why would the stairs be blocked?'

Benny said, 'You live in Newcastle. You're sure to be recognised. You told us three people in the bank know you. Catch you, and they catch us all.'

'We will all be masked.'

'If it comes to the point, will anyone be shooting? The army trained us not to point a gun unless we were ready to fire it.'

'They will not catch us,' I said. 'There'll be no shooting. Now, we went over all this last night. Who is in and who is out?'

When everyone else nodded, flicked a finger, or said, 'In,' I consulted Benny silently with my eyes.

'I'll never get that winery on a tram conductor's wage,' he said. 'I'm in.'

The barn smelled of ancient chicken poo from a long-unused cage and last night's beer and cigarettes. My boys are the roosters. They'll strut around crowing when the papers report the robbery, and after a few days, they'll be clamouring for the cash. As long as I'm the only one to know where the money is hidden, I can control them by feeding it out slowly so they don't splash it around.

Discipline was what we needed now to stay out of prison. I'd do this one job, disappear when the right time came, and, in due time, make sure Gabe knows I did it. No matter where I went in this world, somehow, I'd make it through.

'Where's the ham and eggs?' Horlicks said, clapping his hands.

'I lied,' Skeet said. 'Today, corned beef sangers. Tomorrow, caviar and lobster.'

I came out of the bus swinging my arms. 'No ham, no eggs, and it's raining. You better smarten up, Skeet, if you want to be a millionaire.' I laughed, and the kids shouted and slapped me on the shoulder.

The boss.

26. Queen Elizabeth II & Lesser Distractions

Tuesday, February 9.

My boys drove into the streets of Newcastle early and cruised past clattering police horses, forming an honour guard for the Royals—no doubt they'd be over the top with nervous anticipation and excitement. The 13th Battalion (Macquarie Regiment) had formed a military guard in Watt Street, police motorcycles idled nearby, and the delirious crowd cheered everything that stirred and hooted at a civilian who slipped under the barricade and danced across the road to find a better vantage point.

Horlicks had cleverly disguised the Dodge as an army ambulance to conceal our true intentions, displaying the unmistakable International Red Cross on a white background on its khaki canvas sides and roof. Marty was driving, Horlicks in the passenger seat, Becker and Benny in the rear. The spectators cheered them and applauded to relieve their boredom. Traffic cops blew their whistles and motioned them through every intersection; the bandmaster grinned, and the band struck up the "Can Can". Marty and Horlicks waved through the open windows of the ambulance, tooting the horn at intervals to show their appreciation until they turned off at the rail station and parked in a shared delivery lane behind the Great Northern Hotel.

Aware there was a chance the police might identify me prematurely and end the heist before we reached the starting gate, I intended to sneak in later, join the ambulance team at two o'clock and squat with Benny and Becker under the canvas cover tailored by Horlicks to a snug fit. There, we would sit, quiet as the desert night, not even whispering. Expecting a long wait, I provided sandwiches, a flask of tea to share, and six screw-top jars to pee into.

Billy had arrived at City Hall at six to reserve a space immediately below the podium where the Queen and dignitaries would make their speeches. At midday, Jessica and I joined him, sitting on folding chairs for everyone to see, including Tommo, who waved to me. I stood and flapped a handkerchief, holding an umbrella against the drizzle and, to the envy of the jovial crowd who shouted their disapproval, I held out a sandwich and a flask of tea to him. Tommo shook his head. But he had noticed me.

My morale held until, away from the gang with nothing to do except talk to Billy and Jess, I fretted and re-thought my plans. Should I have left the boys on their own? What if a shot is fired? Why would a man like Gabe calmly give up his money without a fight? What if something went badly wrong and someone dies? People will say I should have planned for such contingencies, but I'm a simple publican on my own, not a general with staff to ask all the questions and find all the answers. Was Kitty's behaviour bad enough to set me off on this madcap heist? But then Gabe viciously attacked Becker or paid Kitty to do it, which is the same thing. Why would I rob poor Tom Halley of his savings?

It was not too late to stop the whole crazy thing.

I tripped on the chair leg as I stood abruptly to run, and Jess threw out a hand to steady me. 'Are you okay?'

Billy stood to search the crowd. 'I've been looking for Franz Becker. Have you seen him?'

'I haven't been looking for him.'

'I thought he'd be here.'

'Oh, he's in Sydney,' Jessica said, dismissing him. 'Don't you remember?'

'I suppose he can't cause any trouble there,' I said. Then, to

Billy, 'Can't you put off the settling? You'll miss the close-ups while the Queen makes her speech.'

'Settling is on Tuesday afternoons until the world stops spinning, and today will be the biggest ever. I've got three thousand in this bag. There's a window overlooking the assembly point at the station. The Queen will be right under our window. I'll be able to reach out and ask why the Brits abandoned our troops in Singapore.' He smirked. 'I'd better go,' stooping to retrieve the bag. 'Catch you after the shindig.'

Panic swept through my head, erasing everything as a feather duster would. Wisen up, Sunni. Trouble will come, and there's no point thinking otherwise. Get through it and come out the other side.

A few minutes after one o'clock, I jumped up and, on tiptoe, put a shading hand to my forehead, peering into the distance, 'Damn. Billy forgot his notebook. He gave it to me to look after. I'll run to Tatts and be back here in fifteen minutes.'

Jess eyed the dense crowd. 'Half an hour, more likely, to get through this mob.'

I hadn't thought of that. My mistakes were mounting.

In the rear of the Dodge behind the Great Northern with Benny and Becker, I waited anxiously for the Royal train to arrive at Newcastle Rail Station, a lookalike for the Michelin Man in my overalls padded with pillows. We listened to the chatter and catcalls of the thirty-thousand outside the station in a misty rain, their excitement vibrating through the canvas. My heart was thumping, my mind filled with fears of failure, and I had not thought to tell Skeet what to do if we failed to return to the barn. The fright was in Benny's eyes and a sparkle and gleam in Becker's as he fanned himself with his cap, hummed a bouncy tune, and radiated a luminescence as soft as the stars and as sharp as the sun. It came to me of a sudden that I loved that boy, and I wondered at life's lunacy that I should crush into a tight space with a boy who was capable of changing in an instant from sweet to fierce, from dancing to violence and whose beauty was breathtaking even while we waited, clamped together, to rob the robbers and for the axe to fall.

He watched me watching him, tapped a foot against my ankle and brought his face close to my ear, 'How is ya doin', partner?'

Partner? Friend? I'll take what's on offer.

Cloud cover and the occasional shower kept the temperature lower under the canvas, but we were cramped on the steel floor, our legs pushed out in front. Benny's tool bag holding our gear and weapons provided a hard pillow. When we needed to move, we would tap on the cabin roof, and Marty would check his rear-view mirrors before giving us the all-clear, and they would shuffle about noisily and talk loudly in the front seat to disguise any sounds we made, then settle again. A walkie-talkie hanging off Benny's shoulder on a cord swung against the canvas with every movement. It was cumbersome and unreliable, crackling and hissing at low volume.

At six that morning, I positioned Horlicks in Watt Street, on the corner of Hunter, to watch for the armoured van delivering cash in deposit boxes from the Commonwealth Bank, and, even that early, he had to scramble to find a place among an excited crowd who had slept all night on the footpath. The stakes were high. Hidden behind a newspaper pretending to read the race commentaries, he had to remain alert, disguised in his raincoat, Akubra hat, horn-rimmed glasses and bushy Greek moustache.

Despite their grumblings at the shed last night, I insisted the entire team wear gloves, except for Marty and Horlicks, in the front seat. They would take theirs off while driving to avoid attracting attention. Driving gloves in the summer heat?

The cash van had arrived at ten-thirty, earlier than usual, because of the expected heavy traffic. That was the final clear-to-go, and Horlicks' instructions were to report to me if the cash did not arrive. Without the cash delivery, we would have aborted. He struggled through the crowd to reach the ambulance, changed into uniform and took over the front seat from Benny. They waited again.

At two-fifteen, the Royal train steamed into Newcastle Rail Station to an enormous and enthusiastic reception. I smelled the smoke of its arrival. The brakes squealed, the huge crowd waiting in the rain outside the station roared, and the Minister of Lands made a long speech to welcome the Queen and the Duke.

Bored with marching music, I scratched my ear and was about to tap on the roof, say something and move to ease a cramp in my leg when a hand banged on the door, and a voice said, 'What you doing here, mate? Having a kip, looks like?'

We sat like tightrope walkers balanced on the wire, waiting for death to claim us, and Marty said, 'G'day constable. Yeah, a short snooze is good as a long beer. What are you blokes up to?'

Marty and Horlicks shuffled awake in the front seat, stretched and groaned. They wore white overalls, long-sleeve white shirts with Red Cross armbands and white caps displaying the Red Cross, and we had practised our response. If the coppers asked questions, we would belong to the army, and we would be a St John's team for the military. The police would have no reason to look in the rear and recognise me, but, if they did, we would be sleeping volunteers and cancel the heist.

'Uh,' Marty grunted and stretched again. 'Having a quiet time while we're waiting for some action.' He removed his cap to reveal a red port wine stain, a birthmark the size and shape of a man's hand covering the right side of his face from ear to chin. The police constable fell silent, probably fixated on the mark. 'Ahh… Expecting casualties, are you?'

'Oh, yeah,' Marty said, his voice seeking their understanding. 'There'll be maybe a hundred collapses. Heart attacks, strokes, falling injuries, broken bones, you name it, mate. Every sort of ambulance from Swansea to Port Macquarie is out today. Our orders are to stay here, out of the traffic, until they call us. From here, we can move north, south, east or west. Someone was thinking right.'

The constable clapped a hand on the roof and landed his booted foot on the running board, 'Good truck, the Dodge. Reliable?'

'Yeah, mate,' Marty said, 'never had any trouble.'

'Spare parts easy to get?'

'Yeah, mate, dead easy.'

The copper had all the time in the world to chat. 'See,' he said, 'I'm looking at getting a ute, aren't I? Don't tell me offsider here,' he added, with a wicked chuckle, 'but I moonlight as a removalist. Plenty of small jobs don't need a big truck. You know, take a fridge or a wardrobe from Raymond Terrace to someone's old grandma at Maitland.'

Marty asked, 'How much would you charge for that?'

The tension in his voice cried out to me. I hoped the coppers had switched off their hearing aids.

'Five bob. Maybe six?'

The policeman ambled to the front of the truck, and we bounced when he checked the suspension. He kicked a tyre, patted the bonnet and returned to Marty. 'What's it like on petrol?'

'Ah, mate. I don't know. How would I know? I don't pay for it, but I suppose fifteen or twenty to the gallon on the highway.'

The constable banged a hand on the canvas cover. 'Plenty of space in the rear, is there?'

'Yeah, mate,' and Marty made a grab for the radio, as it broke into a string of static, abruptly louder as he increased the volume. 'Great Northern to base, come in,' and the radio squawked and stuttered, clicked and snuffled as Benny, in the rear, quietly pressed the transmit button on and off and mumbled into the mouthpiece. 'Great Northern confirming. Roger that. We will go to Readiness One.' Marty pressed the starter button, and the engine stuttered to life.

'Didn't understand a word,' the constable said, screwing his eyes the better to listen.

'I'm used to it,' Marty said. 'The royals have arrived. You'll be able to get a peek at them if you hurry.'

'Yeah. Good luck. See ya.'

Marty spoke to us through the canvas cover. 'Thanks, Benny. We were done. You always were fast on your feet.' Benny double-clicked his walkie-talkie, blew into the mouthpiece and smiled in his shy way.

The commentator's voice built to a frenzy over the loudspeakers hooked up around the streets. 'And here they are, Queen Elizabeth the Second, Queen of Australia, with her husband, Prince Philip, coming out through a bower of ornamental shrubs and native flowers. Her Majesty is waving, and the crowd is delighted. Listen to them cheer. Now, the Queen is walking to the elegant, black Daimler Landaulette.'

At the podium, Jessica jumped to her feet. 'Oh, my God. Billy's notebook? Billy! I joined the dots—a robbery at Tatts. Sunni and Becker and Skeet are planning to rob Tatts. Billy and the bookies.'

But Billy was gone.

'Wait,' the loudspeakers screeched. 'What's happening? The Queen is not entering the car but is talking to an attendant.'

Jessica sat again, shuffling and twisting in her seat.

'She is smiling,' the commentator fawned. He was over the moon. 'The driver is folding the canvas hood to allow spectators to see her, and now the Queen is entering the car.'

Jessica counted off on her fingers, speaking aloud. Sunni, Becker, the Royal Tour, Settling Day, Skeet, Tattersalls. On her feet again, gasping, gabbling to a constable to join the dots. The dots, Madam? I'm not allowed to leave my post to search for dots. Look for the Super at the event headquarters inside the City Hall and tell him about your dots.

The commentator's voice fell to a suitably hushed servility. 'How charming. A small child, a girl, is proffering a bunch of flowers. The Queen is smiling, graciously taking the flowers, and the cavalcade moves off two minutes behind schedule.'

The clouds furled, the sun peeped through, and the Royal procession rolled forward on a sixteen-minute drive to City Hall, and after speeches there, it would wend its way to the steelworks. Their schedule would take the Royal couple past two hundred and sixty thousand admirers packing the streets, some of whom, like Billy, had been in place before dawn.

Police motorcycles led the procession, then came a contingent of police mounted on horses splashing their dung in front of the Royal Daimler, followed by ten cars holding the Premier, the Queen's entourage and the British press. Spectators fluttered flags and threw confetti at the Daimler, dogs barked, children swarmed, Boy Scouts lining the route cheered like crazy, and one little girl was thumped by a rifle butt when troops ordered arms as the Daimler hove into sight.

From every vantage point, five-deep along every kerb, standing on fruit boxes and chairs, hanging from windows and balconies, the crowds cheered and waved and, as soon as the Queen passed by, raced through side streets to watch the procession from another vantage point on the route.

Jessica wedged her way through the crowd, leaving behind a hundred complaining enthusiasts, and saw Sergeant Thomson fifty feet away, perched on a fruit case, his eyes probing the jostling swarm, searching for trouble.

Behind the Great Northern, we huddled in the ambulance, overflowing with adrenaline, cracking with the tension. We were clad in white overalls and ball caps, unaware of the happenings outside, guessing the parade's location from the cheering.

The skies had opened early in the day, and a flooded road or an accident causing a significant traffic hold-up would ruin our escape route. By lunch, it was intermittent showers, and noise from the excited crowd drowned out the band music, but the gutters ran deep with rainwater, and low-lying areas were a foot deep in water.

All eyes were on me, their breathing on hold; the time for murmured good luck passed. I waited for the police constable with ambitions to become a removalist to disappear and for the tail of the Royal procession to pass Hunter Street.

Then I said, as though we were off for a day at the races, 'Toolbag, Benny? Gloves? Away you go.' Benny had to walk twenty-five yards on Scott Street, then round the corner and another thirty yards on Watt Street, past the Great Northern, while we waited, parked in the lane behind, for him to give us the all-clear on the walkie-talkie.

His canvas tool bag held plumber's tools. A second bag was chock full with two submachine guns, two handguns, the cut-off shottie, a hand grenade, a long-handled rebar cutter, rolls of thick twine, a six-pound hammer, pliers and other useful tools. From Watt Street, he stepped through the front entrance of Tattersalls Club.

Benny's job was to open the delivery bay's external door to the lane, and, after Skeet walked it with a stopwatch in hand, I scheduled three minutes. But, after six minutes, we waited in the ambulance, behind time, before we got going. Muscles strained and aching, we crouched on our haunches, ready to spring from the van. I should have trained harder. I ran through the preparations in my mind. All pockets emptied of identification, all bladders empty, all in sandshoes with non-slip soles, all weapons tucked inside overalls out of sight, coloured hairnets, no flesh showing, gloves. I opened the canvas hood, ready to rush in to find the problem, when Benny's voice came through the walkie-talkie, 'In position. The door is open. It's all go.'

Marty reversed the ambulance along the lane to the door, and we piled out of the truck, stepped into the storeroom and closed the door.

'Okay, Benny?'

'Yep.'

'What happened?'

'Lunch guests and staff streamed into the lobby. They were too excited to question me in my white overalls and tool bag. I entered the refrigerator room, found the switch where Skeet said I would, and shut down the refrigerator. I opened the external door when a steward asked if I needed anything and told me to report to reception next time. He wanted to talk about my Air Force moustache and how he had applied to fly Spitfires in Egypt but was too young.'

A baseball cap covered Benny's forehead. Sideburns swept across his cheeks from ears to lips, centring on a ginger mass of hair on his upper lip.

'Good work. Telephones?'

'Cut.' Wires hung from the PMG telephone box.

'Marty, Horlicks, Franz. Gloves on? Weapons?'

Benny knew what to do, but no general had ever lost a battle by repeating the instructions. 'Watch the truck,' I said. 'Gloves on, clean the door handles and anything else you touched.' The truck engine was running. 'Keep the engine idling, watch our backs and be ready to drive. You know the story. The coppers think we are Army.'

'Got it.'

'All ready? Masks on.'

We pulled on papier-mâché masks of the Queen and Prince Philip. Because at least two of our victims knew me well enough to identify me, I first drew on a balaclava as an extra precaution, turned up my collar, and, to top it off, my royal mask. I had trouble aligning the eye holes and stumbled to the door.

Jessica was panting when she saw Tommo's head approaching through the crowd. She stood on tiptoe to wave but snapped her arm down. Crouching low, she hid behind a bus stand until Tommo passed by not five yards away and disappeared toward the City Hall in a mass of cheering spectators. The constable would tell him later about joining the dots.

She arrived at Tattersalls as people returned to the lobby, throwing their arms about, describing their opinions on the Royals and their entourage with great noise and enthusiasm. Entering the hall with the crowd, a bloke in white overalls, sporting a garish orange moustache and carrying a tool bag, laughed excitedly, swapping experiences with a devoted Anglophile in a steward's uniform.

The Queen would be arriving at City Hall, the crowd near the Rail Station had dispersed, and car and foot traffic were heavy in surrounding streets.

Inside the refrigerator room, we were ready to go.

'Benny, check the lobby,' I said.

Benny cracked the door and spoke into his radio. 'All clear.'

I took a grip on my nerves, bounced on my toes, jiggled my mask, pumped my arm and spoke louder than needed. 'Good to go?' A stream of okays, then, 'Go.'

And, wearing a Philip mask, Horlicks led the way to the winding stairs leading from the kitchen door to the second floor. Becker, second in line, tripped on the seventh step, but the momentum from behind picked him up and carried him on.

Last in the line rushing up the stairs to the settling room, I checked our rear. Through the open front door, I glimpsed the busloads of uniformed police and troops lining the parade to City Hall, then to the steelworks. And there, open-mouthed in the doorway, was Jessica. She looked directly into my eyes and clapped a hand over her mouth. The game was up. Panting, I gaped at her and shook my head, unable to believe the bad luck that would put her in the wrong place at the worst possible time.

Her hand fell away, and we stood like statues. Through the eyeholes in my stupid mask, I saw recognition flash. She hesitated with her hand in the air, nodded, and peeped at me over her shoulder as she darted away. I reckoned that meant what I thought it meant.

The time was two-thirty-six. The sighting by Jess had cost me twelve seconds. They hadn't waited for me. Their weapons came out, I caught up, and they burst through the door. We erupted into the room where fifteen bookies and their well-heeled clients had assembled to settle their accounts from Saturday's race meeting. Horlicks rushed directly at the uniformed security guard standing by the wire cage, jammed a submachine gun under his chin, plucked his weapon from the holster on his hip, and tripped his feet. The guard fell to the floor, and Becker stood with one boot on his chest and a revolver inches away from his head.

Horlicks held the gun high with his finger on the trigger and hollered, 'On the floor! Facedown! On the floor! Guns on the floor! No heroes—no one gets hurt. You! Security! Get over there with the others.' Gabe Rosen's ear was pressed into the carpet. 'You have a gun, mate?' Red in the face, snarling. 'I'll be searching everyone. Put it here. Now. Or I'll shoot you stone dead. Easy now.'

Becker knew Gabe carried a revolver, so he swooped on him and kicked him hard in the ankle with his soft-toed sandshoe to focus his mind while he gave up the gun. I saw Becker enjoyed it—a small payback for his broken ribs. I recognised my Billy also. His head stuck deep into the carpet, and if my disguise was not equal to the task, then that would be fifteen years written off. The rest didn't know me as well or see me as clearly as Jess did.

There was a lot of hoping involved in this spree.

Two other guns, a pistol and a revolver, landed on the floor, and I kicked them away. For two seconds, the room was quiet.

There was only the sound of amplified speeches and cheering crowds until Marty stirred the place up. In his Prince Philip mask, he sprang onto a table, held his hand high, and yelled, 'Grenade!' Panicked eyes swung like the pointer of a magnetic compass to the grenade. 'I've pulled the pin,' waving the split pin high on a key ring. 'Screw with me, and we're all dead. Eyes on the carpet. Don't look up.'

Becker had slung his Sten across his chest and, hiding his limp, opened the pantry door with a steel wrecking bar easy as tearing paper, but he made heavy going of smashing the lock on the first of fifteen steel security boxes.

I handed him the six-pound hammer without speaking because my voice would give me away. The locks broke quickly under its noisy assault, the boxes sprang open, and I hurried along the line, emptying their contents into a khaki kit bag.

Everything was going to plan. I checked the room. Plush green carpet with a fleur-de-lis design in dark blue, crystal chandeliers, tables with starched white cloths and piled with cash. Mounds of it in neatly banded bricks, more money than I thought existed.

And everyone in the room was jittery, hyper, and twitchy.

'Eyes on the carpet,' Marty screamed. 'You! Don't move. I've got the grenade. Hey, you. Stop!' Horlicks swung his machine gun, and the room sucked air.

I patted the air impatiently, as masculine as you like. Horlicks retreated, reluctantly, I thought, and joined me. Mass execution avoided.

We swept the cash from the tables into two canvas kit bags. Marty waved the grenade high and hollered. 'Eyes up here. Watch the grenade. Do not open the door when we leave. Watch the grenade.'

He unwound a cord from around his wrist. 'The pin is loose. Don't look at me. Watch the grenade. The Grenade! Look. The pin is in place. It's tied to this cord. The grenade will explode

191

when the door opens. Don't open the door, or you will all die in little pieces. Anything disturbs me, and we're all dead. Eyes on the carpet. Don't look up.'

Horlicks carried the bags to the door. Marty held the grenade up and shouted. 'Eyes up here. Watch the grenade. Do not open the door when we leave. This grenade will explode when the door opens. You will all die.'

A loud knock came at the door, and a male voice shouted. Horlicks spun to me, but Marty answered. 'Ask who it is.'

Horlicks at the door, 'Yes?'

The male voice answered.

'What?'

'Waiter service, I have the coffee you ordered.'

'Not now. I'll call later.'

The coffee service knocked my schedule by two more minutes while we waited to check that he had returned to the kitchen. It seemed a week before we backed through the door, and as Marty left the room, he made a drama of feeding the cord under the door. 'Watch the grenade,' he called.

He banged the door shut behind him, and we clattered down the stairs, armament covered again, to Benny and the ambulance.

By then, the Queen would have concluded her speech at City Hall, and the cavalcade departed for the steelworks where the Press expected an even bigger crowd. Their plans were also behind schedule, and traffic was bumper to bumper and stationary in the city.

We threw the weapons into Benny's tool bag, ripped off our masks, tossed them in with the guns, and breathed out for the first time in sixteen minutes. Horlicks shoved the tool bag behind a stack of cardboard cartons.

'Come on, mate. We can't mess about all day.'

In the rear of the truck, I double-tapped the hood. 'Go!' and Benny got it moving in the lane beside the Great Northern towards Scott Street as Horlicks ran out and clambered aboard. The engine revved noisily; the ambulance rolled and immediately braked. The same copper shouted, 'Street's blocked, mate. You in a hurry?'

'Yeah,' Benny raised his voice. 'Hurry is right.'

'Serious one, is it?'

'Heart attack.'

'We'll get you through,' and two coppers jumped onto the running boards, one on each side.

'No way, mate,' Marty squealed, 'Army regs. Jump off, or they'll have my balls for breakfast.' He hit the siren and Benny pumped the brakes. 'Thanks, mate. Off ya get.'

The ambulance siren hee-hawed to clear a passage into Scott Street, the police jumped off waving their arms to direct the crowd away from the exit, and Benny swung the wheel and accelerated on gravel tracks through the park towards the hospital. I peeked at the road through a join in the canvas. 'Pull the Red Cross signs in. Ditch the khaki cover. Siren off.'

The Red Cross signs retracted through holes in the canvas, leaving a blank khaki canvas. Horlicks tripped six tie wires and pulled the khaki cover inside, and one minute later, the ambulance was gone, replaced by a delivery truck with a spanking white tonneau cover.

'Watch your speed, Benny,' I said. 'No hurry. Follow The Esplanade. Get on to Scenic Drive.' I checked my watch. Seventeen minutes to clear a quarter-million-quid haul. Good going.

I had time to think about Jess for the first time since I saw her at the door. Which way would she jump? Nothing I could do about it. Press on.

27. Our Getaway

Adrenaline was firing as we raced into the barn, the Dodge taking out the rear wall. It had been our sanctuary last night, and now, for no more than ten minutes, would be our refuge from the police already hunting us. I let loose a cheer and slapped hands for a minute but didn't try to contain my excitement and bellowed louder than I needed. 'Great work, everyone. Don't rest yet. Marty and Horlicks wipe the truck. Any fingerprints are yours, so be careful. Use metho and then wipe the bottle. The rest of you wipe anything in the shed that will hold a fingerprint. Look for beer bottles in case we missed one. Bag everything and toss it into the VW.'

According to Skeet's portable wireless, the Queen's entourage was sixteen minutes behind schedule when they arrived at the airport. The rain had given the town another drenching; rubbish from the procession blocked street drains in Hunter Street, causing minor flooding, and water was deep in the gutters. St John's ambulances were busy, and medics did not get through the traffic. They had treated forty collapses, thirteen heart attacks and twenty-five minor injuries. Ambulance sirens wailed across the inner city, frustrated by clogged roads.

Skeet had bagged the kettle and the kerosene heater, sandwich wrappers, crusts, and anything that wasn't there when we first came and packed it into the VW.

'Skeet, wipe the padlock and the door where you opened it.'

We abandoned the Dodge, wiped the canvas covers and Red Cross logos and left them in the shed. Ten minutes after arriving, We locked the door and set off in the VW, Skeet driving and me beside him. On the floor in the rear, Marty bagged his birthmark while Horlicks talked and laughed endlessly.

Benny tore off the ginger moustache and smiled a silly smile. 'I wonder if he noticed my black eyebrows.'

'Right, mate.' I said. 'All they will remember is the driver had a terrible birthmark on his face, you had a flaming ginger mo, and Horlicks wore a bright green ribbon around the forehead on his mask.'

Horlicks asked, 'What about the grenade? I almost shit me pants.'

Marty let out a roar of laughter. 'Dummy grenade. Kept 'em quiet.'

'You might have told us.'

'Overalls,' I shouted, 'into a kit bag.'

Under the overalls, Marty and the bikies wore long trousers and tee shirts. They had stored leather jackets in their saddlebags at Charlestown. I changed into the work clothes favoured by miners, and Skeet had dressed in a tee shirt and jeans.

Two hundred and more thousand had come to Newcastle to catch a glimpse of the Queen and were too excited to hurry away. Taking photos and licking ice creams, they would be roaming the streets in town and creating havoc on the roads.

'Don't slack off,' I called. 'We drop the bikies in twenty minutes. Finish the packing. Stuff the cash into the toolbox. Jewellery and papers into a separate toolbox. Stop, Skeet. Here's the first garbage drop-off. Marty, one bag in the bin. Make sure it's rubbish and not the cash.'

'Cash and papers will take two toolboxes, maybe three,' Benny shouted.

'Jewels in a bag, then. I'll chuck it somewhere. We don't want to get caught with diamonds and rubies.'

'There's some beautiful stuff here,' Horlicks said reverently. 'Worth a mint. I know a reliable fence. Can we keep the best bits?'

'No way. A fence will lead the coppers right to us. Did you hear me? That's what gets us caught. Move it now. Cash and papers into the metal toolbox where the rats can't get at it. Jewels into a bag.'

The VW followed quiet streets in Adamstown and Charlestown, well away from the parade route and escaped the city limits before traffic clogged the roads to the South. While Skeet drove, Benny and Marty counted cash into six parcels, each with twenty quid in one-pound and ten-bob notes.

But Horlicks wasn't happy with that. 'How come Skeet gets a full share? He was behind the lines while we took all the risk.'

I shouted over my shoulder, 'Skeet was the inside contact. He knew the what and the how and the measurements. This heist wouldn't have happened without Skeet taking the risk to search out all the details.'

'Okay. Okay. Keep ya hair on.'

'Hurry it up.' I shouted. 'Don't care if someone gets a bit more than twenty. Splash it out roughly will do—the first month's pay. Go easy on the spending. Twenty is a lot. No grandstanding, and we keep our mouths closed tight.'

'Who's the sixth pile for?' Horlicks asked.

'It's for the sixth man on the team. I told you he's at the hiding place.'

'Just asking.'

'If the police stop you after we separate, you gambled your wages and won on Pride of Egypt, Saturday, at five to one. They'll be looking for four men in an ambulance. I don't expect we'll have any trouble.'

We whooped, whistled, and shouted while the cream VW panel van chugged along lanes and minor roads, heading South for ten minutes. We intended to drop Marty and his Sydney mates at their motorbikes in Charlestown. Horlicks would leave on his bike ten minutes before Benny with Marty on the pillion.

No suspicion should attach to the bikies separated by ten minutes, so they would take the shorter Pacific Highway through Lakes Entrance and Gosford. I planned to go alone to

Dudley, then return to collect Becker and Skeet and take the inland route through Glendale and Tuggerah to Gosford, where I intended to abandon the panel van and take a train to Sydney.

'Two toolboxes will not be enough,' Marty shouted from the rear of the bus. 'There's more than we expected.'

'Pack the cash tight.' Twisting my body to peer over into the rear. 'Use the third if you need to. I have to carry them.'

'Sunni,' Skeet shouted, although I sat inches away. 'We're here.'

The VW slowed and pulled into the kerb at Charlestown. 'Bikies, go,' I shouted, as excited as Skeet. 'Take your cash and nothing else. Don't get picked up for speeding. See you in Sydney.'

When the bikies were out of sight, I said, 'Skeet and Becker, wait here for me.'

'Wait?' Skeet bristled, fluttered his arms. 'Aren't we going to hide the cash?'

'*I'm* hiding the cash. No one other than me will know where it's hidden, and that is the best security we can have.

'But—'

Becker said, soothing Skeet's concern. 'Trust her, Skeet. It's for the best.'

'I—'

I leaned across Skeet, opened the door and encouraged him with gentle pressure on his shoulder. 'Go. Trust me. I promise to be here with you in thirty-five minutes. I promise.'

'Rudy might not be there.' Skeet was inside, holding on to the door frame. 'You'll need me to help you with three boxes and a bag.'

'He'll be there. Now go,' I said, pushing firmly.

Tense and fearful, alone for the first time, I pressed forward, my grip strangling the VW's steering wheel, to Dudley, four minutes away, where I parked on the deserted street beside the vacant block next to The Dudley.

Jess would be at the procession, and her bus would never get through the traffic in time to see me hide the proceeds of the robbery. I found later she had decided to wait and have a hamburger and chips in the city rather than struggle to leave on snarled roads, the traffic moving at barely more than a walking pace. There was no one to take an interest in a VW panel van or the bearded miner in orange overalls and helmet, who calmly strode through the unlocked gate and down the unformed path through wet, knee-high grass carrying two heavy toolboxes.

I came to a depression in the shadow of a spreading Moreton Bay Fig. The buttress roots had cracked the walls of a masonry shed built to prevent entrance to an adit where the rising coal seam had outcropped to the surface. I dropped the toolboxes and knocked three times on the door, fingers crossed that Rudy was on the other side, and gave the rest of the code, four knocks spaced apart.

The heavy door was locked from the outside by a key restricted to the company's security and held in a safe at Head Office. But from the inside, being an emergency exit, Rudy opened it without a key.

The door opened, and I entered a small, roofless chamber where Rudy waited at the top of a five-foot ladder bolted to the coal face. He'd walked underground from the Burwood pit bottom on a circuitous route through mined and unused passages connecting with the Dudley mine, a path he had surveyed, mapped, and tested.

We slapped hands, cheered, and drummed our hands on the toolboxes, and I returned to the van for the third toolbox and a canvas bag. I gave Rudy a three-minute description of the event.

'The perfect heist,' I said. 'Nothing went wrong.' I didn't need to tell them about Jess springing me at Tatts. She'll not bring us unstuck, will she? 'Now, let's get the next few payments ready in case we are in a hurry when the time comes,' and we were laughing again. 'We need about three hundred.' I thrust a hand into the steel box and withdrew a handful of cash.

'Jeez.' Rudy smoothed his hair with both hands. 'What's three hundred look like?' He delved into the box and came out with ten-pound notes.

'Go for the packets of one-pounders,' I said. 'They've come straight from the bank.'

He drew out a packet of ones and flicked a quick count. 'There's two hundred in each pack.' His hands flew to the toolbox, and he produced a bundle of ten-shilling notes.

'Use the small notes until you run out,' I instructed him. 'Less likely to be noticed.'

'Right,' Benny said, 'let's get on with it. Good. You brought the rope. Lower the boxes in the shaft. It's seven feet,' and we slid down the ladder.

Fifteen minutes later, we scampered up the ladder after scrambling through passages with our helmet lamps for light. 'Okay,' I said. 'We've done it, and we're gone. I'll see you in Newcastle.'

A cream-coloured VW panel van kicked up gravel on the road from Toronto to Gosford. Traffic was light. The front seat passenger wore a huge grin, singing happily, a little off-tune, and beating her hand in rhythm on the dashboard. Undeterred by the wind and engine noises, Becker napped against the window in the rear, occasionally yelping and moving in his seat to clutch his ribs, and Skeet sat beside me driving, unable to stop talking about the heist, repeating the description word for word.

'Step on it, Skeet,' I said. 'You need to be in the dining room at Woolloomooloo by seven.'

28. Après Heist

Wednesday, February 10.

'Hard to believe.' My head was shaking without encouragement from my brain, addled with excitement and nervous energy. I folded the *Herald* open to the centre page, the paper rattling in rhythm with the tremors in my hands, and studied the photographs before passing it to Billy, eager to have his opinion as a victim. The two-page, black and white spread showed Tommo dressed up for the media in a pale beige suit that brought out the colour in his hair. He perched on the edge of a table, legs out at full stretch and hands tucked casually in his pockets. He had laid out the robbers' weapons and a canvas tool bag on the table: Sten guns, handguns, grenade.

At screaming point in The Dudley's kitchen, I tried my best to appear calm and collected.

I wore pink pyjamas and a silk kimono with an apple blossom motif, a six-year-old gift from the CEO of a Japanese company, along with a silver and pearl necklace that I had somehow forgotten to give up to Kitty. I poured another cup of tea, stepped to the window and stood looking directly at the fig tree above the adit where I met Rudy and hid our loot yesterday afternoon in daylight. Then, grinning like a clown, I sat at the pine table.

Billy read from the paper:

> According to this, the business centre was a traffic maze. Within five minutes of the Queen's speech at City Hall, police cars and outgoing traffic on Maitland Road were jam-packed, and the Mayfield to Thornton Road was a solid mass of blocked vehicles. By the time police set roadblocks, the

Pacific Highway to Sydney was walking pace as far as The Entrance.

He raised his head when I giggled. 'What's funny?' he asked, in no mood for my giggling.

'I'm thinking it's time for a swim.' And, pointing at the photograph to distract his attention from my inappropriate face, I added, 'The superintendent deserves the sack. I warned him something like this would happen.'

'You're not making sense. Are you talking about Becker again? That snotty-nosed kid did this? No way. He'd get lost finding the Pacific Ocean on a map.'

He wanted a fight, so stupid me gave him one. 'It's a big mistake to call him a kid. He has a man's head on his shoulders.' He would be a prime suspect, so there was no harm in raising his name. 'Did you know that Jessica had a premonition and went looking for Tommo but didn't find him in the crowd?'

Big mistake. Cut your tongue out, Sunni. Billy will never have a reason to repeat her suspicion to Tommo. Will he?

'Tommo finally agrees with me,' Billy said. 'Last night, he told us that Sydney police found Becker in a Woolloomooloo hotel, and there was no way for him to have robbed the bookies, driven to Sydney and arrived in time to be at the hotel by seven-thirty that night when they interviewed him. The traffic was bumper to bumper all the way. A five-hour drive, they say.'

Yawning, he clipped the top off a boiled egg and shook salt and pepper from silver shakers. 'It's too late for roadblocks, but police are watching trains and the airport. Customs are searching passenger luggage on all ships leaving Australia.'

He poured tea, got on with his breakfast, then shivered theatrically. 'Ugh. When this terrorist in a Prince Philip mask held up a grenade, I buried my face in the carpet, and there's nothing I can't tell you about the pattern on that carpet. The grenade was harmless, but no one knew that. We hopped around like squawking chooks when they left, too scared to go near the door while they escaped. I've never been so happy to be tucked up at the old Dudley.'

He read aloud from the newspaper again: 'More police are arriving from Sydney to help with the investigation.'

The cook was clattering about in the kitchen, cracking eggs into a pan and shaking rashers of bacon in another, clanking the pans loudly to let us know it was time we left her kitchen. Billy rested his backside on the window ledge. 'Last night,' he went on, 'Tommo told me Becker had a ticket in his pocket for the Manly Ferry, stamped Tuesday, 1:20 p.m. And one to the Odeon Cinema for the five o'clock session. The receptionist, the ticket seller and the ferry conductor all described him. He wore a red leather jacket and a captain's cap, flashy like that film star, and Skeet had on some sort of floral shirt, tight trousers and oversized tortoise-shell sunglasses at night with shells strung around his neck. Later, they ID'd Becker and Skeet from photos Tommo sent to Sydney.'

I suppose the aftermath of many hours of planning and then the tension of the heist tired me. I shooed Billy away from the windowsill and stood again, looking out at the vacant lot. The grass needed cutting. I considered phoning a complaint to Councillor Fraser.

'It's been a long day and night,' I said, 'and I'm not sure I care who robbed the bookies or how much they lost. It was clever to use the cover of the Royal tour, don't you think?'

In my dressing gown, I thought *I'm* clever enough to do that. I stood and, trying to hide the silly grin that wouldn't disappear, I said, 'How much did they get away with?'

'Tom Halley told me he lost fifteen thousand and some jewellery, but he would claim three thou from insurance.'

'To fool the tax man?' I said. 'I told you—everyone is crooked when you scratch the skin.'

Billy said, 'Tom Halley suggested maybe if we declared twenty thousand lost altogether, the Tax Department would stay away, but if they find it's closer to two hundred, we'll never live to hear the end of it.'

'Two hundred thousand pounds. Good God. And Gabe, did he lose much?'

'More than anyone,' Billy said. 'Close to twenty-five thou. On top of that, he had a lot of jewellery in his box.'

And interesting papers and contracts, which I expect are engrossing. I'm not about to mention that to Billy. I'll get some sleep before I slip and say something I shouldn't.

Later, in the guest lounge at The Dudley, I dipped a biscuit into my tea. 'Don't worry, Jessica. Franz was not involved in the robbery. He's still crippled from the bashing.'

Jessica's face blazed. 'Did I say he was in on the robbery? I asked if you thought it was possible.' She glided towards the door, brushing past my chair. 'Franz was in Sydney. I don't believe the rumour about an international gang. I reckon it was a local job. Probably led by a business person we deal with every day.'

She had not mentioned sighting me at Tattersall's during the robbery, and I let it slide until the day she decided to broach the subject. 'Are you holding a flame for him?' I said, surprised. 'After he ran out on you at the beach?'

At the door, she swung about to confront me. 'I'll hold a flame for Franz if I want to. He is going places. One day, he'll be someone who counts. I'm not stupid, Sunni. I know he has his problems, but he's the most thrilling thing ever happened to me, and I'll hang on to him because he's the one I can look to for glamour and excitement in my life.'

Ponytail whipping, she flounced out, leaving me thunderstruck with my lips parted in a goofy smile.

Tommo came, clearing his throat and fidgeting with the buttons on his jacket, with a search warrant, two Sydney detectives introduced as Detectives Macdonald and O'Malley, and three constables. He ducked his head, 'A witness places you in company with Franz Becker coming and going from Tin City—'

'What is your relationship with Becker?' Macdonald interrupted rudely and, before I raised the spit to speak, added, 'And with Kitty Balushi?'

It's never pleasant being bullied by the police, but I'd practised the art of lying often enough during my Kitty years, and, over the next half-hour, I got more out of them than they got out of me.

They had no other suspect than Becker, and they thought he was incapable, through inexperience and wounding, of undertaking such a complicated heist without direction, so their line of investigation was to cast a broad net amongst those associated with him since his return from the war. People like Gabe Rosen, I suggested.

They exercised search warrants at Annie's boarding house, at Tin City and at The Dudley and cleared all, including Skeet, whose part-time work at Tattersalls had them heaving until they verified his alibi at the Woolloomooloo Hotel.

Since his return from Sydney, Skeet had been wearing a collection of bright Hawaiian shirts, each day in different colours, and trousers fitting tight at the ankles, always with a necklace of flowers or shells. He shocked the elderly in Newcastle, inspired the young by claiming to be a bodgie, and said he bought the shirts in Sydney. He camped it up when the Sydney police came to interview him, and they made crude jokes at his expense but believed his alibi without asking what a bodgie might believe in.

The Army was checking its vehicle inventory after police discovered the Dodge but claimed it would take upwards of twelve months to get an answer. A witness reported suspicious sightings and sounds in the barn, where there should not be any. That discovery led Detective Macdonald to believe a gang from Sydney or Melbourne organised the heist, though he was not eliminating a US or Hong Kong mafia.

Tommo offered the opinion that the robbers would surface soon, attempting to fence the stolen jewellery. Macdonald sneered at stupid criminals for reaching a sticky end after drawing the attention of smarter and tougher criminals who wanted to take the loot away from them. 'Mark my word,' he said. 'These robbing bastards will be dead within the year from shootings and knifings by their own kind.'

29. Living It Up with Suspicion

March-April, 1954.

On a Friday, nearly five weeks after the heist, I lived it up with my gang in the old docker's hotel in Balmain. Becker was cock-a-hoop and crowing about his role in the aftermath of the heist. Tommo and the inspector had come to Sydney the next day to interrogate him again, he bragged, with slight variations in the numerous versions of his story. They bombarded him with questions. Where was he on Tuesday afternoon? Why did he not stay to watch the Royal procession? What did he do in Sydney? Where did he eat, and why did Skeet accompany him on his holiday? And they smirked about one double bed.

Becker bounced up his arm in an Italian salute.

I admired my new Cadillac as a parking boy drove it off. In shimmering fur and form-hugging gown, I held out a gloved hand, 'Becker, Dahrling. Will you join me in a champers?'

A beer bottle clattered carelessly on the table. 'Sunni. Sunni. You were staring into space, mate. I asked what you meant about laundering cash.'

But I gazed through the window at his mud-splashed Plymouth, not wanting to give up my fantasy where I tossed money around in the casino, tipped big, and bought anything that met my eye—silk suits, handmade shoes, a home here, a holiday house in the South of France—and for good measure had Gabe Rosen run my messages.

Detective MacDonald suspected that somehow, through my association with Becker, I knew more about the heist than I admitted to and visited The Dudley frequently and irregularly without warning. He arrived with another search warrant in the guise of looking for illegal gambling. I presumed he had gossiped to Tom Halley and other bookies about Becker's role in the mischief and they alerted him to my tenuous connection to Becker. Having inside information, I had no cause to be alarmed. Hector was in with that group and would report any suspicion attaching to me.

In the third week, the surveillance by plain-clothes detectives had tapered off and by the fifth had ceased, or so it seemed. Macdonald's visits had become more casual, careless and even friendly, and he pushed the line that a Melbourne gang was to blame. No, not in his backyard. But I thought it was too risky to take home the stolen jewellery to admire or the papers to study.

Becker's injuries and inexperience mitigated suspicion. He used a walking stick and worked seven-hour shifts in the Redhead mine three days every week as Rudy's chainman, surveying progress on all three levels. The work was light, holding a tape or a level rod in tunnels and recording it on a map that Rudy kept up to date.

Skeet worked his mine shifts and part-time at Tatts and the Jockey Club, so open and naïve that no question would attach to him.

When it was time for the first monthly cash distribution, Rudy left the Redhead mine with one hundred and twenty quid in low-denomination banknotes in his pockets and boots and inside his surveying equipment. He travelled by train to Gosford—an unlikely place for a police search—stepped straight into the waiting Plymouth and headed on the highway to Sydney with Becker at the wheel. Skeet and I travelled separately in my A70.

In a guest bedroom at the Balmain pub, I passed twenty one-pound notes each to Benny and Marty and twenty for them to give to Horlicks. After our celebration, I would return alone to Newcastle in my A70—I carried only five quid in case Tommo picked me up on some trumped-up charge and searched me. Rudy would travel home by train with a ten-bob note in his wallet, the balance hidden in his socks and a linen pouch hanging around his neck. Skeet and Becker planned to stay overnight and travel in separate carriages to Newcastle on the early train in the morning.

It wasn't the police that worried me. They would need proof, and I'd been cautious not to leave hard evidence. But the syndicate required no sworn statements or justification. Kitty Balushi and the Sydney gangs would know the true extent of the robbery and who the police suspected and would be looking hard at how to get their hands on the swag. They would kidnap and torture to find the money at the merest suspicion of a culprit.

I visited the cache for a quick squiz at Gabe's documents and did not believe how careless he was to store, in the same security box as his cash, papers that risked putting him away for five years and a few corrupt politicians and police with him.

Horlicks was our weak point. He was greedy and flashy. What could I do about it? Too late. I should never have employed him. I needed protection. Who did I trust to protect me?

I strolled on the beach, read at the library, and doodled on a notepad, wealthy for the first time in my life. I had enough to go straight, buy a solid house, have a nice car and never have to work. A voice in my ear asked who I would have to talk to. Who would live in that big house with me? Skeet and the gang? I don't think so. Inevitably, my thoughts turned to Becker.

Jess knew I robbed the bookies but had not mentioned sighting me at Tattersalls, and I stayed well clear of the subject with her. Was a marriage likely? Would she have him? Was he in love with her enough to consider marriage?

Jess would be twenty in May, which was not far off. Would she want Becker if he were poor? Would I tell her about the wealth I'd buried in the mineshaft?

No. Don't be so dumb. I might as well headline it in *The Herald* for all the assassins to gloat over.

Towards the end of March, the police appeared to have lost interest. Rudy and the others worked at the mine three days each week, and Rudy stayed away from the shallow adit running north to Dudley, where I hid the swag from the robbery in one of many mined-out cross cuts intersecting the main heading.

However, with the April payment coming up, we needed to access the cash. I left Billy to close the bar at six o'clock, and while the comings and goings at the front of the hotel took his attention, I hurried in the dusk to the corner of our car park and, concealed amongst the buttress roots and overhang of the Moreton Bay Fig, knocked on the door of the adit. Rudy let me in, and under the light from our helmet lamps, we separated the cash into seven metal, rat-proof boxes.

I tied a string around the last packet. 'One hundred and fifty-seven thousand, six hundred and sixty-two pounds, Rudy. A hundred and fifty-seven thousand, six hundred and sixty-two little quidlets.'

Rudy, quick with arithmetic, wielded a pencil for a minute. 'Sixty per cent to you. That's ninety-four thousand five hundred and ninety-seven for you and ten thousand five hundred and ten pounds for each of us. My God.' Then, in a hushed voice, adding, 'I never....'

I laughed, more excited than Rudy, if that was possible. 'Let's count out the usual twenty quid packets in small notes. Then, I want to take a look at these documents.'

'Rosen's documents?'

The smile froze on my face. I stared at Rudy for a long time, my helmet lamp shining directly into my friend's face. My mind screamed of doubt and betrayal.

'How did you find out?' I demanded. My brain was unable to grasp how Rudy knew Gabe's documents were worth more to me than his cash.

'No need to look at me like that,' Rudy said.

'Like what?'

'As though I were a stranger, a threat.'

'Well,' I said, 'how did you know I was interested in Gabe's stuff?'

'Because I saw you putting some papers in a separate pile. And I read Rosen's name from here. Come on, Sunni. We've been through too much together for you not to trust me now.'

'What do you mean? I trust you. I trust you.'

'The look in your eyes,' he said. 'Your teeth bared as though you were going to kill me.'

'Sorry, mate. It's the reflection from the helmet lamps distorting my grin of triumph. Okay?'

Rudy grimaced. 'Course it is. I should have known that.'

But it was not a triumphant grin. Rudy knew that, and my cheeks burned in the half-light.

'Yes,' I said. 'Rosen's documents came as a complete surprise. What a bonus that was. I've kept them to one side.'

'You have a plan for that stuff?'

'Soon enough, Gabe will conclude it was me, and he'll come after me. I need special protection that you blokes don't.'

'Fine with me,' Rudy said. 'I've already forgotten about it. Will you tell the others the total swag?'

'They're entitled to know. Yeah. Let's get out of here.'

30. Treasure Trove Revealed

Friday, April 9.

Nine weeks after the heist, with the window closed in my bedroom and the curtains drawn, I discovered a treasure trove of evidence among the documents from Gabe's box. I had enough documented proof to expose his involvement in tax fraud and put him in prison for many years and longer for graft and corruption of police, politicians and other government officials. However, the evidence would have no value once used, and employed recklessly would lead to my downfall. Without a solid plan, I would be risking my life. I needed a foolproof way to blackmail Gabe while keeping the upper hand.

Emotions ran high when the gang gathered at the Balmain Hotel for payday and a celebration. The mood in our hotel room was a mixture of anticipation for the money and wariness for the weeks of risk ahead. Bound by a common purpose, we were not out of the deep water yet and had to maintain separation in public. Identify as a gang and spark a suspicion that might bring us down? No sir, Ma'am.

The press had dubbed us The Racetrack Raiders, sensationalising our daring, guessing our haul to be in the millions of pounds, and transforming us into cult celebrities, the twentieth-century Ned Kellys and Thunderbolts. At the same time, they clamoured for our capture, demanded justice and the ousting of the police minister this week and the commissioner the next while relishing the irony of bookmakers losing their shirts to a bunch of thieves. We were notorious yet heroic. Our names whispered in hushed tones as though legendary rebels had risen to challenge the aristocracy.

Underlying the celebration was my urgency to uplift my boys, urge patience and planning for their prosperous new lives and ensure there would be no slip-ups that would put our new wealth at risk. The party was loud, drunken, unabashed, and uncontrollable.

Becker skylarked, danced, and sang. How long would it take Jess to distance herself from him when she discovered the risky life he would lead as one of the Racetrack Raiders, and how much damage would he wreak on her life?

Our lives hung in the balance, poised between, on the one hand, victory, triumph, glory, gloating, wallowing and elation, and, on the other, defeat, tragedy, heartbreak, catastrophe, and prison.

After an hour of partying, we grew more mellow. Marty told us he had made a deposit on a house twenty yards from the beach at Coogee. It was comfortable, he said, but not flashy; stylish, but not likely to appear in *House and Garden*, four bedrooms and two inside toilets and not grand enough to draw attention. The house cost seven thousand pounds, and he would settle the contract and take possession early in August. He also had an order in for a brand-new FJ Holden, another thousand quid.

'I've found a thirty-year-old woman to share my good luck,' he told us. 'She believes a long-lost, wealthy uncle died in Ireland and left me a few bob, and I've found a job as a doorman at the Cricketers Club.'

Rudy had always talked about life in the Queensland sun and the enormous opportunities to be had there and had put a deposit on ten acres of sub-dividable waterfront land at the quiet village of Southport and would settle in August. He planned to operate a caravan park on the way to becoming a legitimate multi-millionaire with four kids to inherit his wealth.

Benny had quietly married a family friend he had been courting before the heist and leased five hundred acres of prime farming land at Pokolbin in the Hunter Valley, New South Wales, where he intended to settle, build a house, and plant grapes when his ship came in. His contract gave him the first right of refusal to buy the property until the end of the year.

Horlicks cheerfully reported he had stayed out of serious trouble but spent every penny of his twenty pounds partying around Sydney, drinking, and generally enjoying the life. 'But, Sunni, don't worry. My friends think I'm spending my father's small inheritance.'

After lunch in the hotel room, eating prawns and sharing a bottle of champagne, congratulating each other and reliving the heist, I said, 'Time to leave. We go separately, remember. We don't know who might be following. If two are together, the followers immediately know two of the gang, and it won't be long before they have tabs on all of us.'

'Okay, boss. Okay. Right again.'

'If anyone notices something strange, send a telegram to Skeet, care of the Newcastle Post Office. You have the box number. Skeet will check the box twice each day.'

Skeet had remained in Newcastle to be close to me and wait for the big day when he would collect and move to Lismore and build his Mum a new house on her dairy farm. I had neglected Skeet to spend more time at The Dudley, but I put that on the back burner while considering my plan for Gabe.

It was Payback Time.

31. Payback Time

O h, how I burned for an audience to witness my sweet taste of vengeance as I ran Gabe out of this town. Today's encounter would be a stunning contrast from when I met him at the dawn gallops. It would not be merely my plundering his wealth and jewellery fuelling Gabe's resentment and not the loss of title deeds to his properties. No, the true devastation would be the blow to his self-esteem and the freefall of his reputation in a domain where ego and prestige reigned supreme.

I deliberately held off to savour the moment, remembering how Gabe callously blew Becker off the last time we met at dawn, then had him beaten half to death.

Today, there was the same rising sun, the same smell of stale horse shit and the mellow music of horses—the creaking of saddles, the clink of iron buckles, the snorts of a baritone stallion. But the tension was unmistakable and had precious little to do with the simpering star at his side. I didn't need to tell Gabe the Sydney gangs whispering behind their hands would openly laugh and mock him if the word got out that a woman had single-handedly taken down the mighty Gabe Rosen. The robbery had provoked contempt for him among his gangland peers, and Gabe, no doubt to salvage some small measure of pride, was deflecting suspicion towards the Chicago mafia.

Despite the heavy artillery he had available to deal with other crises, the documents I held stymied him, and he knew I would not hesitate to use them against him.

'I'll meet you at dawn,' he had demanded, 'or not at all. Come with all the stuff you stole from me, or bring an army, because you'll need it.'

'I'll come alone, Gabe. And don't be such a bully.'

And I came. Alone.

I swaggered forward and held out a hand, 'Morning, Gabe.'

'G'day, Sunni.' He raised a glass mug, 'Join me in a hot toddy. It's a great way to kick off the day. Whisky to warm you, honey to set your body going, and spices to spark the brain.'

'Thanks, Mr Rosen,' deliberately expressing respect, using the title though I lacked the respect. 'But I don't drink whisky at dawn.'

Gabe drank, delaying, and blew out a ragged breath. 'If you try to play me for a fool,' his voice catching on the words, 'you'll regret it.'

'Why do you say that?'

He glanced at me and then away.

I said, 'Would you like to walk for a while?'

A stable hand dressed in white overalls materialised from the gloom and disappeared as quickly when Rosen snarled and flicked his fingers.

'Did you lose a lot of cash?' I asked.

'I have plenty of that,' he said nonchalantly, his hands in his pockets to deny I scared the hell out of him when I told him on the phone he was in trouble with the taxman.

'Rumour has it you have hotels and casinos and nightclubs that the Tax Department doesn't know about, and your financier, Mr Greenwald, might be getting a bit pushy about you repaying the debt.'

'Nah. That's not right.'

I allowed the silence to stress that point. 'But I have a lot to learn from you,' I said. 'I'm ambitious enough to take over your business here and send you to Sydney. You did nicely, in Sydney, until you lost control.'

For a long while, we were quiet. Gabe ran his fingers through his hair, and we listened to horses neighing and men talking in the distance. While we waited, a breeze blew in to disperse the mist and open the way for an autumn sun.

Gabe said, 'You don't know about racing,' his voice taking on an edge. 'You don't know which coppers to pay off, which judges, public servants. You don't know how to handle the casino or the new gambling machines. You know sweet F. A. You are no use to me.'

'Yeah, but you'd be a good teacher.'

'You have a cheek, Sunni.'

'Yes. I suppose. Whoever did the robbery would want to be secure and would need to launder the cash, which they wouldn't know how to. They'd need to satisfy the Tax Department on how their reported income was enough for a flash house, like the one you live in on the hill, and a big car. They'd need to keep the syndicate's loyalty, too.'

'In return for what?'

'I suppose, for one thing, you would not have to give your money to the taxman—or go to prison. That's two things.'

Gabe shuffled his feet. Pushed his hands deeper into his pockets. 'What are you saying?'

'I don't have any proposals because I took no part in the robbery. Suppose you employed me as your next in line with an agreement that I take over your businesses in Newcastle. Gave me an Oldsmobile and title to your house on the hill. I would lease it for six months to avoid suspicious activity and then claim the title. House must be worth a few quid.'

'I haven't the cash left to be generous like that.'

'Yes,' I said, 'but the bastard who robbed you does.'

He waited to find what other clues I might offer, but I wasn't playing his game.

Gabe said, 'I'd need money to move on Sydney.'

'Two thousand should do it.'

'Two?' Flapping the air away with the back of his hand. 'You're joking. Security wouldn't allow me inside my own casino.'

'Well, how much did this bloke steal from you?'

'Cash, you mean? Forty thou, and don't gossip about that.'

'C'mon, mate. That much wouldn't fit in your box. Not with the jewellery and the documents.'

The warming sun was up, the sky clear, and we leant on the fence at the side of the track, with one foot on the low rail. I broke off a stem of green grass, held it in my teeth, and refrained from interrupting his deep thoughts. This was not the time to hurry the man.

After a while, he said, 'I don't believe you have the stuff.'

'Keep your eyes open,' I said, 'and put your hands in your pockets.'

Gabe's hands rushed to his pockets, and one came out with a five-carat diamond and ruby ring.

'You're dead when they find you, Sunni.'

'Dead dumb?' I asked.

'No.' He laughed. 'Dead smart. Would this bastard you're talking about like to come to the Casino Saturday evening and do a deal?'

'No. They'd prefer to wait while all the paperwork gets done by the lawyers. Maybe seven or eight weeks.'

'They'd return all my documents? All my jewellery? Twenty-five thousand?'

'They would keep the jewels a woman might wear and the title on the French cottage the taxman doesn't know about. I bet this robbing bastard would like a little cottage in France like the one described in your deposit box.'

'It's not a fucking cottage. It's a fourteen-room mansion at Neuilly-sur-Seine, near the Longchamp Racecourse.'

'Title to the French mansion, then,' I said with a straight face. 'And ten thousand.'

Gabe squared to me, his hands tucked into the pockets of his jeans. 'Twenty, and I'll throw in my stable, but no horses.'

'Let's say this robbing bastard gives you twelve thousand, and you give them the jewellery, an Oldsmobile, the house on the hill, the casino, the mansion in Paris, and two good race-winning horses. And this bastard gives you the documents but keeps a selection to be sure you don't set your mates on to them or tell the syndicate who robbed the bookies.'

'Half the crims in Australia will work it out and come after you.'

'That's why I'm talking to you. Because they'll think twice if they believe I'm on your payroll. But I'm not. I'm taking over your Newcastle operation. It will all belong to me—all mine. You walk away to Sydney. Half the crims in Australia will not know the real situation. I'll ask the robbing bastard for thirteen thousand, and I'm sure he'll agree.'

'No one takes my casino off me. No one.'

'Forget the freehold, then. I'll own the business and pay a nominal rent.'

'Why would I let you keep some documents?'

'I'll keep stuff that would interest the taxman and land you and the coppers you bribed behind bars at Long Bay Gaol.'

I gave him time to be clear on the way ahead and said, 'I will have Hector Larcombe draw up the contracts. You'll not miss Newcastle, Mr Rosen. It's a little coal town. Sydney is where they keep the real gold.'

32. The Great Pretender

Thursday, May 6.

Hector Larcombe OBE shunned inquisitive eyes that might be witness to our meetings, so we did our business after dark at his home on twenty acres outside Fletcher, a thirty-minute commute to Hunter Street, in a charming four-bedroom homestead that gave the lie to his tatty office.

Gabe had wasted little time mourning his losses and tackled the details of handing over his business to me. Within three weeks, his lawyer had drawn a form of agreement. After intense negotiation among the lawyers—Hector representing me—the six-month lease, the contract to buy his house on the hill, and the horses passed quietly, conditional on settlement of the Neuilly property, to Mary Ang and Co., Pty Ltd, a company registered in Bermuda that no one would easily trace to me. Gabe had already relocated to Sydney.

'Transfer of the Neuilly-Sur-Seine property,' Hector said, 'will take at least another month. The French are slow. For God's sake, Sunni, what will you do with racehorses? You know nothing. It's casting pearls before swine. The horses are a liability, eating their heads off while the trainers and handlers take your money. You need ten times what you have to own racehorses.'

'Thanks for your advice,' I said. 'But I'll keep the horses. I'll hand over half the cash now but none of the documents until my trainer inspects the horses and the French property settles.'

Hector sighed. 'You are such a smart Alec. I shouldn't waste my hard-earned advice, but I will. You tell yourself, do this one job, and you'll be rich and never have to do it again. Except, life doesn't work like that. The excitement burns into your blood until there is only ugliness ruining the lives of everyone around you. If you don't believe that, you are worse than stupid.'

I played along with him, though not believing a word of it. 'As long as you are on a two-guinea half-hour,' I said, 'then tell me what I should do.'

'Find a way to bury that part of you destroying the rest, or you'll never have peace. No crook I know has ever managed that, so it probably will not happen.'

The farm was in the highlands, and autumn was well-advanced. Hector lit a fire and sipped a dark red wine from the Hunter Valley. His was a lifestyle I wanted, and when he offered again, I said yes, I'd try it—a 1948 Rosehill Shiraz.

He described the wine as rich and intense, with an elegant floral nose. It tasted like the red I sold in our dining room, but if I wanted to live the stately life, I would have to learn the ropes, and after half an hour and a refill, I enjoyed the buzz and, strangely, the acid taste disappeared.

Business finished, Hector said, 'Over a beer at Tatts with Dominic Towers and Cam Bacon, the bookies you robbed, your name came up as a possible beneficiary of the heist but was quickly discounted. By spreading malicious gossip, Tommo convinced Dominic it was a Melbourne razor gang.'

'That's funny,' I said. 'There are no razor gangs or gangsters in Melbourne. I'll start a rumour it was a Hong Kong gang.'

Hector swished a mouthful of Shiraz, then continued. 'For now, Chief Inspector Cummins is telling Tommo what to say and muddying the waters, but don't underestimate him. A dingo in a trap has fangs. I don't know how you sleep at night knowing how many people want a slice of you.'

'It's a matter of showing confidence, Judge,' I said. 'Cummins and people like him believe I will hurt them more than they will hurt me.' I think the elegantly nosey Shiraz was answering for me. 'I find it entertaining that you and I are partners in crime. The Judge and the Woman-of-Repute. What an unlikely affair it is. Don't worry. I'll handle Tommo and Cummins and anything anyone throws at me.'

Saturday night, I moped in my A70 in the street outside my new house—though it hadn't settled yet—daydreaming about Albie Fowler and wondering if Tommo did him in. I would be disappointed in Tommo if I found he had. I thought he was a man of high morals. From the hill, I watched the lightning flash on the dark horizon, and, on the esplanade far below me, an older man taking the air was rugged against the cold autumn breeze.

Sleep kept its distance; I hadn't left The Dudley except to drive around and maybe get a hamburger and cuppa, and when I finally dozed, I dreamt of Jess with Becker. Are they in love? Up here alone, outside my new home on the hill overlooking the ocean, with all the money in the world, a vital something was missing. How do I know what love is?

I switched on the wireless and twirled the knob until The Platters were on, singing "The Great Pretender."

33. A Prayer, an Engagement and Jealousy

Sunday, May 9.

I hesitated before stepping through the grand entrance into the cathedral, the dim light embracing me after the change from bright sunlight and the outside chill lingering in the floor tiles and sandstone walls. A fragile believer, my faith wavered with each new day, yet I admit that church bells stirred me to a profound sense of tranquillity and contentment. It was as though every Sunday was another magical Christmas Day.

Since the heist, I attended every Sunday, and, on this day, I paused to search the pews for a familiar face among the congregation. I was a regular donor to church activities at such a generous level that most worshippers forgave my past transgressions or at least overlooked them. I was on nodding terms with many in the diocese. Given my recent activities, I stepped inside gingerly, half-expecting a lightning bolt to carry me off to a warmer, less forgiving place.

And there was Jessica, alone towards the rear of the church. I walked down the central aisle, accompanied by the sounds through the open doors of boys playing football and men chattering, reluctant to join their wives inside, and sat next to her. I leaned in to whisper, 'Happy twentieth birthday, Jessica. I'm surprised to see you here.'

'I've come to pray for Franzi and for guidance.'

'Guidance?' I said, unsure whether to frown or smile.

'He's asked me to marry him.'

The organ struck up a thundering hymn, and the procession of priests and altar boys moving down the aisle joined the seated congregation in singing with vigour and enthusiasm, their combined efforts preventing further conversation,

Silly for Jessica to think of marriage at twenty. Foolish for me to think at all.

Mind your own business, Sunni.

He's a criminal.

Yes, but the bookies are not genuine victims.

The Racetrack Raid makes Becker an entrepreneur and international adventurer—a man on the way to wealth—a man the world had to reckon with.

Have they been to bed together?

After the service, we sat together in a shadowy corner of the nave. 'Don't look shocked,' Jessica said.

I chose my words carefully. 'It's that he's a bit … shady.'

'He wouldn't harm me. You're saying because he has money, he must be dangerous.' Jessica wiped her eyes with a lace handkerchief and peered around the church as though she'd never sat in the pews or admired the stained-glass windows and the timber roof beams. 'At school, Franzi charmed all the teachers. He was funny. You'd have loved him.'

'I did notice you and your Franzi becoming good friends,' I said.

'Now he calls you his adventurer, his buccaneer. "How's your exotic Blackbeard?" I ask, and he laughs. I think he likes you.'

'Come on. It's a lovely day. Let's walk to the river.'

On the water, a pair of sailing dinghies turned about, caught the wind and sped away. Noisy gulls fed on a school of fish. Church bells chimed the midday hour, and I pointed to a cloud, 'What do you see?' I asked.

'A dolphin, but it's changing into a whale and now a puppy. It's funny how clouds change. Like people.'

Bells pealed; the breeze carried freshly cut grass and the river. Footsteps passed by on the concrete path. I wanted to admit that she saw me at Tatts and to describe how I robbed the bookies. I wanted to confess to being The Scarlet Pimpernel who had pulled off the biggest heist of the century, and now, wealthy beyond dreams, I would have a house on the hill and an Oldsmobile, and maybe some jewellery if I could wangle it. Most of all, I needed to warn her that man is a short step up from the wolves that roam the desolate tundra and that her Franzi was a wolf, and they would spend their lives roaming the lonely cities across the world to stay ahead of the hunters.

Then, in my daydream, I wore that dazzling green ball gown again, stepping from my Olds and swanking to the lift in a cloud of Chanel Number Five.

We are given only one life to live.

'Come on, Jess,' I said. 'I'll buy you a beautiful green dress to celebrate your engagement.'

We passed two elegant women strolling on the esplanade, and I wanted to wrap my arms around Jess and boast to her how I put one over Gabe Rosen and had enough to buy her anything she wanted. 'Where could we buy the most beautiful frock in Newcastle?'

'I've always wanted to shop at the Corona building. Some lovely fashion shops there. Rockmans, and Mamselle.'

'For you, anything.'

She drew herself up, puffed out air and smiled. 'I have something to tell you. It must always be our secret.'

Jessica giggled. I raised my eyebrows to encourage her confession.

'Armed robbery,' she said quietly, fear and fury discarded, dealt with. 'I can handle that.'

She raised a hand to halt my exclamations of surprise and alarm.

'With all his comings and goings and the secrecy, and suddenly I'm to have a new dress, and we're to be married and living in a grand style in a grand house. I guessed he was in the robbery with you, though I haven't said anything to Franzi. Why should I be poor and everyone else wealthy? I never want to be poor again. No one will remember after we die.'

'But you're guessing about the robbery?' I said.

'He hasn't confessed or anything, but I saw you.'

'Best to keep it that way, Jessica. For your sake.'

An open-mouthed smile ignited Jessica's face, and she stood to throw out her arms and do a little jig. 'I'll be a woman of wealth and influence. I asked if I should put up with his strange ways or take the money. I tossed a coin, and I went for it. Maybe he'll find love as people say you do.'

Her eyes widened, her face and neck flushed with colour, and she laid a hand on my arm. 'Oh, Sunni, I'm so happy. A girl might do a lot worse than marry Franz Becker.'

I hung a smile on my face. 'Oh, Jessica, if you say your Franzi is true blue, I will go with that. After all, a lot of people out there,' as I flicked a thumb at the congregation chatting outside the cathedral, 'would say I made my money easily, too. But, when you have a few quid to share, people accept you for what you are.'

'Like Mr Rosen,' Jessica said. 'Everywhere he goes, people fawn over him. Important people. Or should I say people who believe they're important?'

'Others are contemptuous.' I stared into space for a while. 'Oh, some sneer at me, too. Behind their hands. Some openly. They flick a finger as I walk past, as though I were a dust mite. Some of the wives get agitated at me, too. But I laugh and carry on. Mostly, they envy me and dream about doing what I did to have a little fun and get a better life.'

'Franz wants me to move into the Dudley with him. Is that all right?'

She wasn't asking about the rent; she was questioning the entire Christian culture that denied the right of women to have sex with men before marriage. Women who cohabited with a man faced ostracism from married and single women of all walks of life while they accepted the man in question. After all, boys would be boys.

I took Jessica's arm. 'I don't have a problem with that, but be sure you understand the risks and take precautions. Pregnancy before marriage can be a rough road to travel. Come on, love. Let's buy that green dress. Then I'll shout you to the best lunch in Newcastle to celebrate. Oysters, lobster and champers.'

After lunch, I would check with Hector. Is it true that a married person cannot give evidence against their spouse? That is, if the snake ever gets into the chicken coop.

34. Why Did the Cock Crow Thrice?

Saturday, June 5.

I needed to celebrate my triumph, to shout aloud my daring. I needed it in bold headlines on the front page of *The Herald* so I could boast that I robbed Newcastle and bested Gabe Rosen, and was unquestionably a woman who counted. Seized by a sudden recognition of the absurdity of it all, I buried my head in the pillow, burrowed under the blanket and suppressed my laughter. Dangerous to think like that.

I left the bedroom in my slippers and warm dressing gown and headed for the kitchen. It was a wintry night, two weeks after Jess came to live at The Dudley and be with her Franzi, and I was sleepless again. It was so strange that I was probably Australia's most successful female bushranger, yet I could not tell anyone; my exhilaration evaporated, and I didn't sleep for worrying.

I thought I'd make tea and toast a slice of bread, but Becker's voice cut through the hallway as I approached the kitchen.

'Do you want to make toast and vegemite for me?'

But Jessica, who was already there, sounded in a sulk as if she hadn't slept either. 'Go and make it yourself,' her voice rising. 'You say you love me, but you don't want to toast a slice of bread for me?'

Their voices echoed from the walls. My skin prickled with the electricity of an imminent storm. I retreated into the hall where I could see and hear as Jessica's frustration boiled over.

She shouted, 'You never listen, Franz. It's like I'm talking to the wall.'

Becker shrugged. 'What's the big deal? Relax.'

Her eyes blazed, she raised a hand to strike. 'You don't love me. Not properly. It's like you don't even care for me.'

He scoffed. 'That's over the top, Jess. It's not so serious.'

She covered her ears and screaming shook her head as though she wanted it off. 'Serious? You don't get it, do you?'

Becker turned away from her. He muttered, 'Fine, if you're gunna be like that, go ahead.'

It seemed to me that The Dudley, once their love nest, was to witness Becker's fall from grace and Jessica's desperate need for understanding.

'I've talked to my friends,' Jessica went on. 'It's not right. Why did you bother to ask me to move in with you? And I'm not your slave girl. Get your own toast.'

Jessica stormed past where I skulked behind my half-closed door and ran to her room. Less than a minute later, she reappeared in jeans and a sweater and fled towards the side door, flushed, almost tripping over me. Then, the doorbell jangled. She faltered and spun about in an uncertain circle once, then again.

The bell rang a second time. I felt like a prying landlady, so I stepped into the dark hall.

Jess adjusted her sweater, plumped her hair and, still angry, threw the door open to Skeet standing on the mat, smiling unconvincingly.

'Can I come in?' he slurred his practised words. 'Becker and me. We're best friends. I need to talk to him.'

'It's late,' Jess said. 'And you're drunk.'

Skeet wiped a hand across his dripping nose and turned cautious red eyes on her. 'S'important.'

'Go right in. Loverboy is in the kitchen, and I'm leaving. You can make his toast and vegemite.' She pushed her way past him into the street.

I watched her sprint downhill towards the beach where a solitary streetlamp cast sparkling reflections on a patch of breaking, white surf in a pitch-black world. Pine trees moaned, their cones and needles tumbling and rustling. A cat screeched. I saw her reach the sand, and her shadow paddling in the shallow water.

Skeet's voice whined from the kitchen, but Becker raced past me and out the door to pursue Jess. Concerned for Jess, I followed.

I heard pebbles rattle in a landslide at the road's edge, and in the soft light of a full moon, saw a figure scramble over rocks, apelike in its silhouette from the streetlamp's reflection. I searched desperately, but the shadows hid her from me. A yelp above the sound of the wind, an obscenity spoken, heavy boots running on shingles, and a darker shadow plunged out of the night in the shape of Cedric, a miner who fished at night to help feed his wife and five children, and, for a fleeting moment, I thought his arm reached out to her.

Becker closed on the sounds of Jessica's scream, and she screamed again above the sounds of punches given and received. Poor Cedric, he was no rapist. I hoped that he would clout Becker.

Becker's voice came from the darkness, 'I'll kill you,' but Cedric's sport was rugby, and he would give as good as he received. There were sounds in the darkness then there was the surf and wind whistling in the pines, and I returned to my home knowing that no damage would come to Jessica.

Ten minutes later, the sweet smell of perfume was followed by Jess and the warmth as she came in through the door. Becker hugged her trembling body close, and I heard their whispered questions and declarations of love, and fumbling kisses as the passion took them, and I fell into bed alone and didn't care that his nose was bleeding. It sometimes takes strange behaviour to excite men.

'Forget the past,' I heard Becker say as their door closed. 'We'll start again.'

Jessica joined me for an early breakfast, looking like a woman whose man had loved her well. She hadn't slept, she said, but Becker was out to it. Before dawn broke, he confessed his sins to her, his cowardice in the face of the violent relationship between his mother and father, how he abandoned his sergeant on a Korean battlefield to be tortured after saving Becker's life, and his role in the bookie heist. He talked about his ambitions and how much money he had. He told her what they would buy with it and vowed to give it all to her if she would marry him despite his strange ways. Jessica thought it wasn't bragging but a true confession and a plea for forgiveness. She took his breath away when, instead of rebuking him, she told him she knew most of it and gave him an unconditional pardon.

'He's had such a hard life with too much violence and may never be good in bed,' Jessica said. 'But I will work with what I've got, and it will all come good.'

Jessica left the kitchen, but before I could go to my room to change, Skeet, hungover and hungry, clumped down the stairs in heavy boots, came into the kitchen's warmth, and sat in the chair she had vacated. He had stayed the night in a spare room—another free-loader.

'Tea.' I slid the pot across the pine table and cocked a thumb at a toaster plugged in on a side bench. 'Toast. Boil as many eggs as you want.'

Skeet sidled about the kitchen, trying to be unobtrusive while taking in the painted cupboards, the cold wood fire range in the old stove recess, blacked and redundant, a separate gas oven and cookers and a tap dripping into the sink overflowing with cups and plates. He rinsed a cup and filled it from the teapot.

'What was so important,' I asked, 'that you had to come here last night and wake us?'

'Uh, I forgot to tell you,' Skeet said. 'Horlicks sent a telegram from Melbourne to me at the post office box. It was long, about ordering a brand-new DeSoto Coupe. I think he was pissed. He's such a bigmouth.'

'And dangerous,' I said. 'A mistake. I'll slip along to Sydney and talk to him.'

Skeet dipped a finger in the honey and sucked on it. 'Sorry I disturbed you, last night.' He was jumpy and anxious, the way veteran soldiers who could no longer handle the brutality of peace behaved before they put a gun to their heads. He probably had more to say, and I didn't want to pressure him, but I had other things to do, and he outwaited me.

'Skeet, is there anything more?'

'Nah. Visiting is all.'

I might have avoided a lot of heartaches if I had waited. But I failed to hear the cock crow three times, and Skeet charged off, haunted by the dread of capture and reprisal.

35. Timebomb Walking

Wednesday, June 9.

Three days after Jess's dramatic departure and subsequent reconciliation with Becker, Skeet stumbled into The Dudley, reeking of whisky and drunk as a wandering parson. His words slurred, his conscience lay heavy, and he complained of having no one to talk to. Behind the bar, with closing time nowhere in sight, I was busy pouring drinks, bantering with my boys, and reluctant to listen to Skeet's ramblings because I knew what he wanted to say. What Skeet may have guessed, but which I had no intention of telling him, was that Becker's love life had found a fresh start with his reconciliation and lovemaking only three nights ago. Things were looking up for Jessica, and Skeet was jealous.

'We are not supposed to mix with others from the gang,' I muttered. 'Remember?'

But Skeet was unusually aggressive. 'Becker is too wrapped up in his love life to talk to me.'

I skated along the bar to fill two glasses and returned after a few minutes.

'Always someone to talk to in a bar,' he mumbled. 'I wouldn't mind having a bar.'

'I'm sorry, mate.' The expression on my face would drag him from his depression or send him on his way. 'If you're looking at me for a job, forget it. This place needs a psychiatrist, not more bar staff.'

With a cheeky wink over the top of his schooner, he chugged his beer and said, 'Own a bar, and you always have someone to talk to. I could go partners in a bar with Mr Rosen now that I've got money. Money attracts money, you know.'

I leaned across the bar and spoke cautiously. 'Oh wow. You know Mr Rosen. Good for you. A partnership, eh? Be careful there. He's the bloke you robbed of his life's savings.'

'He lost a fortune.'

'Yes, and if he gets a whiff of who did it, that's a sticky end for you and the gang who robbed him. Wait there, Skeet.' And I moved to refill empty glasses at the end of the bar.

'Mr Rosen is smart,' Skeet said when I returned, fumbling with his glass and sliding it across for another drink. 'I reckon he would go partners with me. He's high up, you know, but if he suspects Becker—'

I wiped the taps, washed the glasses, and waltzed around pouring beer for other drinkers but frequently returned to keep the conversation going. Let him take out his jealousy on me. I have big shoulders.

'Why would Mr Rosen suspect Becker?' I asked.

'Did I say suspect? Nah, I meant *respect*. But... you know about his world. You know about money and bookies and stuff. I know Mr Rosen from the Tatts Club.'

'So, you did talk to Mr Rosen about Tatts, ' I accused him, alarm bells clashing in my head.

'Yeah, just a few words to feel him out.' Skeet paled. His eyes rushed around the bar, and his hand shook. 'No, Sunni. Not what you think. Not that. Becker would kill me, and, besides, Mr Rosen said I could tell no one he talked to me.'

'What did you tell him about the robbery?'

'No, not that. Mr Rosen told me if I heard anything about Becker to report it to him, and he'd be generous.' He looked around the bar. 'No. I... Buy my bar. Have someone to talk to. That's all. Yeah. I don't know about business. I need a partner is all. Mr Rosen... or you?'

'Another beer, Skeet? On the house.' I had nothing to laugh about. Skeet's gossip had me riveted to the floor. To protect the gang, could I do what Kitty would do without a second thought?

'A whisky, please, Sunni. Make it a single malt from Scotland. I'll pay.' He gave darting glances at the door whenever it clacked open. 'Not on the house—I got cash,' he insisted, downing the single-malt. 'There's no one to talk to now Becker's having it on with Jessica.' He coughed and beat his chest.

I leaned close. 'I know someone to give you the right advice—a good lawyer. Have a chat with him. Might be the best way.'

'Yeah? A lawyer? Nah.'

I shook my head and tried not to sound angry. 'If I were you,' I said, 'I'd stay clear of Becker and Mr Rosen. Becker has all the trouble he can handle. You don't want him to hear you talking about Tatts and Mr. Rosen. Do you?'

'You're smart, Sunni,' he babbled. 'Yeah. No. Did you know Shanks?'

'Lou?' I polished the bar as though it was sterling silver. 'Yeah, I knew Lou.'

'Poor bloke.' Skeet rattled the ice in his empty whisky glass. 'Poor old bloke. How …' The question did not break through to his tongue. 'It's stuffy in here… Wait a bit. I'll—'

I spoke softly, my hand holding his across the bar. 'Skeet, do you know the true story about Lou?' Did I want confirmation to provide an excuse for what Kitty would do?

Skeet held an unsteady finger to the side of his nose. 'Between you and… between me, it wasn't entirely an accident, his death. Not entirely.' He pushed his glass towards me. 'I'll have another one of those. No. Not entirely.' He loosened his hand to belch and put it again on the bar for me to hold. 'Coroner said… weak heart…' His unfocused eyes squinted lifelessly at nothing. 'Gotta go outside. Fresh air.' There was a touch of panic in his voice. On the edge of a breakdown.

'No,' I said. 'Wait here. Have a glass of water.'

Head loose on his shoulders, eyes wild, losing his grip on my hand and maybe on the world, he made a rush for the door.

'Billy, look after the bar.' I came out from behind it, weaved through the crush to the door and found him crouching among bushes in the vacant lot next door, rain driven in from the sea nibbling at the dirt on his face, unsteady, alone, wrapped in the mixed smell of wet grass, rotting mud and vomit. 'Will you live, Skeet?'

He nodded and made a lopsided grin. 'I haven't been drunk like this since the night we celebrated in that Balmain bar. What a night. We cheered, hooted, and brayed at everything and nothing. I drank whisky and champagne until I threw up on the lavatory floor and woke in bed with Tonio.'

'Do you think you should come in out of the rain?'

Skeet retreated to the awning over the footpath at the Dudley, his afternoon wearing on with me keeping an eye on him through the window. Sobered a little from the cool air, he came inside and leant against the bar, raising a heavy hand to miners coming and going and patronising him because they had all been in the same state at one time or another.

A knobbly old miner, his face permanently stained and blackened, ambled over and spoke to him. Skeet coughed and swallowed, sobered a little, mumbled inaudibly, wiped his mouth on his sleeve and held on to the bar for support while the ancient miner mumbled, apologising to me about a pit pony, the electric, and the lights in section six.

Back at his place at the bar, Skeet addressed a spot on the floor at his feet. 'I'm through with Becker,' he said. 'He was the one. I loved him with all my heart, but he's got Jessica now and discarded me like an old floppy mop.'

'There you go, Skeet, love. That's how life goes sometimes. Are you a bit over the top? You want to think about going home?'

'Fowler chased Shanks into the surf, but Becker should have blocked him. I drove the car, and that's all. Becker's... big trouble. I'll have that whisky now.'

So, Fowler had chased Lou into the surf. Skeet was the driver.

'Are you sure, mate? I'd give it a skip. You're a bit gone to be drinking expensive Scotch and telling secrets.'

'No worries. I can afford to drink as much as I like. By the way—'

After a while, I returned from serving another customer and gave him a soda water. 'You said, by the way?'

'Did I? By the way, what?'

I leaned across the bar again. 'Let me guess. Suppose you had murdered someone—'

Skeet shushed me with a finger to his boozy lips and told me he had asked a friend in the police about the death penalty. He described a hypothetical situation—a bank robbery and the guard shot dead—then asked, 'Would the driver hang too?'

Skeet was unhappy with the answer, and it was little comfort when his police friend said the government was introducing a law to stop the death penalty, so, next year, if the politicians sprang off their arses, the whole gang would spend the rest of their lives in prison, the driver, too.

Skeet tried to drink but gulped, and the water went down the wrong way. 'God, Sunni. No. No... not the driver.' Then, spluttering, banging his chest with a fist, he cried, 'By the way, you mentioned a lawyer.'

'Hector Larcombe.'

'I'll remember that.'

'No, you won't. Here's his card. Go to him tomorrow. Wait. I'll come to make sure you get there. Skeet, go home now and don't speak to a soul about you-know-what. Hurry. The bus comes by in four minutes. I'll collect you at eight in the morning.'

'Thanks, Sunni. Thanks.'

'Especially don't speak to Mr Rosen. You're a walking time bomb, and everyone near you will likely cop the shrapnel.'

36. Take Only What You Can Carry

Thursday, June 10.

'Jump in, Skeet,' I said, deducing from the smell of whisky he had breakfasted. Skeet sat gingerly in the front seat of the Ford, hands on his knees, silent, head lowered, spilling furtive glances towards me.

He was scared. Dumb and afraid and ready to admit his sins to the nearest police and beg for mercy. And drinking whisky in the morning. Now, there's a fiery combination.

'Skeet,' I said, 'you need to change your life. First, that nickname. What's your real name, again? Say it slowly.'

'Giambattista Fulvio La Rocca.'

'You'll have to be Gianni or Johnny.'

Skeet shivered. 'I'm innocent, Sunni. I didn't kill Shanks.'

'Who did kill him? I asked gently.'

'It was... it was an accident.'

'Tell me.'

We followed Hunter Street with the river on our left. A North-easter was blowing, and the Stockton ferry was bouncing about in the channel and having trouble docking.

'Albie had a violent nature,' Skeet said. 'He insisted we had to punish Shanks. Becker was half-hearted but said okay. I told them to count me out if there was to be violence, so Becker said they'd only knock him around a bit to teach him a lesson and encourage him to leave town. There was Becker, Albie and me. I drove the car. Shanks was drunk. He said he wanted to go for a swim and took off to the water without warning. He must have reckoned on getting out past the surf and swimming along the coast for a mile, and he'd be in the clear.'

Skeet blinked and choked. 'Albie raced after him. Then, I saw a splash of fluorescence when Shanks hit the water. Albie raced into the water, but it was too dark. I lost track of them. Then, five minutes later, Albie came panting and heaving. His long trousers were wet to the knees. He said Shanks was dead.'

Skeet choked again and was silent for a long while. 'I raced along the beach with Becker to check out the body. Sure enough, Shanks was dead. Albie said he wasn't a strong enough swimmer to catch him, and he was up to his knees in the surf when Shanks threw up an arm and went under. Albie said that when the next wave passed, Shanks was stiff and groaning and couldn't get his breath. Albie swore it was a heart attack. We'd be up for murder if the police... So, we chucked the body into the sea and took off.'

Skeet shivered uncontrollably. Unable to speak, he wept.

'Here we are,' I said. 'Let's listen to what Judge Larcombe says about it. Tell the whole truth, but don't tell him how much cash is coming to you, or he'll take you for everything.'

Skeet hiccupped and said, 'I can't tell him about that. I don't know where it's hidden.'

'There, you admitted you and Becker robbed the bookies.'

'No. You can't say that. It's not fair. You tricked me.'

'Well, be sure the judge doesn't trick you too.'

At the top of the stairs, I said, 'Don't rush this.' Then, to the receptionist, 'Announce me to the judge. Wait. Don't bother. I'll tell him.'

I raised my voice, 'Hector. Come out wherever you are. I have a live client for you. Mr Giambattista La Rocca, from Italy.'

'Sunni, my darling. I knew you'd rescue me from the coils of the working classes.' His aura of whisky competed with Skeet's as he held out four long delicate fingers to be shaken, 'Skeet, my good man, how d'ya do? I observe that you are a man of means. Pay me two guineas upfront and a guinea for every fifteen minutes, and I'll assure you of a not guilty verdict.'

'You'll have your fee from me, Judge,' I said. 'When I'm good and ready. A guinea for every thirty minutes. Now the clock's ticking.'

The judge drew on a cigar, waved us to his office, and sat in a creaking swivel chair, indicating a visitors' bench. 'Sit. You say you know the boy, Becker. There may be a conflict of interest, but let me worry about that.' His eyes tried to focus on me. 'Drink?'

'I'm paying, Judge,' I said. 'There'll be no drinking until we're done.'

'Know Mr Rosen, too, do you, Skeet?' the judge asked. 'Touch you up, did he? If we can make a case, he's good for ten thousand pounds—ruined your life, mental breakdown. At least he was good for ten before the robbery.' He leant back, puffed a cigar stub and contemplated a brighter future through the eyes of a politician. 'Some are saying Becker did the bookie job. If you're in his gang, escape while you can, my boy. No future with him. Likely dead before the end of the month.'

Skeet flinched; his cheeks flushed.

The judge shook ash on the carpet. 'The bookie robbery, then.' He consulted his watch. 'Time flies, and I smell a whiff of sulphur. Tell me about it.'

Skeet drained a glass of water and took a half-hour and two guineas to tell the story—Albie Fowler's accidental death, our planning sessions, claiming credit for suggesting Tattersalls Club and locating the barn, the robbery, driving to Sydney in the VW getaway van and the soon to be shared spoils of the crime.

'You poor boy,' the judge said. 'I had no idea. Give me the names and addresses of your fellow robbers. The police are bound to catch them, and we wouldn't want to miss out on the reward money.'

'I don't know anything except first names.'

'That's the worse for you. The crooks will find you and torture you until you tell or die.'

Skeet turned sharply to me.

'We'll not let that happen, love.' I intended to offer immeasurable confidence, a sharing of his burden, and a hint of deep sadness at the injustice of Skeet's world. What I delivered was a shaky hold on compassion. 'Now, Hector,' I said, surprised at the strength in my voice, 'if you expect me to pay, cough up the advice.'

The disrobed judge flapped a hand at the cloud of accumulated cigar smoke, glared at his empty glass with a tear in one bloodshot eye, and in a booming courtroom voice said, 'Steer clear of Becker, stay away from Rosen and run for your life. Go as far away as you can get. Take what money you have and flee this very day. I shall collect your shareholding and keep it in a trust account until you are able to collect it.'

Skeet looked at him, appalled. 'That's not proper advice. I'm not some scared child. I'm a Racetrack Raider.'

'Skeet's right,' I said, less startled because I had known the judge for ten years. 'There's no justice in that, Judge. This boy has worked hard for his money and deserves to keep it.'

'He stole it.'

'From crooks. He's not the first to take a step off the proper track. Why you, a—'

'Must you bring me into this, Sunni?'

'Look at me,' I said to Skeet. 'I'm not a saint. We are here to live our lives, not to be content doing what the bourgeoisie allows us to do. Take pride in your achievement, and Judge Hector will see to it that you lead your life in the luxury due to you.'

Skeet blushed and did his best to fade into the background. 'Meanwhile,' I said, 'you're not safe here. You will have to take off. I'll make certain Becker delivers your share as he promised.'

Hector said, 'Don't allow him to mix you up in it, Sunni.

You are far too beautiful for torture. I'll take a lien on his share now. Into escrow, and take a twenty per cent fee to cover my risk.'

'Forget it, mate. Skeet has satisfied me about Lou's death. I'll take his money from Becker and charge no fee for the trouble.' I dug into my handbag. 'And here's your three guineas.'

'I am a traitor, a Judas, to talk like that to you,' Skeet said to me. 'But I love Becker. I didn't intend to betray him.'

'There's no betrayal in this, love,' I said. 'You needed someone who would understand that Lou was an accident, and, by some incredibly good fortune, you chose me to be your confessor, your woman's shoulder. Lou was my friend, and I am therefore able to forgive you, on his behalf, for your tiny part in it.'

'Thank you, Sunni,' Skeet said. 'Thank you, Judge.'

'Don't thank that old busybody. You found the courage after everything that happened to you, so take the credit for yourself. Now,' I said, throwing an arm around his waist and leading him out the door, 'I've paid Hector, and we're finished here. I'll drive you to Annie's. One day soon, but not yet, when I deliver your share of the heist, you must go away as far as you can. You have family in Calabria. Take your Mum with you and find a home for her there. But don't tell anyone, even me.'

37. No Time for Love

'But I stayed on,' Skeet confessed, his voice trembling. 'I couldn't abandon you to face it alone, without me. Now... this.'

It was noon. We had gathered in the kitchen at The Dudley, Skeet, Becker and Rudy, the tension suffocating as we braced for an onslaught of bad news. Jess was there, also, one of the gang now. There were no more secrets to separate us, and Skeet had come to terms with that hard truth.

'Now what?' I demanded, trying unsuccessfully to steady my voice.

'It's Horlicks.' Skeet, rocking on his feet, was shocked into near sobriety. His face was a shade of ash, his words barely audible. 'You remember Tonio? The barman at the Balmain hotel. He rang soon after you dropped me home from Judge Hector. He was freaking out. Horlicks is as good as dead. He spent twelve hours with mind-blowing wounds on the night train from Melbourne. He's pleading to meet us in Sydney. Three thugs attacked him. Beat him up, tortured him for hours and almost killed him. He gave up my name and Becker's.'

Jessica sobbed quietly. My world was darker, more dangerous than I had ever imagined possible. We faced torture and death from an unknown monster who knew our names.

'He doesn't know where we live,' Skeet said, 'only my phone number and our names, Skeet and Becker. Not yours, Sunni. Horlicks wanted me to tell you that.'

'They have two names,' I noted, the weight of failure crushing me. 'Soon, they'll have it all. Who gave Becker's name to Horlicks?'

Skeet flinched, his eyes squeezed shut. 'We got on good that night, Horlicks and Tonio and me. I got a bit pissed, mind, and might have mentioned it. He doesn't know any other names, Becker and Skeet, that's it. Where I'm living now, I'm known as Fulvio. I doubt they will find me. I came to warn you.'

It was inevitable that one of us would breach security. There's no point in going on about it. So, who would die because I set out to rob this stagecoach? Marty? Skeet? Jess? And I would finish as Tom Halley predicted—like all bushrangers, dead at the side of the road. I needed time to arrange an escape.

'When did he tell them the names?'

Skeet said, 'Must be the night before last night.'

'They will be on the way.'

Panic in our wake. Stop. Plan a way out. Get yourself under control.

Jess's voice was shakier than mine. 'Franz is known around town. They'll be on to us quickly.'

I liked her use of us, but she was an innocent, out of her depth. Time raced past while I considered the odds. Did I have hours? Days? Skeet attempted to speak, but I cut him off. Without an answer, I peered out for a long time through lace curtains at the front of the hotel and returned to the kitchen. 'They'll organise, make a plan and drive from Melbourne. Say, two days on the road. They'll find this place soon and work out what to do. You did right to warn me, Skeet.'

On the edge of a meltdown made worse by Jessica's saccharine insistence on coming with her Franzi, I hot-tailed it to Balmain in the Plymouth. Three hours later, we huddled around Horlicks, his voice strained and broken, his lips bruised and busted.

'I lifted a… Ahh!... a Chevvy Deluxe sedan in Sydney and delivered it to me mate, Tex, the next day,' he breathed hard, halting after every third word. 'Tex has a dodgy chop shop in a lane in Fitzroy. He's an ex-U.S. Marine, and his friend, Erin, looks like a gorilla.'

Horlicks eyed Becker. 'You gotta understand, mate. I wouldn't have given you up, but look at what they did to me.' And, shivering with shock, face bruised, eyes blacked, he held up two bandaged hands. He was in a terrible state, blood seeping through the bandages on his hands and feet. He needed a break. I went to the bar, and Tonio, the barman, hurriedly made tea.

Sipping the hot, sweet drink, Horlicks spoke through damaged vocal cords. 'Thanks. That shed was cold as a penguin's prick. I wanted him to know I wasn't a common-as-shit car thief. I should have gone home, gone anywhere. But I had to strut around in my new Afghan wool coat. I opened my stupid mouth. I told him I ordered a brand new DeSoto Firedome Coupe.

'He said that was bullshit, and that got me going. I described the car, ugh—so stupidly proud—a V8, one-sixty horsepower, yada yada—red and black—grey upholstery. Tex sniggered, and that pissed me off. I had a chance to stop—get out of it. But no. I had to get into a pissing contest. I told him it had set me back fifteen hundred quid, give or take.'

Horlicks was in such pain, wide-eyed and at the point of collapsing. 'You want a break?' I asked.

He shook his head and went ahead. 'Tex sneered. Where would I find that sorta dough? Full of shit, he said. Alarm bells were ringing, but I lost my rag. Before I thought about it, I blurted out, 'It's no bullshit. You know about the Racetrack Raiders in Newcastle?'

Horlicks sniffled and wiped his face with a bandaged hand. 'Sunni, I'm sorry …' he held up the hand and choked up.

'Rum or a brandy?' I asked.

A brandy brought a little life to him, but it would be temporary. 'I hadn't told a soul at that stage,' Horlicks said. 'But months had passed. It was all settled. I thought, no harm in telling him how I put together a gang from Sydney. Tex laughed at me, so I told him about the ambulance and the grenade and how I risked ending in pieces for a miserable quarter of a million. Straight off, I'd blown it and thought I'd make a run for it. But I had no idea what Tex was like.'

38. Razor's Edge

While Horlicks dozed, time crawled, and I listened to the silence. The hotel room was overcrowded, warm, and stifling. I felt claustrophobic, betrayed, bitter, and overcome by a desperate depression foreign to me. The gaudy red, green and blue room only added to my despair and raging emotions.

I debated whether to wake Horlicks or let him sleep, and there was something I needed to address, something gnawing at me, but the images remained misty. Confused and angry, wrestling with matters beyond explanation, I wanted to lash Becker. Hurt him. Provoke his conscience.

'It all began with you and Moran,' I said. 'So how did you feel about it then? Did you care? Were you amused? Shocked? Horrified? Ashamed to have run off?' I had my arms wrapped tight around my waist and waited, afraid of what I might discover about myself.

Becker was in no rush to respond. Finally, he said, 'When I left Moran, his head was bleeding, and I guessed he was dying. I freaked out for three days—stunned to be part of it. I rushed to the toilet and became jumpy whenever a siren sounded, but I needed to move ahead and live my life like he had never existed.'

Becker's bitterness matched mine. 'What do you expect me to do?' he asked indignantly. 'Confess to the coppers that I left Moran there and ran for it? I'd get at least fifteen years. That would end my life, and I hadn't had my twenty-first birthday. Not old enough to vote. We used to sit—me and my mates—in Korea, playing penny poker, drinking beer and talking about how we'd never work for a wage. We'd grab life by the balls and never be poor again. Do anything to get at the bastards wasting our miserable lives. Kill or be killed was our motto. Life

246

in the fast lane with plenty of women is what Marty wanted. Benny was a Commie and reckoned we were the lickspittles of the establishment, and there had to be a revolution. Me? What I wanted most was sex or celebrity and the riches and power that go with money. One thing we agreed on. No way would our dreams come true by working at Pennys or Woolworths or a thousand feet underground with rats and horses. No way, mate. We would work our way up the crime ladder until the big payday came, and here was Fowler screwing up my plans by whacking Sergeant Moran.'

He was on a roll. I checked my watch, but I had nothing better to do than listen to him.

Becker went on, 'I'm used to hanging around with tough men, but that doesn't mean I have to like them. Some stick around, others come and go, but I needed to do something about Fowler. I'd jump off a cliff to avoid prison time. But I put that aside to worry about later. Three days passed, and there was no sign of the coppers. I had no intention of working in a bank or a mine for an honest day's pay while living in middle-class poverty at Annie's. As Benny often said in Korea, I had done my bit for Australia and the ruling class. In the real world, a civilian again, I planned to think smart, play hard, commit to a life of crime and a quick fortune, then luxury and early retirement.

'So, call me a dreamer,' he said, 'but most people are too frightened to dream. Not me. Not Franz Becker. I was determined to ignore iron curtains and nuclear obliteration and enjoy the life I cared about, starting that night with the fete and a dance at the Palais.

'You asked how I felt about Moran's death. Well, that's how I felt.'

It was as though only we two were in the room while the others slept. He paused. A shake of the head without emotion and a sigh. Then, quietly, 'I met you, and everything changed for me.'

But my real question remained unanswered. I ignored Becker's attempt at intimacy and forced the pace. 'How can you live with yourself after all that killing in the war?'

While the seconds ticked by, the silence in the cramped room grew heavier like a storm cloud waiting to burst, and Becker studied me with the intensity of an athlete awaiting the starter's pistol. 'You want to know, could you pull the trigger if you were at the edge? Is that it?'

My throat tightened as I searched for words that would allow me to live after I spoke them. 'I never thought I'd be where I am today. I must know if I can protect myself and those I love.'

Becker said, 'Sometimes, the razor's edge between right and wrong is blunt. I had no idea how I would react. Until this Korean came at me with his bayonet.'

Then Horlicks was awake and wanted to talk. 'They ambushed me on a dark lane leading from the tram to my flat in the daggy part of Malvern. I rented it to use on my visits to Sydney...'

Winter darkness had fallen on Melbourne when he struggled into his new tan overcoat with the lapin fur collar and, shortly after six o'clock, left the Richmond bar and merged with the crowd on the footpath. Tolerated by the publican for his free spending, he usually stayed behind after six o'clock closing, but he was due at the showroom early next morning to ask after the delivery date of the brand new, two-tone DeSoto he had been boasting about to his mates. 'I brought it on myself,' he told us. 'I should have run.'

Tex grabbed him, Erin whacked him on the head with a sock filled with wet sand, and he went down like a pole-axed Christmas porker.

When he came to, a globe was burning in the hall outside. Light entered through a gap under the door, and the smell of cabbages cooking and burnt cloth hung about the darkened room. A naked dusty bulb swung from the ceiling, a doorless silky-oak wardrobe, scratched and battered, was empty of clothes but overflowing with paint cans and tools. Straw and weathered horse tack littered the floor—collars, harnesses, bridles and bits. As consciousness slowly returned, a strange world of rotting onions, evil-smelling rats, and farm smells came in with three men wearing black ski masks.

Horlicks said, 'They told me to hold out a hand, so I did. I was shaking. My hand was shaking. They seized it. A voice I didn't recognise told me not to struggle. Someone grabbed my hand and gripped it tight as though it was a crocodile's jaws. Another separated my index finger and squeezed it with pliers until I screamed.

'A voice said, "Gag him." The pliers squeezed tighter and I screamed non-stop. The same voice said, "Tell me where the cash is, or I will chop off this finger." I couldn't breathe. I nodded and made choking sounds through the gag. Then, finally, the pliers eased after a lifetime, and the gag loosened. I'm not a hero. I'm a coward. I said I'd tell them everything. But the voice told me that every time I lied, I'd lose a finger.'

Horlicks stared around the motel room, his eyes ready to pop out. 'I told them that the telephone rang, and a voice asked if I remembered the Q Store in Kimpo. South Korea. They shouted at me, "Who phoned you? Who phoned you?"

'"Don't know," I screamed. "Don't know." And then the pain! I couldn't believe the pain. I was crying, spraying snot.

'The voice shouted, "There goes the first finger. Now tell me who phoned."

'"Don't know," I screamed over and over. "Don't know. Don't know." Pleading. Screaming again, sobbing "Wait, Wait." Then the pain. "Noooo."

'And the voice again bellowing in my ear, "Two fingers gone. No more lies."

'I begged. "Please." They took another finger, and I hollered that three blokes met me in Sydney.

'The voice came, but it sounded friendly. "Give me the names." He squeezed the pliers on my middle finger. "Give me the names and the pain will stop." I thought I would get away with only first names. "Marty, Benny." I told them there was a bloke in the van, but I never heard his name. They grabbed my other hand and squeezed a finger. I was begging again. Like, "No. No. Please. Don't do that. Don't do it." Then I surrendered. "Wait. Wait. I remember it was Skeet."

'All three shouted together, "Who was the boss?"

'There was no point saying the boss was a woman—they wouldn't believe me—and I'd lose more fingers. So, I told them the boss was a kid. They took another finger anyway. The voice bellowed in my ear again. "Here goes another finger."

'I yelled, "Noooo!" Then I told them. "We weren't supposed to use surnames. But they slipped, and one of the others called him Becker."

'They wanted to know what happened to the cash, so I told them that Becker said he'd hide it for the six months then give us our share.'

'"How do we find this Becker?"'

'"Don't know." The pain was worse. I can't believe the pain was worse. "That's a toe for the lie. You're lucky it's not a foot. Feet hurt."'

In the Balmain hotel room, Horlicks told us he was left alone with a bottle of cheap brandy to pour on his stumps from the bottle he held with his mangled hands. Then, quiet voices came to him through the walls of the shed. He recognised Tex's accent, and when the conversation ended, he rolled into a ball on the floor and pretended to sleep. But the toe of a boot caught him in the ribs. They wound bandages tightly around his hands and foot. Tex's American accent cut through his daze telling him to keep the hood on for five minutes after they released him. Then, he was to go to the hospital and have them fix his hands. That he had caught them in an electric lawn mower.

They told him to go home and not to say a word to anyone, or he'd lose all the other bits. And if they didn't find the Becker kid, they'd come back, and he would never be interested in cars again.

Horlicks faded away. I checked his breathing, and there was no fresh blood from his hands, so I let him rest.

'Three attacked him,' I said.

'But I got only two names,' Skeet said. 'Tex and Erin. Tex is a Yank.'

I didn't speak, my thoughts drifting while I watched Horlicks's face. There were too many questions and not enough feedback from my fossilised mind. I would have to wing it. 'Skeet, I need you with me for three days. Be Fulvio until we find a permanent solution. They don't know that name. Don't do anything to draw attention. Will you do that for me?'

'Yes. Anything you ask, Sunni.' He shuffled about in his chair. 'Horlicks lost his fingers and saved your life. He told them Becker was boss, not you.'

'Yes. I owe him for that.'

'It all seemed so straightforward at the dress rehearsal in the barn.'

'It always does,' I said.

I leaned against the wall and searched outside the window. It always goes wrong, but the trick is handling the crisis when it comes at you. Now, I had to look after our casualties, Horlicks and Skeet. At the same time, I needed to fend off Tex and the grenades he would hurl at us.

'If I go,' Skeet said, slowly standing and looking about the room, 'you'll have no one to guard your back.'

'Better a possible risk for me than certain death for you. Horlicks knows nothing about Marty and Benny. They were careful to avoid any chance of identification. So, it's you and me and Becker.'

'And how safe is Rudy?'

'Rudy's name never came up. I'm sure of that.'

'What will you do, darling?' Jess asked.

Darling! I squirmed. Becker was the darling in question, but I answered for him. 'I'll ask Marty to hide Horlicks until we sort things out. Then we'll go to Dudley and find somewhere secure for you.'

Fired with energy, I locked the doors and all the ground-floor windows at The Dudley. 'Jess, race upstairs and pack clothes for you and Becker. One case each. Enough for a few weeks. You can't come here until it's over. You take the Plymouth. I have mine.'

'Skeet!' I yelled. 'One last favour. Will you stay at Annie's for two nights? Then go wherever you are safest. I'll give you an extra hundred quid.'

Everyone was speaking, no one listening, the voices growing louder.

I heard Skeet say, 'Three hundred in advance—'

'Done,' I shouted. 'I'll drop you near Annie's in case—'

Becker was bleary-eyed, 'Jess,' he said, 'you'll have to live with your mum and dad until I—'

'No way.'

Skeet examined the floor while massaging his temples. 'There's no safety for us. The word's out. Let's return the money.'

Everyone spoke at once, raising their voices until only fragments were heard.

'Forget it—'

'There'll be no rest for us while you're alive.'

'We're not giving the money—'

'They'll torture Becker until—'

'Trust me,' I hollered. 'Everyone shut up. I'll come up with a plan.'

They'd find Skeet. He knew enough for them to work out the rough location of the first hiding place. I couldn't ask Jess to keep the information away from the police. 'We have no choice but to go on. Stick with me, do as I say, and we'll be safe.'

I addressed everyone in the room. They were quiet, now, shocked. 'Don't wait for them to torture you. Tell them everything you know, and don't try to keep secrets.'

Skeet had no idea I moved the swag to a new hiding place. They'll torture him until he's dead. From the day of the heist, I understood that the pinch would come, and I sought out a second stash for the plunder. When it came to the point of the spear, I couldn't toss a hundred thousand pounds worth of jewels into the harbour. So, I hid it with the cash.

Becker thrust out his jaw and grabbed Jessica's hand. 'Let's go. I'm taking you to your dad.'

'No,' she said, snatching back her hand. 'While you've been talking, I've been thinking. I'm staying here at The Dudley. There's nowhere safe, and here I'm among friends.'

Jess was right. She would not be safe with her parents. They're bourgeois snobs and would open their mouths to everyone in the golf club. Probably phone the police. No good taking her to Stockton—too many know to search there.

'At the Dudley?' Becker's voice sounded the alarm as loud as the doomsday bell.

Jess said, 'I'll be safe with Sunni.'

I folded my arms on the kitchen table and made some decisions. I had everything I ever wanted, and it meant nothing to me. The fantasy had led me astray, and a dose of reality was overdue. I didn't want to be alone, watching for the next attack. I'll need Becker beside me when we are safe again. While Jess is here, he will be, too.

'Yes,' I said. 'You're right, Jess. Stay at the Dudley.'

In the guest lounge, Becker wriggled about on his chair, holding on to a tight-lipped scowl while I paced, and Jess sat on the edge of the divan, kneading her fingers when she wasn't tucking a stray hair behind her ear.

After six, the bar was closed to the public, and I clipped the top off a bottle of Toohey's, refilled three glasses, and raised mine to Jess. 'Here's to Dudley's female bushrangers. We'll be legends like Captain Thunderbolt or Ben Hall.'

In the fragile silence, I stepped across to the parrot's cage by the window. 'Hello, Cocky. What do you make of these dashing Robin Hoods who steal from the wicked and keep it for themselves?'

Becker confronted me with troubled eyes. 'Gabe leaves town with his tail between his legs, and a month later, you are neglecting the hotel, pretending to train his horses, and generally acting like the cat found the ice cream. Supposedly, you've done all that on Gabe's payroll. Did you take everyone for a fool? You retained our money while you chanced our necks and our profits?'

He grabbed Jess's hand, 'Come on. We're going to your dad's place.'

I continued talking to the bird. 'Don't worry, Cocky. Mr Becker will be back. He doesn't know where I hid the loot.'

He retreated to the sofa, his laughter forced and stiff. I glowered at him, my suspicions deepening.

He searched the floor at my feet, and his eyes travelled slowly up, past my high heels, ankles, and long legs and finally settled on my face. 'I know where you hid the cash,' he said quietly and drifted to the window.

He knew the original hiding place. I remained unruffled as water in a fishbowl. 'How did you find out?' I asked calmly.

'A few days before the raid, I came here to listen to the big race. But there were too many people. It was silly to expose myself. So, I waited outside. Then I remembered how Rudy and I once walked underground from Redhead to have lunch at The Dudley. I leaned over the fence and saw the closed-off adit where we exited the mine. Then, Pride of Egypt was racing, and I forgot about it. That is until yesterday. I remembered the adit and you leaving Skeet and me after the heist. You drove off and hid the swag in the adit.'

He poked a biscuit into the parrot's cage. 'Did you think I'd betray you? Steal the money? Leave you in the lurch when the going got tough?'

I glanced at Becker over the top of the bird. 'A boss has to consider every eventuality. If the police were outside the door, we had an escape route underground with the treasury.'

He watched me shrewdly. 'And now, they've caught up with you. You need to run out of town before the Sheriff and his posse arrive to drag you off to the hanging tree. Right?'

'Not the Sheriff,' Jessica muttered, biting her fingernails.

'Of course.' Becker threw out a hand and clicked his finger and thumb. 'It's the gangsters in their black Caddies, with their molls and Tommy guns. But the same hanging tree. How long before they get here?'

'They'll come by road,' I said. 'Allow a day, maybe two, before they finish their work and make preparations. Then a day to drive from Melbourne.'

Becker said, 'The road to Melbourne is only two lanes slow-going. It's rough, potholed, broken, dangerous edges and long stretches of gravel. Most drivers take two days.'

Jess said, 'They'll have to find Skeet before they can do anything. Franz is the one they're after.'

And, I thought, they need time to screw the information out of him. 'So, let's say I have three days to sort everything out.' I shook my head at Skeet. Kitty would throw him to the dogs. But that was a burden I would have to carry.

We drank and figured and worried, until Jess said to me, 'Are you telling how much you took off with?'

So, Becker also held his secrets close. 'Yes. A stack of cash. I haven't counted it yet.' I thought I'd gotten away with that lie. 'And jewellery. An emperor's ransom in jewels. But the most valuable stuff is the legal papers and letters agreeing to pay bribes to VIP officials. Police, politicians, race supervisors, all top shelf in their professions.'

'Jewellery, did you say?' Jessica asked.

'Necklaces worth thousands of quid each. Gabe Rosen's five-carat ring would be worth close to a thousand, but I gave it to him. I've kept the loose gems—rubies, pearls, gold, diamonds. Forty thousand pounds at retail prices.' Another lie. 'But it's all too easily traceable. I'll drop it in the harbour as planned. Not the gold.'

'And,' Becker said, 'you found enough evidence to blackmail Gabe. So, he did a deal with you.'

'Yeah. There's more than enough hard evidence for the tax office to bankrupt him and the coppers to put him away for years. He's not the only one. Those bookies—how they live it up.'

The room was quiet.

Jessica said, 'Imagine a box overflowing with jewels.' Her voice broke. 'Someone will die for our greed.'

That stabbed me like a migraine. 'Overflowing with documented law-breaking, not jewels.' Restless? Conceited? So what? I had Becker to help me. Would he help? I embraced Jess awkwardly, as her heart beat like a bass drum.

I watched Becker, feeling for his weakness. 'This is the home stretch,' I said. 'I can see the finish line, and there'll be no retreat. Are you sticking with me?'

'You don't need to demand that,' Becker said. 'I don't give in that easily. We have two, maybe three days. What's your plan?'

Determined to salvage everything, I said, 'Leg it with the

cash that's left. I deserve it. We deserve it.' The question was, would I dump the jewellery and documents. But while my mind said yes, my eyes held the sparkle in the diamonds.

Full of restless energy, Becker paced around the lounge while I waited for a plan to come to mind, fully organised with all the details. 'I don't want to throw away everything we've planned for,' I said. 'I need time to handle these killers first.'

Becker said, 'And after that, we vanish? Turn to smoke, never to return?'

'I'm coming with you, Franzi, ' Jess said. 'You can't leave me here to face the music.'

I said, 'I am working on a plan, though it has holes in it.'

Becker was wearing a hole in the carpet. 'How close are you with Gabe?' he asked and blushed. 'I don't mean....'

'You mean, can I pander to his base desires?' I laughed to relieve the tension. 'Of course. Do you think I may be out of practice?'

Becker blushed again. 'Would he be prepared to help you?'

I gagged and waggled a hand in front of my face. 'You can't ask for help from a dog you whipped yesterday.'

'But *you* can, Sunni,' he insisted. 'You can.'

'Me?' I shook my head, uncertain again.

'You said you know him well. You know... like bonded.'

'Yes, but—'

'And you're in a strong position to help him and ask for his help.'

My smile was hesitant and rusty but intact. 'Do you have any idea of how Gabe can stop these murderers? He's not a killer.'

'But he's the best negotiator I know.'

I saw a glint of light at the end of a long night, showed my white teeth, and my reluctance dwindled. My eyes burned with excitement. 'After me, that is.'

I fiddled with the cruet set on a table set for dinner, lined up the cutlery, and polished a water glass, an idea taking shape so tenuous I looked away in case I lost it. 'You want me to ask Gabe to help us?'

'Ten thousand quid for him if he can help us escape with the cash.'

'It's not about money, mate. It's about power and wielding that power over others.'

'So, talk to him about some of those documents you were skiting about. That's where your power lies.'

My eyes circled the room again, searching for that life raft Becker had thrown me from a sinking ship. Play Gabe like Becker plays poker? Calculate the chances, then bluff it out.

'Persuade Gabe to meet you,' Becker intruded rudely on my daydream. 'It's urgent.'

'I can do it,' I said through clamped teeth. 'Gabe's at the Horsley Park training track every Friday. So, that's where I'll be at dawn tomorrow.'

My plan was already in motion as I mentally ticked off the steps I needed to take and the words I needed to use.

'Go there. Persuade him, or we're as good as dead.'

I knew there was a good reason I invited Becker to join my heist. More and more, I liked this boy, Franz Becker.

39. Baser and Higher Desires

Friday, June 11.

In the pink freshness of dawn, Gabe leaned against a redwood fence post, arms folded, breath fogging, face scowling rejection before I opened my mouth. 'I remember saying you had a cheek,' he said. 'I should have brought a shotgun.'

'Thanks for coming, Gabe darling,' I thought that would get the meeting off on the right track and remind him of those base desires I had to pander to.

I had no need to drive to Sydney; Gabe had spent the night at a thoroughbred stud outside Scone, a ninety-minute drive from Dudley. Behind him, a pink gravel road led between two fence rows, receding to a vanishing point at the base of a hill cleared at the bottom and forested on one side with native trees and bush. The Hunter Valley was dairy farms, wineries, trout fishing, beautiful scenery, and some of the best horse studs in the world—and coal mines.

'You know my lawyer, Judge Hector Larcombe,' I said.

Gabe inclined his head minimally to Hector but refused to offer a hand. A row of grapevines was at his feet, a chestnut mare nuzzling his shoulder. 'You were persuasive on the phone. But you should have told me you'd be carrying a lawyer.'

'Too many people,' I said, 'are guessing, getting close to the right answer. Time is running out. That's why Hector's here against his better judgment to draft an agreement on the spot. I insisted he come with me. He is sensitive to the smallest suggestion of Kitty.' I slung Hector a cheery smile so he would know I wasn't being disrespectful.

'You're not only cheeky,' he said, glancing at his watch, 'you're an outrageous optimist.'

'Everything's about to come apart,' I said. 'People are after me with finger-cutters and big sticks, and they have a taste for what I've got. They'll go at me until I give up names and details and documents. But you'll be the loser.'

'How's that?'

'You'll lose everything to the toughest blackmailer who finds me first.'

Gabe shaded his eyes to watch a strapper leading two horses from a stable made from cut logs for posts and rusting corrugated iron for the roof and walls. The teenage strapper wore blue jeans, a filthy green half-coat against the morning chill, and a black beanie on his head. He headed in our direction, and the sour smell of horses and manure followed behind.

'Your horses?' I asked with a half-hearted shrug, the opening salvo in my retreat.

'They're not a patch on the two I gave you. Jesus, what idiot would carry those documents?'

'You can have the horses if we can find a deal,' I said quietly and tried a comfortable laugh, cordial, chummy and more invitation than ever before.

'Go straight to the track, Muz,' Gabe shouted. 'I'll see you next week.' And to me, 'Look at that beauty in the home paddock,' pointing to a grey mare and its foal up to their hocks in lush, green grass. 'She's a Melbourne Cup winner if ever I saw one.'

'Your house?' I asked.

'Joking,' Gabe said roughly, a sword concealed. 'It was until you came. Now I'm paying huge interest on the loan, and I'll be knee-capped if I miss a payment.'

'A lovely home,' I said. 'You can have it again.'

We stared, admiring the timber colonial with cast-iron posts and lace balustrades framing wide verandas on three sides. A woman arranged squatter's chairs on the porch to allow the best sun onto the breakfast table. A row of tall, shady ghost gums lined the drive like soldiers on parade.

Gabe misunderstood me, 'I can't just walk in and take it. I'm not the Chicago mafia. I don't go around killing people. I'm not Bugsy Siegel.'

Suddenly disgusted at my timid approach to the negotiation, I recoiled. 'But you are a Frank Sinatra. You know who does the rough stuff and how to get it done.'

'You should be talking to Kitty.'

'I don't have anything Kitty wants.'

'The jewellery. She'd jump through a tramp's fire for the jewellery.'

'Too risky. Fences talk.'

'Not for Kitty. She'd wear it, flaunt it, and there's not a person I know who'd try to take it off her.'

Watching two ponies playing in a field of mown grass, we smirked at taking anything from Kitty, and I detected in Gabe a slender encouragement to go on.

'She'd do it for you,' I said. 'Not for me.'

'Urgent, I suppose?'

'They will arrive today or tomorrow.'

'I know.'

This bastard is playing with me. 'You arranged for them to come?'

'No, but I've done nothing to stop them. I want everything I handed to you, my documents, and the rest of the cash you stole, and Kitty gets all the jewels.'

I said, 'I'll keep the main half-dozen documents. So, you don't come at me when I'm naked.'

Gabe sucked air through his teeth. 'You walk from my life and never come back.'

'You can have the cash I've given you, but no more.'

'Piss off,' he said. 'I'll take my chances with the tax department.'

'And with the bribery and corruption charges? They're worth ten years of your life, but you'll probably not last more than six weeks before a boogeyman gets you.'

Gabe said, 'I'll ask Kitty to put a bullet in your head and chuck you in the harbour.'

'That immediately triggers a release of all the documents to the press and the tax department.' I was not kidding. Hector had his instructions.

A single-engine, high-wing Auster circled low overhead. The pilot waved and headed for a level grass paddock a half-mile away with a windsock I hadn't noticed.

Gabe said, 'What do you want me to do?'

'Have Kitty chase away the Melbourne hoods and clear any opposition out of the way while I leave the country.'

'Where will you go?'

'I'll live in my house in Neuilly-Sur-Seine,' I said, pronouncing French, as I'd learned from Gabe himself.

'Like hell, you will.'

'That's the deal,' I said. 'It's my house, and if you try to take it away from me, I'll release the documents to the press.'

'That Auster is my ride to Sydney. Piss off. Neuilly is my house.'

'Then there's no deal,' I said. 'I'll take my chances against a few Melbourne pansies, and you'll take the punt that my documents won't go to press if I lose that fight.'

I had no intention of trusting Gabe. On the contrary, I was also negotiating a separate deal with Kitty's man. Bart would take a heap of money in return for saving my arse. Then he'd retire to a hole safe from Kitty. Trust Bart? No way.

Gabe pounded his cap again and again against the redwood post, unleashing his frustration with each strike.

But I had only just reached my stride. 'Judge Larcombe will

262

knock up an agreement and transfer documents, and we can sign it in an hour. Then, you fly to Sydney and persuade Kitty to have her people organised by tomorrow at the latest.'

Hector chimed in. 'The contracts were conditional on settling the Neuilly property, so you save on stamp duty.'

I thought I had crossed the line by a whisker and chose not to risk more. I held out a hand. 'Deal?'

Gabe hesitated, held out a reluctant hand and swore. 'Deal,' he said. 'Where will I find you?'

'I'm set for tonight. I'll stay in touch with Hector.'

'Don't try to cross Kitty. She'll get the jewels or come after you, and no matter where you are, she'll find you.'

Preoccupied with the detailed escape plan, I drove from Scone to Dudley with Hector. High on the list of priorities was the need to retrieve the jewels from the mineshaft and conceal them safely on the surface where I stashed the cash and where the jewellery would be available at short notice to give to Kitty.

'You are a mystery to me,' Hector said. 'I am privileged to know only as much information as I can glean from others, and I add what I find to my store of knowledge after making assumptions. Your gangsters have had a run of good luck, but they work in the mine three days a week. Why is that?'

'We don't want to make people jealous,' I said. 'Some people become snaky when others get lucky.'

Hector did not need to know that Rudy carried cash out in his pockets, his lunch box, and inside his surveying equipment until only a thousand remained. And the jewellery was enough to tempt St Gabriel. Sure, I would give the jewellery to Kitty. But the gold and loose gemstones were all mine as long as she didn't know about them.

'I imagine,' Hector said, 'taking over Gabe's savings has made a few people... envious.'

'Only you and Gabe know the true story. The rumour that it is part of my salary is holding up.'

'I dealt with people like you as a judge before I fell out of favour. But most were vicious thugs or plain stupid. You're neither. Do you ever think about your life? That you're a criminal wanted by the police? Can you not tell right from wrong?'

I had a bit of trouble with that, but I said, 'All my life, I've had my own ideas on right and wrong.' But Hector was right. Sometimes, not often, I worried my conscience. 'Believe in sin or heaven or hell, if you want to. By all means believe in saints or devils. But I'm having fun playing on a different team. There's only stuff that people do. Some might say it's legal, some not entirely legal. It depends on which house on the same street you came from.'

Hector grimaced. 'You have it all figured out. You're thirty-two? Already, you have the world sorted into pieces.'

'I'm a big, bad bank robber now, Hector. A bushranger, and one day, the City Council will make a statue of me and put it on a street corner.'

Twenty minutes of silence as we drove on to Newcastle said everything, our opinions poles apart. But the judge cracked first. 'Sunni, whoever you are, publican or thief, don't finish like me. I worked with the syndicate and made one slip-up. Now, there's no more Yes, Milord, No, Milord. I take two guineas an hour and turn Nelson's telescope to who pays me. Move out and stay out. They'll hang you the way you're heading.'

'Not me,' I said. 'They need to catch me first.' I crossed my fingers behind me and my ankles below the dashboard.

The only sign of my good fortune in Newcastle was the big house on the hill, which I had persuaded everyone was a bonus from Gabe—everyone other than Tommo, I suppose, and my boys. In a moment of weakness, I bought the Oldsmobile, which faded out among the wealth in Sydney. And, hesitant to flash my wealth around Newcastle, I retained the old Austin to use there. I garaged the new Oldsmobile at the stylish waterfront townhouse I bought for two thousand quid in Kirribilli, across the street from the Prime Minister's house. I thought it best to keep news of the Oldsmobile or the Kirribilli apartment from Hector.

There was a lot Hector didn't know. For instance, after purchasing the car and apartment, I rented a derelict warehouse in West Maitland and stashed the cash there, including my team's share. So, I had the readies to repay Gabe, and though the Hunter had flooded in the previous two years, the caretaker's room was above flood level.

Rudy had helped me scrape the mortar and remove bricks from the solid wall to create a niche to hide the money and documents. We replaced the bricks and covered the cache with a heavy blackened plank. Being on the main rail link from Sydney to Brisbane, Maitland allowed me to take a train from Broadmeadow to my stash and observe if anyone followed.

'Judge, I have a question of ethics for you.'

'Ethics? Okay, ethics is right up my alley. Go ahead, but don't ask if it's about Kitty.'

'I have partners,' I said. 'One, Horlicks, lost five fingers to torture until he gave up Becker's name. Five fingers.'

'And?'

'And I hid their shares for six months so they wouldn't go crazy and have the police catch them. Know what I mean?'

'Yes, you'll skip town and take their money with you. I know people who would say that's ethical.'

'Not at all. My question is this. Should I punish Horlicks or give him the agreed share?'

'Yes,' Judge Hector said, 'I see what you mean. That's your ethical dilemma. A real bushranger would take the money and skip, and you're asking, are you, or ain't you a proper bushranger?'

'I hadn't thought of it like that.'

'Give me two guineas, and I'll give you my answer in a week.'
'Don't worry. Two guineas! I have the answer.'

It had been a long day, starting with Gabe at dawn. I was tired of driving, and Hector had lost concentration. We stopped at a traffic light, where the two highways met eight miles west of Newcastle, and three motorcycles manoeuvred through the junction.

'Oh, my,' Hector cried. 'Just take a look at those bikes.'

Three muscled, war-hardened bikies astride three muddy bikes. One rode a two-year-old Indian Chief, a custom cruiser with wheel spats and all the comfort features the Americans can build into a bike.

The second rider was on a Vincent Black Shadow, an English bike, spartan, built for business; chrome used sparely on crackling exhaust pipes, a black painted galloper with a single speedo and an old-fashioned round headlight.

The last rider in the trio rode a four-year-old Triumph Thunderbird, a sexy, fire-breathing road warrior.

The first rider brandished a road map. He pointed and shouted to his pals, 'This way to Worimi. We'll check that out first.'

He folded the map. They revved their engines, turning envious heads, and roared through the intersection towards Worimi when the lights changed.

'Cop that Vincent Black Shadow,' Hector said. 'When I was an up-and-coming lawyer, I rode a motorbike. The Vincent is the fastest and most perfect bike in the world. They've come a long way by the mud on their machines.'

'Yeah. I suppose I'd prefer the Indian for a long trip.'

'You'll have to take a long trip yourself,' Hector said. 'I've had Kitty on my tail wanting to know who robbed the bookies, and she had nothing at all to say about ethics. But eventually, she'll not be happy with only the jewels, and now, other bad boys will be in the know and want to take you out.'

'Is that your professional advice?'

'My professional advice,' said Hector, 'is to hand yourself over to the cops, give everything away and crawl into a cell until the bookies die of old age.'

'I may be funny,' I said, 'but the danger excites me. It's like having a tiger for a pet.'

'That's because you've never suffered pain. Kitty is a Sydney big shot. She doesn't care about anyone. She'll become your tiger after Gabe talks to her. Kitty's not a handsome woman by a long shot, but the men flock after her as though she's a princess. She socialises with prime ministers, presidents, and royalty and thinks it's a life worth living. You can keep the cash, but Kitty will never let you rest until she's taken it off you and sucked you dry.'

I was on the Big Dipper while others were deciding everything for me. I didn't care that I was not entirely in control. I didn't know where I would finish. If I lost the easy life, well, it came easily, and perhaps I would be able to grab it again as quickly.

'No one can guarantee your survival,' Hector said, 'but you have allies.'

'You and Skeet.'

'And Becker. Jess is not a stayer.'

'Becker, then.'

'Someone to love you.'

40. A Pitch for Love

Saturday, June 12.

I raced against time to catch the five o'clock train from Broadmeadow to Maitland, my heart pounding, fearing another panic attack. Every detail had to fall into place, including Skeet's arrival on the nine o'clock rail motor. The past two days had been a whirlwind. Chaos. Retrieving the jewels from the mine with Rudy's help, then sitting alone separating the gold bullion and coins and the loose gems that neither Gabe nor Kitty knew about or might recognise, entrusting the finest jewellery pieces to Hector to hold in trust on behalf of Kitty, making the reservations for Becker and Jess to travel to Europe—we had organised passports the day Jess warned me she knew about my part in the heist—and sealing the deal with Gabe. Kitty demanded nothing more—just all the jewellery and nothing in writing.

The greatest challenge, and the most critical, had been finalising the deal with Bart Evans, Kitty's man in Newcastle, whom I needed to alert me when Tex's gang finally appeared and to keep them away from us when they did. The same brute who savagely beat Becker at the racecourse refused at first to meet me. He threatened death or worse and came around to talk only when I made him understand I had an arrangement with Kitty.

Bart snickered when he raised a shoulder and finally condescended to speak to me. 'So? You are in with Kitty. Big deal. What's in it for me?'

'Whatever Kitty wants to give you,' I said. 'I'm handing her thirty thousand in high-quality jewels.'

Bart whistled. 'Jewels? Thirty thou? That much? She told me nothing about jewels.'

'I wouldn't mention it if you want to keep your face and get a bonus.' I thought it best not to mention what Kitty would do if I told her the true value of the jewellery.

'Yeah,' Bart said. 'The bonus. Kitty takes the thirty grand and gives me a toffee apple. She said nothing to me about what to do with you.'

'What's that supposed to mean?'

'It means she don't care if you live or die.'

'Gabe cares a lot,' I said.

Bart sneered. 'Who's Gabe when Kitty's about? You need protection.' He let out a snigger. 'Can I be of service, Your Ladyship?'

'Gabe will report to Kitty, and she'll not be happy.'

'Kitty cares nothing for you,' Bart said. 'Or for Gabe. Let's say three thousand to ensure your safety against the nasty boys coming for you.'

'I don't have three to give away. But I understand your point. What say I pay you a thousand to look after me?'

'Oh, mate,' Bart laughed. 'With three, I'll break from Kitty and get lost, where she'll never find me. Can't do that with one lazy thou.'

'I'm safe until Kitty gets the jewellery. I'll be away and flying by then, and you'll never find me. But, as a token to a friend of Albie Fowler, let's say fifteen hundred.'

Bart said, 'Working for Kitty, I make that in six months. Tell you what. Two and a half. My last offer. That gives me a year to get set.'

'One and three-quarters, or we go to war. If the Melbourne gang grabs me, you'll get nothing. '

Bart spat. 'Two, and we stay friends.'

At first, I phoned Bart every hour from a local bar close to my new hiding place. I went to ground with Becker in the vacant warehouse at Maitland, and every exposure to make a call added to our danger. Three bikies, Bart reported, were cruising about Newcastle, asking around in likely places for Becker; Tex on his Indian Chief, Erin Feely on a Vincent, and their mate, Caddy, on a Triumph. Erin, I found later, was an enthusiastic torturer.

Everyone in town had heard of Becker, but he was holed up out of sight. But bartenders, petrol pumpers, brothel keepers and grocers kept track of the three noisy bikies, and reports of their progress and questions trickled to Bart Evans. Since Newcastle was a country town where three flashy motor bikes stood out, Bart knew within fifteen minutes after Tex tracked Skeet to his usual drinking place, the Crown and Anchor, near the ferry terminal. And, on my next trip to the public phone, Bart reported that a green Morris van had disappeared from its usual parking spot behind a shop in the lane off Brunker Road.

'It's probably your new friends,' he said. 'Hot-wired it.'

Sleep was a distant dream in the decaying, flood-damaged warehouse a stone's throw from the Maitland rail station. Through a filthy window, I watched listless passengers waiting for the rail motor to arrive, huddled on the platform open to the sky with two bare bulbs providing the only light. Steam engines hissed, screeched, and spun their wheels, enough to terrorise me and shake the hair from my head. The Ritz, it was not, but I clung to the illusion of security it offered my overworked brain. Windows were fixed shut, a single-entry door and a built-in obstacle course of broken plaster, wire cables, forty-gallon drums and rusting machinery would trip the unwary, and to capture me, they would then have to get past Becker.

I was scared witless and joined Becker for company, hiding behind the door, armed and alert. I threw my arms around him and squeezed. He laughed and stepped away.

'I need you,' I said. 'We could be dead by dawn.'

He took another step, looked into my eyes, 'Yeah, well...'

and danced past me.

I said, 'Becker.'

He turned away from me.

I said, 'You can't face me?'

'I don't expect you would enjoy the life of a bushranger.'

'You ...' My voice cracked. His heavy breathing was loud in the still air.

'I can't think about it,' he shrugged, waved a hand around the building. 'Not here. Not now.'

'You can't think?' I whispered. Stung by his flippancy, I couldn't hold back the tears prickling my eyes. 'Or you don't want to think of the other men I've been with?'

Becker said, 'I never meant.... No. It's...'

'It's Jess?' I said. 'You can't hold on to her.' I stepped hesitantly to him. 'I'm frightened,' and wrapped my arms around him from behind to hold in the fear. I breathed in the smell of the night and the steam engine and coal dust. He tilted his head and nestled it on my shoulder, the air crushing me. Neither of us took a breath. We stood there, unmoving, waiting for the panic to go away. It didn't.

We touched, his warm breath gasping in my ear, and we rocked in rhythm secretly as though a single sound would give our position away, uncaring of the harsh concrete beneath us, united in passion, and, afterwards, stroking his back, I prayed we would come out from this alive, and even as I moved my lips in a long disused prayer I knew no one was listening.

I whispered, 'I shouldn't have cried. You will think I'm weak.'

'You? Weak? No! Honest.'

Slowly, the railway restored its sounds of shunting and braking, and Becker said, 'How come—?' But he left the question in mid-air.

'How come I did this with so many men?'

'Why?' he asked.

'Because I enjoyed it. I lived such an exciting life—so many adventures, I've forgotten them. Do you think I'm bad?'

"Course not,' Becker said.' You are making the best of your life. But wasn't it dangerous?' He spluttered and giggled and waved his hand to take in the warehouse, the night, and the menace in our faces. We laughed until our nervous energy dissipated.

'Enough with the adventure,' I said, breathless. 'It's best if we are separate.' But I wanted to stay in his warmth. 'I'll go. I'll be up there,' I said, pointing to the mezzanine floor and the steps only thirty feet away. I took his face in my hands, and we kissed and rocked on our heels. 'Soon, this will be over, and you can go to Jessica. If you want to.'

'She may not want me,' he said, taunting me, looking deep into my eyes. 'Not every girl would take a man like this. Covered in coal dust from head to foot and everywhere between, as though I'd been rolling in the coal heap at the wharf.'

Where it all began with Sergeant Moran.

Before settling on my makeshift bed of flattened sugar bags in the caretaker's room smelling of sewer drains and dead rats, I took one final peek through the window, surprised that passengers were sitting on the concrete platform waiting for the rail motor to depart, a rat on the sideline waiting with them, knowing there would be food. Our honeymoon suite. I checked that I had locked the door.

The rail motor's in. Where's Skeet?

Exhausted and on edge, I stumbled over broken boxes containing nothing of value and ten yards beyond a dirt-caked window, a washed-out, sullen woman with dishevelled hair paced, her arms crossed and shivering in the cold. She stared mindlessly towards me in silence. My lips moved to wish her luck, but she needed more than luck. A battle-scarred older man joined her: a tall, thick bloke with a lengthy pigtail and a wispy Chinese beard that did nothing to improve his rat-shaped features. He wore a dark leather jacket and, moving fast like a boxer, sidled up to her and threw an arm around her waist. He looked up at the window, and I stepped back, hoping the darkness hid me.

Rat-face bent to speak to the woman. She tried to smile, to look sensuous, and they slunk away towards some dingy bar on the other side of the tracks, the man looking over his shoulder, his face above the beard pale under a flickering streetlamp.

Music wailed, a train whistled, a passenger on the platform shouted, and the air smelled of greasy rags and my sweat. Worrying that Skeet hadn't arrived, I cleared round stones from a space on the dusty floor, sat on my sugar-bag bed, resting against a wall sloping and buckling from a settlement of the foundations, and peered at the sky through broken window glass. Kids. Why do boys love to sling rocks from a shanghai to break glass? I should know—I did it. Girls, too, had mastered the art of the slingshot. It's the challenge of committing a crime, busting something, breaking away from the rules and getting away with it.

Where *was* Skeet? Maybe it was a mistake to have him come here. He's not what you'd call bright. Drinks too much and wouldn't know if someone was following.

The temperature fell. The floor groaned and cracked and settled again.

Pray the walls will not cave in tonight.

A movement caught my eye, and startled, I squinted at the dark corner and waited with a four-by-two timber baulk in my hand, prepared to fight. A cat meowed. Emerging hesitantly from the shadow, the ginger animal stretched, padded into the centre of the room and sat preening its fur, feigning nonchalance.

'Here, pussy,' I whispered, my memory flashing to Tom, the stray orange cat I adopted on my tenth birthday. 'Puss, puss, puss.' It leapt to a timber crate, examined me, and crept closer until I stretched out a hand to pat it, now purring and stretching its tail. Then, carefully, to avoid frightening it, I unwrapped a sandwich from greaseproof paper, selected a piece of ham and held it out. 'Here.' He took the offering with a delicate tongue and sprang onto my lap.

Warmed by the cat, secure with its weight on my chest and lulled by the hiss of steam, I fell into a doze.

The cat woke me—the subtle weight of its paws as it sprang away. 'Shh, Puss.'

I crept across the floor, down three stairs, and leaned on the handrail to scan the lower floor. There was a metallic clatter, a muttered command. The door smashed open, men shouted words that made no sense, and Becker was in the torch's beam.

A shout. 'It's him: Becker.'

A glimpse of a pigtail, Becker's arms pinioned, a hand over his mouth, and I was close enough, invisible in the darkness, to smell engines and spent petrol on their bodies and clothes. I sprinted up the stairs and gently squeezed the door closed. A crash from below. Heavy footsteps on the timber floor. Hands lifted, carried him out and bounced him into a small van. A body sat heavily on him and trussed him up with electrical tape. His captors exchanged urgent words, and while a loaded train clanked off trailing a lonesome dirge, they careened off the kerb and tore off in the green van, leaving behind Caddy's Triumph.

So much for Bart's security. Or Becker's sentry duty. I raced to the station to telephone for help, only to find the handset cut and the phone useless.

41. Captured?

Sunday, June 13.

Skeet shivered uncontrollably, banging on the warehouse door with a flat hand, shouting my name and screaming the urgency of his message. 'They'll cut off his fingers like they did to Horlicks,' he blurted, raising his voice more. His frightened eyes skittered about. 'Hurry. We can take Caddy's Triumph. We have to move. Come on. Move.'

'Stop, Skeet. Are you hurt?' I raised a hand to his shoulder, but he batted it away. 'Quickly, now,' I said. 'What happened?'

'I came on the rail motor like you told me. From the window, I saw the Triumph. I didn't know then, but it followed me and the rail motor. I left it at Maitland Station and walked here like you told me.'

Skeet tripped and grabbed my shoulder for support.

'Hurry it up, Skeet,' I urged.

'I spotted the Triumph pulling in. The rider dumped his bike and almost caught me when he raced back to the station. I watched from the shadows while he used the public phone and returned to the warehouse. I thought it best to stay clear from you and ran to the public phone to ring Rudy. But the bastard had cut the cord.'

I was in a panic. 'What happened, Skeet? What happened? Quickly.'

'At first, he went into that bar with a woman and watched the door. Then he sat on the path guarding the door with a shotgun. I had no chance to get in to warn you. A small van arrived. An Indian Chief freewheeled in silently behind it. They had a pow-wow, and then all hell broke loose. Three blokes made a dash for the warehouse and battered down the door. They shouted and screamed, and next thing, they dragged Becker out, across the line to the van and threw him in the rear. They had a short parley, then two drove him away. The third followed them on the Indian.'

Racing to the motorbike, I shouted, 'For God's sake, finish the story, Skeet.'

He kicked over the Triumph and revved the engine. I climbed onto the pillion, and we tore off towards Dudley at seventy miles an hour.

Skeet shouted over his shoulder, the wind whipping away his words 'They left this bike, so I kicked it over and followed them. I was a hundred yards behind. Headlight off. Shonky brake cable. At the level crossing near Raymond Terrace, the gatekeeper was closing the gate. But they swerved around him and raced across. Too late for me. I was left on the wrong side. The coal train carried on forever. By the time I crossed the line, they had disappeared. I came for you.'

At the Dudley, Billy was half asleep, but I force-fed him the general outline. To his credit he didn't waste time with recriminations. 'The area is too large and swampy,' he said and sounded ready to give up. 'We'll never find them.'

Skeet said, 'While two tied Becker up, the other yelled to Erin to go left at Hexham. "At Williamtown," he shouted, "take the coast road to where we left your Vincent. Wait there. We'll be five minutes behind you." Something like that.'

I should have listened to Skeet, but he had wasted my time repeating details. I phoned Hector again to alert Gabe and Kitty to the new information, but he had left the office.

'You should have told me,' I barked at Skeet, throwing off his hand. I was already running. 'They are three hours ahead of us.' I had a blinding headache and was having trouble breathing. 'Get working on a rescue.'

I grabbed Billy's shoulder and dragged him with me, shouting, 'You need to search a fifteen-mile stretch. It's dense rainforest. Isolated. Swampy. Remember? We used to go there?'

Everyone was yelling at once, Billy raising his voice. 'They'll be off the main coastal road. Away from interruptions. They'll need to be indoors. To dampen the screaming. Remember the place you used to take me before my divorce? That old forestry hut on the road to Mallabula. On the edge of the creek. It's the only shelter shed in the forest. There's nobody for miles. Becker will scream his head off, with no one to hear him. I don't know where to find it again. It's been a long time.'

'Don't worry,' I said. 'I'll find it. Stay here. Make sure Hector and Gabe organise a search party. Skeet, find Bart Evans. Bring him to us where the gravel track from Tilligerry joins the main coast road. That's as good as any place. It's not far from the forestry hut.'

'Fifteen miles of creek and lakes,' Skeet said, sobering quickly. 'What are our chances of finding him?'

'Slim to nothing. But we better find Becker, or Kitty will lose her jewellery and be up me like an angry hornet.'

Inside the forester's hut, a wood fire had burnt to a red glow in the firebox of a cast-iron Crown stove. I walked the last half-mile and, on my own against three armed thugs, could only watch through the window and wait for help. Becker's face was all wrong. This was not the face that lay beside me on the beach or the mouth that recited Henry Lawson's poem. I thought he was dead. He moved an eye. Blood soaked his shirt and his hair.

I recognised Tex from his American drawl. He said, 'Grab the poker, Erin.'

Erin was sixty with white hair scruffy below his shoulder, a horseshoe moustache stained ginger from cigarette smoke, and sunglasses underpinning his protruding forehead. His arm tattoos, permanently inked above hairy wrists, extolled the virtues of Sylvia and the Royal Navy. He was a proud fourteen stone, all shoulders and bum and a don't screw with me slant to his mouth. He grabbed the wooden handle of an iron poker, tore it from the partly open fire door, its tip glowing red, and screamed, 'Where's the cash? Where's the cash? You wanta another dose of the branding iron?'

Tex lifted the gag from Becker's mouth and smashed a fist in his face. 'You want the hot poker again? Lose another toe? Three gone, and now I'm comin' for the big one. Ya hear me?' slamming Becker's face again.

He shouted at the skinny guy. 'Caddy! Gimme the bolt cutter.'

'He's passed out again.'

When they lowered the volume, most of the words were lost to me.

'… too much blood.'

'Hot ashes. You said that would seal the wounds—'

Caddy giggling.

'Don't wanta kill him—'

'—transfusion if he keeps on leaking.'

'Forget the transfusion.' Tex shouting.

'—tourniquet. Tight, so the blood don't empty out.'

'Keep him—until we have the cash.'

Tex threw a can of water in Becker's face.

'He's out to it.'

'Foxing.' Another bucket of cold water.

'—scrambled his brains—'

'He'll never wake if you don't—'

'—sick of holding him—do with a drink—rum supply?'

'Five left—saddlebag.'

'—nip off a finger.'

Tex, impatient, shouted again, 'He was screaming about Kitty Balushi having the stash. Who—

'Sydney razor gang.'

'Take a swig. Here. There's plenty.'

'Bandage his toes tight—adhesive tape—can't tell us nothin' if he's dead.'

I slid away from the window and peered into the forest's darkness. I knew then Becker was dead or would die, and I would die with him.

42. The Chase

Ileft Skeet at the racetrack and walked the curving staircase in my Neuilly-Sur-Seine house, where I found Jess in a green dress.

'Clear out,' she said, with her hand on her heart, obviously having read Henry Lawson's poem, 'and ride hard for the ranges. We'll bluff them a while, and 'twill give you a start.'

I lingered—of course—then ran for the trees where I'd hobbled my horse. A stern-faced man with an enormous white beard clapped his hands close to my ear. 'Wake up. Get out and away while they're all drunk and asleep.'

Pain sparked a blurred awakening. The first gleam of light opened on a ragged grey mist, clinging to the ground and blanketing the swamp in a musty, earthy smell of rotting vegetation.

I had dozed off, huddled on the ground in long grass beneath a picnic rug while waiting outside the foresters' hut in darkness for reinforcements that hadn't come. A movement in the grass jolted me awake, the dew-damp grass swaying as I held my breath in fear of attack. An animal moved away, hissing. A possum? Overcome with remorse for dozing off, I crept to the window, head down, heart pounding and rose slowly to peer over the sill.

Inert bodies. The stench of burnt flesh. Empty rum bottles. Becker on the floor. Fire damped in the wood stove, a firebrand resting in still-hot ashes—a torture chamber. Let the bastards rot in hell.

God. So much blood. The stink. Burning hair, flesh. My entire body trembled. I exhaled heavily, closed my eyes, and bent with shaky hands on my knees to draw enough oxygen.

In the half-light, an inquisitive bandicoot quivered at the edge of the scrub, nose twitching, ears forward. Dull light reflected off a Morris van. Two motorbikes. Empty rum bottles.

I prayed. 'Let me kill all three.'

Where in hell was my rescue team? Not coming. It was up to me, and I was out of time.

Becker moved a hand, closed and extended it, moved a finger, a foot, rolled over and stayed quiet. One eye opened. He brought his knees up, pushed with his hands, and slid towards the door. He was awake. Broken. Barely conscious and acting on instinct.

I crawled to meet him, the sky lightening in the east, slowly breaking through the mist, white clouds on the horizon. His vomit splashed until he was empty. A motorbike stood two yards away. On hands and knees, he inched towards it.

I reached him, got my hands under his shoulders and dragged him. 'Not the bike.' I had to clear my throat to whisper. 'Too noisy. You haven't the strength. Stand. Lean on me. Into the bush.'

'Can't.'

'You can,' I whispered, struggling to keep from shouting. 'You know how to fight in the bush, how to lose yourself.'

'Thirsty.'

'Left foot. Now, right foot. Six yards to go.'

I was shuffling, gaining pace, Becker moaning. 'No noise,' I told him. 'Here's a track. Move fast. Cut into the scrub.'

Becker coughed up blood. 'Gabe... Double-crossed us.'

'Forget Gabe.'

'Keep documents.'

'Concentrate on walking,' I barked.

'Do not give... to Gabe.'

Behind me, someone is pissing. A fart. A groan. The sky is lighter. A family of wallabies inspects us and pounds away along a track so narrow only the animals are aware of it.

Becker said, 'Follow the wallabies.'

'Any second, they'll discover you've gone. Run!'

'Can't run. Feet on fire.'

'Run.'

'The creek. Leads to the coast. Stay off the track. Into the scrub. Ahh.' Whipped in the face by a low-hung branch. 'Can't.

'Go on,' I urged. 'Faster.'

Shouting arose from behind.

'They've discovered you've gone,' I said. 'Faster.'

It was light enough to see we were in a paperbark forest, and the smell of swamp was overwhelming. The pale tree trunks were two yards apart with low undergrowth of ferns and sedges, the sounds of pursuit muffled by the dense planting. A thorny whip cut across my eyes. Blinded. We limped fast through long grass and came to an open space, loose gravel. I slipped, fell, dragged Becker with me. We rolled down a steep bank—the sudden shock of cold water, and he was drowning.

'Get your head up,' I commanded. 'Hold the edge. Hide in the reeds. Rest for one minute. Stop coughing. They're close by. Quiet.' My hand pressed hard to cover his mouth

Voices above. 'Lost him. No, by God. Spread out. Search. Ahhh.' Sound of spitting. 'Saltwater.'

I was dying of thirst, too.

'Dozy bastard.' The voice of Tex. The American-style bastard with the clipped "a". 'You were on guard. Drank too much rum. Now suffer until you find him.'

A shout, 'Hey, where the hell are you? Where is everyone? I'm lost.'

'Wait on,' Tex shouted. 'We're coming to you. Stand there.'

I held on to a low branch, working my legs and feet in the water, guiding Becker to a shallow bank under cover of a clump of Melaleucas growing to the water's edge. Beyond my reach, hyacinth floated, and waterlilies danced in my ripples to betray me.

Tex called orders and directions to his men. They would find me if I stayed there—the voices and sounds of pursuit moving closer. Be prepared.

Becker said, 'They don't know shit about the bush. Don't be careless,' his voice made stronger by the cold-water bath.

We struck out across waist-deep water to a rocky shelf and a shallow incline leading to tall grass in deep shadow, clambered up the rocks and a low hill behind to find the bank of a broad stream—no escape in that direction.

I was going to die there. The colossal certainty of that struck me, and I crumbled.

'Dig deep,' he said, holding me up. 'Find the strength. Endure.'

'I'll be right, mate.' Shaken, I reached out to him. I had a boat to catch. Get out? How? Walk on water to cross the stream?

'Wasted,' Becker, brain-addled from the torture, said, raising his head.

The sun was up and cutting through the trees. The silence shouted until my ears buzzed, and my mind conjured a squadron of bikies waiting in ambush for me to move.

Becker mumbled, 'My feet and face. On fire. Time to move.'

'What can I do?'

'Go,' he said. 'Can't wait here.'

'Stay. They don't know where we are.'

'Can't think.'

'Think or die—your choice.'

'Don't want... to die.'

Leaves crunching. Twigs breaking. Behind me. They were close.

A noise ahead. Surrounded. I slithered into the shadows. A magpie broke cover, the branch it sat on bounced, the leaves shook, twigs fell. There, behind that tree, a movement.

A body stepped into the open, waved its arms to get the blood circulating, and scrambled away on an animal's path.

My breath exploded out. 'C'mon.' I clambered over a heavy rock and slipped past a fallen tree. A fox disappeared into deep shadows. I crept ten yards through the water, and my hair stood on end. Tex stepped into a ray of silvery sunlight among the trees. Behind a clump of melaleucas, a tattooed thug brandishing a sawn-off shotgun stared about and disappeared into the trees.

The third bikie, the one with a flat head, holding the sawn-off, stood on the path above my head, panting heavily and blocking our escape. Caddy. How could he not smell me?

I crawled through water towards the low bank, but the tattooed thug had flanked us and stood guard. Trapped.

They need me. Won't shoot at me. Save Becker.

I ran. Up the shallow bank at an angle, tripping on uneven ground, hurdling wildly over water channels and across an open space, I stumbled and rolled into a rivulet.

Voices yelled, 'A woman. Cut them off!'

Nowhere to hide, no way to break out.

Running boots converged. A solid branch on the ground. Sharp end. A weapon. The tattooed thug with the sawn-off propped at the creek's edge. His back was to me, most of his weight on one leg, and his mind fixated on a brown snake thick as my arm and a foot from his ankle. I leaned out to get purchase and drove the stick into the flesh behind his knee, the point cutting deep, and stabbed again. He teetered and fell face-first into the water, screaming, "Snake! Snake!" I whacked his head with the heavy branch and the strength of desperation. The branch rose and fell, rose and fell on his bloody face. I stood on his unconscious body, leaned on the pointed branch cutting into his throat, and held his head underwater until he stopped moving.

Caddy. Gone to heaven to rock 'n roll.

Out and running again. My torn feet would not last. In my path, Erin, teeth bared, charging. I stared into his eyes because I didn't want to look at the gun, and I smelled his fear and animal savagery. I dodged. He slipped in the mud. Head over heels, and in the two seconds it took him to recover, I closed in, put a shoulder to him and grabbed the shotgun. Tex broke cover and raised an empty hand, I suppose to protest his death that he saw in my eyes.

Should have raised his gun. I shot him. Big hole in his chest. He should have stayed in Melbourne.

Then a heavyweight behind got a headlock on me, pinning me, a hand clamping on my mouth, twisting my head. I dropped the shotgun. A hard fist punched my head, my kidneys, my face. Locked in a death struggle, unable to shout for help.

The bastard hefted the sawn-off Tex had dropped, stepped away and fired.

Pellets churned the leaves a yard from my head.

'Next time,' Erin bellowed, 'I'll take your head off.'

'Drop the gun.' A voice shouting from the shadows. 'Or I'll put a bullet in your spine.'

Erin's reflexes spun him about. He raised his sawn-off. A shot from behind a swamp mahogany cracked past his head.

A second shot, and he dropped like a busted doll to the ground.

'Billy,' I called. 'Bring that shotgun. Watch him. You creased his skull.'

'When did you learn to use a gun?' Billy yelped.

'Never did. I still don't know how.'

'Franzi!' Jess screamed, hesitating.

Where did she come from?

I lay stretched out on the ground in a confusion of voices. A killer? Me? He would have killed me. Doesn't matter. I'm sorry. Sorry, I killed. Sorry, I started this whole damn thing. But it's okay. Isn't it? Not too far to go for a friend?

Bart's voice: 'What will I do with this bastard holding his bloody head in his hands?'

I shrugged, thinking feed him to the brown snake. But I said, 'Put him on the first train to Darwin.'

Skeet was hysterical. 'Billy pinged Erin. Two dead, one wounded. We win.'

Bart shouted that it all happened too fast for him to get here in time and to get these people to the hut.

Billy said, 'Skeet can keep the Indian Chief. I'll take the Vincent.'

Bart said, 'Get those bodies into the ute.'

Exhausted by the death and greed that had brought pain to my life, I looked at the bodies. To hell with Gabe and Bart and Kitty Balushi and their offhand cruelty. That's not for me. Too tired to care about morals or money or Jessica screaming non-stop, I closed my eyes.

But then I said, 'You can't keep the bikes. Their friends in Melbourne will report them missing.' I panted with the effort of speaking. 'They've been all over town looking for Becker.'

Bart made the decision. 'Bikes can go into the shaft with the bodies, then. What do you want me to do with this bloke?' He repeated it, flicking a finger at Erin. Passing the buck.

Not my problem. I'd be leaving town on the first coach out. 'I'm exhausted.' I said. 'You look after it. It's what I paid you for. I've gone as far as I can go.'

43. Here's Missing You, Kid

It is misty, nothing straight, nothing on the flat, and a strange musical whistle fills the air. I walk up the curving staircase at the Neuilly-Sur-Seine house and meet Jess in a green dress walking down.

With my hand on my heart, I tell her, 'Clear out and leave the dress. It's not yours. Call Becker. He'll tell you. It's mine.'

But the old bloke with a white beard laughs—not a word does he say as he kneels by Becker's side.

I came to life lying on the sofa in my suite at the Dudley, listening to voices. The door crashed open. I recoiled and cried out, the tension of a sleepless night remaining.

'Don't let the bugger die,' Gabe said, storming into my room. 'If he does, all the stuff against me comes out. That's what you said.'

'Yes,' I replied, exhausted. I'd told Gabe that big fat lie and wasn't comforted by the knowledge. There would be more casualties before the game was over. 'You're all heart, Gabe Rosen.'

'Yeah, well,' Gabe said, breathing heavily.

Becker's eyes were half-closed, Jess fussing over the bandages on his foot, his hands twitching.

'Fix that kid,' Gabe said, 'and hide him out of sight before the next lot come searching for him to make their fortune. I'm outta here.'

And he slammed the door behind him.

Jess finished bandaging Becker and set to work on my feet. 'Look at this. Bruises, thorns, cuts and slashes.'

I groaned, fluttered my eyes. 'We're leaving tonight. What's the time?'

Jess said, 'Franz can't leave. He'll not be able to walk.'

'Tell Skeet to phone Marty,' I said, before adding, 'Please. Get Marty and Benny on the two o'clock train to Maitland. Rudy will meet them at Maitland station. Travel separately. Skeet, come with me.' I lay back, sighing. 'We're leaving, Jess. Get packed in a hurry.'

But Jess had been thinking, too. 'I'm not going anywhere. You are crazy if you think I'm hanging around with Becker until the next gangster takes a shot at him. Or at you. I've had my fill of excitement and adventure, and plenty of boys will want to marry me, now I've got money.'

'What are you saying?' I asked.

'While you slept, I told Becker I'm finished with him. What girl in her right mind would marry him? He'll not live more than a year if he's lucky. Or finish up crippled for life. I don't want to be anywhere near him when they take pot-shots at him.'

'Are you saying the engagement is off?'

'Exactly,' Jess said. 'Franz understood. He was kind and insisted I take half of what he stole. I said no, but he persuaded me, so now I'll be well off.'

I told her Becker needed oversized sandshoes, sandals, and crutches, and, when she hesitated, I said, 'Here's the money. Leave now. No time to mess about.'

'Where are you going?'

I said, 'We will decide that when the time is right. Go.'

'You will make it through,' Jess said then turned a half-circle. 'Won't you?'

'Yes, we'll make it.'

'You'll need penicillin,' Jess said, opening the door and looking over her shoulder. 'Sulphur ointment, painkillers.'

'Thanks. Take what money you need and go to the pharmacy.'

Jess rushed off.

I put my head around the door, 'Billy. Billy.'

'Yes? What is it?'

'Bring the car to the side door.'

'I'm busy.'

'Billy!'

'Okay. Okay.'

'Help Becker into the car. Strap the wheelchair to the roof.'

Jess arrived at the old warehouse with crutches and medicines just as Skeet busted into the wall with a six-pound hammer and cold chisel and revealed my cache.

'Let's sit on the floor,' I said, opening the cloth jewellery bag. 'Oh, my. What I wouldn't give... Elizabeth Taylor would swoon.' Next to the bag, I placed a pile of documents. 'Jess, take this lot,' I said, pointing at the jewels, 'to Hector, please?'

'You can't trust Hector,' Becker said. 'Who are the jewels for?'

'Kitty Balushi.'

Becker grinned. 'I suppose you'll have to trust Hector. He wouldn't dare. And the papers?'

I handed the documents to Jess. 'Seal these in an envelope, address it to Gabe Rosen and give it personally to him.'

'I will definitely not read them.'

'That would be best. Thanks for everything, Jess.'

'You know, I fell in love with you as well as Becker.'

'Oh God,' I said. 'You're not the first, and you'll not be the last. I fall in love every day. I'm in love with love and have plenty to spare for everyone. Becker was the adventure I asked for, and he gave me excitement with a bang.'

With a cheeky look, Jessica hummed a tune. Her voice grew stronger until she sang in full flight. 'He robbed the wealthy outlaws, their assets to destroy. A terror to the bookies was the wild Colonial Boy. Man.'

Becker said, 'I suppose you can call me a boy. I don't care anymore.'

'I'll miss you, Franzi,' Jess said.

'And I'll be missing you, kid,' he said in a fair imitation of Humphrey Bogart.

Under Jess's unblinking gaze, I gave Becker a kiss. A small one, not lingering on it. That was for later.

'I've changed my mind,' Jess said. 'I think I'll go after all. Someone has to keep Franz away from this scarlet woman.'

44. Rush of Pale Men

Sunday, August 1.

A tipsy bushranger and her sober accomplice stood at the rail admiring a stunning sunset and watching the water glide past the bow of the *SS Roma*, picking its path through the small boat traffic in Bombay harbour. The wind carried a perfume of jasmine from harbourside gardens, mixed with the bitter tang of rotting mud and the litter of millions. The adrenaline rush of torture and murder had leaked out over four thousand miles of tropical ocean, drifting off somewhere into another world, leaving me weighed down with my conscience.

Becker said, 'In the same situation, we'd do it all again.'

Remembering the look in Tex's eyes and the shotgun swinging around to meet me, I said, 'Do you think so?'

'You're worried about shooting him?' he asked. 'The scumbag who tortured me?'

I nodded.

'Forget the jungle,' Becker said. 'You can live by civilised rules, now.'

'True,' I said, searching his eyes, the ghosts of torture permanently marked in them. 'Where the big cats cannot get us.'

Two passengers had joined the ship in Bombay—the Archbishop of Bombay, and an Italian man with dark olive skin tones, silver hair and shadowy bags under his eyes. I smiled as they strolled past. The bishop returned my smile with a wave, but the Italian ignored me.

Becker said, 'They'll still come after us. The big cats.'

'Sure. Some day. In the faraway land of Oz.' I took his hand, and we waltzed towards the dining room.

People like Gabe and Kitty would pass through the cracks for a while. They'd kill and wound and make lives greyer and lonelier, but the jungle would catch up with them sooner or later. Civilised people trade their souls for the pretence of security. They close their eyes, and Kitty wins. Gabe wins.

What does that make me?

Before we departed from Maitland, I gave my boys the balance of unspent cash, amounting to ten thousand five hundred and ten quid each, and a packet with Horlick's share for Marty to take to him. I put a thousand of mine into a hat for Albie Fowler's daughter and handed the hat around. Rudy would deliver four thousand to her, including a donation from Horlicks.

Too many in Newcastle knew about Skeet's part in this robbery. I had booked him on the three o'clock train north to his mother at Grafton, and soon he would take her to a new home on Rudy's estate at Southport. There was no time for emotional speeches; we split, and I told no one where we were going.

From the Maitland station, Becker and I travelled to Brisbane in a sleeping compartment and took a taxi directly from South Brisbane Station to the Hamilton pier in time to board the liner. I planned the escape a week before, reserved and paid for first-class berths on the train and two staterooms on the SS *Roma*, and the purser didn't raise an eyebrow when I changed Jessica's name for mine on the door of Becker's suite.

Justice, of a sort, had prevailed. The crooks got what they deserved. We would hide among the crowd in the streets of Rome, Paris, or Berlin. Shipping schedules put Kitty at least a week behind us, and, surely, they would not bother to follow.

Fate and luck were with me, and we spent seventeen days in a luxury stateroom fitted out with all the style and flair of Italian designers. In the evenings, we sat on the upper deck holding hands under the stars to watch old movies in the open-air cinema. With my dedicated love and attention, Becker's feet were healing, and, though he would forever be partially disabled, he was walking, and the crew treated us like royalty.

Rose petals covered the tables in the first-class dining room of the Flotta Lauro cruise ship *SS Roma*. The dinner dance was a happy occasion attended by all the first-class passengers who wanted to come, with champagne and laughter by the bucketful. I waltzed through the dining room door, and Becker's eyes shone through the soft glow of candlelight dancing on polished mahogany tables. He wore a tailored blue suit and floppy bow tie, dapper as James Stewart, and shifted uneasily as though concerned that I might not have come. But a breeze carried to him the perfume of Arpège he had bought for me, 'so I will know you are with me,' he said when he handed me the gift-wrapped parcel.

I found my pearl-white, satin tea dress by chance during a one-day stopover at a department store in Singapore. Designed by Pierre Balmain and imported from Paris, the fabric, a delicate tapestry of woven florals in pastel shades, was shot through with threads of shimmering silver and nestled at the small of my back a dainty pink bow whispered of love's playful intricacies—a dance I would savour, a joy I would share, and I believe to this day that fate had worked its magic for me to unearth such an exquisite gown. I crossed my fingers.

As I drew nearer, he beckoned me with a gentle gesture of his hand. Our fingers brushed, intertwining naturally, and, in that touch, I belonged beside this man. He laid a playful hand on my arm, and I said, 'A penny for your thoughts?'

Franz Becker stooped, his lips met mine, and I sighed, contented with my life.

The violinist played a Strauss melody, moving us into a slow waltz, his arm around my waist, my head on his shoulder, his limp forgotten. Behind us, a low-pitched voice spoke, and a woman's soft chuckle joined Herr Strauss. When the music receded, we held hands and glided on air to our table, where a red rose rested in a silver vase on the white tablecloth. The ship's captain stood in our honour and joined in the applause for our dancing.

The new Italian passenger kept himself to himself and took his meals in his room, for which I thanked the Angel Gabriel. He emerged occasionally, so sombre and sad that I told Becker he must be in mourning. He would appear as if from nowhere, wearing a rumpled jacket over an open-neck shirt and needing a shave. On the occasions we did meet on the ship's deck, I would try to engage him in conversation, but he would tip me a nod and move on, his ghastly smile suggesting that was adequate recompense for his trouble, while I would feel the cool of a cloud on the horizon and cling to the shawl about my shoulders. But Becker took a disliking to him, suggesting I steer clear of him.

'Why?' I asked.

'He's from Sicily. Mafia territory.'

'Are you known to the Sicilian mafia?'

'No.'

'Neither am I. You're being paranoid. Stop worrying.'

The archbishop, a worldly man who often travelled this route on his frequent trips to the Vatican, entertained our table with stories of India and flattered me by searching out my company on the sun deck and at the bar.

'Next stop, Port Said,' I said to the bishop as we stood on the deck watching India recede, 'then Malta, Messina and Naples.'

'I know Naples well,' he said. 'I would be delighted to show you the sights and look after you while we wait for the train to Rome.'

In our stateroom, after a post-lunch romp, Becker suggested we spend a week in Rome.

'We'll pass through Paris,' I said, 'and I'll arrange to sell the house at Neuilly-sur-Seine. It's a weakness. Kitty will track us there if she decides to come after us.'

'Why would Kitty do that?'

'I held on to some of the jewellery. There was a pearl necklace and a diamond brooch that would have dazzled The Shah of Persia. Kitty has this need to win and will demand punishment.'

'She'll not miss them.'

'Fingers crossed that Fred Hetherington's one-nighter didn't attend a bookies' night out with the brooch pinned to her chest.'

As the cruise drew closer to Italy, Becker carried a revolver in his trouser pocket or a white cotton towelling bag. I ribbed him about it, but he ignored my remarks, and I sensed an uneasy undercurrent until my enjoyment of ship life swamped it.

On the night before we docked at Port Said, the ship's captain, strolling past, paused and tipped his hat to me. 'Be sure to find time to visit Cairo and the Pyramids, Ma'am.'

Ma'am. That's me. Sunni Sinclair, paid escort and bushranger. Ma'am, not Miss. A somebody already.

'The sea is building, Ma'am. Don't stay out too long. The deck can be dangerous.'

I laughed at his idea of danger and a ghostly image of Tom Halley reading Henry Lawson's poetry and wondering who robbed him at Tattersalls. Or did he know?

'We're fine, Captain,' I said. 'We'll take our chances.'

We stopped for a day and two nights at Port Said and spent the daylight hours in Cairo, strolling and shopping, and the shopping was fabulous. Amid the poverty, couturiers from Paris and Rome, jewellers from Holland and London displayed their most gorgeous products and milliners from Barcelona, Prague, and Rome showcased their hats. I had the money, and when

I arrived at the Roma, I carried the most splendid array of shopping bags ever to be taken aboard this ship.

It was a perfect Italian summer day when we landed at Naples. I watched from the rail as the gangway came down and the crowd on the dock surged forward, shouting and laughing with that joy and enthusiasm Italians bring to their lives.

At our stopover in Cairo, I bought a sporty outfit by Schiaparelli—a soft, sheer, self-patterned white silk suit with an oversized ruffled collar to the shirt and a whimsical matching scarf, a sculptured white felt hat shaped and moulded with a huge eccentric brim, and I wore the necklace of multi-coloured Tahitian pearls from Kitty Balushi's collection. I was a celebrity, a movie star, a duchess. Braless, of course. After all, this was Italy in the fifties.

Putting aside his increasing tension, Becker joined the fun in a cream linen suit, Panama hat, and white shoes. I embraced him, breathed in the smell of his skin against my face, and we laughed at everything and nothing. Being here together was enough, and we laughed at the children hopping and shouting and the joy of the elderly Italians who, nine years after the war, had come to meet family who had escaped to America or Australia. And we laughed for the sheer joy of being alive.

Our luggage emerged from the hold in a net suspended from a crane hook and landed gently on the deck.

The Captain suggested it was time to go. 'Take care in Naples,' he said. 'It's a hard town under the thumb of a Calabrian mafia family, and no one is safe in the streets, not even a bishop.'

He took our hands in his, gave me a smile and led us to the gangway, the other passengers following noisily, laughing with the same joy for life as the Italians.

We had hours to spare before our train departed for Rome, so we went with the bishop to the cathedral, and, though I'm not much of a believer, and Becker is not at all, we were converted to the faith by the magnificence of the gold-leafed dome, the

296

marble statues and the paintings by famous artists whose names I can't begin to remember, the fourteen centuries of history, the angels in blue cloaks and frescoes, and the mosaics of the baptistery that got me all clucky for a baptism.

I lit a candle in the gloomy sanctuary, bowed, and prayed for safety and happiness for Becker and me.

We came to the front door, and there, by the holy water font, was our elusive Italian fellow passenger. I smiled at him. He nodded as though we were still aboard but must have had a bad tooth day because he didn't smile. After the dim light inside, I shaded my eyes with my hand against the harsh glare of a busy street. As I moved out to the top of the steps, one rude fellow shoved through the crowded pavement, shouting words I didn't understand. A strong hand pushed me forward. I twisted my head to find the Italian behind me. And Becker was hollering, and the rude fellow coming towards us pointed a pistol at me and screamed, 'Balushi! Balushi. Balushi,' and Becker knocked me aside, and I was falling. I felt the heat of the bullet meant for me, heard an explosion close to my ear, and the Balushi fellow was clutching at his body, blood gushing, his weapon flung into the air, dropping into the crowd, and Becker's weight crushed me as he fell.

The bishop dragged Becker off me and laid him on the step. His hand held the revolver he had shown me in Maitland, his blood pumping and pooling under his body, his white shirt now crimson. The bishop knelt to anoint his forehead with a cross and murmured in Latin the words of forgiveness and reconciliation. I searched among the crowd for the Italian from the Roma, but he had disappeared.

Becker stared with the light fading from his eyes and gazed into mine. I didn't need a doctor to tell me there was no helping him, and I bent my head to hear his last words. 'Just kiss me— my girl— and—I'll—chance it,' he said.

And so the game ended as Henry Lawson had foreseen:

> They chased, and they shouted, 'Surrender, Jack Dean!'
> They called him three times in the name of the Queen.
> Then came from the darkness the clicking of locks;
> The crack of the rifles was heard in the rocks!
> A shriek and a shout, and a rush of pale men—
> And there lay the bushranger, chancing it then.
>
> The sergeant dismounted and knelt on the sod—
> 'Your bushranging's over—make peace, Jack, with God!'

But there is another round left to fight. I am coming for you, Kitty Balushi. If it takes a lifetime, I will find you, and you will pay with your life for this poor darling boy who once was mine.

www.ingramcontent.com/pod-product-compliance
Lightning Source LLC
Chambersburg PA
CBHW011758010726
47497CB00013B/3257